T0036598

"Atmospheric . . . Taylor creates a rich and gothic atmosphere, with the ocean beating against the treacherous, windswept cliffs. . . . *The Drowning Sea*'s gorgeous backdrop and stalwart sleuth will satisfy and impress mystery readers, particularly fans of traditional whodunits."

—*BookPage*

"Taylor is adept at balancing police procedure with the domestic drama of Maggie's mixed family, and her descriptions of the Irish coast and the small town where Maggie is staying will have armchair travelers itching to grab a pint and head to the local pub. Readers will be looking forward to more from this heartfelt series."

—*Publishers Weekly*

"Tana French fans will love this intricate, relationship-fueled crime story and its strong women characters."

—*firstCLUE*

"A taut and thrilling mystery . . . [that] held me spellbound up until the nerve-racking finale. Maggie D'arcy, who combines her policing skills with the psychological insight of a mother, is fast becoming my favorite sleuth."

—Carol Goodman

Praise for *A Distant Grave*

"The result is a fast-paced, tension-filled yarn filled with twists the reader is unlikely to see coming."

—Associated Press

"Taylor combines complex layering of plots with depth of characterization, lovely Emerald Isle color, and prose that often rises to lyricism. . . . Taylor further burnishes her bona fides as a practitioner par excellence of literary crime fiction."

—*The Free Lance-Star*

"Complex, slow-burning . . . Taylor has crafted another believable and intriguing installment of Maggie's story." —*BookPage*

"[*A Distant Grave*] is as intricately plotted as *The Mountains Wild*."

—*Library Journal*

"Taylor pulls out all the stops—subplots, threats, red herrings, warning bells—to keep the pot boiling till the end."

—*Kirkus Reviews*

"Tana French fans will be eager for the next series entry."

—*Publishers Weekly*

"The Irish setting takes center stage. . . . A solid series."

—*Booklist*

"Lyrical, haunting, and impossible to put down . . . Absolutely do not miss this." —Hank Phillippi Ryan

"Sarah Stewart Taylor commands the most complex of emotions—grief, guilt, love—with ease to deliver a story that, like a chill off the water, gets in your bones." —Tessa Wegert

Praise for *The Mountains Wild*

"A valentine to Ireland, delving into its beauty, history, and varied landscape . . . *The Mountains Wild* is a terrific series launch."

—*South Florida Sun Sentinel*

"Gripping." —*Christian Science Monitor*

"Sarah Stewart Taylor has written a beautiful, bittersweet novel about loyalty and loss and how they can blind us to the truth."

—*Star Tribune*

"This fantastic novel has something for everyone: mystery, murder, police work, family drama, and even romance. Fans of strong women protagonists and crime drama will love this chilling page-turner." —*Mystery Scene*

"The atmospheric, intricately plotted story builds to a stunning, unforgettable conclusion. . . . This outstanding book will please fans of mysteries set in Ireland and readers of police procedurals."

—*Library Journal* (starred review)

"This mystery, evocative of the Irish diaspora, interrogates both a young woman's disappearance and the meaning of homeland."

—*Kirkus Reviews*

"Layers of Dublin details will ensnare biblio-travelers, and this series starter offers a compelling introduction to Maggie D'arcy as she faces her life's mystery." —*Booklist*

The Drowning Sea

Sarah Stewart Taylor

Minotaur Books
New York

Published in the United States by Minotaur Books, an imprint of
St. Martin's Publishing Group

THE DROWNING SEA. Copyright © 2022 by Sarah Stewart Taylor. All rights reserved. Printed in the United States of America. For information, address St. Martin's Publishing Group, 120 Broadway, New York, NY 10271.

www.minotaurbooks.com

"Swimmer" from *The Orb Weaver* © 1961 by Robert Francis, published by Wesleyan University Press. Reprinted by permission

Excerpt from *A Stolen Child* copyright © 2023 by Sarah Stewart Taylor

The Library of Congress has cataloged the hardcover edition as follows:

Names: Taylor, Sarah Stewart, author.
Title: The drowning sea / Sarah Stewart Taylor.
Description: First Edition. | New York : Minotaur Books, 2022. |
    Series: Maggie D'arcy mysteries ; 3
Identifiers: LCCN 2022003367 | ISBN 9781250826657 (hardcover) |
    ISBN 9781250826664 (ebook)
Subjects: LCGFT: Novels.
Classification: LCC PS3620.A97 D76 2022 | DDC 813/.6—dc23
LC record available at https://lccn.loc.gov/2022003367

ISBN 978-1-250-82667-1 (trade paperback)

Our books may be purchased in bulk for promotional, educational, or business use. Please contact your local bookseller or the Macmillan Corporate and Premium Sales Department at 1-800-221-7945, extension 5442, or by email at MacmillanSpecialMarkets@macmillan.com.

First Minotaur Books Trade Paperback Edition: 2023

10 9 8 7 6 5 4 3 2 1

I.

Observe how he negotiates his way

With trust and the least violence, making

The stranger friend, the enemy ally.

The depth that could destroy gently supports him.

With water he defends himself from water.

Danger he leans on, rests in. The drowning sea

Is all he has between himself and drowning.

II.

What lover ever lay more mutually

With his beloved, his always-reaching arms

Stroking in smooth and powerful caresses?

Some drown in love as dark water, and some

By love are strongly held as the green sea

Now holds the swimmer. Indolently he turns

To float—The swimmer floats, the lover sleeps.

—From "Swimmer" by Robert Francis

One

The narrow trail disappears into the low grass, as though whoever or whatever walked there before us suddenly disappeared, or turned around, or rose up into the sky like an angel. Far below the path, the coastline curls and winds around the base of the cliffs, a brilliant blue scarf of water, edged with lacy white surf.

Ahead of us, my boyfriend Conor's son, Adrien, and my daughter, Lilly, forge a path of their own, Conor and Adrien's corgi dashing around their feet, barking and trying to herd them away from the edge. Conor's hand is warm in mine. We can't stop smiling, at the hot day—unusual for Ireland even in July—and at the summer unspooling ahead of us, a whole two months on this gorgeous, remote West Cork peninsula in a rented vacation cottage. Lilly and I flew to Dublin two weeks ago, right after school ended, and we all drove down to West Cork the next day. The stretch of glorious sunny weather has felt like a miracle, day after day of clear skies and blue water.

A bird passes overhead, its gray wings and body a cross against the paler sky, and Conor shields his eyes from the sun. "Peregrine falcon!" he calls out. "If Beanie were a mouse he'd be in fear of his life." Mr. Bean barks and we both laugh.

I first saw Ross Head from the passenger-side window of Conor's car as we turned off the narrow coast road in the nearby village and slowly crested the hill that leads to the peninsula. I felt my heart leap at the dramatic cliffs and the tall golden grass and the rocks dotted here and there with fuchsia and white wildflowers.

Ross Head is one of the smaller peninsulas along Ireland's southwest coastline; only two miles around the peninsula road that traces its outlines along the steep cliffs. At the mouth of the peninsula is a big gray stone manor house called Rosscliffe House, once grand, now disheveled-looking, though Conor has told me that it's in the process of being turned into a luxury hotel. The house was built on the ruins of a castle or stone fort and the over-grown gardens are dotted here and there with small stone struc-tures and the remnants of rampart walls and towers with views of the sea in almost every direction.

The same developer who's bought the house for a hotel has built five huge modern holiday houses along the cliffs and has started building more of them. At the construction sites, we can see steel girders shining in the sun; views of the ocean show through the skeletons of the huge structures.

Sheep dot the cropped green of the hills on another peninsula across the inlet, and where the peninsula meets what passes for a main road, there's a village called Rosscliffe with a smattering of houses and buildings, a horseshoe-shaped beach in a protected cove, a little harbor and sailing club, a few shops and two pubs, and holiday cottages and farmhouses strung along the roads.

"Our" place, as I've already come to think of it, is a cozy white-washed cottage perched at the edge of the cliffs across the penin-sula from Rosscliffe House and the new houses, with a hearth for turf fires, a cozy kitchen and sitting room, and three bedrooms in an extension that opens on to a stone patio looking out over the inlet. We've been here less than a week and I already feel attached to it in a way that makes me want to call our landlady, Mrs. Crawford, and make an offer. Conor says to wait until the stretch of fine weather we've enjoyed comes to an end.

We stop for a kiss, the sun hitting my cheek as I lift my face to Conor's, the wind swirling around us, rippling the grass. I'm full of that delicious feeling you get at the beginning of a vacation, everything still before you, the days not yet finite, the span of time not yet winding down. I formally resigned from my job as a detective on the homicide squad of the Suffolk County Police Department on Long Island in April, and for the first time in decades, I have no job to go back to, no calls or emails from my team building up, no one waiting for my return. The long-reaching implications of the case I worked in February, the one that led to me resigning from my job, have left me traumatized and anxious, though I can feel the sharp edges of the case's aftermath softening, as though they've been worn away by the wind.

Our cat died of old age in May. Lilly, Conor, and Adrien are all here with me. Only my uncle Danny is back on Long Island, but he moved in with his girlfriend, Eileen, in March and though he keeps sending me and Lilly texts about how much he misses us, I know he's just fine, better than fine actually, finally living again after twenty-three years of mourning his daughter without knowing that's what he was doing.

The sun is strong and direct at noon and I can feel it soaking into my body, giving me energy, warming me from the inside. There's a lone figure with long reddish hair on the path ahead of us, a birdwatcher, I realize when she lifts a pair of binoculars to her eyes and scans the sky over the ocean, and I wonder if she saw the falcon. I stretch my arm a little, testing my shoulder, which I sprained badly in March. I continue to have pain off and on, but it's mostly healed now. Conor is watching me and smiling, his worn green shirt bringing out specks of gold and olive in his brown eyes. His pale Irish skin is a little burned from all the sun and he looks windblown and handsome.

"What?" I ask.

"It's just nice to see you relaxed like this," he says. "It's very . . ."

"Unfamiliar?"

"Yes, but very nice. I worried, you know, that you wouldn't know how to be on holiday." His eyes crinkle a little at the edges, his mouth trying to hide the grin. His face still delights me, its novelty a legacy of the year we were long distance, I suppose, but also of the twenty-three years I didn't see him at all, years when I imagined his face and lived off memory and the few pictures of him online I was able to find. I feel a surge of love for him, a surge of gratitude for the circumstances, tragic as they were, that brought us to each other twenty-three years after we first met, after I first began to love him.

I smile at him. "Being on holiday? What's that? Is it a skill you can learn, like playing the recorder?"

"Oh, yes. I can give you pointers if you need them. I'm very, very skilled at being on holiday." It's true. Conor, a history professor, has a lot of work to do this summer on the book he's writing on Irish political history of the 1950s, '60s, and '70s, but he's doing it on the patio behind the cottage, surrounded by piles of reference works and notebooks and cups of tea. More than once, I've found him on the chaise longue, wrapped in a blanket, walled in by books on all sides, looking perfectly contented and pleased with the world. And when he puts his research aside to go for walks or swims or to sit on our patio and look at the view, he seems able to disconnect from his work in a way I've never been able to manage.

We turn around at the end of the peninsula, stopping for a moment to look at the visual spectacle of the five huge modern houses perched close to the cliffs like elegant seabirds, and then start back, Lilly and Adrien and Mr. Bean dawdling behind us, checking for whales or dolphins. Rosscliffe House looms ahead of us, and as they watch the water, Conor and I walk over to the house for a closer look.

It stands proudly and defiantly at the crest of the rise, a gray stone fortress with three stories of empty windows, an imposing columned facade, and what feels like a half-hearted attempt at decorative detail above the entrance. It's as though the architect took one look at the site and knew he'd have to trade beauty for stalwartness against winds political and meteorological. The house seems to be crouching there, bracing itself for the gusts sweeping across the peninsula.

When we walk closer we see a couple of NO TRESPASSING signs and one reading NEVIN PROPERTIES, FUTURE SITE OF ROSSCLIFFE HOUSE HOTEL, A LUXURY RESORT AND WEDDING VENUE. I think someone has tried to tame the overrun gardens all around it a bit, but otherwise it doesn't look like they've started the renovation.

"How old is it?" I ask Conor.

"From the 1780s, I think I read. It's a good example of Georgian architecture, built by some ancestor of the painter Felix Crawford next to the ruins of what had been a thirteen-century Norman castle. We'll have to see what else we can learn about it."

"It's magnificent but ugly," I say. "You know what I mean?"

"Mmmm. They were meant to be imposing, these Anglo-Irish Big Houses. They had to be. Their builders were uneasy here, trying to cement their claim over a place they had no claim to."

We stand there for a minute, looking up at the house, then walk over to a floor-length window on the terrace and look inside the large, empty room on the other side of the glass. Suddenly I feel as though I'm being watched. The wind is snapping around us, doing funny things as it rounds the stone structure. The sound it makes is almost human, like a wailing baby, and I take Conor's arm as we walk around to the back, finding a stone terrace and covered portico. One of the floor-length windows is open a little, a rock wedged in the gap.

Something rustles and we both jump. "Just the wind," Conor says. The terrace is covered with dead grass and leaves and there's some trash there, too, and graffiti on the back wall of the house. "Well, someone's been here since the 1780s, anyway," he says, pointing to a blanket in one corner and a pile of empty bottles opposite.

"Not a bad place for teenagers to meet for romantic assignations."

"I don't know. I think I'd find it a bit creepy." We both take one final look up at the house and then he tucks my hand under his arm and says, "Let's go find the kids."

We catch up to Lilly and Adrien on the final stretch of the walking path and we all stand there for a few minutes looking back at the view. It's stunning, the almost turquoise blue water against the white of the waves and the vibrant green of the grass. Across the peninsula, the three white cottages, ours in the center, are tucked cozily into the landscape rather than defying it.

"We saw you up in the window of the mansion," Lilly says suddenly. "How'd you get up there? Is it open?" The wind whips her dark hair all around her face; she's impossibly vibrant, her cheeks pink, her body strong and upright against the wind.

"What?" Conor turns to look at her. "What do you mean?"

"We saw you up in one of the windows," Adrien says. "Just now. What's it like up there?"

Conor and I look at each other, confused. "We were looking at the house," I say finally. "We didn't go inside, though."

Lilly pushes her hair off her face. "Well, someone was up there," she says casually. "Right, Adrien? We thought it was you."

Adrien looks up and meets my eyes. "It looked like a woman, but maybe . . ." He turned seventeen in May and his face has thinned since the last time I saw him. Tall and gangly, he has his mother's blond hair and heavily lashed blue eyes, shy and intelligent behind his glasses, but there's something about the shape of his mouth and chin now that's all Conor and his gestures are Conor's, too. He's been so conscious of Lilly's feelings since we arrived, for which I'm eternally grateful. I can see him thinking, his eyes intent behind his glasses, trying to figure out if this is something we shouldn't talk about around Lilly.

"Maybe there was someone hiding up there," Lilly says. "You didn't hear anything, did you?"

Conor smiles. "I don't think so," he says. But now I'm thinking of the sense I had of being watched.

"Probably just the light," I say in what I hope is a reassuring way.

Conor nods. "Come on, Adrien, I'll race you back. We'll meet you two at the cottage," he tells me and he calls to Mr. Bean, who barks and chases after them.

"You ready to head back?" I ask Lilly. Before we went on the walk, she told me that she was tired because she didn't sleep well. "I'm going to stop at Mrs. Crawford's cottage to get eggs and bread. You want to come with me?"

"Sure. I like that bread we got from her."

Lilly and I walk in silence for a bit through the tall grass and then she says, "Mom, I was thinking I might want to run cross-country this fall."

"That's a good thought, Lill. We can talk about it. There's still a lot of time before then." I don't look at her.

"What?"

"Nothing, just . . . that's great. Maybe we can run together this summer. This is a gorgeous place to train. I saw there's a 10K in August in Bantry. Maybe we could do that." I try to make it sound breezy.

But she's alert to my hesitation. "What's wrong? We're going back, aren't we? We're going back to Long Island at the end of the summer?"

"Of course we are, sweetheart. And then we can talk about it."

"Talk about what?" She stops on the path, her hands on her hips, her legs long and lean in black leggings. Her thick brown hair is loose, rising all around her in the air.

"We can do this later, Lill. We're on vacation."

"*What?*"

The wind picks up again, whipping the tall grass back and forth. The ground beneath us is spongy, making me feel uncertain about my footing. "Well, part of us spending the summer here is to see if we might like to move here. You could go to school in Dublin and we could get some . . . some space from everything. You know, the past year has been—"

"What, and live with *Conor*?" Her face is incredulous.

"Well, yes, that's the idea. Their house in Dublin is big enough for all four of us and you liked the city when we spent those two weeks there in April."

She stops and stares at me for a long moment. Her eyes are dark, her face stony. "So what, you're just going to, like, become an Irish cop?"

"Well, I'd have to figure all of that out. Honestly, sweetie, nothing's been decided. It's all just—"

"What about school?"

"There's a really great school called St. Theresa's. It's right near Conor's house. They have room and you can walk and—"

"You talked to a *school*? Without telling me?"

I turn to her, my hands out, but she steps away. "No, we were just getting information, to be prepared. Nothing's been decided, sweetheart. We're here for the summer. That's all."

The wind shifts again. I'm furious with myself. Lilly's therapist said I should wait until later in the summer to talk to her about moving to Dublin. Lilly's been doing so much better, almost back to her old, sunny self the last month or so once we got past the one-year anniversary of Brian's death, but the therapist said that Lilly's biggest fear right now is not being in control of her life after her father's suicide. If her dad, if her whole idea of who he was, could be taken from her just like that, what else could be taken from her? I've fucked this up about fifty different ways.

"Why can't Conor and Adrien move to Long Island?" she asks. "Why do we have to move?"

"Well, sweetie, Conor's work is here. His area of research is Irish history after all, and you know, Adrien's mom is in Ireland, so they can't just—"

"Oh, so because I'm the one with a dead dad, I'm the one who has to move?" She's half crying, her hair whipping across her face in the stiff wind. Her cheeks are reddened now, her eyes dark and gleaming with anger. I want to reach out and lift her, bring her to me. I can feel her pain, her rage, her fear in the air between us. "You're so fucking selfish!" she throws out and runs back along the walking path toward the cottage. "It's all about you."

I stop myself from sprinting after her and let her go, telling myself she'll cool down. She disappears in the tall grass, so quickly it shakes me a little.

Letting the wind flow over my face, calming my heart rate, I stand there looking out at the view for a moment. It's stunning, all the visual elements combining to form a pleasing composition, but suddenly I'm aware of the sharp angles of the high cliffs, the treacherous distance down to the water. And when I look back at Rosscliffe House, checking the uppermost windows to see if I can figure out what optical illusion made Lilly and Adrien think there was someone up there, all I can see is the dark bulk of it, imposing and vaguely threatening against the endless ocean.

Two

I walk slowly along the road ringing the peninsula, feeling lucky to be here despite Lilly's mood and my own uneasiness. Conor and I were planning on staying in his colleague and friend Grace Murphy's house on Ross Head for a week back in the winter, before the last case I worked wrecked our vacation plans and left me unemployed for the first time in my adult life. This summer was supposed to be a do-over since Grace and her husband, Lorcan, were going to be in France. But at the last minute they decided to spend the summer in West Cork and put us in touch with a woman named Lissa Crawford, who owns the three cottages. A cancellation meant ours was available for July and August.

"She's a bit eccentric, Lissa Crawford," Grace told Conor, once we'd decided to sign the lease. "Quite a talented painter, but she's odd. She says odd things. You'll see. She sells fresh eggs and does a good brown bread, too. Anyway, the cottages are lovely and you'll be close to us. There's a bit of social life on the peninsula and the village is lively enough now. Sam Nevin, who built our house and the other houses on Ross Head, has been investing in Rosscliffe, trying to make it a real tourist destination like the other towns and villages in that part of West Cork." She explained that Lorcan, who is a banker in Dublin, has been helping Nevin put together investors to finance the holiday development and the fund for the hotel renovation.

Lissa Crawford lives in the biggest of the three cottages, a cheery, whitewashed one-story surrounded by flower beds and a chicken coop, with a glass-walled extension that she uses as a painting studio. We met her the day we arrived, when we stopped by to get the key. As we waited in the entryway for her to fetch it, we all looked around in astonishment. The walls were crowded with her paintings, abstract compositions with bright splashes of color that reminded me of Rorschach inkblots. In their simple frames, they climbed the white walls like glorious stains, spilled wine or paint or candle wax on a tablecloth. She was wearing an artist's smock covered in paint, her braided silver and yellow hair on top of her head and a long strand of glass beads in bright colors around her neck. I turned forty-six in March and I take her for only five or ten years older than me, but she seems both much older and somehow ageless, enveloped in a cloud of creative energy and the bright colors of her work. Lilly and I walked down the day after we arrived to buy a loaf of bread from her and she showed us her paintings as her chickens clucked outside the open windows.

Walking home, with the loaf of still-warm bread, Lilly said, "That's how I want to be when I'm older, like, I just don't give a shit, you know?"

I smiled at her. "How do you know she doesn't give a shit?"

"You can just tell, right? Like her hair, and she's just, like, doing her thing. Painting her paintings. She doesn't have a husband or anything. She's her own person."

"*I* don't have a husband," I said.

"But you have Conor and you wear, like, regular mom clothes."

She gestured dismissively at my jeans and tank top and I took the comparison as a criticism. I wasn't bohemian enough, didn't dress right. Lately, Lilly has been communicating strongly that she finds my job vaguely fascist.

I sigh. I'm in one of the most beautiful places on earth . . . with a teenage daughter who seems intent on making me feel bad about myself in any way she can.

As I approach Lissa Crawford's cottage today, though, I see something that makes me forget about Lilly's digs at my clothes and job. There's a car, still running, parked in front of the cottage, and a man and a woman—he in a dark blue Garda uniform, she in plainclothes—are standing outside talking to Lissa. The Garda Síochána is Ireland's national police service, and I assume that the woman in plainclothes is a detective. I can read the scene, the tension in all three bodies, the crackling of a radio through the open window of one of the cars. This isn't just a social visit. These guards, as officers are called here, are responding to a call or an incident.

Something's happened.

They've seen me now and Lissa gestures toward me and seems to be explaining something. They all look up in expectation.

"Is everything all right?" I call out.

"This is Annie Tobin," Lissa says as I come closer, pointing to the woman in plainclothes.

"Detective Sergeant Ann Tobin," the woman says. "I'm a Garda detective posted in Bantry, but I live here in Rosscliffe." She's my height and my age, with brown hair, silvering at her temples and cut in a no-nonsense but still stylish short bob, and sad brown eyes that turn to take me in. Her outfit is too big on her, her blue linen blouse loose and baggy, as though she's lost weight suddenly. The young guy next to her, awkwardly tall and thin, his face still troubled by teenage acne, rocks back on his heels a bit as she introduces him as Garda Broome. He's not comfortable in his uniform yet; he keeps fiddling with the waistband of his pants.

"Mrs. D'arcy is renting the middle cottage for the summer," Lissa explains. "They've only just arrived. She's a police detective as well." I don't know how she knows this. Grace must have told her.

Tobin nods.

"I've just been telling Lissa that we'll be conducting a search on Ross Head today. Unfortunately, a Belgian tourist found, em, human remains down on Crescent Beach this morning." Crescent Beach is a popular swimming spot close to Ross Head.

"Oh, how awful," I say. "Do they know who it is?"

Lissa jumps in before Tobin can say anything, talking too fast, tucking a strand of hair back up into her bun. She's upset, I think, babbling to stave off strong emotion, fear, or sadness. "There was a young man, Lukas, who worked for Sam Nevin on the building sites. Such a nice lad. He disappeared and they thought he went back to Poland in April, but it looks like maybe he . . . didn't," she says, her eyes wide. "Oh, poor Lukas."

"Yes, well, we don't know anything yet. We'll have to do some more investigation," Tobin says quickly, giving Lissa an annoyed glance, then looking back at me. "We hope you won't be inconvenienced, but we'll be asking all the residents to stay off the cliffs today."

"We've just finished walking," I say. "We'll stay away as long as you need us to." They must be thinking he went off the cliffs into the water, I realize. We've been warned about walking on the cliffs and apparently it's not uncommon for tourists to slip and fall. April. The remains would be almost completely unrecognizable by now. They'll need to use dental records, possibly DNA, to make an identification.

"Thank you," Tobin says. They're waiting for me to explain what I'm doing here.

"I'm so sorry," I say. "I don't mean to intrude, but I was just coming down to see if I could get some eggs and bread."

"Of course," Lissa says. "I can just go get them."

Sergeant Tobin says quickly, "I'll leave you then." She gives Lissa a meaningful look. "We'll let you know when we have concrete information. No need for rumors to get started."

Lissa frowns, understanding the reprimand.

Tobin nods to me. "Nice to meet you, Mrs. D'arcy. I'm sure I'll be seeing you around." She and the young guard get into the car and head back toward the village.

"How awful," I say once they're gone.

"Yes." Lissa leads the way toward the cottage. "I'll just get you some bread and eggs now. Can I make you a cup of tea? I need one myself. That's been a bit of a shock." And then as though Tobin hadn't said a word about not speculating about the remains, she goes on. "Lukas. When he went missing back in April, we all thought maybe he'd fallen from the cliffs, but then when they didn't find him, it seemed more likely he'd returned home. A lot of young people, from Poland, or Bulgaria and sometimes Ukraine, they work as builders or at the hotels around here. We have a lovely group of Polish workers in Rosscliffe. They must get awfully home-sick and we just thought . . ." She trails off, thinking out loud.

I hesitate, but I'm a bit shaken now and not ready to go back and face Lilly. "Maybe a quick one. Thank you. I'm so sorry." She nods and leads me inside. While she makes the tea, I wander through the kitchen and sitting room, looking at her artwork.

The layout of the cottage is open, the kitchen at one side of a large, sunny room painted white, the extension serving as her studio on the other. As on our last visit, the paintings are everywhere, bright, saturated blobs of red and orange and green on white canvases, sketches and quick studies on paper taped here and there. Her worktable is messy, covered with tubes of paint, brushes, wicked-looking little knives, and other tools. When I get closer, I can see that she's approximated the texture of cloth on some of the canvases with finely applied oil paints, and used vibrant, saturated colors to create what look like stains. There's something beautiful but disturbing about the paintings, the splashes of color accidents on the perfect white, spilled sauce or ink . . . or blood.

She hands me a mug of tea and a little pitcher of cream, then leads the way out to a small patio behind the cottage. The yard is crowded with plants, tall grasses, roses, and bright pink cosmos. I make a little exclamation of pleasure and she says, "I love gardening. I grew up with gardens. Things grow beautifully here, don't they? The cottage blocks the wind." I see what she means. This side of the peninsula is on the inlet, where the long finger of Ross Head meets the mainland. The landscape is gentler and it's quieter here without the constant sound of the wind and the surf on the Atlantic side. I understand why the new houses are out there on the high cliffs, each view more spectacular than the next, but I imagine it's noisy.

She takes a deep breath and lets out a little hum of happiness as she looks around at her flowers. I see what Lilly meant, though I don't think it's that Lissa doesn't care about anything. I think it's that she doesn't have a filter; I can see thoughts and feelings flitting across her face as they occur to her. She looks back toward the peninsula and something occurs to her that causes her face to cloud over for a moment. "I'm so sorry this had to happen," she says, gesturing toward where we'd been standing talking to the guards. "But how are you liking the cottage?"

"We love it," I say. "And Ross Head is so beautiful and peaceful."

"Really?" Her gaze is intense now, as though she's misjudged me. "I don't think it's peaceful at all. It *is* beautiful, and invigorating, I think, but peaceful is not a word I'd use. The wind. It's always there, and the sea is so *angry* here. The sea is always claiming lives, in one way or another." Her eyes are fixed on me.

"Did you know him well, the man who . . . was found?"

"Lukas? Yes. He's been living here for a few years, working on the building sites, the houses. The *monstrosities,* some of us call them. They're horrid. But I don't hold that against the young people who come over to work on them . . ." Her face clouds over. "Lukas was so friendly. I always enjoyed chatting to him."

"Do you think he . . . slipped?" I ask.

Her eyes troubled, she says with a shrug, "He was depressed, his friends said, missing home."

"You think it might have been suicide?"

"Maybe." She looks away. I feel panic sweep through me. How am I going to tell Lilly?

I change the subject. "Have you lived in this cottage a long time?"

Her smile is tight, ironic, holding something back. "Oh, I was born in the Big House," she says after a moment, gesturing toward Rosscliffe House.

"We wondered if Felix Crawford was your father," I say. "So you grew up here on Ross Head?"

"We left when I was ten. I moved back almost twenty years ago now. The cottages were part of the property, and when I inherited, I decided to renovate them. One for me and two to rent. I had to sell Rosscliffe House and the land though. Of course, I regret it now." She looks down toward the new houses. There's much more behind the words, but I have the sense it's a closed topic, so I don't follow up. She looks out over the water. I don't know what to say and the silence is starting to feel awkward when she says, "How about a hot drop?" and before I can respond, she tops off my tea with more from the pot.

While I finish it, she tells me the names of the flowers in her garden, pointing to each and giving me the Latin name and the common name. When I look at my watch and say, "Oh, I really should be getting back. They'll be wondering," she smiles and takes the seven euros I hand over and brings me a carton of eggs and a loaf of brown bread wrapped in wax paper.

"I hope you won't be bothered by all of this," she says. "I don't know how long it will go on . . . I'm so sorry."

"Please don't worry," I say. "It's not your fault and they're likely to be finished quickly." Something in her eyes makes me add, "I'm happy to explain it to you, what they'll be doing or anything about the investigation. Let me know if you have any questions. It's my line of work after all."

Lissa looks up quickly, her gray eyes fixed on mine, and I think she's about to take me up on my offer. But then she hesitates and thanks me, saying she may do that at some point. We exchange goodbyes and I walk back along the path, curious now about what the local guards *are* doing. Sergeant Tobin said the remains had been found by a tourist walking on the beach. It was likely the unlucky tourist called the emergency line and the local guards responded, setting up cordons on the beach and looking for evidence where the remains had washed up. If the body has been in the water since April, though, it's unlikely there's any evidence to be found. At this point, the remains are likely to be not much more than a skeleton dressed in what's left of the sodden clothes, most of the soft tissue eaten away by fish and crabs.

Even though it seems likely the death was a suicide, they'll have to check for evidence along the cliffs, anything indicating that this Lukas didn't go in on purpose. They'll have to look for places where there might have been a struggle or where he may have slipped or grabbed at the grass or plants along the cliffs as he went over.

But I know there won't be much of an investigation. When this much time has passed, and the scene is outdoors on top of that, you do a search for evidence out of a sense of responsibility, not because you think you're actually going to find something.

Lissa's cottage sits on the highest point of the peninsula and I turn to look down toward Rosscliffe House and the open Atlantic beyond. She has a good view of the house and the cliffs and the new houses as well as the three construction sites, and I wonder what it's like to look out every day at the place where she grew up, now owned by someone else, someone she seems to resent for developing her childhood home. I'm betting there's a complicated story there.

I turn around and follow the path to the edge of the cliffs and stand there for a moment looking across the inlet, feeling the wind on my face. Suddenly, I'm seized with vertigo as I imagine falling through space, hurtling toward the rocks below, and I step back, a little breathless, then return to the road.

Outside our cottage, I take a moment to steel myself for Lilly's onslaught. I'm going to have to explain to her why there are guards everywhere, and the one thing I don't want to have to tell her is that someone died of an accidental or suicidal drowning a few hundred yards from where we're spending the summer.

But when I walk in, she seems to have forgotten all about our fight. Sprawled out on the couch watching a video with Adrien, she's now wearing jeans and a black T-shirt and eye shadow and mascara and she looks ready for a night on the town rather than a cliff walk in the country.

Conor's cleaning up from lunch and he takes the eggs and bread I hand him and puts them away. Whispering so the kids won't hear, I tell him about the remains and he hugs me and says, "Oh, Maggie. I'm so sorry. What do they think happened?"

"It sounds to me like a suicide in April and the remains just washed up. He was from Poland, a construction worker on the houses. Poor kid. I don't suppose it will be a big story, though. They'll probably keep it quiet once they confirm his identity."

He hugs me again and I rest my head on his chest. I'm tired all of a sudden and overwhelmed thinking about planning something for dinner and finding activities to keep Lilly from dwelling on this new death.

"Let's go out for a meal in the village tonight," Conor says suddenly. "We haven't been yet and Grace says that one of the pubs, The Net, is a sort of gastropub, does really good food, won an award last year. We can celebrate you and Lilly being here, have a look around. What do you think?"

I lean into him, smelling him through his shirt, feeling the warmth of his body, the satisfying solidness of his chest. He pulls me in and strokes my hair away from my forehead.

"I think that you are a very smart man," I tell him. "And I think you have very good ideas."

Three

....

Detective Sergeant Ann Tobin pulls the car into a spot in front of the Garda station and shuts it off, the engine hissing as the air conditioner slows and stops. Broome opens his door and starts to get out, then looks back when he realizes she hasn't moved to take off her safety belt. It's hot today. She can already feel the heat outside seeping into the cool interior of the car. She knows the superintendent will be waiting inside. He'll want to know what she's got. He'll want to know what her plan is. She closes her eyes and leans back in the seat, overwhelmed by all that's ahead.

"Em, everything all right then?" Broome asks, hesitating. He's only been posted in Bantry for a few months now and he's got a prim Wexford accent that annoys her unreasonably. But then everyone annoys her unreasonably these days.

She hesitates, then asks him, "You saw the remains, down on the beach?" He nods, looking nauseous. Broome's face paled when he saw them and Ann worried that he might be sick right there. "The skin was fairly intact, don't you think?"

He just looks confused. "You mean . . . ?"

"The face had been chewed on, but not as much as I would

expect," she goes on, thinking out loud. "Ah, well. He should be at the hospital by now. You go. I'll be in in a minute."

He looks concerned—Broome always looks concerned—but he gets out and goes inside, tripping on the footpath and just barely catching himself before he falls to the pavement. She gets a pack of cigarettes out of her purse and lights one, blowing smoke out the window and ignoring the distasteful glances of the tourists walking by on their way to look at Bantry Bay.

She's been up since seven, when the call came through. The poor woman who found the remains, a grandmotherly type from Brussels out for an early morning walk on Crescent Beach, wanted to talk when Ann arrived. Ann sent Broome and the other officers to secure the scene while she listened to the woman process her experience, describing over and over again how she'd at first thought someone had dumped a bag of trash, but as she got closer, she recognized a hand, then a foot, and then . . . She started crying when she got to the foot.

The remains were not as far gone as Ann might have thought for being in the water all that time. It was undoubtedly Lukas Adamik; Ann lives in Rosscliffe and used to see him around the village. Even with the state of the body she recognized something of the remains. But of course they'll need to be sure. Lukas's girlfriend can do the ID, or Sam Nevin or Tomasz Sadowski, who had been his supervisor on the building sites.

And Lissa Crawford will have the village holding his wake before they've made the formal ID. Ann sighs. She didn't sleep well last night; she never does anymore. The exhaustion is settled into her bones, permanent now. She'll have to go back up to the cottage and ask Lissa not to speculate too much. And then there's Maggie

D'arcy. Ann already knows about her from Danielle Donnelly at the village shop; Danielle, always looking for excitement, tells anyone who will listen about the American cop staying on Ross Head for the summer. "You know, the one who saved the girl in Wicklow. Apparently they're pals with the Murphys. She's got a lovely daughter as well," she told Ann. Danielle is a gossip. If she gets wind of this, she'll have the entire village talking about Lukas Adamik.

Ann hopes that having a cop in the mix on Ross Head won't complicate things. Probably not. Maggie D'arcy seemed a bit too curious, natural, of course, for a detective, but not inclined to jump in where she's not wanted. Ann will have to keep an eye on that, though.

She tosses what's left of the cigarette out the window and gets her things together, locking the car behind her. The super's likely already rung Dublin. They're going to need tech assistance. The chances are small that anything's left after all this time, but they'll need to do whatever they can. And she knows that once Dublin gets wind of the location there'll be additional attention paid.

Ann tries to call up a picture of Lukas's face in life rather than the mess on the beach. He was blond, round, young-looking, jolly. When his girlfriend, Zuzanna, reported him missing back in April, she told Ann that he'd been homesick, but not in a way that made her think he wanted to harm himself. Poor girl. Once they set the wheels in motion, Ann will have to go find her at The Net and talk with her.

It's going to be a long day. Ann puts a hand into her pocket and rubs the smooth stone she keeps there for luck. She's going to need it.

But a thought lodges itself in her mind, and as she rubs the stone, she's conscious of its power, its dangerous allure: *Justice.* Maybe this is it. Maybe he's slipped up and this is the chance they need. For the first time in a while, she feels a little sliver of something like hope. *Steady on, Ann,* she tells herself. *You need to play this right.* And again she thinks: *Justice.*

Four

....

We've all gotten a little dressed up, Lilly and I in jeans and sandals and fancy tops and Conor and Adrien in trousers and nice shirts. I gave Lilly the bare minimum of information, just telling her and Adrien that there's an investigation going on because someone had an accident on the cliffs and that it will be over soon and isn't something they need to worry about. She seemed unconcerned, and though I know I should take her aside and talk to her, get some closure on our argument, it seems so much easier to let it go that I do, playing along with her sudden good mood and excitement about going out to dinner.

We walk the ten minutes down to the village, instead of driving, and the warm summer evening and purply sky at seven make us all a little giddy. There's no sign of the Garda investigation and I breathe a sigh of relief as we push open the door of the pub, the one Grace described as a "gastropub," with the good food. It's called The Net and it has a studiously authentic but recently made-over feel about it, the menu written in chalk on a board hanging on the salmon-colored walls, old Guinness ads and black-and-white photographs of Rosscliffe village and Ross Head positioned next to framed reviews of the gastropub's food. The hostess is showing us to a table when we hear, "Conor! Maggie!"

It's Grace Murphy calling to us from one end of a long table at the back of the pub. Her husband, Lorcan, waves us over and says, "Come join us. We've had a no-show, so there's room for the four of you." Conor and I exchange a glance. I was looking forward to a quiet dinner, but there isn't any way to decline the invitation. We nod and the hostess smiles and hands us our menus.

Grace is a colleague of Conor's in the history department at Trinity, an assistant professor specializing in something to do with French medieval history. Lorcan is a banker. Their daughters are a few years younger than Lilly and Adrien, and while I like Grace's down-to-earth intelligence and style, Conor and I both find Lorcan a bit egotistical and grandstanding. He wears suits even when he doesn't have to and loves to talk about how much money he's made, causing Grace to cringe visibly. Lorcan's been involved in the development at Ross Head; he's organized the financing for the new construction and hotel renovation, and he and Grace bought one of the houses here before it was even built.

"We're just settling in. Have a seat," Lorcan says. "Lilly and Adrien, you go down with the rest of the young ones. We'll just bore you." I check Lilly's face to make sure she's okay with that; she seems fine, already greeting the other teens, who are looking at something on one of their phones and laughing.

"Say hello to Conor and Maggie," Lorcan announces to our side of the table. He points to an older couple at one end of the table, the man in a crisp white shirt and olive green windowpane blazer and the woman in a lighter green linen dress, and introduces them as the Dicksons, Carol and Harry. "They're from London and they were the first investors on Ross Head. We roped them in early!" Lorcan says, a bit too loudly.

Then he gestures toward the handsome man sitting next to Harry Dickson. "Have you met Sam Nevin yet? He's the brains behind the whole development. And this is the lovely Rochelle."

Sam Nevin stands to shake our hand. "Rochelle's really the brains behind it all," he says with a charming smile, nodding at his wife. "Lovely to see you. We're so glad you'll be on Ross Head this summer."

I saw a photo of him online when I googled Ross Head before Lilly and I flew over. In the photo, he was appearing before some sort of zoning board and he looked older, elegant in a dark suit, holding a stack of papers. Now, casually dressed in a crisp button-down shirt and dark trousers, he's still polished looking but more approachable, his expertly cut salt-and-pepper hair glossy with a styling product, something kind and good humored in his blue eyes. He must be in his mid-fifties, but Rochelle Nevin can't be older than forty.

She smiles and gestures for me to sit in the empty seat between her and Grace, who leans in to give me a kiss on the cheek. Grace told me that Rochelle was an actress in the early days of her marriage. Her face is oddly smooth, improved by either plastic surgery or expertly applied makeup, her dark hair in studied messy waves that don't seem to move, and she's wearing a fuchsia pink jacket and pants with shiny gold zippers down the sides.

But her smile is genuine as she turns to me. "Perfect. Now we're a real party. Is everyone having wine?" Her accent isn't Irish, but American or Canadian with a tiny, adopted lilt.

I check on Lilly, who seems perfectly happy next to Adrien at the end of the table with the other teenagers. The two Nevin sons are blends of their parents, dark-haired, the older one about Lilly's age, almost as tall as his father. He's leaning toward her, saying something that makes her laugh.

"So, Maggie, how are you finding West Cork?" Carol Dickson asks after we've ordered drinks from the young waitress.

"Ross Head is absolutely beautiful," I say. "We love our cottage, and the development is stunning. We'll definitely be coming back to stay at the hotel when it's finished."

"Hear that, Sam?" Lorcan booms. "We've got a paying customer already. Now we just have to get the hotel project off the ground, so."

Sam Nevin gives him a small, tight smile and I wonder if the discovery of the remains is on his mind. It's not exactly the publicity you want for a brand-new hotel.

"Has it been an adjustment, Maggie?" Rochelle asks. "Are they treating you well? I found it difficult to make real friends when I first moved here from Canada. But now they're all right, I suppose. If you like that sort of thing." She winks at her husband and everyone laughs. "It's nice to have another North American around."

"I like it a lot. Conor and Adrien have been great about showing us the sights."

"And Grace says you may be moving over in the fall?" Carol adds in.

When my eyes dart to the end of the table to see if Lilly's heard, I find her deep in conversation with the Nevins' sons and Adrien. The older son is telling her something and she's listening raptly, as though it's the most interesting thing she's ever heard.

"That's one of the options," I say. "We're still working out the details. Now that I've seen West Cork, though, I'm thinking about just moving here by myself." I smile at Conor across the table. "Cut out the middleman."

"I knew it," he says. "Just when I've convinced her."

"I love to come down here by myself," Rochelle says. "It's so peaceful in the off-season."

"Hey there, Rosie, what are you having?" Sam asks Rochelle as two waitresses come around to take orders.

I turn to Grace. "I thought it was Rochelle," I whisper. "Is that her nickname?"

Grace reaches up to tuck in a strand of strawberry blond hair that's fallen out of her French twist and scratches her nose, dotted with freckles. "No, Sam just likes to call her that. She was an international Rose of Tralee when they met and he finds it quite funny."

"That's the beauty contest, right?" I remember reading an article about how they were updating the Rose of Tralee contest for the twenty-first century, with contestants who coded and did scientific research.

Grace whispers in a gossipy tone, "Mmmm, celebrating Irish heritage and that. She was the Toronto Rose and came over for the festival and that's how she met Sam. She couldn't have been more than eighteen and he must have been thirty-five."

We chat about things to do in the area and Carol promises to make a list of her favorite shops for me and Lilly. The waitresses bustle around, filling everyone's glasses, and I feel my wine taking effect, shaving the edge off the constant stream of worry that's been running through my veins since I saw the cars in front of Lissa Crawford's cottage. Then Harry Dickson says offhandedly, "Did you see they found the Polish fella who was missing there back in the spring? Sam, did the guards bother you about it?"

Sam looks up from his conversation. I see it again, the worry on his face, and sadness, too. "No, it's all straightforward, it seems," he says quickly, glancing toward the two waitresses. "Very sad thing. He was a good lad."

Rochelle waits for the waitresses to leave and then says in a quiet voice, "He was a lovely boy. We've known him for a few years now. Sam had him working on the projects in the village and then the houses. His friends thought maybe he'd gone home to Poland; he'd been quite depressed." She looks up. The waitresses are coming back with trays of food and she raises her eyebrows and puts a finger to her lips. "They're upset about it," she whispers. "One of them was dating Lukas."

Our plates are put in front of us and for a bit everyone eats happily and makes the requisite sounds of approval. The food *is* good; my duck, raised on a farm nearby, is perfectly cooked and my "tangle of garden lettuces and edible flowers" delicious enough to be forgiven for the pretentious name.

"Barry has a new chef," Sam says. "I'm quite happy with him so far. Irish fella, but he's been in San Francisco for years. Ah, look who's here." A tall guy with short, curly gray hair comes to the table and asks how everything is. There's something a little rough about him; he's got a boxer's nose and a chipped front tooth, a wounded wariness in his eyes. "This is my brother-in-law Barry Mahoney," Sam tells me and Conor, obvious pride spreading across his face. "He manages the place for us and he's making a great job of it!"

I meet Conor's eyes. It seems Sam Nevin doesn't just own all of Ross Head but some of the village, too.

"You're very welcome," Barry says a bit stiffly. "Hope everything was good for ya."

"It was delicious," I tell him. "Thank you." He doesn't make eye contact but looks pleased with the praise.

When he's gone, the waitresses go around the table pouring more wine and one of them asks, "And you, Mrs. Nevin? Will you have some more wine?" Her accent is Eastern European, I think. She's lovely, willowy and dark-haired, wearing a pair of colorful, folk-art earrings.

"Oh, yes, please, Agnieska," Rochelle said, pronouncing it *Agneshka.*

"I love your earrings," I tell her.

"Oh." She reaches up with her free hand to touch one and smiles. "Thank you. They're Polish. The designs are from *wycinanki,* like designs made of paper."

"Agnieska, Zuzanna," Rochelle says to the two women. "Have you met Maggie and Conor yet? They're in Lissa's middle cottage so I'm sure you'll see a lot of them. Take good care of them, all right?"

"All right, Mrs. Nevin." Agnieska, the brunette with the earrings, nods to me. "You're very welcome to Ross Head."

Zuzanna, blond and stockier, says, "I hope you will like it here. It's very beautiful and the people are very nice." She breaks into a hesitant smile that reaches her blue-green eyes. "Especially these people here. Have you been bathing yet?"

I say that we haven't, and she recommends a beach we might like.

When we've finished eating, they come back to take our dessert orders. Sam orders plates of cheese and biscuits for the table and the teenagers all order from the dessert menu. I catch sight of a large painting hanging on the wall at the other end of the room. "That's Rosscliffe House, isn't it?" I ask. "What a beautiful painting of the peninsula."

"That's a Felix Crawford," Grace tells me. "Rosscliffe House was the family seat. He wasn't a terribly famous painter, but he had his fans. His paintings of Ross Head are really lovely."

"You know, your landlady is his daughter. What do you think of her?" Carol asks me. "She's an odd one, isn't she?"

Something about her tone puts my back up. "I like her," I say. "I like her paintings."

Grace jumps in. "Aren't they lovely? She's started showing at some galleries in Dublin. You'd know, Conor. Doesn't Bláithín still work at the College Street Gallery?" She looks suddenly embarrassed at her mention of Conor's ex-wife and Adrien's mother. "Anyway, she's very talented." Conor mentioned once that she and Bláithín were close friends and I wonder if she's resentful of me being here. She's been nothing but welcoming though she's seemed distracted. When I asked Conor about it, he said that she's been struggling with a book she's supposed to be working on and that one of her daughters is going through a challenging period right now.

I look up at Felix Crawford's painting again. "We walked all around Ross Head today and looked at the house and he's captured it perfectly. It has a real atmosphere."

Lorcan asks, "Did you see the ghost?" and breaks into a huge grin when he sees my face. "I'm only messing. Carol's convinced there's a ghost in the house."

"Oh, she's imagining it, of course," Harry Dickson cuts in.

"It must have just been the light," Carol said, giving us a weak smile. "I was walking out there and I could have sworn I saw someone in a window. But maybe—" I check to make sure Lilly's not listening, but I can't tell if she's only pretending to look at her phone. Carol goes on, "There are stories, you know, in the village. About the—"

"Oh, everyone needs to try the cheese," Rochelle interrupts her. We look up to see Agnieska and Zuzanna standing there with platters of cheese, fruit, and biscuits. Zuzanna looks stricken, her face pale, her eyes wide. "It's made right in Rosscliffe," Rochelle says. As Zuzanna leans over to put the platter on the table, Rochelle gives her a quick little pat on her back. Zuzanna must be the one who was dating Lukas. The gesture, understated but sensitive, makes me like Rochelle. "Have you all seen the shop?" she asks us. "We helped to get it up and running a few years ago and they've already won some awards for Irish cheesemaking."

Everyone tries the cheese and exclaims over how good it is. "Maggie, will you be working as a guard in Dublin?" Rochelle asks me.

I look up, aware that all the adults are listening. No one has said anything to me about the Niamh Horrigan case or the murder of my cousin Erin, but they must all remember the coverage of the cases last year. You would have had to have been completely off the grid to avoid it.

"It's unclear," I say. "I'd have to do some additional training. It wouldn't be a lateral thing. We'll see." I try to sound breezy, though in fact I know exactly what the requirements for working for An Garda Síochána would be. My friend Roly Byrne, a detective in the Garda's criminal investigation bureau, responsible for major crimes like murder, has outlined the whole thing for me. Garda Training College for thirty-four weeks, then an assignment somewhere in the country in uniform, some additional detective training and practical experience, and then maybe, just maybe, he'd be able to get me an expedited posting on a specialty team on the basis of my career in the States and my work on the Niamh Horrigan case. It's far from a sure thing, but he's started the process for me in case I decide I want to do it.

I haven't decided.

"Well, it was such an incredible thing, you finding that poor woman like that," Carol says a little breathlessly. "How is she doing? Do you know?"

I look up and catch Conor's eye from across the table. He's listening, too, worried about Lilly hearing, worried about me.

"She's doing well," I say, looking away from the gossipy glitter in Carol's eyes. The truth is more complicated. Niamh, who was assaulted for days while waiting to be found, has reached the point in the process where she's angry, raging at the way her life was hijacked. It lasts for a while, in my experience, and some people never get past it, but anger is better than the alternative, where it turns inward and eats you up. I have experience with that, too.

Agnieska and Zuzanna are clearing the table when Barry Mahoney and another man appear. Barry looks worried. The man with him is quite a bit younger, maybe in his late twenties, very tall, blond, and high-cheekboned, wearing a leather jacket. He has a scar on his forehead, a raised seam that looks like a knife wound. Something about the way they stand, waiting, catches my interest, and I watch as Sam Nevin notices them and exchanges a glance with Barry. He pushes his chair back, makes an apology to the table, and follows them up to the bar. I'm aware of Rochelle following him with her eyes and I wonder if it's something related to the Garda investigation.

My phone vibrates and when I see it's Uncle Danny calling, I excuse myself and step outside on to the sidewalk to take the call. I've been trying to reach him and I've missed him a few times over the past few days; I just want to make sure nothing's wrong. "Hey, Uncle Danny," I say. "Everything okay?"

"Yeah, Mags, just wanted to make sure you guys are having a good vacation." I breathe a sigh of relief and tell him about Ross Head and the cottage. He says he and Eileen have been going for walks a lot and that things are good at the bar. I tell him I need to get back but that we'll talk soon. I've just put the phone back in my pocket when I look up to see a car parked right in front of the pub. It's idling, the low hum of the radio seeping out the open passenger-side window and a thin stream of cigarette smoke following it. The man sitting in the driver's seat looks up and meets my gaze. Immediately, he gives me a detached smile, and tosses the cigarette out the window. My cop brain makes note of the car: a late-model Mercedes, dark, the chrome shiny and well cared for, Cork registration, a small stuffed whale or dolphin hanging from the rearview mirror. And it makes note of the guy, too, late forties or early fifties, heavyset, crew cut. I turn and go back into the pub.

Sam Nevin is back and the other two guys are gone when I return to the table. Conor and I exchange a glance as everyone starts to get up to go. "Should we settle our bill at the bar?" he ventures.

"It's all taken care of," Sam says. "You're all my guests."

I know Conor well enough to know he doesn't like it, but we thank Sam and are getting ready to leave when Lilly calls over to us from the other end of the table, "Mom, Jack says there's a really good band playing at the other pub, the one across the street. He knows some of the guys in the band. Can we walk over and go listen for a bit?" Jack must be the older Nevin son. He's watching Lilly with more than casual interest, I think.

I look at Conor, who nods. "Sure," I say. "That sounds great. You can head over and we'll be right behind you." The teenagers tumble out of the pub and we say our thank-yous and goodbyes.

Rochelle Nevin touches my arm. "I'm so glad the kids hit it off. Maggie, it was lovely to meet you. Someone told me you're a runner. I am, too. Maybe we can run together sometime and you can tell me all about your plans."

"I'd like that," I say. But thinking about those plans gives me a sudden rush of anxiety. What *are* my plans? There are so many things to be decided between now and some undetermined date at the end of the summer when Lilly and I might make a decision about moving to Dublin.

I look over at Conor. When he feels me watching him, he raises his eyebrows and gives me a funny little twist of a smile. I'm flooded with love for him, for his graying hair, flopping onto his forehead, for his concern, for the way his arms feel around me. *For now.* That's what we said when we decided on this summer. *For now.*

Five

....

Conor and I walk across the street to the other pub, a more traditional village gathering place called McCarthy's, holding hands
and debriefing on the evening. "I think the kids had fun, don't
you?" I say.

"Yeah, every time I looked down at their end of the table, they
were laughing and chatting away," he says. "Even Adrien." Adrien's
shy, and while he's quite comfortable around adults, Conor worries
about how he gets along with people his own age. "So, what did
you think of the local property tycoon? Lorcan says that the Ross
Head development and revitalizing the village are Sam's great passion."

"He's charming, but there's something a little slick about him. I
liked her better. She's smart."

"You just like having someone around with a similarly horrible accent." He winks and I make a face at him. "Yeah, I feel a
bit funny now that Sam's bought us all dinner. Feel like I owe
him, you know."

"They seemed stressed about something," I say after a minute.

"Well, they're probably just a wee bit stressed that someone's
body was found on the beach. See, who's the better detective
now?"

I turn my face up and he stoops for a kiss. "You're a very good detective," I say as we push through the door into the warm and close interior, already crowded as we squeeze past the bodies toward the bar. Sure enough, there's a band set up against one wall, playing a rock and roll version of an Irish tune I vaguely recognize, and I can see Lilly and Adrien and the Nevins' teenage sons standing and listening to the music. Conor goes up to get us each a pint and we watch the band from the other side of the room and let Lilly and Adrien do their thing.

The band is good, really good actually, a group of guys in their late teens or early twenties, playing covers of classics, a few original songs, and some Irish standards, too. The bass player is a goth-looking teen in a leather jacket and there's a keyboard player and a kid with a fiddle and another holding a bodhrán. The lead singer and guitar player is a tall, blond baby-faced boy with high cheekbones and longish hair and luxurious lips and eyelashes. His voice is something special, a clear, croony tenor that, on its own, elevates them above your usual local kid bar band.

"Do you think Lilly's gotten over your argument from earlier?" Conor asks me when the band takes a break. The pub is absolutely packed now, not a square foot to stand in up near Adrien and Lilly, so we stay where we were, our pints resting on the table in front of us.

"Hell if I know," I say, trying to make myself heard over the noise in the pub. "She perked up at dinner, but I think that's because she was sitting next to Jack Nevin."

"She's not talking to him now," Conor says, and we both look up to see her huddled with a tall blond boy. The lead singer of the band, I realize.

"Hmmmm. She abandoned poor Adrien?"

"He'll be all right," Conor says. Lilly is laughing at something the blond guy is saying. He's leaning toward her, completely focused on her and talking animatedly with his hands.

I watch as he says something and nods and she smiles as he heads back to his guitar. "Thank you," he says into the mike. He has a slight accent, Eastern European, like the waitresses. "I'm Alex and we're the Mountaineers." He hesitates, then says somberly, "We want to do a special Polish song tonight in honor of a friend of ours who passed away. This is a song about a town by the ocean where the singer's love is waiting for him. This one's for you, Lukas." He raises the pint glass he's put down on a stool and the other band members and a few other people in the pub raise their glasses, too. "Lukas," they all say, and then the band launches into a slow, sad, folky ballad. Alex sings the words in Polish, a language I don't understand, and yet I don't need to recognize the words to feel it: love, grief, homesickness. Somehow it all comes through. When it's over, there's a round of respectful applause and a chorus of "To Lukas." Lilly is clapping wildly and gazing at Alex now. I don't see Jack Nevin anywhere.

I scan the pub, trying to figure out who's here. It looks like a mix of locals and tourists, the locals at the back of the room and the tourists sitting at the few tables in the pub and clapping enthusiastically for the band. Standing in a small group of men next to the bar, I notice, is the blond guy with the scar on his forehead who came over with Barry Mahoney to talk to Sam Nevin. When Grace and Lorcan squeeze in next to us, I ask Grace who he is.

"That's Tomasz, right?" she asks Lorcan.

Lorcan takes a long sip of his lager and looks back at them. "Yeah. He's Sam's building manager, I think. Polish fella. Lot of the lads who've been working on the development are over from Poland, Bulgaria, and Albania. Tomasz keeps 'em in line. Very capable fella. He's been over here a good few years now, working for Sam. Sam depends on him."

"Sam seemed upset about something at dinner," I say.

Lorcan says quickly, "They're racing to finish the three houses that are underway and get started on the next seven. Not to mention breaking ground on the hotel renovation. We're waiting on the permission from the Cork County Council. And then this thing with the body and the guards keeping the crews out for part of the day. They're a bit antsy about it. Tomasz must be wondering when they can get back on the sites. Every day they're stopped, it's thousands and thousands of euros gone. You know how building goes."

"Thank you," the lead singer says when they've finished the song they're doing. "As I said, I'm Alex and we're the Mountaineers. This is my friend Billy on bass and Stephen on drums and we've got Daragh on the keyboard there and Mac on the fiddle. Now, we have a special guest tonight, all the way from America. She's going to give us a song. Her name is Lilly. Lilly Lombardi. Here she is."

I feel my stomach contract in panic. "Oh, God," I say to Conor. "Usually she's terrified to sing in front of people. Is she drunk?"

Conor looks panicked, too. "I don't think so." We've been in bars when drunk American tourists have gotten up to sing Irish tunes they barely know the words to. It always embarrasses me.

"How did she even . . . ?" I turn to Lorcan and Grace. "Should I try to stop her?"

"No," Grace says. "Let her sing. What's the harm?"

Conor looks around for Adrien, to see if he knows anything, but Adrien's off to the side, looking as surprised as we are.

Lilly steps up to the microphone stand and Alex-the-lead-singer smiles at her, though he looks a little nervous, too. She takes the microphone and closes her eyes. I wait for "Wild Mountain Thyme" or an Irish tune I know she knows the words to, but instead they take a long moment, gathering our attention, and then the keyboard player plays a few bars and Alex strums a few chords. They're familiar, but I don't have it yet, not until Lilly is singing, *"A long, long time ago / I can still remember how that music / Used to make me smile."* She opens her eyes and smiles broadly, confidently, then goes on.

Conor and I look at each other. Her voice is pure and clear, the familiar words coming out like drops of sunlight, her face so perfect and smooth in the low light that I can't stop looking at her. Lilly. My Lilly.

By the time she gets to *"bye, bye, Miss American Pie,"* everyone in the bar is cheering and singing along and her voice has evolved, a little husky, a little bit of a country twang in there that mixes perfectly with Alex's tenor and raucous guitar and the steady bass and drums and keyboard and fiddle. They're improvising, creating something new, the six of them and Don McLean. Lilly and Alex are watching each other while they sing, taking cues from each other's eyes as though they've known each other for years. They're making the song their own, giving it something that makes me feel the lost innocence and sadness of it all over again, as though I've never heard it before.

What I can't help thinking, what I'll come back to later when I think about this night, is that I'm watching my daughter fall in love.

I'm just not sure if it's the guy, or the music, or the feeling of having the audience under her power.

Maybe all three.

"You were brilliant, Lilly," Adrien says as we walk home along the peninsula road, the night finally almost dark, the bright stars picked out in the sky overhead. Gulls call over the water. The ocean rushes beneath us. "You should do it for real, like."

"Hold on a second," I say in mock horror. "Are you telling my daughter to quit school and join a rock band?"

"Yeah," Adrien says. "Do it, Lilly. Do it!"

"Watch it, Kearney." I turn around and swat him and he smiles at me, a sweet, shy smile full of something, hope I think, that our bad luck has passed, that things are going to be better for all of us. I feel a surge of love for him that surprises me. It feels somehow inappropriate, but it's there nonetheless, the affection for the part of him that's Conor, but also the part of him that isn't, too. Even the part of him that's his mother. I smile back.

"I love you guys," I say without thinking about it. Conor squeezes my hand.

From behind us, Adrien says, "We think you're all right, too, Maggie."

Lilly is looking dreamily toward the cliffs and Rosscliffe House, a tiny half smile on her face. The moonlight makes her face pale and pearly and her smile is secret, full of hidden things.

"Mom," she says suddenly. "I was just thinking about the person we saw in the house. And what they said at dinner about the ghost. And you said they found a dead person in the water. You don't think that's what we saw, do you? Like the ghost of someone who died?"

"Oh, Lilly, no, of course not," I say, too loudly. "No, no. And we don't even know what that was, what they were talking about with the house."

Lilly looks out toward the cliffs again. Rosscliffe House looms, a dark blockade against the marble of the night sky. Lilly doesn't say anything; her mind is somewhere else now. I feel a surge of love and worry for her, and a flash of caution.

The windows of the house are empty as we turn toward home.

Six

Sitting on the patio with my coffee the next morning before Conor and the kids are up, I find an online Cork area news site and search for a story about Lukas Adamik and the remains.

> *Human remains were found yesterday by a tourist walking on a beach near Ross Head. Gardaí have not confirmed that the remains are those of Lukas Adamik, a local man who went missing in April after walking on the cliffs at Ross Head, but sources confirm that they are operating on the assumption the remains are Adamik's. Adamik was working as a builder on the development at Ross Head when he went missing. He was known to have suffered from depression and one theory was that he had returned to his native Poland.*
>
> *Gardaí remind walkers to be cautious when walking along cliffs and to wear shoes with good treads to avoid slipping.*

I check my watch. Eight o'clock Sunday morning. But he'll be up. I dial Roly Byrne's cell phone number.

"Hi, D'arcy," he answers, cheerful and wide awake. "How's the holiday?"

"Nice. It's been sunny. How are you?"

"Ah, good. I've gone out to get some pastries for the lady of the house, now. She likes the big almond ones. Yeah, it's been quiet here. Kids are all on school holidays and we're going to San Sebastian in a few days now."

"Oh, that's right. I forgot you have the holiday coming up. You ready for some time off?"

"I am, I am, right enough. Some sand, some sun, some sangria . . ." I can see his face, his huge grin, his mischief-filled blue eyes staring off into space as he imagines himself on a Spanish beach.

"Well, look, before you go, I'm wondering if you can do me a favor. A tourist found a body on the beach down here yesterday. Actually, it probably wasn't much of a body anymore. It looks like it was a local guy, originally from Poland, a builder who had been working on this big development down here. He went missing in April and, well, it seems he fell or jumped off the cliffs."

"Shite, on your holiday, like? You and Lilly weren't there when they found it, were you?" Roly knows how worried I've been about Lilly's mental health.

"No, but I . . . well, I want to be able to tell her exactly what happened, you know? So she doesn't speculate and get too in her head about it. Does that make sense?"

"Absolutely. Okay, I'll ask around. What's the place called?"

"The village is Rosscliffe, the Ross Head peninsula."

He hesitates. "Ah. Okay. Give me the day and I'll get back to you." I'm almost positive he recognized the name.

"Thanks, Roly. Take care now."

"No worries. Been meaning to ring you, anyway," he says. "To let you know there's a place for you at Templemore in September if you want it." The Garda Training College, where every police officer in Ireland does their version of police academy, is in Templemore, an hour and a half southwest of Dublin.

"Seriously? Wow. When do I have to let them know?" I feel panic wash over me. We've just gotten here. I don't feel ready to make the decision.

"You've got a few weeks, anyway. Have a think about it. What does Conor think?"

"He's all for us moving here. He's not sure about the part where I'll have to live in Tipperary during the week for the better part of a year."

"Okay, then. Have a chat with him. Take care. I'll be back to you as soon as I can."

I take Mr. Bean for a walk along the peninsula road, letting him off leash to do his own thing while I stroll and relish the mug of strong coffee I've brought along. The morning is wet and fresh, the ocean calm this morning, and I'm feeling surprisingly at peace. Lilly seemed in high spirits as she went off to bed last night and I let myself fantasize about her working hard to get into a music conservatory or deciding to sing opera. I've gotten as far as Conor and I in glamorous clothes sitting in a box at La Scala before I start laughing at myself. Lilly will figure out what she wants to do, but it felt good to see her so happy last night, surprised by her own talent, excelling at something in public.

And my anxiety about the investigation has dissipated, too. The body found on the beach yesterday seems to be nothing more than a sad case of suicide and it seems like it should be resolved fairly quickly.

I walk along the road, watching Mr. Bean's squat little body rising and disappearing in the tall grass, and I'm startled when I hear my name and look up to find Lissa Crawford standing in front of her cottage, also holding a coffee mug and waving at me.

"Would you like to come in for coffee and a scone?" she calls out. "I'd like to speak with you about something if it's all right with you."

I call Mr. Bean over and put him back on the leash. His short legs are tired out from his romping and he flops happily beneath my chair in the kitchen, panting heavily while Lissa brings me a fresh cup of coffee and a warm oatmeal scone, dripping butter onto my plate, and offers the little dog a dish of water, which he laps gratefully.

"I hope you don't mind me waylaying you like this," she says nervously. "It's just that you said, yesterday, that if I had any questions about the investigation, I should ask and, well, it's not about Lukas, but it occurred to me that you might be the perfect person to help me solve a . . . well, a mystery."

Surprised, I say, "I'm happy to help if I can." I wait expectantly, but she seems to be gathering her thoughts, figuring out how to say it.

Finally she says, "As I told you, I was born at Rosscliffe House." She gestures vaguely at the cottage's front window. "It was in my family for many generations, as these houses were. My father, Felix Crawford, was a . . . well, I suppose a well-known painter in his way. He and my mother tried to live the life that they'd been raised to live, but there wasn't money for that life anymore and my childhood was odd. In a way that is perhaps particular to people of my . . . well, to a certain kind of Irish person, I suppose.

"Maybe it's hard for an American to understand. Rosscliffe House was *The Big House*. Around here. It always has been. I don't know how much Irish history you have, but you understand what that means? For centuries we were the landlords here, we were in charge of things, and then we weren't?" I nod. "I suppose in some ways we still were in charge, but by the time I was born, it was gone mostly, that way of life. Some of the families were . . . clinging on, in our houses. In our case, the money was all gone, but I suppose I didn't know that. The benefits of a country childhood, I suppose. There was always something to do, something to eat." She smiles a radiant smile.

"Blackberries, you know, along the lanes, and fish we would catch from the rocks. My parents were fairly social, so we often had people visiting, friends and family and other, well, other families like ours. The summer of 1973, I was ten, my brother fourteen, and we had some distant cousins called the Allertons, who stayed with us, and some other people were here, too. West Cork is a bit like that, I suppose, more than other parts of Ireland. It's . . . somehow looser out here. Or it was then. They were just living with us, a bunch of adults, artists, and just people, too, who, I suppose, had nowhere else to go, or just liked West Cork in the summer, and we children ran wild. In 1973. You can imagine. Mrs. Nevin, Sam's mother, who cooked for us sometimes, tried to exert a little discipline. But otherwise, it was all very . . ." She waved her hands around. "Free. The house was crumbling around us. That I knew. I have this vivid memory of a strip of wallpaper peeling off the wall while we were eating dinner. It rolled right down and hit the floor and there was rot underneath, black, like lace, and no one said a word."

She stops speaking for a minute and I sense that she's trying to get her story in order. Then she says, "Memory is funny, isn't it? I recently . . . thought of something I hadn't thought of in many years and now I can't stop thinking about it. When I woke up, I wasn't sure at first if it was only a dream. It felt so real and then I realized that it *was* real. It was a memory, if that makes any sense. The dream had sort of . . . dredged it up."

She looks at me expectantly, as though I should understand what she means.

When my face makes it clear that I don't, she takes a breath and goes on. "That year we left Rosscliffe House for good, my father died in a fall from the cliffs." She looks up at me. "We never went back.

"The memory, well . . . I think I may have found a piece of evidence. A cloth with blood on it. In my dream, I was wandering through the house and I was going up the stairs to the third floor, where my room was, and in this little sort of pocket or compartment in the molding next to the stairs—that part of the dream is oddly vivid, the little pocket, like a secret door. I saw that someone had stuffed a piece of cloth or linen inside, something nice, and it was stained with blood, absolutely soaked with it. I picked it up and brought it back to my room. I thought it was beautiful, you see. The red, the vibrancy of it. For the last few years, I've been painting these canvases that are exploring the idea of stains, of . . . well, you've seen them. I didn't understand why I was painting them, only that I had to. And then . . . the dream. Except I don't think it was a dream. I think it was a memory. Does that make any sense?"

I just nod and let her go on.

"Everyone was very upset later that day, but no one said anything about it. There was just this silence and strangeness and all the visitors left over the next few days, and then at the end of the summer my mother and my brother and myself, we left for Dublin, and my father was coming after us with Charles Allerton, his cousin who had been staying with us. My father went for a last walk on the cliffs and . . . something happened. He slipped. We didn't get word until we were back in Dublin." She looks away, in the direction of the cliffs.

"How awful. I'm so sorry."

"Yes. I don't know, but the more I think about it, the more I go over it in my head, the more I think that when I found the cloth, there must have been some sort of terrible accident or . . . injury. Doesn't that seem to you like the only explanation?" Her face is pale, stricken.

"Perhaps," I say. "It's hard to know without more information. What happened to the cloth?"

She frowns. "I don't know. The memory isn't very clear after that. Only . . . Do you think it could have been a . . . a murder?"

I force myself to wait a minute before responding. "I don't know about that. It's much more likely to have been a kitchen accident or something more pedestrian," I say soothingly.

She nods. "I know that. After the dream, I couldn't understand why I'd attached that word—*murder*—to the memory. Of course, it might have been an injured animal, menstrual blood, or as you say a kitchen accident. But it wasn't. I don't know how I know that, but I just do. I haven't wanted to go back into the house. I had to, when I returned to live here, to find some papers and things and . . . well, I didn't understand it then, but I had the most terrible feeling going back there, like I wasn't wanted, like I would be *driven* out. I knew I would never go back again. There must have been something terrible, don't you think?"

She looks so distressed that I have the urge to reach out and pat her hand. Instead I say, "If there had been a . . . an unnatural death, there would have been a body to report, the guards called to the house, or someone would have been missing."

She swallows, then looks up at me, and I can see the fear in her eyes. This, whatever she's going to say next, is the thing that scares her. "Well, that's just it," she says. "I only just remembered this part. There was a girl, a young woman, I suppose, who was living with us and taking care of me and my brother sometimes, like a sort of governess. She was kind. I liked her, and I've put it together since the dream that she . . . well, she was gone the next morning, after I found the cloth, just gone, and no one would talk about it. She . . . disappeared. I never saw her again. Everyone seemed upset the next day. Nobody would answer my questions about where she'd gone. And then it was just a few days later that my mother said we were leaving and then . . . my father."

"You said she was a governess?"

"Well, not formally. She may have been a friend . . . I'm not sure. I forgot all about her, for many years. And then, well . . . I'll show you." She stands up abruptly and goes through to a room off the kitchen. I finish my scone, scratching Mr. Bean's head when he wakes up long enough to beg for a few crumbs and then lies back down again. Sun streams through the windows of the kitchen; the inkblot paintings are the colors of cherry Popsicles and yet now I can only see blood. There are a few framed photographs of Ross Head and West Cork on the walls, but very few of human beings. The only exceptions are a framed photo of a cute blond boy of about ten and a formal portrait of a woman who resembles Lissa Crawford a bit around the mouth, both on the mantel.

"You see, I was writing up an introduction for a little book the tourism council was publishing, about the art scene here in West Cork and the artists whose studios you can visit and so forth," Lissa says, coming back into the room and placing a photocopy of a newspaper clipping in front of me. "And I asked one of the librarians in Bantry if she could find some photographs and stories about Ross Head in the old days. I thought I might find some little stories about painters and pot makers and weavers who have worked here. I found this."

I look down at it. It's a copy of the front page of a local West Cork newspaper from June 30, 1973. There's a photo printed on the front of a group of people sitting on the ground on blankets, an old-fashioned picnic basket in front of them, and the caption reads "Picnickers at Ross Head."

Lissa points to a woman with long dark hair, a white streak at her temple, and says, "Her name was Dorothea. It came back when I saw her picture. That's her. She lived with us that summer and then she disappeared."

I don't know what to say, so I wait to see if she's going to say anything else. Finally, I ask, "Have you tried to contact her, this Dorothea?"

"No, I don't know her surname, you see. I wouldn't know how to begin. She was Irish. I remember that."

"Could anyone from your family shed any light?"

"My mother died when I was fifteen, of uterine cancer, and my brother died young," she says. "He's been gone for years. There's no family left." She looks out toward the sea and I see grief flash across her face. "I did ask Annie Tobin, the guard you met, about it, to see if there was anything in her files about a woman gone missing, but she said there was nothing. Of course, if no one reported it, well, then . . . there wouldn't be a report, would there?"

I see where she's going. "You're concerned there was a crime and it was . . . covered up," I say.

She sits down again and her fingers fiddle with the fringed edge of her napkin. "It's terrible to think of, but, you see, the dreams keep coming, the paintings. I feel I need to *know*, if you see. And that's why I wanted to talk to you. I'm wondering if I could hire you, as a sort of private investigator."

I take a deep breath. "I'm sure there's an explanation for the cloth and Dorothea's disappearance. Often these things tend to be much less dramatic than our memories make them out to be. Children project the very worst on to slightly mysterious situations. I've always thought it's best to tell them the truth for that reason, so their imaginations don't create something much worse than the truth." I'm a hypocrite, of course, keeping from Lilly the fact that I'm planning on moving her to Dublin. "I'm happy to help you in any way that I can, but you don't need to hire me. Maybe you could try to make a list of everyone who was in and out of the house that summer. As a place to start. It's a technique I use when I'm interviewing witnesses. You can go through each room of the house and try to see all the people associated with that particular room. Then you could ask them if they remember anything."

Suddenly, Mr. Bean, refreshed from his nap, jumps up and whines at me. Lissa Crawford says, "Oh, I've kept you so long, but that's a good idea," she says. "I'll try that."

"My family will be wondering what happened to us," I say. *My family.* "But let me know how the list goes and we can take it from there."

Tucking a few strands of cascading silvery blond hair into her bun, she walks me back out to the road and bids me goodbye. When I turn around to wave a final time, she's standing there with her feet firmly planted and her hands on her hips, looking out across the peninsula that used to be hers. She can see everything from here: the gleaming new houses on the cliffs, the building sites, Rosscliffe House, a few vague islands in the distance, and the Atlantic beyond, melting into the horizon toward North America.

I can't help seeing Lissa Crawford as a lady of the manor out of history, surveying her property, as far as the eye can see.

The day is hot and sunny and we drive to the beach Zuzanna told us about, where we sit in chairs on the sand, reading and dozing. The ocean is still cold—Conor says it never really warms up—but we all go in once and come out invigorated to sit in the sun again and let it warm our goose-bumped skin. Adrien and Lilly walk along the stretch of shoreline and return with little pink shells they've collected; their excited smiles remind me of children collecting treasures. In the evening, Conor makes grilled chicken and the four of us sit out after dinner, playing Scrabble on the patio and watching the sun set in the west. There's no more sign of the Garda investigation and I assume they've wrapped it up, accepting that any evidence there might have been in April is now lost to the wind and the waves.

After Lilly and Adrien go inside to watch a movie, I tell Conor about my conversation with Lissa Crawford.

"Do you think there's anything in it?" he asks me.

"I have no idea. There's clearly some real trauma associated with the memory. I took this class a few years back, on the psychology of trauma, and the way she told the story of finding the cloth, of remembering that moment so vividly but not what came before or after, it was clear that *something* happened."

"But wouldn't there have been a missing person's report if this woman really did disappear? If she worked for the Crawfords, wouldn't they have gone to the guards?"

"Well, unless they were covering it up," I say. "That's clearly what she's worried about. She said she asked Ann Tobin—she's a detective out of Bantry who lives here in the village—and nothing was in the files from 1973. I told her to make a list of everyone who she remembers being at the house that summer. It's a place to start, anyway."

Conor reaches for his wineglass and raises his eyebrows. "Surely there must be an explanation. Some sort of an accident and she was sent off to hospital and decided not to return to the job, something like that."

"Yeah, I hope Lissa figures it out. It's clearly been troubling her since she found the picture. Though the paintings that came out of it are lovely." I grin at him. "Hope she makes some more before she resolves her deep-seated trauma."

"Mmmm," Conor says. "The quality of the art really declines when the therapist gets involved, like." He reaches out and takes my hand and we finish our wine before going inside to do the dishes.

Adrien is alone on the couch, reading a giant math textbook he brought along to prepare himself for a class he's taking next year. "Where's Lilly?" I ask him. A fleece blanket is in a heap on the couch next to him, as though she's just thrown it off.

"On the phone," he says, pointing in the direction of her room.

"Oh," I say. "You know who? Zoe or one of her friends from home?"

He shakes his head but doesn't look up at me. When Lilly comes out again, she doesn't say anything and something on her face stops me from asking.

Conor washes and I dry. When we arrived and realized the cottage didn't have a dishwasher, we all complained for a few days, but I've come to love the repetitive nature of washing and drying the dishes by hand, the way my brain quiets down and then floats free while I soap and rinse and dry. The cottage has open shelves for tableware on one wall and seeing the clean and cheerfully painted bowls and plates stacked next to one another in their places engenders a deep sense of peace, if only for a moment.

Seven

Monday morning, I wake up at six to get a long run in before it gets too hot. I'm running through the village, just starting to loosen up, when I hear my name and look up to see Rochelle Nevin, also in running clothes, waving from the little parking lot next to the pub. She's bent over, tying her shoes. "Hi, Maggie," she calls out. "Beautiful morning for it, isn't it?"

It *is* a beautiful morning, the pale blue sky deckled with wispy clouds, a slight breeze touching the grass. I slow when I reach her and she falls into pace next to me. "Do you mind if we run together?" she asks. "I suspect we're taking the same route."

"Of course not," I say. "I'm still learning the routes."

She laughs. "There are only two really, one where you run half the miles you want to go south and one half the miles you want to go north. And you're taking your life into your hands either way."

"I know. These narrow roads. It's lovely, though." We reach the main road, and when I point north, she nods and we set off. We're well matched. She keeps up with me easily and has no trouble talking while we run.

"Thank you again for dinner the other night," I tell her. "It was delicious and it was fun to meet everyone. The food was so good."

"Well, we're proud of the pub. It was one of our first projects here. Sam knew if it could get some notice for the food, it would bring people here, make it seem like a viable place for a holiday home. We've been working on revitalizing Rosscliffe for ten years. The hotel opening is going to be the end of a long journey." She presses something on her watch and it beeps back at her.

"Really? Ten years? That's a long time," I say.

"It's felt like a hundred years at times."

Because I'm curious what she'll say, I venture, "I'm so sorry about the boy who worked for you."

She doesn't seem reluctant to talk about it. "Yes, it's awful," she says. "A lot of our employees from the pub and some of the other businesses were friends with him. They were a tightly knit group. He was a lovely boy. It's so unfortunate and it's been bad for morale. I think everyone really did think he went back to Poland. But in retrospect, we should have known. He'd been quite depressed, and he had some . . . personal problems, and maybe he'd been having some conflicts with his girlfriend, Zuzanna, who you met the other night." She looks up as a car approaches and she falls back so that we can run single file. "How long have you been running?"

"Forever," I tell her. "I ran cross-country in high school and college. I started doing marathons twenty-five years ago and I still try to run one every few years. I saw there's a 10K in Bantry later this summer."

We're settled into a good pace now. "Maybe we'll do it together," she says. "I started running as therapy after my boys were born. It was my excuse for getting out of the house, but now I'm addicted to it. It's becoming quite popular in Ireland. People don't look at me strangely now. Everybody's got their water bottles and sports bras now." She laughs. A small blue car passes us, a hand waving out the window. "Oh, that's Jack. He's been to Bantry to do an errand for Sam."

We do three miles at an ambitious pace, then take it down a notch when we turn around as the road winds close to the coast.

"This is great," I say after a bit. "I usually have a hard time finding running partners."

"I know." She grins at me and wipes a sheen of sweat from her forehead. "Everybody's too slow or wants to talk too much on the way out."

I'm breathing harder now, but our pace is sensible and we settle into a comfortable silence after a bit. She asks me how Lilly likes Ireland and I say I think she's happy, but it's been an adjustment.

She regards me shrewdly. "It must be difficult," she says. "She's such a lovely girl. And I hear she has a beautiful voice."

"The pub? Yes, she loves to sing, though she's never done it in public before, other than in school."

"Well, from what I hear from my boys, she's a natural." She grins. "I think Jack may have a bit of a crush actually."

I smile. "Lissa Crawford told me Sam's mother worked at Rosscliffe House. I didn't realize he grew up in the village."

"Oh, yes, Sam was raised here. The boutique is his sister Ellen's. And you met his brother-in-law Barry, who manages the pub now, which has always been his and Ellen's dream. He used to manage the building sites, but he always wanted to be a restaurateur. Sam was able to make that happen."

She goes on. "Sam's quite cosmopolitan now, but his roots are here. That's why he's been so passionate about the development. He wants to do something for the village, bring it back to life. Even if there have been times when it didn't make any sense, financially,

I mean. Or for our family. We still live in Douglas—that's a suburb of Cork—during the school year, but Sam's been spending more and more time out here so that he can keep an eye on the development. At least we have the house now." Something crosses her face and I get the sense that her feelings about Rosscliffe and Ross Head are extremely complicated.

We're running back through the village now and she points out the businesses they've helped to start. Lilly and I have been meaning to go into the shop next to The Net, a boutique called My Blue Heaven with a cheerfully painted Caribbean-blue exterior. It has local crafts and knitwear and some pretty women's clothes, too. "Ellen always had a good eye," Rochelle says. "She just needed the capital to start the shop. She's done very well there." We've been into the bakery and cheese shop already, and as we pass by, I tell Rochelle that we loved the local farmhouse cheese we got from the shop.

She points to the row of small terraced houses just past the last of the shopfronts. "That's where they were raised," she says. "Right there. Sam and Ellen's dad was a mechanic and their mother worked for the Crawfords up at the Big House as a cook, when the Big House could afford it. Her mother worked in the kitchen as well, in the old days when the house had cooks and kitchen maids and a housekeeper and everything. They raised seven children in that house."

"Does she ever talk about working there?" I ask her. If she was working at the house then, Mrs. Nevin might remember Dorothea and know what had happened to her. "I've gotten interested in its history."

"They're both gone now, but Sam knows a few of the stories. I'd say she would have told the girls more about working at the house, so Ellen might know. They were good people. They were kind to me when Sam and I first got together. I was this brash young thing. You should have seen me." She smiles. "But we were in love and they accepted me. Anyway, I'll leave you here. I've got to check on a staff situation. As you can imagine, there have been some . . . issues since Lukas was found." She looks troubled. "We have Barry managing, of course, but for the time being, Sam and I feel like we need to be a bit more hands-on. Managing staff is my least favorite part of the job."

"Good luck," I say. "I don't envy you. I need to wake up my own household and see if I can manage them a bit."

I leave her and jog back up along the narrow lane, standing on the rise for a moment and looking out across the headlands.

The birdwatcher is out again this morning. She's got her binoculars up and she's clearly tracking something. When she brings the binoculars down, she sees me watching and waves. I wave back and scan the sky, wondering what she was looking at. There are a few dark shapes in the early morning sky above, but nothing that looks particularly interesting to me and I turn to look at the view of Rosscliffe House with the sea behind it, nearly the same scene depicted in Felix Crawford's painting. The early morning light shifts and sparkles on the water and for a moment it looks like there's a phantom chandelier inside one of the windows, lighting the interior as the sun rises in the other direction.

Eight

Agnieska Tarnowski is thinking about love.

All of the movies and songs and books, the poems and paintings, all of them get one thing wrong, she's realized. They miss the discomfort of love, the way it feels like a rock in your shoe or an eyelash floating in your eye, something you can't ignore, something you can't forget, even when you need to. She has always worked hard, every day of her life since she was twelve and got a job working for Mrs. Babiarz next to her grandmother's. She has never not wanted to work, never not wanted to make money.

But love makes you lazy. It makes you soft. It makes you distracted and tired and it just makes you want to lie around all day, thinking about it, thinking about love.

She laughs at herself and gets out of bed, banging on the door to Zuzanna's room to wake her up. Zuzanna has been down since Lukas went missing and Agnieska hopes that now that he's been found, she'll be able to start dealing with it. Anything will be better than her thinking he just left without a word, that he stopped caring about her, stopped loving her. Even death is better than that.

Love, Agnieska thinks. Just like an eyelash in your eye.

They have to make breakfast for the guests of the bed-and-breakfast, then clean the rooms and start getting the pub ready for the dinner service. They don't have to wait tables tonight because they're on breakfast duty, but they work for Mrs. Crawford sometimes too and Agnieska said she would clean the far cottage before the new renters arrive.

Agnieska sighs and goes to the window to look out to the stretching finger of the peninsula. Ross Head. She remembers when she first got here, how she thought Ross Head was an island. When she's out there, on the headlands, she still feels far away from everything.

Humming to herself, she knocks on Zuzanna's door again and then opens it and goes through. *"Obudź się!"* she calls out. Zuzanna groans. "Come, sleepyhead, wake up." Zuzanna groans again and sits up, rubbing her eyes and looking out at the sunny day. Her room is messy, clothing strewn all over the floor, the drawers of her bureau pulled out and overflowing. Agnieska resists the urge to tidy it up for her. She has enough cleaning to do today without adding this to it. She glances at Zuzanna, trying to gauge her mood, but she's still staring out the window. She looks deep in thought.

"Aga," Zuzanna starts, using her nickname for Agnieska.

"Yes?"

"Do you remember the day Lukas disappeared?" Her blond hair is all ratted from sleep, her eyes swollen. She's wearing a Hello Kitty nightgown.

"Oh, Zuz. You have to stop. You're just making yourself sad."

"But do you?"

"I think so. I remember the next day when you went to his flat and he had not been home and you were worried."

"I keep thinking there was something about that day, about when I went to the flat, that I am not remembering, but I don't know what it is. Something that doesn't make sense. Okay, I must get up." She sighs and rolls out of bed, disappearing into the small bathroom in the hallway.

Zuzanna loved Lukas. Agnieska is sure of this. Was it the same as Agnieska's own love? Who can know?

Love, Agnieska thinks. *Without love, there is no grief.*

Nine

....

Lilly and Adrien and I are out walking Mr. Bean on the headlands later that day when Roly calls me back. I let it go to voice mail, not wanting to talk about the discovery of the remains in front of the kids.

"Does Mr. Bean retrieve?" I ask Adrien, watching the dog trot ahead of us. "I've never seen your dad throw a stick to him."

"I tried to teach him once," Adrien says. "When he was a puppy. I tried for hours in the park, throwing sticks. He just stared at me. I don't think corgis are very good retrievers."

"Mom, remember that dog the Vinsons had?" Lilly asks me. She turns to Adrien. "Our neighbors had this dog and he was so into retrieving sticks. He used to stand out in front of their house with a pile of sticks and when you walked by, he would stare at you until you picked one up and threw it."

"It was so funny, Adrien," I say. "If you didn't throw a stick, he would just stare at you with this judgmental look on his face. Everyone in the neighborhood was really superstitious, like if you didn't throw the stick, the dog would curse you and you'd have bad luck. What was his name, Lill?"

"Snoopy," she says. "He was obsessed."

Adrien laughs. "Maybe we should try again with Beanie." As if he knows we're talking about him, the little dog turns around and cocks his head, then barks at us. Lilly kneels down to scratch his head. "Yes, Beanie, we love you. Even if you don't retrieve," she says as Mr. Bean wags his furry hindquarters in delight.

I wait until everyone's settled into their own activities in separate corners of the house before I listen to Roly's message: "D'arcy, I found out a little bit about your remains down there now. Anyway, I sent a couple of things over to your email. Fella left the building site where he was working a few months ago, in April, and never returned. They searched for him pretty intensely for a couple of days, coast guard and so forth, but there was no sign of him. Normally, a body that went into the water there would wash up on the beach in a few days. It's happened before. You can see it in the piece I sent you. But this one didn't. He'd been depressed, according to people who knew him and worked with him. So when they didn't find him, they assumed he'd gone back to Poland. But . . . you know yourself now. Seems that he didn't. Anyway, have a look and see what you think. By the way, behind the scenes, there was some talk at the time that this fella might have been involved with some drugs activity down there. That he might have disappeared back to Poland because he knew something or that he'd been disappeared by someone who didn't want him to talk. You'll see why. Your little village there is on our radar, for good reason, too. Okay, then? Give me a ring if you've any questions."

Intrigued, I plug my laptop into the outlet next to the kitchen table and open Roly's email. No message, but he's pasted in a couple of links to online news stories. The first one is similar to the one I found searching on my own, about Lukas Adamik's disappearance and the search conducted off Ross Head in the immediate days after it was presumed that he fell from the cliffs. It's a bit more comprehensive though and contains some additional details about the search, which involved the coast guard and includes a sidebar about where the coast guard has found the bodies of other people who have fallen from the cliffs on Ross Head and some of the other nearby peninsulas. There's a map and a quote from a coast guard representative saying that the tides generally move "objects in the water" from the west side of Ross Head to the beaches along the south side of the neighboring peninsula. Reading between the lines, I can figure out what they're trying to say: they looked in all the places it made sense to look. It's not their fault they didn't find him right away.

The second one is an older story, from 2013, about something called "Operation Waves." I scan it and get the basics. It seems the gardaí had an informant inside a drug trafficking organization out of West Cork and learned that there was going to be a drop in the water right off Ross Head. There had been a high-profile one the year before and a few more over the years. The gardaí seized five bales of cocaine as the traffickers, two British citizens who were arrested and charged, transferred them from a yacht that they'd piloted from the Caribbean on to a smaller boat one of them had rented earlier. That's all.

I put the kettle on for tea and do a search for "Sam Nevin developer" and "Rosscliffe House." After my run with Rochelle, I'm curious about how Sam went from living in a council house in the village, his mother working as a cook at the Big House, to owning the Big House and planning to turn it into a luxury hotel.

There are a few stories from some of the local papers and one each from the *Irish Times* and the *Irish Independent* about his developments in Kildare and Cork City. His first major real estate purchases seem to have been fifteen years ago, a small housing estate in Kildare that went under in the financial crash and then a series of purchases in the years after the crash. There are a couple of articles about him buying the land for the Ross Head development and then buying Rosscliffe House four years ago.

"Did you know that Sam Nevin grew up here?" I ask Conor when he comes in looking for a cup of tea at four. I do it properly, the way I know he likes it, pouring the hot water over two tea bags in the pot just after the water boils, then pouring it out into cups and adding two sugars to his and only a tiny drop of milk, murmuring "just a *titim bainne*" the way he always does. He smiles, not sure if I'm making fun or not.

"Grace must have said," he says. "It makes sense, I suppose. Seems like he's buying up the whole village. It's a good bit of symmetry, isn't it? The cook's son taking over the Big House. Generations of colonialism undone with a flourish of the mortgage lender's pen?"

"You really are a writer. When was Rosscliffe House built again?" I ask him.

"In the 1780s. I've been doing a bit of research. The first Crawford, a Cromwellian villain no doubt, was granted all this land here. He was a soldier and would have accepted the land instead of his wages, which Cromwell couldn't pay, and whoever was here before him living in that castle—O'Mahoneys maybe—would have been executed or sent away. That original Crawford's children settled it and then the Earl of Rosscliffe built the house in 1780. He was a brutal landlord, according to the book. It's on the shelf in there. Their estate wasn't very fruitful—not exactly prime agricultural land out here, but he married the heiress to a much more valuable Anglo-Irish estate farther inland and shored up the family fortunes that way."

"I'm trying to picture it. Who else would have been living here then? Besides the Earl of Rosscliffe and his family I mean?"

Conor thinks for a moment. "Not many people on the peninsula, I'd say. Too windy out here for subsistence farming. Poor soil. They would have been fairly isolated. Off the peninsula, however, it would have been very densely settled, especially in the 1820s, 1830s, the years leading up to the famine. Ireland's population was growing exponentially then and most of the land off Ross Head would have been under tillage with the Earl of Rosscliffe as landlord. You would have seen families living everywhere you looked, barely getting by. In the later 1800s, there would have been lots of parties at Rosscliffe House, all of the Anglo-Irish aristocracy from County Cork coming for visits, garden parties and children's parties, and so forth."

"What about my great-great grandparents? They were from West Cork, more inland, I think, near Bandon. They weren't going to the parties."

"No, they weren't. They weren't invited. They were probably digging potatoes on a piece of land owned by the Earl of Rosscliffe or his local equivalent. When the potato crop was blighted, they would have had few options to feed themselves and they may have been evicted. That's when the tidal wave of emigration started. That was probably the beginning of the end for whoever their landlord was, too. We'll have to drive over someday and see your home place," he says. Conor has told me about the Irish concept of the "home place," the spot where your family lived or came from, and I find it intriguing to think that I have one I've never seen.

"Yeah, it would be fun to show Lilly." I top off my own cup of tea. "I wonder what the backstory is behind Sam Nevin buying the house from Lissa," I say.

"I don't know specifically about Rosscliffe House now," Conor says. "But a lot of the Anglo-Irish Big Houses come up for sale these days, many of them quite cheap. They're mostly in bad repair, need updating. Of course, lots of them were burned during the War of Independence and in those years after, too. They came on the market in the seventies and eighties, when the families ran out of funds to keep them going. Except for the really wealthy families, who could afford to keep them up, and that's when they started to fall apart. Do you know what Grace told me? Local lads tried to burn Rosscliffe House in 1920, but it wouldn't light." He grins, delighted with the historical anecdote.

"It's so interesting," I tell him. "Lissa Crawford is clearly resentful of the hotel and the development, but presumably she's the one who sold it to Sam, or someone in her family. But why? It doesn't quite make sense. And then there's her memory and the mysterious Dorothea. It's really interesting to me."

Conor takes a long sip of his tea. "It *is* interesting," he says. "I'm sure you'll sort out all the layers of intrigue. Now, for something less pleasant. Bláithín is coming on Wednesday to get Adrien." Conor's ex-wife is taking Adrien to see her family in France for a week. "She's bringing her new boyfriend and she just texted to say they'll be here around five. Should we invite them for dinner? They're taking a late flight from Cork. I hate to put you through it, but . . ."

"No, of course we should invite them," I say. I check to make sure Adrien's not listening and then say, "I'll think of something really special to make."

Conor grins and whispers, "Poisoned mushrooms?"

"Mmmm. Chicken with just a hint of botulism. No, it will be nice. Send Adrien off right. We're going to miss him. Lilly was complaining about how bored she'll be the week he's gone."

Conor's face clouds over a little. Adrien isn't excited about the trip with Bláithín and her new boyfriend and Conor's anxious about him being with them for a whole week.

"It will be fine," I say, rubbing his back. "You know how it is, the transitions are the worst. Once he gets on the plane he'll be just fine." I remember how Lilly used to get sad the day before she was going to Brian's house. I worried about it so much, but she was always fine once she got there.

"I know. And I'll be able to get some work done. You sure you're okay with me trying to finish a chapter this week while he's gone?"

"Completely," I say. "I'm kind of interested in local history now. Maybe I'll write my own book. *Maggie D'arcy's History of West Cork*. Give you a run for your money." I kiss him and go to check on Lilly.

As it turns out, I don't need to write my own history of West Cork; looking through the bookshelves in the cottage later that afternoon, I find the book Conor referenced. It's called *In Times Gone By: West Cork as We Knew It* and it's an entertaining oral history of the area and includes accounts by a variety of residents about the towns and villages from Schull to Bantry, including Rosscliffe. I get a sense of the progression of history here, the failed burning of Rosscliffe House in 1920, the mining industry in nearby areas, the growing popularity of sailing and tourism and in the 1960s, the arrival of artists and "blow-ins" who even built a few communes around Rosscliffe, Ballydehob, and Schull. "Even now," the book tells me, "West Cork is known as a home and destination for people from all over the world, giving our little towns and villages an international flair."

After dinner, I get on the phone for a quick hello to Conor's parents. "You all right, Maggie?" his mother, Breda, asks. "How's your holiday among the rich and famous?"

"It's posh down here all right," I tell her. "When you come to visit, we'll show you all around. How are things there?"

"Ah, good. Ciaran says hello and to mind you don't burn. The sun's very strong."

"I'll be careful," I tell her. Conor rolls his eyes and I leave him to settle in for a chat. I take Mr. Bean for a walk while Adrien and Lilly stare at their phones and resist all my entreaties to come along with us. I walk out on the peninsula, past the construction sites of the new houses, letting Mr. Bean off leash to sniff the grass and chase imaginary cats along the path. The first of the new houses belongs to Carol and Harry Dickson and as I pass the drive I hear classical music coming from an open window. The night is calm and warm and I keep walking, enjoying the feeling of moving my limbs, enjoying the solitude, and by the time I turn around the sun has sunk down toward the line of the ocean and the islands in the distance. As I approach Rosscliffe House, the last sliver of orange light slides away over the turn of the earth, throwing the house into relief.

And then I see her, a woman standing in one of the third-floor windows, looking out at the peninsula. She's a dark, static profile. I wait for her to move, but she's absolutely still. Mr. Bean barks and I turn to call him, shaken despite myself. When I look back at the window, the figure is gone and I stand there for a moment, waiting to see if she returns. Finally, I call Mr. Bean again and head for the cottage.

Ten

Katya "Griz" Grzeskiewicz snatches the hot cup of tea from the cute guy behind the counter and flashes him a smile. He's young enough to be her little brother, but he always flirts with her, for which she's oddly grateful, and she thinks he might have even tried to ask her out once, bungling it by asking her if she'd seen a film she said she had, in fact, seen and then failing to come up with his next line.

"Thanks. I'm so late, Liam. I'll chat next time, okay?" He nods and pushes a scone wrapped in a paper napkin over the counter, mouthing, *On the house.* "You're lovely," she says, flashing him what she hopes is a platonic smile. Camden Street is busy at half eight, commuters looking dazed at the unfamiliarity of the hot weather in Dublin making their way to their offices, wearing their most airy professional clothes, carrying bottles of water like Americans do.

She sips the tea as she walks fast toward headquarters, her workbag banging against her hip as she goes. Sullivan is an early bird, always in his office at eight, and Katya doesn't want to be late. He doesn't like late.

The other detectives in the department call him "the gaffer" and she does sometimes, too, but she still struggles a little with the slang. She remembers her first days in school, how the little bit of American English picked up from movies and TV shows before they came over seemed to fall to dust beneath the version of the language her schoolmates spoke.

She knocks on the glass and goes in when he looks up and beckons.

"Morning," she says, shutting the door behind her. "Hot out, isn't it?"

He doesn't agree, though his forehead is shiny and there are circles of perspiration staining the fabric of his white shirt. Sullivan's looking physically old to Griz suddenly, increasingly white-haired and paunchy. He must be thinking about retirement, though he's as sharp as ever.

If he hadn't told her the meeting was about a case when he asked her to come in this morning, she would have been much more nervous, thinking she was going to be sacked or upbraided. But when he rang her last night, he said, "I want to talk to you about a possible assignment, nothing definite yet, but something for you while your man's giving himself skin cancer."

He's talking about her friend and sometimes partner Roly Byrne. They both came up from Serious Crime Review, the Garda cold case squad, about six months ago and they work together often enough that Sullivan uses the version of *your man* that means *your partner*.

"I told him to take his sunblock," she'd said last night on the phone.

Now he shakes his head. "It's not definite yet. Roly got a heads-up and I want to give you the background in case it comes through. Do you remember that thing down in West Cork a few years ago? Drugs operation?"

"Maybe. Haven't there been a few of them?"

"So there have. This is the one where they staged a big operation with the Portuguese and all and then there were only five bales on the yacht. Assumption was, they missed the bulk of it. They've got a death down there now, might be something, might not. If it is something, it could crack open some suspects we've been wanting to pin down for years."

Griz waits. There's something else, something he hasn't told her yet. She watches as he flips a stack of papers on his desk. "How's your Polish these days?" he asks after a few minutes. "Like, I know you spoke it as a young one, but can you still speak it? Could you do an interview?"

She shrugs. "Yeah, I think so. I speak it to my mother. Not every day, but maybe seventy percent of the time."

"Okay, good. I don't know yet. They're waiting on a few things from the pathologist, but it may be we'll need someone. Guy who died was a builder on a site down there. Lukas Adamik was his name. There's a bit of a community of Polish workers might need interviewing. I thought it might be a good one for you, with Roly gone and all." He looks nervous, like he's not sure how she'll take it. She feels a little flash of annoyance rise up. *Am I going to get stuck taking witness statements, just because I speak Polish and they'll trust me?* She pushes it down and smiles.

"Sounds good. When should we know more?"

His eyes are careful. He knows, but he isn't going to tell her, not yet. "Soon."

Griz stands up and takes her tea off the end of his desk. "I'll wait for you to tell me," she says, then thinks of something and grins at him. "*Do widzenia!*" she says, enjoying the smile that catches him by surprise, lighting up his face, then turning into a laugh.

"There ya go," Sullivan says. "Fuckin' *do widzenia!*"

Eleven

On Wednesday morning, Lilly surprises me by asking if we can walk down to the village to go shopping together. She's been in a better mood since her triumphant night in the pub, and I smile at Conor over her head. Maybe this is the beginning of a nicer, friendlier Lilly. I say that of course we can and we walk down after lunch, leaving Adrien to pack for his trip and Conor happy and preoccupied with his piles of research materials.

We stop in at the little café in the village and I treat myself to an espresso. Lilly gets an iced coffee and we sip as we walk up and down the tiny main drag. In the cheese shop, we chat a bit with the teenage girl behind the counter before choosing a block of cheddar and some locally made crackers to serve tonight. Outside again, I notice that a few of the signposts along the main street are decorated with posters reading DON'T DEVELOP ROSS HEAD! and SAVE ROSS HEAD!

Lilly says she wants to see what they have in My Blue Heaven, the little boutique next to the pub, so we go in and browse, smiling at the woman behind the counter, who I assume is Sam Nevin's sister Ellen from something familiar around her eyes. She's wearing jeans and one of the artsy screen-printed Ross Head T-shirts she has for sale, and she points out the different sections and tells us to ask if we have any questions. The shop has a nice selection of T-shirts and linen tops and knitwear, and while Lilly tries on dresses upstairs, I wander around looking at the ceramics and artwork that are displayed downstairs. There are a couple of Lissa Crawford's flower paintings hanging on the walls and I study them for a bit. One of the paintings is an abstract red shape, a star or a starfish on white, the paint feathering out onto the textured creamy background. Now that I've heard her story, it makes me uneasy.

Lilly's voice comes from the stairs. "Mom? What do you think of this?" The woman behind the counter and I look up and find her standing there in a tightly fitting black knit dress with a lace inset on one shoulder. She looks years older suddenly, beautiful, her body filling out the dress, her hair streaming down her back.

"That's smashing on you!" the presumed Ellen Mahoney exclaims. "Absolutely gorgeous!" And it is.

I must look uncertain because Lilly says, "What, Mom?"

"Nothing. It *is* gorgeous on you. It's quite formal. Where will you wear it?"

"You never know," she says breezily. "Can I get it?"

"You ought to get it," the woman says. "It was *made* for you."

"Of course," I say. "Go change and I can pay." I wander around some more and choose a hat from a display by the door and take it to the counter.

"I'm Maggie D'arcy," I say, putting it down. "In case you can't tell, we love your shop."

"I thought you might be. I'm Ellen Mahoney, Sam's sister. Rochelle said you might be in. That's a lovely hat."

"Yeah, I'm happy to find it," I say. "I didn't really bring enough clothes for the beach. It's been so sunny."

She smiles, her eyes and dark hair really reminding me of Sam now. She's tall, makeup-less, very down-to-earth, and I wonder how she and Rochelle get along. "It's not always like this. We're lucky to have a really hot day here and there. But it's been such a lovely stretch of weather."

I point to the wall of Lissa Crawford's paintings and the paintings of Rosscliffe House and Ross Head. "I'm obsessed with her paintings. We're in one of her cottages and I've seen some of her other works. They're really beautiful."

"I sell quite a few of them," Ellen says. "Especially lately, with the houses and more visitors in town, it's brought attention to Ross Head. Once the hotel opens, I expect it will bring a lot of attention to her father and to her paintings, too."

"You grew up here, right?" I ask her. "You and Sam?"

"Yes, we did grow up here," she says, smiling. "I always thought I'd get out, but I married Barry Mahoney, didn't I? He wasn't going to leave Rosscliffe. Sam got out, but I got stuck. Anyway, he's back now, in a way. And Barry's managing the pub and I'm here. It's all worked out, thanks to Sam." Her smile is open, joyful, as though she can't quite believe her good fortune.

Sometimes when I'm questioning people and they talk about their lives, I can feel the regret and sadness about the things they haven't done. But Ellen Mahoney seems at peace with the way her life has turned out.

"Someone said your mother worked at Rosscliffe House," I say. "As a cook. That must have been interesting. I keep wondering what it was like when it was still a family home."

She shrugs. "It wasn't exactly *Downton Abbey*. She did what she could. She was a great woman, God rest her soul, but there wasn't much money and they always had people turning up she hadn't planned for. She always said thank goodness she knew how to stretch a pound, having fed seven children at home."

"What was the house like back then?"

"It was already falling in by the time I came along," she says. "Our oldest sister, Bridget, helped with the cleaning and she said it was like sweeping sand on the beach. You couldn't get it clean, no matter what you did. It was all rotting to pieces."

"Does Bridget still live here?" I ask. Surely she'd remember Dorothea.

"She's up in Kildare," Ellen says quickly. "No, the best thing that ever happened to Rosscliffe was Sam coming back and building those houses, buying the pub and this lot." She gestures to the row of shops along the street.

I point to the lamppost outside and say, "Not everyone agrees with you."

Her eyes narrow a little and again I see her brother in them. "No, but for people who need to *earn* their living, anything that brings people to the village is a good thing. If you don't need to earn money, well, then, of course you have time to go about posting signs. People who have spent their lives here understand that." There's real resentment in her voice and her implication is clear: those who are protesting the development didn't grow up in Rosscliffe.

I think we're both relieved when Lilly comes down with the dress. Making small talk in order to defuse the tension, I pay for everything and we thank Ellen and take our bags down to a health food store at the other end of the street, next to a little thrift shop. I'm hoping I can find some spices I couldn't get at the other market in town, but it's mostly vitamins, herbal tonics in glass bottles, and little boxes printed with German I can't understand. Lilly picks out a ginger-scented body lotion, and when I ask the older man behind the counter about bulk spices, he says I'll have to go to the natural foods shop in Skibbereen. He's got an aging hippie air about him with his long gray ponytail and purple linen vest over a blue-and-white-striped grandfather shirt. "Where are you staying then?" he asks. "Here in the village?" He has a soft accent that I recognize as Welsh when he introduces himself as Gwynedd Williams.

"Yes, we're renting one of Mrs. Crawford's cottages," I tell him.

"Oh, good. They're lovely, they are." He purses his lips. "You've had a bit of drama out on Ross Head."

"You mean the man who passed away?" I ask quietly, glancing at Lilly, who's still sniffing lotions.

"Mmmm. Very strange thing. Very sad. I knew the lad a bit, from around the village. You can't hold the monstrosities against the poor foreign workers who are forced to build them."

"The houses?" I ask. He's used the same word Lissa Crawford had.

"I'm biased, of course. We fought the development proposal as hard as we could, but capitalism always wins in the end, doesn't it?" He shakes his head sadly. "It always does." He points to the bulletin board behind the counter, where one of the posters is hanging. "Yes, we fought hard for many years, but here we are at the end of our battle." He sighs, but the expression on his face isn't resigned. If I had to guess, I'd say that he still has some fight left in him.

It's four now. Bláithín will be arriving soon. Lilly waits outside on the street while I duck into the market to get some milk and cereal and some more wine for tonight. We did our big grocery shop in Bantry the day after we arrived, so we've only been into Donnelly's, the village shop, for a few things here and there. It has the feel of a seasonal vacation town market, a bit dusty, not much fresh produce, mostly basics, with a good wine selection and luxuries thrown in here and there for the visitors.

Lorcan is coming out as I go in. He's got what looks like a bottle of wine in a bag and he's smiling, looking delighted at the nice day and the pretty main street of the village. He greets me enthusiastically and tells me to say hello to Conor.

I'm on nodding terms with Danielle, the thirtyish woman behind the counter, now—Conor introduced ourselves and told her we're staying on Ross Head the first time we went in—and now she says, "You've had lovely weather, haven't you?" Her frosted blond hair is cut in a stylish short pixie and she's wearing tight jeans, heels, and a red blazer that matches her fresh lipstick. Unlike Ellen Mahoney, I have the strong feeling that Danielle Donnelly isn't happy being stuck in Rosscliffe. When we told her that we were enjoying Ross Head and the area, she muttered something about how it wasn't as nice as some other places.

"Have you been busy?" I ask conversationally.

"Yeah, with the weather we've had loads of tourists in." She turns to the back of the shop and calls out, "Aidan, bring us some more of those bottles of veg oil!"

"I imagine you'll be really busy once the hotel's open," I say.

"God willing." *Another supporter,* I think.

"The history around here is so interesting," I say. "You're too young to remember it, of course, but Rosscliffe House must have been something in the old days."

"I was raised in Clonakilty," Danielle says. "Never came up here until I married my husband, but he said they used to break in when he was a kid, since no one lived there. They'd drink in there, mess around. It's a tip, he says."

"It must have been creepy."

She raises her eyebrows. "Kids, you know. There were stories. Things they saw. That will be sixteen euros twenty, please." A middle-aged man with stooped shoulders and a dejected air comes out from the back of the shop with a box of bottles of oil and starts to unload them onto the shelves. I assume this is her husband, but she doesn't introduce me.

I hand over a twenty-euro note and Danielle gives me my change. I'm about to ask what she means about stories to see if she'll elaborate when the bell on the door jingles and a young guy and two little kids in flip-flops come in. "It's too early for a choc ice. You can get a juice though," he says in an English accent.

The kids' dismay, freely expressed, fills the shop and I thank Danielle and go back out to the street to meet Lilly, who's sitting on a bench with our packages around her, her face turned to the sun. We're gathering everything up for the walk back to the cottage when I notice Ann Tobin standing on the street talking to an older couple. I imagine she's asking them if they saw anything back in April when Lukas Adamik went missing. She won't get anything of value. People's memories are unreliable two or three days after the fact. Three months renders any scraps of memories they might still have murky and imprecise. She nods and keeps going, stopping to ask someone else a question, and then she disappears into the boutique.

But as we start to walk away, something else catches my eye: the black Mercedes, parked in the same spot in front of the pub it was parked in the other night. The same man sits in the driver's seat, smoking, the engine idling. As we pass the car, I see the little whale—it *is* a whale—dangling from the mirror. As though he can feel me watching him, he slowly turns and meets my eyes, nodding and smiling the way he did the other night. I put my arm around Lilly's shoulders and steer her toward our route home.

Twelve

"Okay, Janet, thanks very much for the help. I'll see you," Ann says, leaving Janet Ford on the footpath, beaming because Ann let her take out a packet of photographs of her new granddaughter in Westport and show each one to her.

Janet didn't have anything to offer in the way of information about how Lukas Adamik's body came to be found on the beach and Ann should have made an excuse to extricate herself, but she knows Janet's daughter Ciara had three miscarriages before this miracle baby's arrival and she wanted to let Janet bathe in the glow of grandmotherhood a bit.

She looks down toward Donnelly's, her next stop. She'll see if there's anyone in the shop who might remember what they were doing on the tenth of April, the day Lukas Adamik disappeared. As with Janet, she doesn't expect anything really useful, but you never know. Danielle might have something, even if it's just second-hand gossip.

But then Ann catches sight of Tomasz Sadowski coming out of the takeaway. She waves and calls, "Tomasz," and he stops and smiles, waiting for her to reach him. She likes Tomasz. He has a straightforward quality that she appreciates; he doesn't smile at you if he doesn't like you. He's holding a bag that smells enticingly of fresh chips and she pushes down the hunger she's only now aware of. She's forgotten to eat again and the salty, oily smell emanating from the bag is irresistible, even if she makes it a practice not to go into the takeaway.

"Do you have a minute?" she asks him.

"Yes, just getting something to eat. Too hot to cook," he says, lifting the bag.

"Ah, yeah, I know what you mean. How's Alex doing? Is he still thinking about the music course in Dublin next year?"

She sees pride come over Tomasz's face as he nods and says they're still getting the details. He should be proud. He raised his brother singlehandedly, in a country not their own. While he talks, he reaches up to scratch the scar on his forehead, and Ann tries to remember how he got it. A construction accident, she thinks someone told her once.

"As you know, we're investigating Lukas's death now that his remains have been found. We'll need to have everyone come down and give formal statements, but since you were one of the last people to see him, I was just wondering if you've remembered anything that might be helpful."

He looks off toward the peninsula, thinking. "I don't think so. I was picking up supplies, but the guys said he seemed fine that day, before he and Piotr went to work at the other site."

Ann remembers those initial interviews. With the help of a translator from the Polish community in Cork and an Albanian woman from Dublin who also spoke German, she talked to the builders and was able to create a picture of the day Lukas disappeared. He and another worker named Piotr Bielka had been working alone that day. Around 4:00 P.M. Bielka said he started to feel nauseous and threw up on the building site. He didn't get any better, so he told Lukas he was going home. That was the last he saw of him. It was the last anyone saw of him. Lukas's girlfriend, Zuzanna, went to his flat that night and again the next morning, but there was no sign of him.

It was difficult conducting the interviews through the translator; not being able to read the way they answered her questions, their exact choice of words, Ann felt as though she was working without one of her senses. Her impression was that Bielka and the other men were scared and at first she wondered about that, but the translator said they were worried about losing their jobs and that they all seemed happy to talk about the last time they saw Lukas. A few of the men said he seemed depressed, that he had been arguing with his girlfriend, Zuzanna. When Ann talked to Zuzanna, she said their argument wasn't a big deal, but Ann sensed she was processing her own guilt over possibly causing Lukas's departure or suicide. For her part, Zuzanna had said right from the beginning that he hadn't gone back to Poland. "I know him!" she told Ann. "He wouldn't do that. He wouldn't." Zuzanna's insistence was partly why they'd called out the coast guard, expended so many resources looking for Lukas in the water.

"Piotr Bielka still around?" she asks him. "I may need to interview him again."

"His father died in May and he went home," Tomasz says. "I thought he was going to come back, but . . ." He shrugs.

"Well, thanks," she tells him. "I'll need to have you come in and give a formal statement, now we know he's gone." He nods. She's about to leave him to his chips when she remembers her last conversation with him. "Ah, Tomasz? The thefts up at the building sites? Have there been any more of them?" There had been a few last summer. Sam Nevin had reported the first one, a missing drill and some valuable saws that had disappeared from Ross Head. Then, this spring, Tomasz called and reported another couple of instances of theft and vandalism. The details were blurry now. They'd installed a security camera and Ann had asked for a few nighttime drive-bys, but nothing had come of it. She wondered if the incidents had actually stopped or if they had just gotten tired of reporting them.

He shrugs. "I haven't noticed anything missing, but . . ."

"But what?"

"Well, things have been . . . they go wrong, I guess you say. Problems."

"What do you mean, problems?"

He thinks for a minute. "Like, the nails would be switched, in the boxes, or cords sliced so the electricity does not get through, things like that."

"The security camera didn't catch anything?" He shakes his head. "Why didn't you report it?"

"These things, they were . . . silly," he says. "Sam said we should just ignore it. And the guys, the men who work for me, they . . ." He's embarrassed now. He doesn't want to say whatever it is.

"What, Tomasz?"

"They said it was the ghost." He smiles, embarrassed. "I don't believe in it, but some of the guys, they say there is a ghost."

Ann rolls her eyes. "They've been listening to the oul fellas in the pub."

Tomasz shrugs again. "It is not . . . too bad, these things. Just silly. They slow us down. I have to buy a new hammer sometimes."

"Okay, but let me know if it happens again or you want to report any of it. And thanks. Let me know when you want to come in to give your statement."

He says he will and goes off in the direction of his flat at the end of the high street.

Ann hesitates. Anton Dorda owns the takeaway and she tries to stay away, but it's the only one in the village and the chips and cod are good, hot and crisp and salty.

Tomasz Sadowski is right. It *is* too hot to cook.

Thirteen

Back at the cottage, Conor's car is parked closer to the front door than usual, the tires oddly turned. Two strange suitcases sit just inside the front door. Voices filter from the kitchen and we go through to find him at the stove and Adrien sitting at the kitchen island. When Conor sees us, he looks up, a warning and an apology in his expression, and he nods toward the table by the window, where I see Bláithín Arpin sitting in a halo of sunlight, her long blond hair in a cascade of curls. She's cuddled up to a very fit bald man in a tight T-shirt.

"Maggie and Lilly! Here are Maggie and Lilly," Conor announces awkwardly.

"Hi," I say, suddenly conscious of my jeans and raggedy T-shirt and sandals. "I didn't see the car."

Bláithín stands up and smiles at me. She's wearing crisp white pants and a bright yellow silk top with interesting angles and an asymmetrical hem. Her pink sandals gleam like candy and she looks like a high-fashion model dropped into a traditional Irish cottage for a catalog photo shoot.

"Hello, Maggie. The car's not here because the car is a piece of crap and it broke down outside of Cork. Lilly, it is lovely to finally meet you." She smiles and runs a hand through her hair, throwing an annoyed look at the tight T-shirt guy.

"Hello?" says the guy with her, who I assume is the French boyfriend. "It's just temperamental because it is a piece of art manufactured in 1962. It is *not* a piece of crap." I check Adrien's face to see if he's okay. He looks a bit shell-shocked. Conor looks furious. Lilly, on the other hand, seems amused, her eyes darting from me to the other adults and back again. Bláithín rolls her eyes and says something to the guy in French. He gives an indignant snort.

"The car broke down, so Adrien and I went to get them while you were in the village," Conor says. "We just got back. Unfortunately, it won't be repaired until tomorrow, so they changed their flight—"

"So," Bláithín interrupts, "we will stay at a hotel in the village and pick up Adrien in the morning."

"I think I remember hearing that the bed-and-breakfast over the gastro pub is booked up weeks in advance . . ." Conor glances at me apologetically. "They only have a few rooms."

"Lilly can sleep on the couch," I say quickly. "You can have her room."

"You're sure?" Bláithín asks me. "You won't find it awkward?" She meets my eyes directly and I can't help remembering the first time I met her, when she stopped by Conor's house in the middle of the night and found me there and realized who I was. Things have been tense between her and Conor. But she was instrumental in helping me solve the mystery of my cousin Erin's disappearance and I've softened toward her during the past year except for when she makes Adrien unhappy.

"No, of course not," I say, trying to keep my voice even.

"I don't mind." Lilly smiles a Cheshire cat smile.

"Well, it's only for one night," Conor says, a little too forcefully.

"Since no one will introduce me, I guess I must introduce my-self," Bláithín's boyfriend says, standing and coming around the table. "Maggie, I'm Henri. It's lovely to meet you." Before I know what's happening, he kisses each of my cheeks. Then he takes my hand and looks deeply into my eyes. He's a stylish man, his jeans fashionable, his brown leather shoes shiny and expensive-looking.

"Nice to meet you, too." I'm sure I'm blushing and I go to the sink to get a glass of water to try to hide how flustered I am, by his familiarity, but mostly by the prospect of the night ahead. When I look up, both Lilly and Bláithín are watching me and then he gives Lilly the same treatment and tells her she is even more beautiful than he's been led to believe, which makes her blush, too.

"Well, what do you think about that chicken?" I ask Conor, to end the awkward moment. "It's not in the oven yet, is it? Does anyone want wine?"

"No, I completely forgot," he says. "We just got back. I'm so sorry. Should I stick it in now? No, it'll take hours, won't it?"

Bláithín jumps in and says that she'll pour wine for everyone and that Henri is an excellent cook and will figure out the chicken. After some half-hearted protesting from me and Conor, Henri takes my simple roast chicken with lemon out of the pan, hacks it to pieces with a cleaver, lovingly pats salt and pepper on it, and then rummages in the fridge for vegetables and makes a delicious-smelling concoction of broiled chicken parts with lemon, potatoes, and greens that's done in thirty minutes rather than two hours. I'm left feeling vaguely incompetent but also hungry and buzzed from the wine I downed too quickly. All of us lubricated by more wine, dinner is surprisingly lovely, Henri telling us about his job as a produce merchant for Paris restaurants and Bláithín talking about her work at an art gallery in Dublin.

"Our landlady here is a painter," I say. "Her name is Lissa Crawford. Someone said she shows at a gallery in Dublin."

"Oh, yes," Bláithín exclaims. "I know Lissa Crawford. She does those inkblot paintings, doesn't she?"

"Her house is full of them," Lilly tells her. "They're really cool. I like them a lot." ·

Bláithín bestows an approving smile upon Lilly. "You have very good taste then, Lilly. A colleague of mine just sold one of those paintings for ten thousand euros. Where's her house? I'd love to see what she has."

"The car won't be ready until the late morning," Henri said. "We could go down and see."

Conor looks uncomfortable and I say, "I had no idea she was so successful. I wonder why she still lives in the cottage then?"

"Maybe she just likes it here," Conor suggests.

"She grew up in the Big House," I tell Bláithín and Henri. "That's what I'm really interested in. It must be so strange, having grown up there, and now she's living in one of the tenant cottages. And she looks across at the house every day."

"Irish people and their houses," Bláithín says. "My father always says he doesn't understand why Irish people are so obsessed with land and houses. My mother says it's because it was taken from them. It's a concrete symbol of freedom, right? Owning land?" Her father is French, her mother Irish, and despite her father's apparent disregard for real estate he owns a gorgeous modernist house in Wicklow where Bláithín and Adrien have been living until recently.

In the kitchen, while we're clearing the table, Conor gives me a hug and says, "I'm so sorry. Are you okay? It's just for one night."

"It's fine," I whisper, hugging him back and settling my head against his cheek. "Dinner was actually nice. Seriously, it's fine." But I'm on edge, vigilant for another snide comment from Bláithín, too aware of Adrien's obvious dislike of Henri.

Lilly drifts off to her room and we're clearing the table when she comes down, dressed in jeans and boots and the black leather jacket I bought her last spring. She's wearing more makeup than she was an hour ago, glittery eyeshadow and mascara and lip gloss, and she smells faintly of perfume.

"Lilly, you look gorgeous," Bláithín says. "I adore that jacket."

"*Très belle*," Henri agrees. "You must have special plans."

"Why are you dressed up?" I ask her, but before she can answer, the doorbell rings and she gives me a guilty glance and mutters something about going to hear music. "With who?" I call after her.

"I'll get it," she says when the doorbell rings again.

I follow her to the door, and when she opens it, it takes me a minute to recognize the boy standing there, a friendly smile on his face.

It's the lead singer from the band at the pub.

"Mom, this is Alex," she says, not meeting my eyes. "We're going to hang out for a little bit. I won't be back too late." There's a car running in the drive behind him, a small battered-looking red Ford, and he smiles a broad smile at me and sticks out his hand. He has light blue eyes, longish hair that flops over his forehead and gives him an innocent rakishness, and he's wearing a worn corduroy jacket ready for an album cover photo shoot.

Rock-star material for sure.

"Hello, Mrs. D'arcy, it's nice to meet you," he says.

I shake his hand and say, "Nice to meet you, too, Alex. Lilly, you didn't tell us you were going out tonight." I try to give her a look that says, *Come into the kitchen and talk to me, Lilly,* but she completely ignores me, planting a fake kiss on my cheek and pasting on a fake smile to go with it and says, "I'll be home by ten. See ya," in a falsely breezy tone of voice I have never, ever heard her use before.

"Lill," I call after her as they head out the door.

But she doesn't hear me and there's nothing I can do but watch them get into the car and take off down the road toward the village.

"That was the singer from the pub that night Lilly sang. Did you know about this?" I ask Adrien.

He blushes and says, "I know they've talked a few times, but she didn't tell me about tonight."

"Did you know about this?" I ask Conor.

"God, no." He holds his hands up in mock defense.

"What should I have done? Should I have stopped her from going?" I ask him.

"Why?" Henri asks. "She's young and beautiful. She should have fun, enjoy the life."

I want to kick Henri right in his perfectly toned stomach.

Conor just shrugs and puts an arm around Adrien's shoulders and winks at us. "I don't have a lot of experience with these things. Since Adrien's got no social life to speak of."

"Thanks for that, Dad. Really, thanks a lot," Adrien says. But he's smiling.

"Oh, he's a late bloomer," Bláithín says, coming over and kissing him on the cheek. "He'll be with all the girls before you know it." Adrien blushes and it does something to my stomach to see the three of them looking like a happy family. Henri just looks amused.

We get out bowls for ice cream and I try to shake off the feeling that I should have stepped in. Lilly has always had her head on straight; she's never been reckless. She's seventeen now, two years away from college if she starts school here in the fall.

The truth, though, is that after what she's been through in the last year, I have no idea what kind of judgment Lilly has anymore.

At ten thirty, I'm still lying awake, listening for the sound of the door, and when I get up and put on a sweater and then check the couch I made up for Lilly in the cottage's small den, it's empty, the covers smooth and white in the low light from the hall. I slip on my sandals and go outside, checking the driveway. The night is cool, the wind off the ocean scented with ice and salt, a full or nearly full moon risen overhead. The white exterior of the cottage gleams and I wrap my cardigan more tightly around my flannel pajamas and walk up the road. Suddenly, I wish I had my running shoes on; I want to take all my nervous energy, my annoyance at Lilly, my guilt for not stopping her, and pound it into the ground. Instead, I walk fast along the road and then out onto the broad expanse of Ross Head, following the barely discernible trails through the grass. The houses are mostly dark along the cliffs, though I spot a few lights here and there. I keep walking until I'm nearly to Rosscliffe House.

The moon looms against the gray sky and the empty windows are dark, the grass all around sparkling with condensation. I think about walking right up to it—I'm feeling reckless, wanting to do something that will engage all my senses so I can ignore my worry about Lilly—but in the end I'm too much of a scaredy-cat and I stand in the wet grass looking out across the Atlantic, trying to decide what to do about my errant daughter. Then someone shouts and I whirl around to find Lissa Crawford standing fifty yards away from me. I can just barely see her walking toward me in the milky light from the moon.

"I thought you were a ghost," she says, but she's grinning. "You should see yourself, standing up there, all in white."

I look down at my long white cardigan. "I'm so sorry. I didn't mean to scare you. I was just . . . my daughter's out and she isn't home yet. She was supposed to be home at ten. Instead of stewing at the house, I thought I'd get out for a bit of fresh air."

She's wearing an oversize plaid overcoat that reaches nearly to her ankles. "Isn't it beautiful up here at night? Especially when there's a bit of moonlight? I love to come out here when I can't sleep. Something about the wind. It's so pure. There's nothing to stop it. Where's your daughter out to then?"

"I don't know actually. She just . . . went. This boy showed up at the door. He's in a band."

She smiles. "I don't have children myself, but I know they cause awful worry. What's this boy's name then?"

"Alex. She didn't even let him come in and meet us, just hustled him out before we could get a look at him. All my friends complained about their teenagers and I thought I was so lucky because Lilly hasn't really had boyfriends. Turns out she was saving up for tonight."

She puts a hand out and touches my wrist. "Oh, Mrs. D'arcy. You have nothing to worry about. That's Alex Sadowski. He's quite, well, trustworthy. Inside himself, you know. He's a lovely boy."

"It's just that I don't know anything about him," I say.

She smiles. "He arrived ten years ago from Poland with his older brother, Tomasz, and some of the men who were building the houses. Tomasz and Alex lived in the far cottage when they first got here, Tomasz working on the roof in exchange for rent, so I got to know them quite well. Alex was alone after school most days and he began to come over to watch me make paintings. He helped around the cottage, feeding the chickens, pulling weeds. He would sing for me." She smiles and I think of the picture of the blond boy on her mantel.

"I don't think I could be more fond of him if he were my own flesh and blood. He's quite a remarkable child. He had to navigate a new place, a new school, and improving his English, everything. Tomasz did the best he could, but he had to work to support them. Alex handled it all quite cheerfully, quite competently. One of the teachers at the school recognized his musical talent, gave him lessons, got him involved in the local trad scene, and he's been playing all around here. He's left school now, but he's auditioned for a place in a music course in Dublin and he's quite serious about it."

"Well, that's a relief, I guess. But she's still late."

She laughs. "I'll let you handle that." And then, as though I had asked the question, she says, "I did what you suggested. I made a list of everyone I could remember being there that summer at Rosscliffe House. It was difficult at first. I was so young, but they started to come back. Anyway, just making the list, it got me thinking, remembering things. Quite amazing, really. I wrote down pages and pages of things that came back to me, names and so forth. If you're passing one of these days, I wonder if you'd stop so I can show you."

I tell her I will and say good night, leaving her standing in the path looking back toward the end of the peninsula.

The wind picks up, and as I walk back, I feel a few drops of rain, then more.

It's 11:30 now, and my annoyance is turning to alarm. Back at the house, I make myself a cup of chamomile tea, but it doesn't calm me at all. I can still hear the rushing of the ocean and now the patter of raindrops on the roof.

At 11:45 I try Lilly's phone again.

Suddenly, I hear a car and then voices outside and when I peer through the windows next to the front door, I can see them coming up the walk, hunched under an umbrella, the dark shapes of their heads leaning toward each other. Lilly is smiling, laughing at something Alex says as they walk to the door. I feel a pang of pain and joy. I haven't seen her laugh like that in months now.

And then they're reaching for each other and I turn and tiptoe down the hall to our room so I don't see them kissing, the sky behind them huge and wide, the jagged clouds jousting violently as the storm rolls in behind them.

Fourteen

It rains in the night, but by the time I wake up at eight, the clouds have moved out over the water and a weak sun is up to our east. Alone in the kitchen, I make a pot of espresso and read the news on my laptop. I want to be sitting here when Lilly comes out of the den, ready to whisk her off for a lecture about trust and why curfews are important. I'm going to keep very calm and ask her why she didn't let me know where she was, why she didn't answer her phone when I called. I'll explain that I'm fine with her going out with a friend but that I need to be able to believe her when she says she'll be home by ten.

I'm practicing it in my head when Bláithín comes into the kitchen, wrapped in an aquamarine silk dressing gown that makes my sweatpants and hoodie, Lilly's castoffs, look even more worn out than they are. "Thank goodness you made coffee," she says, rummaging for a cup and emptying the rest of the espresso pot into it. "That's one good thing about Americans, anyway. The tea here. My God! I hate tea with a passion." She sits down across from me. "Thank you for letting us stay. It's not exactly the way you planned to spend your holiday, I know. Ah, the rain has stopped. It was wild last night, wasn't it? Here's Adrien. Hello, darling."

Adrien nods silently, switches the electric kettle on, and curls up on the couch to check his phone. Mr. Bean paces and then jumps up and cuddles next to him.

"You sleep okay, my love?" Bláithín asks him.

"Yeah," he says, still staring at the phone. "The rain was crazy though. Beanie was barking at it. It woke me up." I hear the toilet flush and then Conor comes in, says an awkward good morning to Bláithín, and tousles Adrien's hair. In the kitchen, he gives me a discreet kiss and asks if everything is okay. I raise my eyebrows and say, "Well, yeah, until I lay into Lilly."

"What time did she come home?" he asks quietly as he pours the water for his and Adrien's tea.

"Almost midnight," I whisper. "Should I wake her up and yell at her?"

"I don't know. Maybe wait until she wakes up and see what she says?" He looks up as Lilly comes in, rubbing her eyes and yawning. "Morning," she says, as though nothing is wrong.

"Lilly?" She looks up at the sound of my voice and rubs her eyes again.

"Hey," she says, smiling sleepily. "Is there coffee?"

Conor makes himself busy adjusting the teapot and getting milk out of the fridge. "Can I talk to you?" I say in what I hope is a meaningful voice. Bláithín picks up on my tone and smiles just a little, hiding it behind her coffee cup.

Lilly widens her eyes and reaches up to lazily scratch her neck, in a casual way that makes me furious. "Oh, yeah, sorry I was late. We had *so* much fun and I lost track of time. We were singing at this pub and then Alex drove me around to show me some really cool cliffs." She smiles a huge, delighted smile at me and I think of her as a child, how she would do something she wasn't supposed to do and then grin up at us in a way that always dissolved my and Brian's resolve.

Not this time though.

"Well, you promised me you'd be home by ten. So I'd really like to—"

"*So much fun,* she says. Look at that smile. I would say you did have fun," Henri calls out. He's bare-chested and wearing a pair of green harem pants that seem dangerously close to slipping off his waist. I'm not sure where to put my eyes.

I resist the urge to tell him to shut the fuck up. "Lilly," I say again. "Let's go outside and chat for a minute."

"Oooooh," Henri teases. "Did you miss your curfew, Lilly?"

Adrien is listening from the couch now but pretending not to.

"Lilly," I say. She follows me outside, and before I can say anything she says, "I know I was late. I'm sorry. But we were having so much fun and I lost track of time. I'm really sorry."

"Why didn't you text me and let me know?" Mr. Bean bursts through the open door and runs across the drive and into the tall grass across the road.

Lilly smiles a glorious, joyful smile at me. "I know . . . just, like, I didn't want to take my phone out and, like, text my mom, you know? We were talking and then we went for a walk and . . . I'm sorry, Mom. It won't happen again."

"Mr. Bean, come back here!" I call out. "Lilly, you need to let me know what's going on, especially if you're out with people I don't know. Okay?"

"Okay," she says. But she's already thinking about something else as she goes back into the house, Mr. Bean following her and wagging his rear end. I stand there, not sure what to do with all of the overflowing worry and relief and anger left over from last night. It rises in my blood, making me dizzy for a second before I turn away from the now bright morning sun.

At one, Conor runs Henri down to the village to get the car and when they're back, Bláithín, Henri, and Adrien leave for the airport in a flurry of reminders and checks for tickets and wallets. Adrien seems nervous, moody, and Conor gives him an extra-long hug before saying, "Have fun. You'll be back soon enough. I'll pick you up in Dublin in a week, so."

Adrien gives me and Lilly quick hugs and then they're gone and I can see the desolation on Conor's face. I hug him and nod when he says he's going to go and read on the deck.

"Lilly," I say. "Do you want to go for a swim with me? It's getting hot."

She shakes her head. "Alex is coming to pick me up in an hour. He's going to show me around and then he's playing at that pub again tonight and he wants me to come."

"Well . . ."

"Well, what?" She looks up at me with a vaguely challenging glare. Her cheeks are pink, her eyes bright and direct.

"Nothing, just . . . we don't know Alex, Lilly. What's he like? How old is he?"

"He's really nice," she says. "He's a really good singer. He, like, grew up here after he and his brother came from Poland. He's moving to Dublin in the fall to take a music course." Her tone is flat, but she can't keep a small smile off her face.

"How old is he?"

"I don't know, like thirty or something." She widens her eyes in mock innocence.

"Lilly!"

"Just kidding. He turns eighteen in October."

"Okay, well, what are you going to do today?"

"I'll be home later," she says. "We might practice a few tunes so we can play at the pub tonight."

"McCarthy's? Where he was singing on Saturday?" She nods, wary now. "Oh, maybe we'll walk down later and we can hear you."

A look of distaste crosses her face.

She presses her lips together and heads for the bathroom throwing a curt "It's a free country" over her shoulder as she goes.

Zuzanna and Agnieska are just leaving as I walk up to Lissa Crawford's cottage. They're holding mops and buckets filled with cleaning supplies and I remember Lissa telling us that new people would be arriving at the other cottage soon. "Mrs. Crawford was going to ask you if you wanted your cottage cleaned today," Agnieska says, smiling a shy, lovely smile that makes her suddenly beautiful. "We can stop after we finish the other one."

"That's okay," I say. "I think we're in good shape for now. Maybe in a week or two?" She nods, the brightly painted earrings she was wearing the other night swinging cheerily. Zuzanna looks up and I can see that she's been crying; her round blue eyes are bloodshot and there are tears on her cheeks that she reaches up to brush away. They must have been talking about Lukas. She gives me a wan smile and they walk along the road, bottles rattling in their buckets.

Lissa is pouring hot water into a teapot, and when I knock on the door she looks up and beckons me in. "I just made tea," she says. "Sit down, sit down."

I accept a cup once it's steeped. "I thought I'd come by and see if I could help with the list you mentioned last night," I say. "My daughter made it home and now she's off with Alex again. Conor has work to do, so I'm a bit at loose ends."

"Well," she says. "As I told you, I was surprised by what I remembered once I sat down and went right through the house, just as you said, Mrs. Nevin in the kitchen and my father in the study and so forth." She stands up and goes over to a desk facing the wall in the sitting room, returning with a handwritten list, black ink in an elegant hand on a piece of watercolor paper. The list reads: "Mrs. Nevin, cook. Bridget Nevin, clean/kitchen help. L. Crawford. F. Crawford. E. Crawford. A. Crawford. Allertons staying. How many? Rachel Allerton. Rodney and Tommy—sons. Mr. Charles Allerton. Another son? Dorothea (Surname?). Mr. Mahoney, gardens, etc. Boys from the village, Sam, Barry, Jason, Dessie. Young people from Eden????"

"What's this?" I ask, pointing to the word *Eden*.

"Oh, there was a sort of commune out on the Dureen Road," she says. "Ten or so young people who were living there and a few of them became friendly with my parents. They fancied themselves artists, you see. They liked to be around my father and I think they made him feel young."

"Have you tried to talk to any of the people on the list?" I ask her. "Rochelle told me Mrs. Nevin's passed away, but what about the others?"

She looks down at her hands in her lap and then says, "I don't think most of them would, well, speak honestly with me. If you see what I mean." A hurt expression comes over her face. "I sold Rosscliffe House to Sam Nevin a few years ago. I didn't want to do it, but I had my reasons, and I, well, I thought I needed the money. There was resentment about that from some, but you see Sam told me he just wanted the property to preserve the views and the wildness of the peninsula, to make the houses more attractive. I didn't know he wanted it for a hotel. I spoke out against it and then, well, those who had been against me for selling were still against me and those who supported the development were against me for speaking against it."

"So everyone's mad at you," I say. I feel sorry for her. It must be terrible to feel that no one's on your side in a small village like this one.

"Well, yes. When it comes to the house, anyway. It's a small village after all. I thought perhaps you could ask around for me, just to see if anyone remembers Dorothea's surname or anything about her. Then we could, well, track her down, I suppose. Or not track her down and then we'd, well, we'd know something, wouldn't we? Your . . . Mr. Kearney is a historian after all. You could say you are helping him with a paper or something of that sort." She's clearly thought it through and I have to stop myself from laughing. She's handling me like an intelligence asset, complete with a thoughtfully prepared cover story and a suggested collaborator.

I take the list and read it through again. "Could I make a copy of this?" I ask her.

"You can have that one," she says, smiling primly. "I copied it out twice. Oh, Mrs. D'arcy, I so appreciate it. Thank you. I really do think that if I could just *know,* for sure, I would be able to put it behind me."

But as I walk home, I can't help wanting to go back and tell her that investigations rarely finish so neatly that you can leave them behind, never to be thought of again. More frequently, they dredge up the past in such a way that you can't help but take the exploded pieces of it with you.

Fifteen

"I can't believe you're actually dragging me along to the pub so we can spy on Lilly and her new boyfriend," Conor says, squeezing my hand as we make our way along the peninsula road after dinner.

"Well, that's not the only reason," I say. "I also want to pump the locals for information about whether a gruesome crime occurred in Rosscliffe House forty years ago and one of them covered it up."

Conor laughs. "Date night with you is . . . interesting," he says. "Do you not think that if one of them committed a gruesome murder he might be evasive?"

"Well, I'll know, won't I? I am literally trained to detect evasion. I'll be all over him. You better never try to be evasive with me, Kearney, okay?"

"No worries there," he says. "But I might get you to screen some of my first-year students. The excuses for late essays they come up with . . ."

We cross the quiet main street to McCarthy's. If The Net is looking toward the future, McCarthy's is happily stuck in the past. There's no trendy menu, no overt nods to the tourist trade, just a quiet village drinking spot, four old men who look like regulars clustered around the bar, half-drunk pints in front of them; a few hill walkers, sunburned and happy, drinking up front; and a group of musicians, including Alex, starting to gather for a session at a grouping of tables and chairs in the back. Lilly waves at us. Conor nods toward a table, but I say, in a loud voice, "No, let's drink up at the bar. I bet these gentlemen have some good stories to tell us."

A round of laughter. "You wouldn't want to hear the stories they've got to tell," says the barman, who I recognize from the other night we were here. The old men don't introduce themselves or invite us to join them, but they subtly make room, turning their bodies just a little to indicate we're welcome. The barman pulls our pints of Guinness three-quarters of the way and sets them to settle, then walks away unhurriedly to wash some glasses.

"Now you're the American cop lady staying up in the cottages, aren't you?" A white-haired man in a shirt, red tie, and gray suit jacket points his finger at me. "C'mere, I'll tell you a story now, if you want a story. This is a good story now. About crime." He waggles his eyebrows. "There was a man who used to live near Durrus who had two families, like. Like he had one family in Durrus and he had another family in Bandon, and he went back and forth. Must have had a lot of energy, that man."

Someone asks him where the man lived and they discuss that for a bit while our pints settle. We know he'll get back to it though.

When the pints have been finished and put in front of us, he continues, "Well, he keeled over. At first they thought he had a heart attack, but they found out—I don't know how, some sort o' Garda sorcery, I suppose—that he'd been poisoned. Something awful, it was, meant for treating cattle. Well, the guards looked to see did he have enemies and then they found out about the second family in Bandon and they thought, ah, maybe it was the first woman, his wife, and maybe she'd found out about the sec-

ond. They talked to everyone they could, they couldn't find a—"
He winks at me. "Smoking gun, so to speak. It wasn't until a couple years later that one o' the kids mentioned to a neighbor that the two women knew each other. Well, someone went asking and they'd known each other all along. They both got tired of him and killed him together."

"Did they go to prison, Jim?" one of the other men asks.

"Ah, no. The neighbor never told the guards. It got around the village he'd said it, but when the guards went knocking, he denied it, o'course, said they must have gotten it wrong. Sure, that man, he was a terrible bastard. He probably deserved it."

Everyone sighs at the well-told tale. There are a couple of "Very good, now, Jim"s and then everyone turns back to their pints.

I go over to say hello to Lilly, and Alex stands up and shakes my hand. "Hello, Mrs. D'arcy, how are you?" he asks.

"Hi, Alex. I'm fine. Hi, Lilly. Did you have a nice day?"

She smiles, looking happy and a little sunburned. "Yeah, we went to Bantry. We had the best lunch."

"Do you have a favorite tune we can do for you tonight?" Alex asks me, smiling charmingly. "Lilly's a fast learner. She'll sing it for you." Lilly rolls her eyes but grins.

"I'll leave it to you," I say. "But I like the dark ones, right, Lilly? Murder, mayhem, betrayal."

"Daragh knows them all," Alex says, nodding to the middle-aged guy tuning his fiddle. "He'll find you a good one."

When I get back to the bar, Conor has inserted himself into the men's conversation and he's telling them about a construction project in a Dublin suburb that cut off six houses when they put the road in the wrong place. The men are delighted by the flagrant government incompetence and Conor gets a round of appreciative grins and sighs when he's done.

It's warm in the pub now that it's full of bodies. The atmosphere is good, comfortable and celebratory. The artifacts behind the bar tell the story of Rosscliffe, photographs of Rosscliffe House and fishing boats and copper mining and villagers swimming off the pier in what looks like frigid weather.

Another round of drinks is bought and this time we're included in it. "What do you think happened to this Polish fella they found?" one of the other men asks the man named Jim. I can feel the attention of the group shifting, everyone listening but trying not to seem too invested in his answer.

"You know what I thought of when they found him?" Jim says. "Your man from Dunmanway there."

"Which one was that now?"

"Your man who was kilt right around the time of our local event," Jim says, raising his caterpillar-like eyebrows meaningfully.

I tug at Conor's sleeve. He takes the hint and obliges with a "Sorry, local event?"

"Ah, did you not know you've come to be at your leisure in a den of fuckin' iniquity?" Jim says, lowering his voice to a mock whisper. "International drugs trafficking like." Everyone laughs as though it's the funniest thing they've ever heard. He winks at me. "Don't worry now, Detective. It's all very quiet here. In the past, our coastal waters have been used for the transfer of illegal goods, but that sort of thing has settled right down. You've nothing to worry about."

I know he must be talking about Operation Waves, but I play dumb and say, "You can't leave it at that. Now I'm intrigued."

"He'd tell you all about it," one of the men says very quietly, nodding almost imperceptibly toward the end of the bar. I wait a second to look, and when I do, there's a man working on a pint of lager at the end of the bar, his eyes fixed on a wall-mounted television on which men in bright shirts are silently chasing a soccer ball around a field. He's tall, barrel-chested, his arms below the sleeves of his tight black polo shirt stenciled with tattoos. It's the man who was sitting in the Mercedes outside The Net the night we had dinner there and the day Lilly and I were shopping in the village.

Jim smiles. "He's a Polish fella," he says. "Anton Dorda. He's all right. Been living here a lot of years, has a few businesses. People talk, don't they, Matt?"

One of the other men, a stooped, sad-looking guy with curly white hair and wearing a dirty yellow cardigan sweater, looks bothered by that, but he nods at Jim. "Here now," Jim says, to change the subject. "Which o' those cottages are you in?"

"The middle one," Conor says. "It's lovely."

"I was raised in that cottage," Jim tells us. "How about that? It was owned by herself, well, her parents in the Big House, but my grandparents had the lease of it. Lived there a lot of years. My father was born in that cottage, too."

I try to keep my voice casual, a little teasing, but serious, too. "Someone told me that there are stories in the village about the peninsula being haunted. You ever seen a ghost out there?"

"Ah, sure, loads of times," Jim says, winking at me. "She likes to walk around in resplendent nudity. Or maybe that's just the movie star who was renting one of Sammy Nevin's houses." Everyone laughs and he winks at me again. We're in league now.

"My granddad saw her once," says another man. "He swore to it now."

"If you see her, it's said you'll die within three days. Did he die within three days, Christy?"

Christy, a plump guy in a perfectly ironed dress shirt, hesitates, building up the drama, and then holds up four fingers. "Four days," he whispers. Everyone sighs. They fall back to their own conversations, done with us for the moment.

The door opens and Tomasz Sadowski enters the pub and nods to the bartender, who wordlessly pulls him a pint of lager. To-masz looks around the bar, his eyes alighting on me and Conor. He nods, but doesn't come over to say hello, and then he sees his brother and Lilly and the other musicians and goes to the back to join them. The old men all raise their eyebrows at one another. "I bet *he* knows what happened to that fella," the man named Christy says in a low voice, meant only for his friends.

"Why would that be now?" Jim asks, his eyebrows raised. "Are you saying that just because he's of Eastern European extraction, like your man in the water, that he knows what this other fella is up to? That's awful xenophobic of you now."

"I didn't mean it like that," Christy grumbles.

"Fella likely slipped and fell. Annie Tobin will figure it out," the guy in the cardigan sweater mutters.

"You're right, Matt. Poor Annie Tobin," someone says, and every-one agrees, a murmur of sympathy going up among the men.

I'm curious about this, but there's no way to ask about it, and the conversation flits and skims and then the music starts, a fast reel, Alex playing guitar, someone on pipes and a few fiddle players keeping it going. Conor and I stand the next round and the pints disappear quickly. If I'm going to ask the old guys about Rosscliffe House in 1973 and the mysterious Dorothea, I've got to do it now.

When there's a break in the music, I say, "We've been hearing about what it was like in Rosscliffe back in the seventies, when Felix Crawford was here. Someone told me there was a hippie commune in Rosscliffe. Do you all remember that?"

"Remember it? Christy here was one of 'em!" Jim gives him a little shove.

"Ah, now," Christy says, blushing and looking sheepish.

"He had a mad love affair with a German girl, Brunnhilde, wasn't that her name? Ah, now *she* liked to go about in the altogether." The men all laugh, Christy still looking sheepish and murmuring, "Hilda, just Hilda," and I realize I'll lose them if I don't get to it.

"Did people from the village spend much time at Rosscliffe House?" I ask. "Would you have gone for visits or anything?"

"Not the likes of me," Jim says. "Matt did the rosebushes and so forth though, so he'd be the one to tell you what it was like." He nods to the sad-looking guy in the yellow cardigan. This must be Barry's father, Matt Mahoney, I realize, seeing the resemblance now that I know.

"You were the gardener," I say. "You're Barry's father."

He nods, his eyes darting around the pub. "That's right. Some of us came up to work at the house. Not many."

Jim considers for a moment, then says, "They kept themselves to themselves, the Crawfords. Few o' Christy's friends from the commune were around the place, I suppose. Gwynedd and that one with the braids. But they didn't invite people from the village into the house." He takes a long drink of his pint.

"Do you remember a woman named Dorothea?" I ask. "She was a sort of governess for the Crawford children."

Matt Mahoney looks alarmed, but Jim claps him on the shoulder and says, "I remember her. She had a white streak in her hair, like a witch. Sure, there was something funny about her all right. My Margaret thought she was a particular friend of Felix's rather than a governess. Something about her never quite added up."

I look over at Matt Mahoney, but he's busy looking down at the bar, and when the music ends he drains his glass and says he's to be getting home. "Ellen will be worrying now," he says. "They'll have the guards out after me." He puts on his cap and shuffles toward a cane leaning against the back of a barstool; he's a bit unsteady on his feet as he makes his way out the door.

Something makes me check on Anton Dorda. He's watching Matt Mahoney go and he must feel my eyes on him because he coolly raises his pint in greeting. I'm not sure why, but it flusters me, the little gleam of a smile at his mouth. He's not a conventionally attractive man, but there's something powerful and charismatic about him. I'd put him at about my age; his gray hair is thinning and he's cropped it close to his skull. His neck is stenciled with tattoos that reach down into his collar.

When they're sure Matt Mahoney is gone, the other men shake their heads sympathetically. "Poor oul bastard," Jim says. "The Parkinson's is a terrible thing now." He sees someone across the pub and goes over to talk. The little fraternity has broken up and Conor and I drift to the back of the pub to listen to the music. They do a reel and then a jig, and when it ends, everyone claps and I see the other musicians urging Alex on.

"Okay, okay," he says. "But Lilly has to sing with me."

"No," I hear her protest. "I don't know all the words."

Conor and I watch. Someone props a piece of paper in front of her, with the lyrics to the tune printed on it, I imagine, and she takes a look and nods. The fiddle player starts up and Alex starts playing and he and Lilly start singing "The Black Velvet Band," the words familiar to me but made new by their voices. She's hesitant at first, but by the time they get to the chorus, she's got the rhythm of it down and she and Alex are owning it. *"Her eyes they shone like diamonds / I thought her the queen of the land."* It's simple and lovely with Alex's and Lilly's harmonies and the gentle fiddle and guitar in the background, a tale of love and betrayal.

"That your girl? She's very good now," Jim says from behind me with something like reverence. "Alex, he's been singing in here since he was a little lad. Couldn't get enough of it. You could see he loved it right from the beginning. That fella." He points to Tomasz, who's sitting silently and listening to the music. "He used to bring him in the evenings after he finished up at the building site. He'd make a little bed, in the corner, so Alex could go to sleep, but he wasn't having any of it. He wanted to listen. Someone found him a tin whistle and he started on that. That fella over there, Daragh, he's very good himself and he saw Alex had something and gave him a guitar. He taught him."

When they're done, Conor and I clap with the rest of the crowd and I throw Lilly a kiss. She's grinning, delighted, her face shining and open as she gazes up at Alex while he gets ready for the next tune. I feel a little stab of discomfort. She looks so vulnerable, besotted with the handsome boy next to her.

I'm up at the bar ordering waters for me and Conor when Gwynedd Williams from the health food shop comes in, followed by a group of teenage boys, Jack Nevin among them. The boys have clearly gotten an early start; they have that elated, buzzy energy that comes from early drinking, the night still ahead of them. They know they won't get served here, so they've probably been doing shots in someone's car or off in the bushes. They make a beeline for the back of the pub and the music, and remembering what Rochelle said about Jack having a crush on Lilly, I watch as one of the boys points in Lilly's direction and gives Jack a little shove. He looks embarrassed and slaps the other boy's hand away.

"Hello then," Gwynedd says to me, catching the bartender's eye and pointing to the taps. "Having a nice night?"

"We are," I say. I switch course and order two more pints, and when his lager comes, I say, "We were just talking about ghosts on Ross Head."

"Ha! A load of bollocks. The only thing haunting the peninsula is Sam Nevin's unbridled capitalist impulse." He frowns into his beer.

I laugh. "You really don't want this hotel built, do you? Wouldn't it be good for your shop? Fancy tourists need remedies and vitamins, too."

He scowls. "I wasn't born here. I wasn't raised here, but I've been living here for almost forty years and I care about this place more than any of this lot." He gestures around the pub. "So many of the towns and villages around here have become not much more than tourist destinations. Rosscliffe still has a bit of village life. Unspoiled headlands. We look out for one another." He frowns. "Sam Nevin wants to change us."

I take a long sip of my own pint. "Can I ask you something? I don't understand why Lissa Crawford thought Sam wasn't going to develop the house." I'm thinking about what she said to me. *I didn't want to do it, but I had my reasons and I, well, I thought I needed the money.*

Gwynedd says, "Do you know, I've always wondered about that. It didn't make sense at the time. A few of us were furious when we heard she'd done it. She implied they had some sort of an agreement and he'd broken it. But she doesn't like to talk about it." The tune ends and there's a round of applause.

"I heard you were here in 1973," I say. I catch Conor craning his neck, trying to figure out where I've gone, but I don't want to lose my chance.

"I arrived in 1971," he says, smiling. "I fell in love with an Irish lass in London and followed her here. We lived with twelve other young people in an old house out near Dureen. Those were good days."

"Was that the commune they were talking about, Eden?" I ask. "That was you? Rainbows and free love?"

Gwynedd laughs. "I suppose you could call it that, but that makes it sound wilder than it was. There was a lot of gardening and a lot of cooking, not as much drugs and sex as we'd been led to believe." He smiles. "Many of us were artists and we were quite serious about our art."

"Are you a painter?"

"No, I'm an herbalist," he says proudly. "My artist's materials are all of Mother Nature's bounty."

"And what happened to the Irish woman? Did you stay at the house with her a long time?"

"She moved to America. But then she moved back. We've been married ever since. I opened a shop in Bantry in 1980. Finally moved it here as the village grew a bit." He frowns and I can hear the ambivalence in his voice. He doesn't like owing Sam Nevin anything.

The fiddlers start in on a jig I recognize as "Out on the Ocean." When I turn around to look at Lilly, she's tapping her foot and listening, smiling at Alex as he plays.

"You must have known Felix Crawford then," I say. "Did you ever go to the house?"

He frowns. "Once or twice. They kept themselves to themselves. Of course, we knew who he was, but they seemed to invite friends from outside Rosscliffe to stay."

"Did you meet a woman named Dorothea? In 1973? Apparently she was staying with them."

I watch his face as he thinks about it. "It's a bit familiar," he says. "There was an . . . odd woman who was a sort of a governess or something. Very tall. As I said, it was only once or twice we went up there. It wasn't at all what we were expecting. The house was in quite a state of disrepair, not at all grand. Why do you ask?" He looks curious now, alert to my ulterior motive.

"No reason. I've gotten a bit interested in local history."

"You know, I always thought there was something off about Crawford myself." He turns his head to watch the musicians at the back of the pub, but he's being serious. There's something there.

"Off how?"

He looks at me. "He was just . . . odd. He stared too long. A few of the girls said he gave them a bad feeling. I wondered . . . Anyway, it was a long time ago." I ask a few more questions, but he doesn't have anything more specific than that and I excuse myself to take the pints to Conor.

"I thought you were getting waters. What's the plan then?" he asks. "To get me so drunk I can't walk home?"

"That's definitely the plan. No, I wanted to talk to the guy who owns the health food store," I say, as I look up and see Agnieska and Zuzanna coming through the door. They must have just closed up over at the gastropub. The women seem in good spirits, laughing and bringing their drinks over to listen to the music. Jack Nevin and his friends say something to them that makes Zuzanna turn around and give them a dirty look.

"Ah, look now," Jack says, loud enough that I can hear. The barman's head snaps over, checking for a problem. Alex stands up and says something to Jack. The barman's still paying attention. So am I. Jack's face clouds over and he turns to leave, followed by his friends.

The music gets louder and faster. I'm the other side of buzzed and Zuzanna hugs Alex and then says something to Lilly, who laughs. Lilly already seems part of the social scene here and I'm not sure how I feel about it. Agnieska looks up at me and says something to Tomasz. I've had too much to drink. I'm not thinking straight, seeing conspiracy where there probably isn't any. Gwynedd Williams wanders over to listen, then buttons up his loose linen coat and goes out into the night. I watch him leave. Anton Dorda's gone now, too, his spot at the end of the bar empty, his half-full pint glass still there.

Conor and I finish our drinks and go over to the table where Lilly is sitting and talking to the musicians. "Lilly, we're going," I tell her.

She looks up at me with puppy-dog eyes. "Can I stay just a bit later, please? We're going to sing another song."

Alex gets up and joins her, smiling broadly. "I'll make sure she gets home, Mrs. D'arcy," he says. "I'm not driving tonight, but I'll walk her up."

Zuzanna jumps up and puts an arm around Alex's shoulders. "He is a very nice boy, seriously. You can trust him." She laughs and Alex rolls his eyes and shrugs her arm off.

"I'm sure I can," I say. "Are you having a good night?"

Zuzanna shrugs. "I suppose. Have you been to the beach yet?"

"Yes, we loved it. Do you go there often?"

"The water's too cold for me." Pain flashes in her eyes and I know she's thinking of Lukas.

Zuzanna smiles up at me sadly, her eyes somehow reassuring. For some reason, the middle-aged men and women also sitting at the table make me feel better. I know where she is. There are lots of other people here, women who will look after Lilly. Not much can happen between here and our cottage. "All right," I say. "But home before midnight, okay?"

Lilly grins. "Thanks, Mom," she says, and they go back to the group. Tomasz has been listening to us and I nod to him, feeling like I should introduce myself, but he's glowering, the scar on his forehead giving him a slightly menacing air, and I get the sense that he doesn't want to talk.

Outside, the village is quiet and dark and we're almost past the shops when I see Barry Mahoney and Anton Dorda standing in the middle of the street, talking. There's tension in their bodies; Barry has his hands at his sides and his shoulders thrust forward. Dorda has a hand up, one finger pointing at Barry. When they see us, they step back, Dorda smiling and waiting for us to pass.

"Lovers' spat?" Conor whispers.

"I don't think there's much love there," I whisper back.

It's nearly dark as we turn onto the peninsula, the sound of the ocean receding into the background. "This night," Conor says, rubbing the top of my hand with his thumb. "It reminds me of when I used to go to the Gaeltacht for Irish college in the summers. We'd go out and run around in the evenings and then we'd be walking back to the *bean an tí*'s house, the host family, like, and the nights would feel like this. Sweet, you know? It stayed light for ages. My first kiss was on one of these nights. Girl from Sligo."

"What was her name?"

"Helena," he says. "*She* kissed *me*. I never would have chanced it."

"Helena," I say. "Romantic."

"It was. Summer. Young love."

"Was she a good kisser?"

"I can't remember exactly. I was pleased, anyway."

Rosscliffe House rises from the peninsula, the castle ruins like little islands in the pool of black around the house. We've crested the rise of the hill when a figure appears out of the dark walking from the direction of Rosscliffe House. Conor whispers, "I think that's Lorcan. What's he doing out here this late?"

"I don't know," I say. "He doesn't look like he's out for a stroll."

We watch him go, and once he's disappeared, Conor says, "I didn't want to call to him, like, you know?"

"He was probably just going for a walk," I say weakly. We both know it's not true. There was an unmistakable furtiveness about Lorcan. He was somewhere he shouldn't have been.

"There was something in that pub," I say after a minute. "An atmosphere, like all the things between people, for years and years and years, were running just under the surface."

"Makes sense, doesn't it? They've known one another for a long time. Did you find out anything about Mrs. Crawford's mystery?"

I tell him about Gwynedd Williams's memories of Felix Crawford. "Didn't you think Matt Mahoney seemed nervous about something when I was asking about Rosscliffe House?" I say.

"I don't know. Maybe. You're the one with training in spotting evasion. I was fully expecting you'd take that poor young fella aside for an interrogation before you'd let him walk Lilly home."

I give him a playful smack, then ask, "Do you think I'm being overprotective, worrying about Lilly?" We're passing Lissa Crawford's cottage and I turn to look for her in the windows. The house is all lit up and I imagine her painting in her studio, transferring the contents of her imagination on to the canvas.

Conor squeezes my hand. "She just wants to see him. You remember how that is."

"Are you thinking of the beautiful Helena?"

"No, I'm thinking of you. Remember when you were waiting for me outside of the arts building, just sitting there when I came out, and I saw you and—"

"You looked up," I say. "And I didn't know what you were going to say. I'd left so suddenly. I'd realized I was in love with you and I needed to tell you, and I was nervous, but I knew somehow, I knew we had to be together. I knew we would."

His voice is soft. "I saw you and I felt . . . gratitude. Overwhelming gratitude. Just *thank you*. I wanted to *be* with you. To be around you. That's what I remember. That's what love is."

"But she's only seventeen," I say quietly. "She's known him less than a week. She doesn't know anything."

Conor just raises his eyebrows. "You think seventeen-year-olds don't fall in love?"

"No, I know . . . It's just . . . I want to protect her, Conor. With everything going on, this feels dangerous. It feels risky."

He turns to look at me. "Love is dangerous, Maggie. Don't you know that?"

We're quiet, walking home and watching the sky. The ocean pounds the rocks below us.

Sixteen

Agnieska makes her way carefully along the edge of the path, her eyes cast down and scanning the thick grass growing out of the wet ground along the cliffs for her missing earring. The sun isn't quite up yet and there isn't enough light to search for the earring properly, but it's going to be time to start cleaning rooms at the bed-and-breakfast soon and this is the only chance she'll have to look without anyone seeing her. The rich people who live in the new houses along the cliffs love to go for walks in the morning; she wants to do her searching before they're awake.

The earrings are little wooden circles, painted with colorful *wycinanki* flowers on a glossy black background, and they were a gift from her grandmother, her *babcia,* the last time she was home. They're not fashionable; she thinks of them as something visitors to Poland take home rather than anything Polish women actually wear, but they're better quality than the ones you find in touristy gift shops, the painting more intricate and skillful, the hooks made of real silver rather than wire, and they remind her of her *babcia* and home. She would never wear them in Poland but here in Ireland they've taken on a different significance, one she can't put into words.

Now she retraces her steps out along the cliffs, searching the dark green thatch for the telltale brightness of the earring. She knows she had it last night, when she and Zuzanna walked over to McCarthy's. Zuzanna was saying something about the cars parked outside the pub, which ones she liked and which ones she didn't and who in the village they belonged to, but Agnieska was distracted because she'd reached up and felt the earring missing. The hook was too big and it kept slipping out. Zuzanna had stopped talking about cars to tell Agnieska the earring was stuck in her hair and to put it back for her.

So, she lost it last night. She wants to find it before someone else does. Maybe she's paranoid, but it seems suddenly important that no one knows she was here. She doesn't know who might be watching her.

The sun is clearing the horizon now and the sky is a milky pink, with traces of orange at the waterline. She rarely gets to see it like this, since she starts working early and finishes late. The ocean and the sunrise and the little islands in the far distance are peaceful. Something about the changing colors, the promise of the light, makes her smile as she watches the line of sun at the point where the water meets the sky.

She keeps her head down, looking, until she reaches Rosscliffe House. Perhaps it was picked up by an early morning walker or blown over the cliffs by the wind. She walks closer to the edge and looks out at the sea.

When Agnieska was a child, she went to the beach at Rewal with her parents and her sister. Her sister liked to run into the waves, confronting them, challenging them, but Agnieska liked to just sit on the sand, watching the waves come in, following the white crests as they came closer and closer and then disappeared. Far below her, the waves come and go, forcing her heart rate down, calming her as she gives herself over to their timing, their rhythm. *In. Out. In. Out.* She watches the line of pale froth move closer and then break.

At first, she thinks the shape is a piece of wood, a tree branch that slid into the ocean, or one of the seals people say you can see off Ross Head. Then she realizes.

Someone's in the water.

It's a body, a dead body. She can tell from the way it drifts, unmoving, the way it shifts on the surface as the waves lap at the rocks far below.

Agnieska looks down to make sure, feeling dizzy, like the water is rising up to her, but her instinct was right. It's a dead body, floating facedown in the calmer water of the little cove below the cliffs, the brown coat dark on the water.

And then recognition tears through her: she knows who it is.

"Help!" she calls out, fumbling for her phone, even though there's no one there to hear her. The houses all along the cliffs are too far away, their glass windows reflecting the rising sun. "Someone help me!" She manages to dial the emergency number, but when the dispatcher answers, she can only think of Polish words and it's a long moment before she's able to say to the confused woman on the other end of the phone, "I'm at Ross Head! I need help out here."

Behind her, the sunrise spreads out across the sky.

Seventeen

I'm making coffee the next morning when I hear a knock at the cottage door. I shush Mr. Bean and look out the window over the sink to see a car in the driveway. When I open the door, I find Ann Tobin standing there, looking worried.

"Good morning, Mrs. D'arcy. I'm sorry to bother you."

"Is everything okay?" I feel a flash of panic, thinking *Lilly,* then remember that I heard her come in last night. The boots she was wearing are next to the door. Relief floods through me as I take in Tobin's grim expression.

"Well, I need to ask some questions. I'm here because, unfortunately, a young woman out walking early this morning spotted human remains in the water at first light and we deployed the coast guard."

She takes in the shocked expression on my face and says, a bit more gently, "It seems there may have been an accident last night on the cliffs."

I stare at her. I'm cold all of a sudden, my vision too sharp.

"What? Another one?"

"Yes, unfortunately." She looks drained, the skin beneath her eyes puffy, her face pale.

"Who was it?" I ask. "Who's the victim?"

"I'd like to come in if I could," she says. "It sounds like your family was at McCarthy's last night. I'd just like to ask you a few questions." I know exactly what she's doing. She's not going to tell us who drowned until she's established where we were—or say we were—last night. She wants our recollections clean. She wants to see what we know before the name is on the table.

"Of course. Please come and sit down. I just made coffee. Can I get you a cup?"

"Yes, please." When I put the coffee in front of her, she tips in a splash of cream and drinks it gratefully. While we wait for Lilly and Conor to get dressed, she asks me to recount my movements last night. I tell her about eating dinner at home and then walking down to the pub. As she makes notes on a pad of paper, I list everyone at the pub. I tell her about Jack Nevin and his friends and about seeing Barry Mahoney and Anton Dorda in the street as we walked home. She looks very interested at that. "Were they fighting?" she asks as Conor and Lilly join us.

"No, not exactly, just . . . there was clearly tension there of some kind. They were discussing something."

"And then you walked home?" I nod. "Did you hear anything during the night?"

"Just Lilly coming in at midnight. That was it. Oh, and we saw Lorcan Murphy out walking on our way home."

"In the village?" She's alert now.

"No, on Ross Head. Heading home, I think."

She has Conor recount his version of the evening, which is identical to mine, right down to his description of Barry Mahoney and Anton Dorda in the street and seeing Lorcan walking home. "And you, Miss . . ."

"Lombardi," I say. "Lillian Lombardi. She's seventeen."

Tobin looks at Lilly for a second. "Miss Lombardi, can you tell me about last evening?"

Lilly's wearing a pink sweatshirt over pajama pants. She pulls her legs up so she's cross-legged in her chair and reaches for the mug of coffee I poured for her. "I was with, uh, Alex. Alex Sadowski? We had lunch in Bantry and then practiced some songs at his apartment and then walked to McCarthy's, in the village, around seven. He was playing music with a bunch of other people, but I don't know all their names. Daragh was one, he's, like, an older guy. We stayed there until eleven thirty and then he walked me home." Tobin asks her who was at the pub and Lilly names everyone as best she can. When she's done, she looks up at Tobin with wide eyes and says, "What happened? Why do you need to know this?"

Tobin hesitates. She knows she needs to tell us now. She's gotten what she can. It's time to see how we react to the name. "I'm sorry to have to tell you that Zuzanna Brol was found in the water below the cliffs this morning. It looks like she went in sometime last night or early this morning."

Lilly gasps. "She's a friend of Alex's. She was at the pub last night. We were talking to her, oh my God." She's crying, gulping for air, the tears running down her cheeks. I put an arm around her and pull her close to me, feeling her chest heave as her breath comes in raggedy mouthfuls.

"I'm so sorry," Tobin says gently. She waits until Lilly wipes her eyes and sits up and then asks us, "How did Zuzanna seem last night? Could you tell how much she'd had to drink?"

"She seemed to be having a good time," Conor says. "I saw her laughing at one point. But she wasn't visibly intoxicated."

"Yeah, she was smiling when I saw her," I agree. "Maybe a bit buzzed, you know. Maybe she was a little subdued, but I don't know her well. She didn't strike me as drunk. Lilly, you were sitting with her."

"She seemed okay," Lilly says uncertainly.

"You said you were talking to her. What about?" Tobin sits back in her chair, relaxed, then scratches her nose and reaches down to pat Mr. Bean on the back.

"Nothing, really. The music is all I remember. I guess she was talking to Alex more." We all wait, but Lilly just sniffs and doesn't say anything more.

"Did she leave before you?" Tobin asks. Lilly nods. "How long before?"

"Maybe a half hour, so around eleven."

"Alone?"

"Um, I think so. Yeah." Lilly looks down, picks up a spoon, and turns it over in her hand.

Tobin studies her for a minute. "Okay, I'm going to leave you all. If you think of anything else that might be relevant, please let me know."

I walk her to the door and step outside, putting a hand up to shield my eyes from the strong morning sun. "There's something I need to tell you," I say. "Lissa Crawford asked me to look into something that may have happened at Rosscliffe House in 1973. She found a cloth with blood on it and she thinks there may have been a young woman living at the house who disappeared. I asked a few questions last night at the pub, didn't really get anything."

Tobin looks out across the water and then back at me. "I looked into it for her a few months ago. There was nothing in the files from that summer, no missing person reported, no report of violence. Nothing. But she's clearly upset about it. Probably a misunderstanding, but you'll let me know if you find anything, yeah?"

"Of course."

"Can I ask you something? Anton Dorda? You said he was at the pub. Did he talk to anyone? Did he talk to Zuzanna?" There's something desperate in her eyes. She's intensely focused on my answer, but she's trying to keep her voice from sounding too eager.

I think for a moment. "I didn't see him talking to her, but I think maybe he was watching her and everyone else who was listening to the music. And I told you about his . . . standoff with Barry Mahoney in the street."

She nods, disappointed. "Thanks for your help."

Back inside, Conor nods to Lilly's room and pantomimes holding a phone to his ear. When she comes out, she tells me that Alex is going to pick her up in a half hour. "He wants to go for a walk on the beach." She blushes. "He's sad about Zuzanna and he said I cheer him up."

"Okay," I say. I know the guards will be crawling all over the peninsula today and she's probably better off away from Ross Head. "But you need to answer your phone and you need to come home when you say you're going to come home, okay?"

She nods, but I'm uneasy. She's only known him a few days and now she's going to provide him with emotional support, and for a presumptive suicide? Lilly's own mental health is still fragile. Surely this is expecting too much.

"Does he have an adult to talk to?" I ask her. "Something like this is, well, it's a big deal."

She shrugs. "His brother, Tomasz, I guess. Their parents died, so his brother is sort of like his dad. He's pretty close to Mrs. Crawford, too, and the Nevins. They've helped him out a lot. He's friends with Jack." This doesn't make me feel much better. Tomasz Sadowski didn't look much older than twenty-six or twenty-seven and there was obvious tension between Alex and Jack Nevin at the pub.

"Well, pass on our sympathies, okay?" When he pulls up out front in the old red Ford, I step outside and wave to him as Lilly dashes out and gets into the car. I want to say something, to tell him I'm sorry about Zuzanna, but he just waves back and turns to Lilly, completely focused on her. He backs out and drives off toward the village at a sensible speed. I watch them go until I can't see the car anymore.

Out of sorts now, I decide to go for a run, both because I need to burn off my anxiety and because I'm curious about what Ann Tobin is setting up in terms of an investigation. There are a couple of marked cars in front of Lissa Crawford's cottage, which they seem to be using as a staging area, and I can see a team of gardaí in yellow reflective coats walking slowly along the path on the cliff edges, presumably looking for evidence.

Just as with Lukas, they'll be looking for anything to indicate that Zuzanna slipped on the cliffs or went over against her will, footprints in the muddy ground and broken blades of grass to indicate she tried to save herself before falling. They'll be looking for biological evidence, hair or torn fingernails, from her and from anyone else. I'm assuming that her friends told Tobin that she was depressed and that the gardaí are interviewing her friends and family, if they're nearby, and gathering information about her state of mind. Before it's ruled an accident or a suicide, they'll want some definite evidence that she had been depressed or despondent, a note or a text, along with physical evidence from the scene. Our accounts—and the accounts of everyone who was at the pub—about her state of mind will be part of the record.

Breathing hard now, I stop for a second on the side of the road and dial Roly's number and leave a message, just to keep him in the loop. He may be able to find out something for me, too.

Then I do a fast five miles and, on my way back, I stop and knock on Lissa Crawford's door. I want to ask her about Matt Mahoney and see if she's ever talked to him about her memories. I'm not sure how I'll handle Gwynedd Williams's comment about Felix Crawford being a bit creepy, but as it turns out, I don't need to worry about that. There's no answer and the cottage is dark.

Back home, I stand for a moment in the empty kitchen, just listening to the quiet. For days, I've been wishing for some solitude. Now I have it and I can't settle down. I need something to do, so I take Conor a cup of tea on the patio, pulling a chair up next to him and angling it so I'll have the full force of the sun on my face. It's a little colder today; the breeze coming off the ocean means business. He's set up with his laptop and notebooks on the table, stacks of books surrounding him like little brick walls. When he looks up at me, he has the dreamy look he gets when he's working. His reading glasses have slipped down on his nose and his brown eyes catch the sunlight. His hair is messy and he smells of the sea and coffee and books.

"Where's Dunmanway?" I ask. "Those old guys in the pub said something about Lukas Adamik reminding them of someone from Dunmanway."

"Ah, back toward Cork City, I think," he says. "Not far from

Kilmichael. There was a famous ambush there in 1920, you know. Tom Barry and his men. I can tell you all about it. It was quite important really, both strategically and in terms of morale. The West Cork IRA hadn't had much success until Kilmichael . . ." He goes on for a bit and finally I lean over and kiss him, feeling the softness of his lips and the scratchy start of stubble on his cheeks. "I love you," I whisper, so quietly I'm not sure he hears until he turns and whispers, "I love you, too."

Eighteen

Ann bends down to look at the footprints at the building site, the six boot prints leading to the big silvery skip, filled with construction debris, where someone has sprayed the words LEAVE ROSS HEAD ALONE! NO HOTEL DEVELOPMENT HERE!! in orange paint. The techs have already photographed the scene, but she wants to look at it again. Something was bothering her when they responded after one of the uniforms noticed the graffiti during the evidence search this morning. They confirmed with Tomasz Sadowski that it hadn't been there when he left the site at six last night, so it seems clear someone was up here in the night making a political statement.

She looks back toward Rosscliffe House. She hates coming out here, avoids it whenever she can. There are good reasons for that, of course, but she hated it even before she had those good reasons. It's because of the house. The house gives her chills every time she sees its gray bulk staring at her from its superior vantage point on the edge of the peninsula. She and Sean used to live in a cottage out along the road to Letterlickey, where she couldn't see the sea or the house at all. But though there are many things she loves about the simplicity of her flat in the village, the views to the west aren't one of them. The house seems to spy into her window at all hours of the day and night. She closes her curtains most of the time and yet she can still feel it there somehow. Lots of people would value the view; on fine days, the water sparkles, reflecting the sky, and the house is proud and grand. But she only took the flat because she needed something fast.

Some might see it, her hatred of the house, as a political statement; Ann, an Irish Catholic, resenting the symbol of her nation's long oppression, but it isn't that at all. There was an abandoned Anglo-Irish country house near where she grew up in the midlands, a Gothic Revival mansion outside of town that was referred to affectionately as Belinda's Castle after some young woman who had lived and died young there in the distant past. The castle was quite beloved in Ann's town and people would picnic out there, take visiting relatives to walk in the overgrown grounds, or propose in front of it. Ann's mother rang her up excitedly a few years ago to say that some Americans had bought Belinda's Castle and were living in it. They've kept part of the grounds open to the public, and if possible, it has become even more popular.

But Rosscliffe House is something else.

She turns away from it, back toward the cliffs, where Broome and the guards they've borrowed from Bandon are doing a fingertip search of the grass. If they find something, they'll send the techs down, but everyone seems to be assuming that both of these deaths are suicides or accidents. They get a fair number of people falling off the cliffs around here. Sometimes you don't know, of course. There was an accident a few years ago, a young medical student from Pakistan who had been under a lot of academic pressure. The official ruling was that he slipped while taking a picture, but Ann thought that maybe he was looking for a way out of the overwhelming workload, the homesickness, the loneliness.

It was suggested she was projecting, so she gave up.

The results from the postmortem on what's left of Lukas Adamik should come from Cork in the next couple of days. Then they'll do Zuzanna Brol's. If one or both of the deceased had drugs in their system at the time of death, that might be grounds to re-question some of the witnesses and suspects from the Operation Waves investigation. But if not, and if there's nothing on the postmortem, she knows they'll likely get classified as suicides or accidental deaths. They'll all move on.

Ann doesn't want to move on.

And she knows there may be someone else who doesn't want to move on, either.

The superintendent has already had a call from Dublin. She saw the name on the message: *Detective P. Fiero.* He would have seen the location of the deaths, would have wondered about the state of the bodies. She knows exactly where his mind is going. She even knows what he's feeling: hope, elation, but shame, too, because he sees these new deaths as an opportunity, because he doesn't really care about the lost lives, only the evidence they may have created, the connections to the other crimes.

The one that got away.

She tries to keep her expectations in check, but she feels it, the little buzz of awareness. Crime scenes have atmosphere and she feels in her bones that this is a crime scene, right here, on the cliffs. She feels the presence of something dark and evil here, as though it has seeped out of the house and into the grass.

And what about the graffiti? Kids most likely, but if they were up here, they might have seen something. She looks out across the peninsula, feeling that little spark of hope reignite.

She needs to get back to Bantry to check in with the superintendent. She thinks about what she'll say to him, how she'll present the evidence. She'll start with a timeline. Re-interview the witnesses.

She starts to plan.

Nineteen

Conor is already working hard out on the patio the next morning when I stumble out with my coffee at seven. When I ask him to tell me about the chapter he's working on, he starts with a long explanation about intraparty politics in 1950s Ireland that must make me glaze over because after a few minutes he says, "You're regretting that you asked, aren't you, now?"

"I like watching you talk about it," I say. "Even if it's all going over my head."

He reaches out and squeezes my hand. "What are you up to today?"

"I'm going to drive down to that beach Grace was telling us about and go for a bracing swim. Want to come along?"

"I like my swimming something less than bracing," he says. "But enjoy. Shall we go for a walk this afternoon?"

"Mmmmm. That would be great. Have you heard from Grace about whether the party's still going forward tomorrow?" We've been invited to a cocktail party at the Nevins' house for tomorrow evening, but I assume that because of Zuzanna's death they'll reschedule it.

"Right, I forgot to tell you. They're going ahead with it. Apparently Rochelle wasn't sure what to do, but so many of the investors had already made travel plans that they felt like they couldn't cancel. Are you still up for it?"

"Yeah. Lilly said if it's still on, Alex's band will play and she might do a song or two." I hesitate. "How does she seem to you? Do you think she's okay?"

He grins and says, "I think she's more than okay. Can you not tell me you wouldn't have wanted this to be your summer when you were her age?"

I smile, but I'm still uneasy. A breeze has come up; the weather's changing. I go to get dressed for swimming.

A ten-minute drive from Ross Head, the hidden, horseshoe-shaped beach is in a little protected bay and is accessed by hiking down a steep path from a crude car park in a field. It's empty at seven thirty and I strip down to my suit and stand for a moment just looking out at the water, gathering my courage.

I started swimming off the beach near my house on Long Island again a couple of months ago, the first time since my ex-husband, Brian, died in those waters, despite me trying to save him. At first I had to force myself to wade in. The smell of the salt water, the sounds of the gulls, and the waves hitting the beach would bring me back to that awful night and I would start to panic. But eventually I got so I could dive beneath the surface and swim out before the memories got to me. The water has started to be a haven for me again, the way it was when I was a child and my cousin Erin and I would spend entire days at the beach. I look out at a different bay, thinking about the fact that it's the same water I swam in at home,

the same ocean, the same tides. I'm about to plunge in when someone calls my name and I turn around to find Grace, Ellen Mahoney,
and Rochelle Nevin coming down the path.

"Great minds think alike," Rochelle calls out. "It's so nice to see
you, Maggie. Swim with us?"

"I'd love to. I was just standing here, getting my courage up." I
feel myself grinning, suddenly happy for company.

"There's only one thing for it," Grace says, throwing off her
robe. "Okay, lads, one, two, three." We all run and dive in.

"Oh, Christ, it's cold," I gasp, coming up for air.

"But doesn't it feel good?" Rochelle asks.

It *does* feel good; the cold water is exhilarating and the open bay
ahead of us makes me feel ambitious. I start swimming, enjoying
the pull of my muscles against the water. "I'll race you," I say to
Rochelle, and she grins and executes a fast crawl stroke. We swim
hard for five minutes and then stop, laughing while we tread water.
"I think you won," I say.

"I don't know about that. Well, maybe. But you gave me a good
race."

We float on our backs, buoyant in the soft, green salt water.
The sky is gray-blue overhead, wispy clouds shifting, their shapes
changing from cotton-candy tufts to animals to abstract leaves.

"Let's see who can get to the hot tea first," Grace calls out, and
all four of us set off for the beach, swimming hard until we feel
rocks under our feet again. The cooler air hits my skin, goose-
bumping it, as I wade out and onto the beach. It feels good to
laugh with a group of women in the early morning sun, shouting
and splashing like children. It's been a long time since I've done

something just for fun with friends, I realize. What with my job and Lilly's problems over the last year and then knowing we were probably moving to Ireland, I've let my connections slide a bit and I feel restored by the swim and the company.

"Ah, that was great," Grace says, breathing hard as we wrap ourselves in our towels and Ellen pours out the hot tea into the cups she's brought. My skin feels cool and soft, the warmth of my towel an intense comfort.

"That was invigorating," I tell them. "I want to do that every morning now."

"Morning sea swims are lovely, but evening ones are nice, too," Ellen says. "You'll have to come along sometime, Maggie. Rochelle brings cocktails after."

"My favorite thing is when it's really cold," Grace says. "The first winter we had the house here we did the Christmas swim. It was painful, but glorious. Maggie, you and Conor need to visit at Christmas. The whole village does it, everyone in, screaming their heads off at the temperature. It's mad fun."

We all sip our tea for a bit, my skin still tingling, my brain wide awake. The beauty of the new day is all around us, sunlight catching ripples on the water, the shapes of sailboats beyond, the vibrant green of the fields on a nearby peninsula, the pearly gray rocks and bright white shells along the beach.

"That's my favorite drug," I say. I feel elated, all my senses alive.

"Isn't it?" Rochelle asks. "There's a triathlon training club in Baltimore. I've been threatening to do one. Maybe I can convince you, too."

"I've got the running and the swimming down," I say. "It's the biking part that scares me, especially on the other side of the road, but right now I'd say yes to anything."

We sip our tea in silence. "How's Lorcan?" Rochelle asks Grace finally. "He seemed stressed the other night." I check Grace's face, remembering how suspicious Lorcan seemed when we saw him on Ross Head. What had he been up to?

Grace makes a face and looks out across the water. "He's being an arsehole. I understand they're worried about the development and the investors, but he takes it out on us and I loathe him. Is Sam as bothered by all of it?"

"He's stressed," Rochelle says. "He's just better at hiding it. Don't worry. Once they break ground on the hotel, everything will be back on track. I think we're getting close to planning approval and then everything is going to line up. We've been going back and forth about the do tomorrow, but we're going to go for it. The investors have already planned their travel. I think it's the right thing." There's something a little too hopeful in her voice and I wonder for the first time who Sam Nevin takes his frustration out on when *he's* being an arsehole. Rochelle sounds desperate and it makes me wonder why.

Grace just shrugs. "How are you, Ellen? How's Barry?" she asks, slipping her robe on over her suit.

Ellen sighs and says, "He's been down about Lukas and Zuzanna and everything. He liked her, of course, she was a sweet girl and she's been at the pub for two years, and it's just so sad. And, of course, it's created a lot of staffing issues, too."

"Have the guards told him *anything*?" Rochelle asks.

"No, though Barry knew she was depressed about Lukas. I

think that's why he's struggling so much. He feels guilty, like he should have known, since he saw her every day."

"Poor Bar," Grace says. "I hope they get some answers soon."

"These men," Rochelle says, reaching out to touch Ellen's shoulder. "Have you ever noticed how they couldn't get along if it weren't for us always being there to save them?"

We all laugh.

"Maggie, you don't need to worry about any of this, of course, since Conor's perfect. He never seems to get stressed about anything," Rochelle says a bit archly, pouring more tea from the thermos.

I hesitate before saying, "Well, he's pretty stressed about his book and I think he's worried about Adrien, off with his mother and her new boyfriend in France."

Grace looks up. "I'm sure he's fine. Adrien and Bláithín are so close and he's always loved spending time with her family."

"You know Conor's ex-wife, don't you, Grace?" Rochelle asks, narrowing her eyes. "What's she like?"

"Bláithín is . . . Bláithín," Grace says, waving her hand. "The divorce was tough on her, but she seems really happy with Henri now. She's quite nice, really."

I can't help feel it as a dig somehow. Grace has known Bláithín for years. Conor said they were good friends at one time. I shouldn't have said anything about Conor being worried about Adrien. Now I'm worried about it getting back to him.

Rochelle smiles and reaches up with both hands to fluff her hair dry. "How's Barry really doing, Ellen?" Something passes between them, a whole history around Barry that I'll never know.

"I guess I've been a bit worried." Ellen looks up at Rochelle forlornly. She pulls her knees up and wraps her arms around them. "I thought maybe he was drinking again, but he says he's not. But . . . I smelled it a few times and he's been having trouble sleeping and that was always his sign that things had gotten too much to handle."

"Ah, El," Rochelle says. "Tell him that Sam and I are here if he needs anything."

Ellen sighs and says to me, "Barry's an alcoholic, Maggie. A few years ago we went through a bad time and he . . . well, he stopped drinking. But I'm worried about him relapsing with the stress."

"Sounds like you're doing all the right things," I say.

"She is," Rochelle says kindly, rubbing Ellen's back.

But Ellen seems troubled now, her face clouding over as she puts on a long-sleeved shirt over her swimsuit. My glow of well-being and contentment is gone and suddenly I feel remarkably lonely. There's no way I'll ever have shared history like this with anyone here in Ireland. It's hard enough to make new friends at this stage of life without moving to a completely new country. Subdued, we clean up the tea and hike up to our cars for the drive back to Rosscliffe.

At the house, I pull into the driveway just as Lilly comes running out, saying she's going to meet Alex in the village so they can practice for the party tomorrow night. She gives me a quick hug, but when I tell her to have fun, I think I detect a hint of worry in her eyes.

"You okay?" I ask her.

"Yeah. Fine. See ya." And she's off, striding along the peninsula road, tall and strong and swift.

I watch her go. As I told Conor, I'm trained in spotting people who are being evasive.

I'm pretty sure my daughter just qualified.

Twenty

After lunch, I tell Conor I'm going to drive to Bantry to go to the library for some reading material. I've been thinking about Lissa Crawford and her memory and I want to know more about her family and their history on Ross Head. I park and I'm following the walking directions on my phone to the library when I see Ann Tobin crossing the street.

I stop, looking at my phone, and then greet her as she walks toward me, calling out, "Hi, Sergeant Tobin. I thought that was you."

She doesn't look happy to see me, but she smiles and says, "Hello, Mrs. D'arcy."

"Anything new on the case?" I ask innocently. I know she won't tell me, but I want to see how she answers the question.

She looks up with mild panic in her eyes. "The investigation is progressing," she says stiffly. "That's not why you're here, is it?"

"No, no. I'm going to the library. Also, I need all the driving practice I can get. It's hard. I've started to find it absolutely ridiculous that they just turn rental cars over to Americans at the airport and let them hit the roads. There must be loads of accidents."

She smiles. "Not as many as you think. Probably because you all drive forty-five kilometers an hour. Even more dangerous are the Irish people who get annoyed and try to go around you." Clearly distracted, she says she has to get back to the station, and we say goodbye.

Bantry's public library is at the end of the main street, an oddly shaped building that looks like a spaceship with a waterwheel out front. It's warm and welcoming inside and I spend thirty minutes browsing among the new fiction, choosing a couple of novels I've been meaning to read and then a favorite Dorothy Sayers for Lilly, who's discovered mysteries lately.

On my way to the circulation desk with the new library card I applied for with Conor's address the last time I visited, the LOCAL HISTORY sign beckons. I leave the novels on a table at the end of the aisle and look through the library's sizable collection of local history books, far beyond the book I found at the cottage. There are lots of local history books about Bantry and Skibbereen and the other bigger towns, but I also find a book called *Rosscliffe: Then and Now* that has a number of old pictures of Rosscliffe House from the 1800s and early 1900s, through the period when Lissa Crawford's family was living there, and then most recently in 1996, when the house stood empty. The caption below that picture reads "Rosscliffe House, empty. It is sad to see a once stately home fall to the ravages of time." The book also has a couple of chapters about Felix Crawford. Reading, I develop a fuller picture of the family and its history in the village and West Cork.

There are quite a few references to Lissa and her family. As Conor said, her ancestors built Rosscliffe House in 1784 on land given to their ancestor for his military service in Ireland. Over the next one hundred and fifty years, from their dubious seat on the peninsula, they presided over a landed estate of thousands of acres of farmland. The Crawfords were thought somewhat eccentric for siting the house on the peninsula and the cliffs, rather than farther inland, and my sense is that the family's bad luck over the generations was blamed on this eccentricity.

And, from what the book says, it was blamed on how they treated the tenant farmers in their land in the mid-nineteenth century. "When the potato blight ruined the crops of the Crawfords' tenant farmers in 1846, locals noted that the landlord gave no mercy to those who could not pay their rent. One particular incident remained in the minds of all who heard of it: a farmer whose wife and infant lay dead in the dooryard, his skeletal children like small ghosts haunting the lane, digging for scraps of food, was dragged from his cabin by men the Crawfords had hired to carry out evictions."

During the War of Independence, when a lot of Anglo-Irish Big Houses were burned as symbols of the ruling ascendancy, a group of men broke into Rosscliffe House and tried to set it alight one summer night, but, according to the author, "as soon as they lit curtains or pieces of furniture on fire, the flames would extinguish and the men eventually gave up on their task." The family sold off parcel after parcel until only the peninsula was left and it could not be farmed. Lissa Crawford inherited when she turned eighteen in 1981 and returned to Rosscliffe in the 1990s, but the house had been empty for forty years. Sam Nevin buying it in 2013 seemed like the logical result of centuries of decline.

I go back into the family history. Lissa's father, Felix Crawford, was born in 1940 at Rosscliffe House. He went to Trinity and then married a woman named Elizabeth Fielding who was the daughter of an Anglo-Irish family from Tipperary. They settled at Rosscliffe

House with Felix's parents, who died in the 1950s. Lissa's brother, named Arthur, was born in 1962 and she was born in 1963.

The section contains a cheaply produced pamphlet of portraits of local artists and craftspeople and, toward the end of the book, a photo of Lissa Crawford painting. There's a little statement below it: "I am inspired by the natural world and the sounds and scents of the sea. I spent the early years of my life here in Rosscliffe and it seems like fate that I should come back to paint in a little cottage at Ross Head, near to what was once my family home. I paint images that come from nature and are inspired by nature, as I am."

My reading confirms what Lissa told me about the house. I check the Cork paper's archives on my phone and find that the 2013 sale was reported in the local paper in December of that year. It strikes me again, though: If she didn't want the peninsula developed, why did she let go of the house and the land? I suppose it's possible that her paintings hadn't really started to sell yet; in 2013 she might have needed the money.

Just to be thorough, I search for "Dorothea" and "Rosscliffe House," but the archives only go back to the early 1990s. I'm about to check out the books when I remember I've been meaning to look up the "your man from Dunmanway" reference, so I use the library computer to search for "unnatural death," "Dunmanway," and "2013," but I don't find anything that could be it until I replace "unnatural death" with "murder."

I find something almost immediately.

It's just two small stories, the first reporting that a twenty-three-year-old man named Colin Nugent went missing in June of 2013. Right after Operation Waves, I realize. His residence is listed as

Dunmanway and there is a reference in the story to his having been charged with possession of cocaine the previous year. Four months later, his remains were found by a fisherman near Skibbereen, though the story notes that his body hadn't been in the water the whole time.

I check out *Rosscliffe: Then and Now,* along with my stack of novels, and I'm back on the road by four.

I tell Conor about my research over dinner on the patio. Lilly is still out with Alex, so we take a bottle of wine and leftover chicken out into the glorious summer air, eating on the chaise longues and holding hands while we watch the sun dip lower and lower.

"Ah, it's nice to relax finally," I say, sighing and looking out at the peninsula across the inlet.

"It's true, this holiday hasn't been quite as relaxing as I was hoping it would be," Conor says.

"Unexpected ex-wives and suspicious deaths aren't relaxing?" I ask, rubbing the top of his hand with my thumb.

"Not in my world." He grimaces. "I'm so sorry about our unexpected overnight guests."

"It was fine. Look, I think it was worse for you than it was for me. And it gave me a break from worrying about Lilly and moving and everything. What a couple of days, huh?"

"She hasn't said anything more about your fight or about moving, has she?" Conor asks after a moment.

"No, and I wouldn't be surprised if she said she's *dying* to move now," I tell him. "As long as we can stay here, near Alex." Conor smiles, and I wait a moment and then say, without looking at him,

"Roly told me a couple of days ago that I can have a place in the September training class."

"Really?" He turns to look at me. "What did you say?"

"I told him I need to talk to you." I wait. When we talked about it briefly in April, Conor was enthusiastic about me training to be a guard in Ireland until I got to the part about having to be in residence at the training college in Templemore during the week for almost a year and then doing a year or so in uniform somewhere else in the country. To be fair, he didn't say he didn't want me to do it, but he went silent on the subject after the conversation.

He goes silent again now. "I know it's so hard to think about," I say. "But I'd be home on the weekends and Roly said that he thinks we could make sure I get posted in Dublin, as long as I don't piss anyone off up the chain of command."

Conor squeezes my hand. "Yeah, because I'm sure that's not going to happen."

I smile. "I'll be good. I just . . . It would be leaving a lot on your shoulders. Lilly's first year at a new school . . ." As I say it, I can't imagine leaving her alone in Dublin during the week. What am I thinking?

Conor starts to say something, reconsiders, then reconsiders again. "You mentioned something about the possibility of consulting work, maybe the FBI, something about doing some European investigations for them."

One of my FBI contacts from the case I worked in February suggested that I consider doing some investigations in continental Europe for them while I figure out what I want to do. I know what the work would be like, a lot of financial cases, probably, some discreet assignments where I would deliver a report on some small part of an investigation and then never hear about the outcome. But it would be more convenient. I could be based in Dublin and take short trips over to the continent or even take on jobs in Ireland or the UK. I don't get a rush of enthusiasm when I think about it though. It's not the same as being a homicide investigator, managing a team, shepherding an investigation from the initial crime scene to the moment you hand it over to the prosecutor.

I sigh. "Yeah, let me get some more information about that. There might be training involved with that, too. Shit, why couldn't I have been an accountant or a graphic designer or something. You can do that from anywhere." I look at Conor and smile. "Or a college professor."

"Oh, Jaysus, you don't want to do that. Getting a job in academia these days is worse than your thing."

"Yeah, although Roly did say something about the possibility of me teaching firearms procedures at the training college or something. I'll get some more information and then we can talk about it again."

"Sounds like a plan." But I can hear everything he's not saying.

We watch the sun drop and as the sky colors, I ask him, "Do you believe in ghosts?"

A surprised grin lights his face. "Do you?"

"I don't think so, but I think there are things we can't explain. I tend to assume we just don't have the scientific knowledge to satisfactorily solve some mysteries yet."

"If there is a ghost on Ross Head," Conor says, "who do you think she is?"

"Well, this Dorothea perhaps. Or I don't know. An eighteenth-century Crawford daughter, prevented from marrying her true love, the poor farm boy? Or one of the evicted tenant farmers, set on haunting the Crawfords into eternity."

He takes my hand and we turn around to watch Rosscliffe House and the peninsula until it's dark, but no ghost, lovelorn or otherwise, presents itself.

Twenty-One

The weather turns the next day, dark clouds settling in over the peninsula and the temperature dropping into the fifties. I try Roly again and catch him as they're getting ready to go to the airport. "Ah, D'arcy, I'm just sitting here on my suitcase, waiting for Cecilia to decide which twenty bikinis she wants to bring. You need twenty now, you know, because you might want to wear nineteen of 'em at once." I hear Cecilia complain about his teasing and then more voices in the background. "I can't really chat," he says. "But I saw there was another death down there."

"Yeah, there's a weird angle on it, too." I'm about to tell him about my conversation with Lissa Crawford.

But he breaks in before I can. "Listen, you be good and stay out of this, right?"

"Why? Do you know something, Roly?" Something in his voice, the seriousness of his warning, makes me pay attention. They've got something. There's been movement.

"The only thing I want to know about is how hot it is and how many sangrias I can drink next to the pool." But he lowers his voice. "I'm serious, D'arcy. Enjoy your holiday. Leave it."

"But look, Lilly went out on a date with this kid who's a member of the Polish worker community down here. He seems like a nice kid, a very talented singer, but it all makes me nervous."

"Oh, you're in for it now. When your daughter starts walking out with the boys, that's when the trouble starts. Ow! Áine's after hitting me. Anyway, I've to go so we don't miss the taxi. Good luck. *Stay out of it.* Griz will let you know if anything's happening, right? Try to have a nice holiday."

And he's gone.

I tie a windbreaker around my waist for my run and I put it on for a stretch down toward Mizen Head on the narrower local roads. I run hard, focusing on speed to clear my head.

"What time does this thing start tonight?" I ask Conor once I'm back.

"Six," he says. "I'll get some work done and then we can walk up later, that okay?" His face looks funny, hesitant, his eyes distracted.

"Yeah. I think I'll clean this place up a bit. You okay?" I touch his shoulder and he takes my hand, squeezing it and rubbing it worriedly with his thumb.

"Yes. No, only I just spoke with Adrien."

Concern rushes through me and I put a hand on his shoulder. "Is he okay?"

"He's grand, but Henri proposed to Bláithín last night. In front of her whole family while they were supposed to be celebrating her niece's tenth birthday. Adrien thought it was in bad taste. She said yes. He said she seems delighted. I'm just . . . I'm worried she's going to want to move there, Maggie."

"Did Adrien say anything about that?"

"No, but . . . I know her." He looks troubled, his forehead wrinkled in worry, his glasses slipping down on his nose. I feel a strange little stab of emotional annoyance. Is he jealous? Is he having regrets now that Bláithín has moved on?

"What about her job? That's based in Dublin."

"It is, but she's been complaining about it lately." *When?* I want to ask him. He hasn't mentioned he's talked to her about her job or about anything other than Adrien.

There's something else he wants to say, but before he can, Lilly comes into the kitchen, smelling of soap and shampoo, her ear buds in. "When does Adrien come back?" she asks, too loudly, opening the refrigerator and scanning the shelves, then taking out some soup from a few days ago. "I miss him." She takes the ear buds out and puts the soup on the counter.

"Thursday," Conor says. "If you'd like, you can come to Dublin with me to pick him up."

"If you can leave Alex that long," I say, giving her a little shove. She makes a face at me, but she's blushing.

It's downright chilly by six, but we decide to walk down to the Nevins' across the peninsula. Lilly is wearing her new black dress and sneakers, carrying her heels. Conor's holding the bottle of prosecco we're offering, and though the air is shiver-inducing, it's a pretty evening, the sky a darkening blue and the ocean busy below us.

I lean into Conor and we walk along the road, our hair blown all around our faces by the stiff wind. Lilly's humming to herself, giddy, practicing for tonight.

We see the protesters when we're almost to the house. Gwynedd Williams and a small group of men and women and children are standing on the road just before the turnoff to the Nevins' drive, holding a few large DON'T DEVELOP ROSS HEAD signs, the children with handmade signs saying SAVE OUR PENINSULA and DON'T BUILD ON OUR GROUND.

Sam Nevin, dressed in a dark suit, Jack standing behind him, is talking to them. He has his hands out and I can hear his pleading voice before I reach them. "Just for tonight," I hear him say. "Please. In the morning you can start up again and do what you like, but this is an important event for us. The investors will be arriving and all I'm asking is that you leave it for tonight." We all look back and see a big gray car approaching along the narrow road. Sam's face falls.

"You and your investors," I hear Gwynedd say. "We're not telling them anything they don't already know. There is *not* community support for this project. You haven't been here, Sam. You don't understand. We have the right to stand here and make our voices heard." He's wearing an Irish grandfather shirt and a purple vest and the contrast between him and Sam is almost comical.

Sam is facing me now and I can see rage sweep across his face. He shifts his weight onto his front foot and his hands curl into fists at his sides. I feel my body tense up, the old cop muscle memory that shows up when tension and conflict threaten to erupt in violence. Sam starts to say something, then stops. I can see his hands flexing. He's trying to get control of his anger. Jack Nevin puts a hand on his shoulder and that seems to shake Sam out of it. He steps back and his shoulders relax.

A tall man in a green, waxed jacket steps forward and says, "We want them to know that the local community doesn't unanimously support your development. We're just informing them of the feelings of the local people, like. That's well within our rights."

"Look, tell ya what," Sam says, stepping back and forcing a smile onto his face. "I'll buy you all dinner at the pub if you'll go down there right now. It's on me. Coupla rounds, too."

The guy in the green jacket looks tempted, but Gwynedd Williams says, "You can't buy us off, Sam Nevin. Your money can't make this go away. You made a promise and you're not living up to it!"

"Yeah," someone shouts. "You can't buy us off. Capitalism isn't king here!"

Sam turns away, cursing under his breath. He's given up. We nod to the protesters. I feel awkward all of a sudden, as though I'm crossing a picket line. I can tell Conor does, too. He waves sheepishly and I can feel every socialist fiber of his body resisting the fact that we're with the real estate developer rather than the rabble-rousers. Lilly just looks excited to get inside.

"I should have known it was useless trying to talk to them," Sam says. He and Jack fall into step with us on the drive. "I thought I could get them to clear off for tonight. It's so frustrating. I've offered to create a little park and keep most of the peninsula open for walking, but it's the idea of it they don't like. Ah, well. I guess I just have to let it go." He seems relaxed now, past it, but I know what I saw: just a few minutes ago, Sam Nevin was furious. I'm pretty certain that under different circumstances, Gwynedd might have ended up with a broken nose.

Strains of a guitar and a drumbeat drift out to us. "I'm sure it will be great night anyway," I say reassuringly. "Lilly is going to sing with the band and they've been practicing for days."

"It'll be great, like," Jack says, looking Lilly up and down. "That's a fantastic dress." They walk ahead of us, talking about music.

We round a turn in the drive and the house comes into view. "Now, welcome to our little cottage," Sam announces.

"Oh my God, it's gorgeous," Lilly says breathlessly. It *is* gorgeous, or the setting is, the house perched right at the end of the peninsula on the cliffs, ocean views in almost every direction. The entrance calls up a traditional Irish cottage, a small rectangular mud room and entrance hall with an archway leading to the very modern main part of the structure. When I looked up Ross Head online, I saw some photos of the Nevins' house from a fancy life-style magazine. But the photos didn't do it justice. It seems to be made up of four separate sections, each one like the mast of a sailing ship, a towering triangle of limestone and glass, the central one opening onto a patio reaching toward the cliffs. The structure is impressive, but it makes me feel very unsettled, the soaring peaks of the roofline aggressive and dangerous, the drop from the cliffs vertigo-inducing.

"Thank you, Lilly. Make sure to get Rochelle to give you a tour." Sam goes around the side of the house, where Barry Mahoney is standing, watching everyone come in. Sam's preoccupied, waving Barry over and giving some instructions that I suspect have to do with the protesters. Barry nods and goes off in the direction of the road.

Inside, we find Agnieska and a few other young women in white aprons offering us trays of hors d'oeuvres. I say hello and she smiles and waits while I take a slice of fried leek wrapped in bacon.

"I thought it was just casual drinks," I whisper to Conor, immediately conscious of my jeans, gauzy blue top, and comfy brown leather sandals. I've brushed my hair into a low ponytail and put on some lipstick and mascara, but I feel dowdy next to Rochelle, who spots us and swoops over in a flowing green dress revealing her tanned shoulders.

"I guess this is their version of casual," he whispers back.

"Conor, Maggie, hello!" Rochelle calls out. "So glad you could come. Let me show you where everyone is." She brings us through a huge living room, one entire wall made of glass windows looking out at the Atlantic, minimalist leather couches arranged in a U shape on an abstract woven rug, and we step through open French doors into the night air to find the other guests standing or sitting in chairs on a deck and looking at the view.

"How are you?" Rochelle asks. "Did you see the protesters outside? Sam was beside himself." She rolls her eyes. "He's so devoted to Rosscliffe and doing things for the village and he can't understand how anyone could be against him. My father was a developer in Canada and he always had people fighting him, so I know it's nothing personal." But I think of Gwynedd's face and Sam's anger and I think she's wrong. It *is* personal. These are people who have known each other a long time. They're fighting about their home, ancestral land. How could it not be?

Lilly brings Alex over to say hello, blushing and self-consciously smoothing her dress over her hips, but looking delighted when he shakes our hands and asks if we're having fun. "I hear you're going to play for us," Conor says. Alex is wearing a dark suit and he looks like a magazine model. Lilly keeps glancing over at him with a pleased smile.

"Well, our reputation has improved since Lilly joined the band," Alex says charmingly. "It is funny how we've gotten more requests since she started singing with us. I will try not to be hurt by that." He and Lilly smile at each other and go over to finish getting ready with the other guys. Jack Nevin watches them set up, and when Agnieska comes by with a tray of wineglasses, he takes one and whispers something to her. She smiles but looks vaguely uncomfortable.

Grace and Lorcan wave at us, but continue talking animatedly to a small group of couples who I assume are the investors Sam Nevin wants so much to impress. It's a lovely party: attractive people, glorious setting, good food and drink, but I'm feeling crabby and preoccupied for reasons I can't quite identify. "I'm off to find you a drink," Conor says. "I think you need one."

I make boring small talk about the party and the hors d'oeuvres with a German investor until Conor returns with my drink and Lorcan and Grace come over to say hello. "The protesters gone?" Grace asks. She's wearing a coral silk dress that makes her green eyes look luminous.

"I think so," Conor tells her, looking uncomfortable.

"Sam sent Barry out to glare at them. He's good at that," says Lorcan with a little smirk. "Of all the nights." He swears under his breath and shakes his head. "Sorry, Maggie. I'm just fed up with ungrateful people who don't realize we're trying to help the village. Do they even know how many jobs the hotel is going to create?"

Conor and I glance at each other. "Perhaps they like the idea of leaving it as is," he offers.

But Lorcan doesn't seem to hear him. "Have you heard about this eco-village idea that's gotten about? I'm not sure what the plan is to fund it, but apparently that's the alternative they're pushing to the council. There was a hippie commune here in the 1970s. It must be nostalgia for that that's driving this. Can you imagine?" An investor from Dublin joins the conversation and Lorcan fawns over him, complimenting his suit and asking him if there's anything he needs.

I feel like I'll scream if I have to listen to their superior tones, especially Lorcan's, any longer. Gritting my teeth, I excuse myself and say I'm going to go look for the bathroom.

I follow a labyrinthine hallway behind the house's entryway, stopping to look at the art on the walls. It's mostly photography of West Cork and a few other places that I recognize: Greece, Paris, the Grand Canyon. But there are a couple of oil paintings, too, and I recognize one as a Felix Crawford, a simple scene of a sailboat moored in what I think must be one of the bigger towns up the coast. There's another Crawford just outside the small powder room, a watercolor of Ross Head looking out toward the sea. I stare at it for a long time. There's something there that holds me in place: a sense of gloominess. The height of the cliffs is exaggerated, I think, and they convey vertigo, even in only two dimensions.

I shut the door of the powder room behind me, push the curtains aside, and look out at the minimalist garden, with a patio table and chairs on a small stone terrace. Someone—one of the Nevins' sons, I assume—has left a rugby ball on one of the chairs, but otherwise nothing's out of place; even the vaguely modernist spiky green plants in the small flower beds along the terrace are perfectly in keeping with the aesthetic of the house.

I'm checking my lipstick when I look out again and see Grace coming around the side of the house. She looks angry, walking quickly, twisting something in her hands, and a second later, Lorcan comes around the corner, holding his drink, following her. They've clearly been fighting and I wish I could hear them through the thick window glazing. He says something, and I watch as she blanches, then responds with something that causes him to frown and go back the way he came. It feels wrong, but I keep watching as one of her hands flies to her mouth and her shoulders fall. She's crying. She covers her eyes with a hand and I feel a pang of sympathy. She can't let herself lose control here. I wish I could poke my head out the window and give her a sympathetic word, but of course I can't.

Back on the terrace, the band is playing a series of jazz standards, and I'm frankly impressed by their versatility and the way Alex's voice adapts to the requirements of each song yet stays recognizable. He's an impressive talent, and when Lilly joins him, the easy way they harmonize is something special. I'm filled with pride but also a little bit of caution at the way they look at each other, the way they already seem to be a pair, a unit. There's something so intimate about the connection between them; it excludes the audience, the rest of the band. It excludes me.

"I'm glad to see the dress worked out for her then," Ellen Mahoney says, coming up behind me as I watch. "If I'd known it was for a real gig, I would have given you a discount."

I laugh. "If I'd known, I might not have let her get it. She was a bit shady about the whole thing."

"Ah, well, teenagers are a bit shady by nature, aren't they?"

"Do you have kids?"

She hesitates. "No. We never did." She looks up and I see her watching Barry across the room, talking to Lorcan. "Sam and I were raised in a family of seven, so I had my fill of there never being enough space or money."

"And it sounds like your mother took on even more children. Lissa Crawford said she was the only one trying to exert any discipline at Rosscliffe House."

"I don't think it did much good. Bridget used to talk about how spoilt the children were. There were always people in and out of the house, no one sitting for their meals." She looks up and smiles as Grace and Rochelle come over.

Rochelle asks if we're having fun and we say it's a beautiful party. "Everyone seems to be enjoying themselves," I tell her.

"I hope so. I'm just so annoyed at Gwynedd and Mairead and the protesters." For the first time since I've met her, Rochelle seems uncertain. "Sam has so much riding on this. Why would they pick tonight, of all nights, to stand out there."

"The guests hardly noticed," Grace says, soothing her. "I think it's been a big success." She seems composed now, not a hint of her tears anywhere on her face.

Ellen touches Rochelle's shoulder. "Sam seems quite happy. It's a lovely party."

We all look up to find Barry coming over. "I guess it's time to go," Ellen says. "He gets funny at these things."

"You ready?" he asks Ellen, ignoring the rest of us.

"Yes. You've met Mrs. D'arcy, haven't you, Barry?"

"Please. Maggie," I say.

He meets my eyes and nods. "Yeah, hello," he says impatiently. He's distracted, ill at ease, the fingers of his right hand drumming a rhythm on his leg. His negotiations with the protesters must have been contentious. He turns to Ellen and I get a whiff of stale alcohol. I think Ellen smells it, too. "I need to check something at the pub," he says.

She mouths *Sorry* and thanks Rochelle and kisses her on the cheek, then follows Barry out the door.

I find Conor and then Grace takes us over to an older couple and introduces them as German investors in Ross Head. "They've flown over from Berlin to see how their house is coming along," she says. It's the same guy I was talking to before, but he doesn't seem to remember, introducing himself and his wife again. "We've been coming to West Cork for years," the wife says. "We jumped at the chance to be part of the development here. We're hoping our house will be finished soon." Her husband glances at Lorcan and I have the sense that they've been talking about the delays in construction.

Conor and I get some food and listen to the band play for a bit. Lilly and Alex sing a swingy version of "I've Got You Under My Skin," and then, at eight, Sam and Rochelle gather everyone on the patio. Agnieska and the other waitresses go around pouring champagne and passing hors d'oeuvres.

"Thank you so much for being here," Rochelle says, smiling out at the crowd. "We have so many wonderful friends and supporters here tonight."

"First of all," Sam Nevin says. "I'd like to thank our investors. You saw the potential here when no one else did and I can't thank you enough for your faith and trust."

"Just make us rich, Sam!" someone shouts.

"We are waiting for planning approval from the county council and then we'll be beginning the extensive renovation of Rosscliffe House, as well as the completion of ten more houses like this one," he says. "It's been a long journey and we hope to have the hotel up and running next year and start booking weddings soon thereafter. So if there's anyone here who's thinking of proposing, maybe wait a little and think of us." Everyone laughs.

The crowd is warm, a little drunk, well fed. Looking around at the faces, I recognize a few people from the village, but it must be mostly investors and business associates. I'm scanning the attendees when I spot Anton Dorda in the very back, standing alone on the lawn. He has a small smile on his face and though he's separate from the party, I have the sense he wants people to see that he's there. He's not hiding.

"I have to thank my friends and family here in Rosscliffe. We know it's the best place in Ireland and now everyone else will, too. And finally to Rochelle and to our boys. You have all put your blood, sweat, and tears into this development and I couldn't be more grateful or love you more." He looks over at them and I swear there are tears in his eyes. It makes me like him a little more. Applause ripples through the crowd, Alex sings "You'd Be So Nice to Come Home To," and when I turn around, Anton Dorda is gone.

I tell Conor I'm going to get some air outside and wave him off when he says he'll come with me. I want to be alone. The walking path winds away from the house along the cliffs and I walk for a few minutes and then stop to look out at the view. The sun is mostly down now, just a thin line of light appearing above the horizon. I close my eyes and listen to the waves. I think if you put me down here, my eyes closed, and told me to guess where I am, I would know immediately that it's Ireland. There's something about the quality of the air, the smell of it. Suddenly, I'm so homesick I feel like I might vomit. I take out my phone and dial Uncle Danny's number. It rings a few times, but he doesn't pick up, so I leave a message and dial the number of my old partner, Dave Milich.

"Mags!" he answers on the second ring. "How are you? How's everything over there?"

I tell him a bit about what's been going on and then say, "Get this. Lilly is in love. With the lead singer of a band. She's singing with them at this party we're at tonight. You should see her, Dave, she looks about twenty-five. It's freaking me out."

I want Dave to tell me I need to shut it down, that it's too risky to let her get close to someone I don't know well. But instead he says, "But at least she's happy, right?"

"Yeah, how are you, anyway? What's going on over there?"

"Not too much. It's been quiet since that last case I told you about. Heather's moving in next week. Did I tell you that?"

"No, that's great." Dave met Heather Thornton during our last case together and they started dating soon after. "Well, look, tell her I say hi, okay? I just wanted to hear your voice. I'm feeling homesick tonight. I've been thinking about Marty lately."

"Me, too. We miss you on the Island," he says.

I hesitate. "Anything on Anthony Pugh?"

"Not really. They're keeping an eye on him." He says it quick, skating over the next part. "He went by your house a few times, but you're not there, right? I bet he'll stop. Anyways, we've got it. We'll know if he leaves the country. Asshole."

"Thanks, Dave. Take care, okay?"

I stand there looking down at the cliffs for a few more minutes and thinking about what Dave said. A serial rapist and murderer, Anthony Pugh got off easy after I arrested him a few years ago because his victim committed suicide before she could testify. We've never been able to get him for a series of other murders, though I know he was responsible for them. Over the last year, he's driven by my house on Long Island a few too many times for comfort. Watching the water, I try to slow my heart rate, telling myself there's an ocean between him and me, between him and Lilly. Uncle Danny's not there anymore. But the waves seem to rise up for a second and I have to take a few deep breaths to slow my racing heart rate.

I step back from the edge, feeling dizzy. Lukas and Zuzanna must have plunged from spots just like this. It's easy to see how you could slip; in places the path goes very close to the edge and if you took a wrong step and couldn't pivot your body back to take advantage of gravity, it would be very easy to go over. The drop is sheer. Once you started falling, there'd be nothing to grab on to to save yourself.

Unless you meant to go over, I tell myself. And, of course, it would be easy to push someone off, too. All you'd have to do would be to give them a shove. If they weren't expecting it, you could send them over with little effort.

The sky above me is huge, the stars picked out here and there in the dark purple night. Clouds drift eerily across the moon.

As I near the house, I can hear the band playing, faraway strains of Lilly's voice singing a song I don't recognize, and the house looks like a spaceship, all lit up and hanging out over the water in dark space. I feel like an explorer, coming upon a strange new land after wandering, alone, in the wilderness.

I see them as soon as I come around the turn in the road, three marked Garda cars and a few unmarked vehicles blocking the drive. The cars' headlights illuminate the faces of the officers standing around, talking and pointing to the house. My heart speeds up. It looks like a crime scene, the bodies moving around in a choreography I know all too well.

There's a familiar figure in the midst of it all, too.

My friend Katya Grzeskiewicz, known to most as Griz, is standing by the front door, talking to a small group of uniformed officers and a guy in a black jacket. Ann Tobin's there, too. When she sees me staring at them, she nods in my direction. Griz looks up; she's not surprised to see me.

"Griz," I call out. "What's going on?"

She breaks away and comes over. She doesn't hug me, but her smile is warm and she seems happy to see me. "Hiya," she says. "Sorry, I would have told you I was coming if I could have."

"What's going on?" I ask again.

"We got the postmortem and some additional evidence from Lukas Adamik's remains last night," she tells me, her eyes serious. "It'll be public soon enough, but it's between us for the moment, now, yeah?" I nod. "He's been dead for a while, probably since he disappeared, but the remains had only been in the water for a couple of days." She waits while I take that in. "This is a murder investigation now."

Twenty-Two

The entire peninsula is a crime scene: the building sites, the walking paths, the roads, the cliffs. Except, as Griz acknowledges when I raise my eyebrows and look out at the expanse of rock and grass, they likely won't find anything because so much time has passed. But they need to try.

"They didn't make Roly come back from the beach? I was picturing him on the plane, sunburned and still clutching his sangria."

She grins. "No, I guess they think we can handle it here."

"Which you can. You think someone here knows what happened to Lukas Adamik?" I ask her.

She looks away, tracking the movement of a guy in plainclothes across the driveway. "We don't think anything yet. All we know is we got a request for assistance. The detective here got word yesterday on the postmortem."

"What about Zuzanna Brol?"

She shakes her head.

"Where do you think Lukas's body was all that time?"

"No idea, but we need to secure whatever's left of a crime scene. And don't quote me on any of that, okay?" The look she gives me is actually stern.

Someone calls out, "Can we get another room for Detective Fiero?"

"I'll see," Tobin calls back.

"Thanks," the guy in the black jacket yells back to them. He's about my age, with a graying crew cut, quite obviously not from around here. "I can try somewhere else, but it would be handy if they've a room."

Griz looks exhausted. "I'll talk to you tomorrow, Maggie, okay? Roly said you were asking about this. Sounds like your instinct that something was off about this place was right."

I wait until Conor and Lilly have both gone to bed to get out my laptop and search for "Detective Fiero" and "Garda Síochána." I'm pretty sure he's not on Roly and Griz's team and I'm even more sure he isn't a local detective, so I want to know what he's doing here. The Italian surname is uncommon enough in Ireland that I figure he'll be easy to find.

He is. I say a silent thank-you to whatever circumstances saddled him with such a name. Detective Sergeant Padraig L. Fiero is on a professional networking site and I find a couple of articles referencing his work on a big drug seizure in Cork City a few months back and a few more articles about his work on some other big operations, one in Bandon and one in Skibbereen. Then I find his LinkedIn page, confirming what I already figured out.

He's a member of the Garda Síochána's National Drugs and Organized Crime Bureau.

I search again, this time looking in the archives section of the *Irish Examiner*. His name shows up once, when he testified during the trial of the two traffickers arrested during Operation Waves.

The men were convicted for their roles in the attempted illegal importation of cocaine that was interrupted by Operation Waves off the coast of Ross Head on May 8, 2013. I go back to the article that Roly sent me about the seizure. It says that the operation was coordinated by the Garda's National Drugs and Organized Crime Bureau and some sort of European anti–drugs trafficking task force based in Portugal. Fiero's name doesn't appear, but if he testified at the trial he must have been involved in the operation.

There's got to be a connection here between Operation Waves and Lukas Adamik's death. The details—a body stored somewhere before being dumped in the water—are similar enough to the Colin Nugent murder that it can't be a coincidence. The involvement of a drugs and organized crime detective who worked on the seizure makes that clear. But what? Was Lukas Adamik dealing drugs? Was Zuzanna involved, too, or had she known about his involvement? If so, there are two possibilities. One is that Zuzanna was so depressed about getting sucked into something criminal or watching her boyfriend get sucked into something criminal that she killed herself. The other is that she was killed because of her involvement or what she knew. I'm sure Griz, Tobin, and Fiero are looking into both possibilities.

I save the articles on my desktop and go up to bed, thinking about where Lukas's body might have been for three months and trying to figure out what it might have to do with Zuzanna's death. As I'm drifting off to sleep, the events of the last few days are all mixed up in my brain: Lissa Crawford's story about the mysterious Dorothea, the ghost, Lilly singing at the Nevins' party, Padraig

Fiero, Anton Dorda, Roly telling me to leave the whole thing alone. It feels like my brain is trying to tell me something, trying to put all the pieces together in a way that makes sense, but for the life of me I can't figure out what it is.

Lissa Crawford is outside feeding her chickens when I stop in on my way down to the village the next morning. It's an overcast day despite the heat, a stiff warm breeze whipping the tall grasses out on the headlands and threatening to knock over the blooms in her garden. Beyond the expanse of green, I can see figures in bright yellow walking slowly along the cliffs, searching the grass.

"Do you have bread today?" I call out. "My family is completely addicted to your bread now."

She shakes her head. "Not today. With all the . . . excitement, I haven't had a chance to bake. I'm sorry."

I think quickly, wanting to draw out our conversation. "I'd take some eggs if you have some."

"Of course. They're just inside." She sends another handful of grain cascading over the fence to the chickens, who rush to peck at it, squawking and bobbing their heads.

"They're such interesting creatures," she says. "People think they're stupid, but they're not. Did you know you can train a chicken to come to its name?"

"I didn't know that." I watch them peck at the ground. She has many different varieties, black ones and red ones and a brown and black one with feathers sprouting out of its head. "I like that one," I say, pointing to it.

"That's a Golden Polish. Zuzanna liked that one. She said it was her sister, since they were both Polish." She smiles and tears rush to her eyes. "Oh, I can't believe she's gone." She reaches up to wipe them away. "Poor Agnieska."

"I've been thinking about you," I say. "I tried to stop in the other day, but you weren't here."

She studies her chickens through the fence. "I've been so upset about it," she says. "To think she was so *desperate* and I didn't know. Oh, Maggie. I feel horrible, like I should have known and stopped her, and now, all this . . . hullabaloo with the guards. Did you hear? They think Lukas was *murdered*. I can't quite believe it . . . Do you want to come in for some tea and I'll get your eggs?"

"That would be lovely," I say. "It's been quite a shock. We were at the Nevins' last night when the guards arrived."

Lissa frowns and leads the way inside. The cottage is a mess this morning, dishes in the sink and pieces of paper and painting equipment strewn all around.

"Sit down, sit down," she says, pushing sheets of watercolor paper out of the way. She's been painting Ross Head, I see, dreamy, pastel versions of her father's studies of the cliffs, the ocean in shades of blue and purple, the sky red and orange at sunset. There are a few interiors, too, an elegant living room with furniture upholstered in floral fabric and velvet, huge arched windows on one wall with the familiar views of the sea on the other side.

"These are lovely," I tell her. "Is that Rosscliffe House?"

"Mmm," she says. "I've been painting from memory again. And I thought maybe it would help to shake things loose if I, well, went inside, if you see what I mean."

"Did you remember anything more?" I ask. "I had a few

conversations in the village that I wanted to tell you about. If this is a good time, that is."

"Oh, yes, yes. Well, let me make the tea and you can tell me." She seems nervous, bustling around the kitchen frenetically, searching for clean mugs and muttering to herself as she looks for tea bags. She's wearing a gingham painting smock over her clothes and she keeps wiping her hands on the skirt, picking at the fabric and the flakes of dried paint crusted on one side. When the tea is ready, she brings it over and sits down across from me. I take my mug and pour a bit of milk in. She's still nervous, so I start.

"I talked to Matt Mahoney at the pub," I tell her. "And some of the other men with him. I had the sense he didn't want to talk about Rosscliffe House. When I asked if he remembered someone named Dorothea, he looked strange, like he did but wasn't going to tell me. I had the feeling that he knew more than he was telling me. I was wondering if there was anything there that you remember. He was the gardener, right?"

She sips her tea. "Yes," she says. "Matt's father had been a proper gardener for my grandparents and great-grandparents. Matt learned as a boy and took care of things. My mother loved flowers and she tried to keep the gardens up and he helped when they could afford it." She smiles. "He told me the names of flowers and he knew which ones we liked and would bring bouquets up to the house. It's odd you should mention Matt."

"Why? *Do* you remember him being there that summer?"

Her eyes are wide. "When I was painting the rooms, I thought . . . of something. It's like a piece of film, cut off from everything around it. Just a piece of a memory, I think. My mother was standing in the entrance hall and Matt came in with yellow roses. Those were her favorites. They grew beautifully in the gardens. I must have been coming down the stairs because I remember the carved posts at the bottom and I was sort of seeing her through those. And he was standing there holding the roses and she said, 'Oh, Matt.' Just like that, *'Oh, Matt'* and I stopped, because something in her voice told me that I shouldn't listen, that it was private. I stopped and sat down so they wouldn't see me on the stairs." She's looking off into space, back in the house on that long-ago day.

"What happened?" I ask gently.

"She began to cry," she says. "She began to cry and he said something like 'Oh, don't worry, please don't be sad,' or something like that. And I heard her gasp and I knew she was crying. And that's it. I don't remember any more."

I wait to see if she'll say anything else and when she doesn't, I say, "Do you think they were in a . . . relationship of some kind?"

"Perhaps. He'd never admit it. He was married then. His wife only passed a few years ago. If there was something like that . . . well, I'm sure he wants to keep it hidden. Besides, he never talks to me. I think he resents me for speaking out about the hotel. He's quite loyal to Sam Nevin, and if you speak out against Sam, well, Matt doesn't like that at all."

"Is that because Barry Mahoney is married to Ellen?" I ask.

"I guess so," she says uncertainly. "Sam has helped Barry out quite a lot. He had him as his building manager and then he renovated the pub so that Barry could manage it. He'd do anything for Ellen. I suppose Matt appreciates that. When I sold Rosscliffe House to Sam, he said he wouldn't be developing it anytime soon, that he just wanted to make sure someone else wouldn't develop it. He was worried about the value of the houses, you see. I needed the money or . . . thought I did and I believed him. I've always thought Sam was trustworthy, but last year I heard he was going for the planning permission. I was so angry at myself." She shakes her head, her eyes distressed.

"But if you needed the money, surely you can't blame yourself," I say gently. "Lots of people find themselves in that situation."

"Well, it wasn't for me exactly. And as it turned out, everything was okay. So . . . I went to the council and told them that a hotel development would ruin the village, the history here. I told Sam I'd buy it back. Gwynedd came to talk about the bird and plant life on Ross Head. I don't know if I convinced them. They should be making their decision quite soon."

I think about the party last night, the determined faces of the protesters, Lorcan's worried face as he talked about the approval. I glance at the chickens pecking at the ground. Sam Nevin may be counting his before they hatch. And is it a coincidence that Griz and her team arrived an hour later to declare the peninsula a crime scene? It occurs to me that if you wanted to stop progress on the hotel development project, a Garda investigation would be a good place to start.

I tell Lissa that I'll do some more asking around about Matt Mahoney and Dorothea and walk slowly down to the village, thinking about what she told me. If Elizabeth Crawford and Matt Mahoney were having an affair, had someone found out? Dorothea? In that case, it makes sense that my asking about her would have made Matt nervous.

The village is quiet at ten. I think I can feel the tension as I walk along the high street, people peeking out of windows, staying inside until they have more information. There's a marked car parked in front of McCarthy's and a few other cars with Dublin registration plates. I'm passing the cheese shop when I see Griz coming out of Donnelly's. "Hey, Griz," I call out.

She grins and crosses the street to hug me. "Good to see you," she says. "I had to be all professional-like last night, but I was hoping I'd see you today."

"Where are you staying, anyway?"

"Bed-and-breakfast over the pub," she says. "They had some rooms open up. I was just getting something to eat at the shop." She opens her carrier bag and shows me a yogurt and a bag of apples. She's cut her hair shorter since the last time I saw her. The short bangs suit her, show up the planes in her face and her wide blue eyes. She's got a nice suit on, too, navy linen in an expensive cut.

"That's not enough for lunch," I say. "You should come up to our cottage and I'll make you a chicken sandwich."

"Nah, I'll be okay. I've got to get back up there and see if they've found anything from the search." She looks back up toward the peninsula.

"Any sense of where the body was all that time?" I don't actually think she's going to tell me, but I want to see what she says.

"They're looking at a few different things," she says cagily. "How about you? You've been here. You have any ideas about this?"

I see Padraig Fiero coming out of the market and walking toward us. I look back at her. "I don't know. There's a weird tension between Sam Nevin and some of the people in town," I say, telling her about the anti-development protest. "Half seem really happy about the development and half don't. I have the feeling that a few of them are a bit bothered by the Polish workers, garden-variety xenophobia, nothing that felt like more than that to me, but you never know." I tell her about my conversation with Lissa Crawford. "It might be worth looking more into whether anyone in the village knew this Dorothea who went missing in 1973, but I'm betting there's an explanation."

Griz isn't really listening though. "Maybe. I think we already have some good leads," she says diplomatically.

"Like with Detective Padraig L. Fiero of drugs and organized crime and whatever Lukas Adamik's connection was with Operation Waves?" I ask her, with a little smile as he stops walking toward us to check his phone.

She laughs. "You overheard his name and went and looked him up. I knew you would! I knew you'd do it!"

"Look, it was all public information," I say. "I was just curious. He has a look about him. Definitely drugs."

Griz just smiles at me. "What are you like? You need a job, you."

We step out of the way to avoid a woman passing hand in hand with two toddlers. "Come on, what's going on, Griz? He was involved in that big seizure in 2013. It sounded to me like the guards think someone knows where the rest of the drugs went. It was *right here,* so there must be a connection. And then there's Colin Nugent. The similarities are not escaping me here. Was Lukas Adamik involved in drug trafficking? Are any of the other Polish workers here involved, too?"

She raises her eyebrows. "Come on, Maggie. You know I can't comment."

"Lilly has been dating Alex Sadowski, Griz. She's obsessed. I know you can't tell me anything, but we don't know him very well and I just don't know how to handle this thing with her. Do you have any sense if . . . ?"

Her eyes narrow. "If the Polish guy Lilly's dating is connected with the Polish drug dealer and the Polish victims whose deaths we're investigating?" she cuts in. "Because Poles come over here to deal drugs, right?"

"I know how that sounds. They were friends though, Lukas Adamik and Alex Sadowski, and I just don't know what we're dealing with here. Has Alex or his brother, Tomasz, ever crossed Fiero's radar?"

She sighs. "Look, part of why they sent me down as the point person is to try to figure out what all the relationships are. I've spoken more Polish this morning than I have in years. Honestly, I don't know yet. I'd keep an eye on things there, with the Sadow-skis, yeah? Alex seems like a nice lad, but Lukas Adamik had a pos-session charge back last, fall and he was living here in 2013. That's all public, yeah? But don't go around quoting me. Whoever's responsible, someone knows where his body was for three months while everyone thought he had gone back to Poland."

She thinks for a moment, weighing things. Then she says, "You're right about Fiero. He was part of Operation Waves. They got the guys who brought the stuff on the yacht from the Caribbean, but they never figured out who the local connection was. There had to be one. The fellas on the yacht wouldn't talk. The feeling was that they were either afraid or they knew they'd have a payday coming when they got out if they keep their mouths shut. And anyone you talk to will tell you there must have been more than five bales. It wouldn't have been worth it otherwise. The thought is that whoever the locals were who were working with those fellas, they may have offloaded a larger amount at some point before the seizure and successfully hidden it."

"They have any idea about who it might be?"

"Probably more than one person. But Fiero seems convinced the mastermind is a local fella named Anton Dorda. Have you met him?"

"I think I know who he is. Why does Fiero think it's him?"

She shakes her head. "I'm not going to tell you that." But it confirms there's something specific. An informant, I think. He probably had an informant who told him Dorda was behind it. "If you want to keep Lilly away from someone, that's who I'd pick."

"I've seen him around the village," I tell her. "He drives a black Mercedes. He was at the party last night. And he was at the pub the night Zuzanna died. And I did mean it about you coming up to the house. I'm making seafood pasta for dinner tonight. You're welcome to join us."

"Maybe tomorrow," she says. "We've got too much to do today. In the meantime, you go find a hobby or something. How about knitting? Or birdwatching? Lot o' birds around here." She looks exhausted and I remember my sense in February that something was bothering her.

"You okay?"

"Yeah, just . . . tired."

Padraig Fiero is done with his phone and he comes up to us, rubbing a hand over his closely cropped hair. His body language is shut down; he crosses his arms and doesn't smile or introduce himself. His blue eyes are cold. He's not in the mood to make a new friend.

"Hi, I'm Maggie D'arcy," I say, sticking out my hand.

"Ah, yeah." He shakes my hand, but reluctantly, as though he's afraid he'll catch something, and only because he can't avoid it. "Detective Grzeskiewicz? We should be getting back. They're waiting for us." His accent is Dublin, fast and blunt.

"Nice to meet you, Detective Fiero," I say cheerily, enjoying his look of distaste. He doesn't want me knowing his name. I'm betting that's because he was undercover at some point and that his job with drugs and organized crime brings him into contact with a lot of people who'd love to know his name and everything about him. Old habits die hard. I turn back to Griz. "Detective Grzeskiewicz, let me know when I can make you dinner. Detective Fiero is very welcome, too." He scowls and it makes me unreasonably happy. Guys like him are all ego and testosterone. I like taking them down a peg.

My Blue Heaven is nearly empty and I wave at Ellen behind the counter and pretend to carefully peruse the pottery offerings before choosing a mug printed with Celtic designs and take it up to the counter.

"I've got to go swimming again," I tell her as she rings it up and tucks it into a bag for me. "That was so amazing. And with everything going on, I feel like I could use some cold-water therapy."

"Yeah," she says. "It's been a weird couple of days."

"Do you think they know anything more?" I ask her.

She shakes her head.

I say casually, "I met your father-in-law at McCarthy's the other night. He's a character."

"Matt? I suppose. Was Jim Duffy with him? Now *he's* the real character."

"He was. We got some good stories out of him. He seems to know everything that happens around here." Ellen just smiles and keeps wrapping. "Do they live in the village still? Barry's parents?"

"Mmm. Barry's mam has passed, but Matt's next to us in a little cottage we built a few years ago. It's nice for him to be close as he gets older."

"Matt was talking about working at Rosscliffe House when Lissa Crawford's parents still lived there. He seemed a bit, well, sad about that time. It made me wonder if he was there when something happened to that woman I was asking about. I asked him whether he remembers her—Dorothea her name was—and he didn't want to talk about it. I just wondered if he's ever told you about something that happened then, or if Barry remembers anything about what it was like at the house when he was a boy."

Her eyes narrow and she purses her lips together, stepping back from the counter as though she wants to get away from me. She hands over the bag and says, "Not really. That's all in the past."

"I know, I was just wondering if he's ever said anything. I think it would really help Lissa if I could tell her a bit more about—"

She cuts in, saying, "Here you are then," and hands the bag over abruptly. "I've things to do now."

I stammer out a thank-you and as I turn to go, she says, "Sam and Barry are trying to bring some life back to this place, to make it a place people, real people, can live. I don't know if Lissa Crawford is telling you lies to try to stir things up and get Sam's planning permission denied, but I'd stay away from it if I were you. You're not a guard here. That house and what happened there is none of your business."

I stare at her for a minute. "I didn't mean—" I start to say. Her change of mood is so abrupt that I'm having trouble processing it. But she's already started walking toward the back of the store. Out on the street again, I stand there for a moment, dazed and trying to decide what to do. I feel guilty about Ellen—she's someone I'd begun to think of as a friend—but I'm also extremely interested now in why she had such a strong reaction to my questions. She clearly wants me to stay away from the whole subject of Rosscliffe House.

The fish market in Bantry has a good selection and I get what I need, then tell the woman behind the counter I'll pick it up in a half hour. I wander around a little, looking into the shops along the high street that are open for tourist traffic on Sunday. There's an arts and crafts gallery that has beautiful jewelry and I pick out a necklace for Lilly, a delicate chain with a silver cockleshell dangling from it. One whole wall of the gallery is covered with landscape paintings of various West Cork locations, as well as more abstract pieces, and I find a little grouping of Lissa Crawford's paintings, the color blots vibrant and visually appealing. After her story, though, I can't see them as anything other than bloodstains.

It's an intriguing idea, that Lissa Crawford witnessed something in her childhood that lodged itself in her subconscious and then came out in her artwork many years later. What if the solution to the mystery is somehow to be found in her work?

Say, for the sake of argument, that something did happen to Dorothea. She was killed, or there was a terrible and bloody accident, and the family didn't report her death. Maybe they buried her on the grounds of Rosscliffe House? If that was the case, then someone in the village might know about it, or suspect something. Maybe Sam Nevin's mother or his sister Bridget, who worked there, too. Ellen said she lives in Kildare now. I could try to look her up, though I can't imagine Ellen would be very happy if she found out.

As I drive home, I'm thinking of Lissa Crawford's list. Both Bridget Nevin and her mother were on it. But so were a lot of other people.

Who on that list knows what happened to Dorothea?

Twenty-Three

Griz looks down at her notes again and then back at Agnieska Tarnowski. "You said that Zuzanna seemed happy the night she died, Agnieska. Is that right?"

"Yes, we were at McCarthy's and the music was good. We were listening and she had a drink and she seemed happy."

Griz finds herself thrown because Agnieska reminds her of a cousin, Griz's childhood playmate, now married and living outside Krakow with her mechanic husband and four children. She started out trying to speak Polish, but instead of creating a bond, it seemed to make Agnieska nervous, so she's gone back to English.

"Why didn't you go back to your rooms at the same time? It was just across the street. I would think you might have walked home together." Griz keeps her voice casual, just asking, though of course this is the question on everyone's mind.

"She wanted to go for a walk," Agnieska says. "I told them. She liked walking out on Ross Head. She liked the wind." She looks up quickly, her blue eyes guarded.

A strand of hair falls across her cheek and she brushes it away, giving Griz another jolt of recognition. She thinks of her cousin, whose beauty was legendary in their family, and the way the aunts would shake their heads about the kind, plain plumber she married and seems to love.

"And what about you? Did you walk straight home after the music stopped?"

Ann Tobin has already told Griz that she thinks Agnieska is lying, that her claim that she walked around the village a bit before going back to her room at the pub to sleep, that she didn't hear Zuzanna come in, is, if not an outright lie, incomplete at the very least. Griz wants to see what she'll say.

Agnieska picks nervously at the cuticle on her right pointer finger. She looks up. "I was feeling homesick," she says carefully. "I wanted to walk around a little, to see if I could make myself feel better."

Griz waits. Agnieska has to know she can't leave it at that. But the blue eyes come up, narrowed. She's not giving anything else unless Griz comes and finds it.

"So you walked up and down the main street of the village?" A nod. "Did you see anyone else while you were walking?"

"Maybe a few people, walking home. I did not know them though."

"So you walked up and down the main street of the village and then you went to bed?"

The eyes flash, calculating. "Well, I may have walked along the road, too. I don't really remember. I was in a kind of fog, thinking about home."

"What time did you return to your room?"

"Midnight. About."

Griz studies her. "So your statement is that after you left the pub, you walked around for a while but you didn't see or meet anyone, anyone at all? And then at midnight you returned to your room over the pub and you went straight to sleep?"

There's a long silence and Griz can see the battle taking place in Agnieska's head. She tries to hide it, keeping her face turned down toward the table, but her fingers freeze on the cuticle and her leg, which has been jiggling under the table, suddenly stops. She considers and finally, slowly raising her head, she looks at Griz and says, "Yes, that is where I was."

Twenty-Four

Conor and I work together on dinner, listening to the Rolling Stones on Adrien's Bluetooth speaker. Lilly's out with Alex at a movie.

"Do you think Griz was telling you everything she knew?" Conor asks as we cook, dumping his cutting board of expertly chopped garlic into the giant cast-iron frying pan we found in the cottage kitchen.

"Not everything. They seem to be following a pretty specific line of inquiry. It seems like it might be connected to this guy Anton Dorda and the drugs seizure off the coast of Ross Head in 2013. Do you remember that?"

Conor touches my hip to move me out of the way of the stove. Mick Jagger's singing "(I Can't Get No) Satisfaction." "Ah, yeah. It was big news. There have been a few of these, I think. One at the port of Cork a few years ago. They bring it in from the Caribbean or Venezuela. There was one where the traffickers almost drowned. Gardaí had to save 'em."

I carefully slice thin ribbons of red and green peppers. The knife is sharp and the sound it makes cutting through the vegetables' flesh is inordinately satisfying. "It's so quiet and beautiful here. I had no idea this area was such a hotbed of crime."

"It's not really. But think of the map of the North Atlantic. If you're bringing drugs to Europe from the Caribbean or South America, West Cork is the first place you come to. If you can off-load the drugs here, then you can take them to mainland Europe without any customs checks. And it's fairly remote out here, especially in the off-season."

I light the stove, directing a couple of glugs of oil into the pan, thinking about it. They must think that Dorda killed Lukas and held the body until it was dumped. I wonder if they've searched Dorda's house or businesses yet. That's where I'd start.

Conor and I are watching a Hungarian art film he's been wanting to see when Lilly and Alex come in at ten. The film, beautifully shot, is also so surrealist that I have no idea what's going on and I can't hide the relief with which I greet them and tell Conor to pause the movie.

Lilly is subdued, her eyes darting to Alex and then back again, and before I can ask if everything's okay, she blurts out, "Can we talk to you? I mean, can Alex talk to you? He doesn't know what to do. It's about Zuzanna and I thought you could give him, like, advice."

Conor and I exchange a glance.

"Of course. Let's sit down in the living room." Conor goes to make tea and we sit down across from one another, Lilly and Alex next to each other on the couch and Conor and I in the armchairs. It's the first time I've really been able to study Alex. He's younger-looking up close, the rock-star hair and leather jacket distracting from his babyish face and thin arms. Lilly's gripping his left hand, letting him know she's there, and I feel again the sense of them as a unit, that he's relying on her. He clears his throat and glances over.

He doesn't seem to know where to start. Finally I say, "Alex, how long had you known Zuzanna?"

Grateful for a question that's easy to answer, he raises his eyes to meet mine. "Three years, I guess. She and Agnieska came to Rosscliffe right after the Nevins opened the gastropub. Barry needed workers and they knew some of the guys on the building sites. Zuzanna . . . made you happy, because she was so happy all the time. She likes jokes." He smiles, remembering, not noticing the present tense.

"How did you find out she had died?"

"The next morning," he says. "Agnieska rang the flat."

"Alex and his brother have a really cute flat in the village, over the store where I got my dress," Lilly explains.

"She rang after she saw Zuzanna in the water?" I ask him. I'm wondering if Ann Tobin questioned her right away or let her go home first.

He nods. "Yeah, after the guards finished asking her questions. Agnieska was really upset and she talked to Tomasz and then Sergeant Tobin came to ask us about how Zuzanna seemed at the pub that night. I think she had talked to Marcus at McCarthy's. He's the barman. He must have told her everyone who was there and she came to talk to us about nine."

I wait for him to go on. Whatever he's going to say, he's getting himself ready. He's arranging things. It puts me on my guard. There's a part of the story he's afraid to tell.

"We were at McCarthy's and we finished playing and we were having a laugh, like, and then everyone started going home. Zuzanna asked if she could talk to me. I said sure and she said she wanted to step outside because it was private. I told Lilly I'd be right back and we went outside." He glances at Lilly. "I was in a hurry. Lilly didn't know anyone in the pub and I didn't want her to think I was . . . Zuzanna is just my friend." Lilly puts a hand on his arm and he goes on. "Anyway, we were outside McCarthy's and Zuzanna asked me what I remembered about the day Lukas disappeared. She said she didn't think everyone was telling the truth about his disappearance. She asked if I remembered anything about that day, if I had seen him, and I said I just remembered that the next morning Tomasz told me Lukas hadn't gone home and that he told me Zuzanna was worried. She said something about a car and that she was going to try to talk to someone and she said she knew that Lukas didn't kill himself and this would prove it."

I can feel my cop brain switch on. I lean forward and fix my eyes on him. "Did you tell Ann Tobin this?" I ask.

He shakes his head and glances at Lilly. "I . . . I was still in shock when she was questioning us and I didn't want . . . the guards, they think the Polish in Rosscliffe are doing bad things, always, and I thought if I said something, then maybe she would think . . ." He looks terrified and very young. "They questioned Tomasz and me, too, about Lukas when he disappeared. If I told them Zuzanna thought someone was lying . . ."

"You were worried it would put attention on your brother?" I finish.

He glances away. "Or me," he says after a minute. "It was stupid. I didn't want her to focus on us. The guards are always bothering the Polish here. Back home, the police were . . . Tomasz doesn't trust them. But then I told Lilly and she said she told the detective who lives in the village, Mrs. Tobin, that I was talking to Zuzanna and I have to tell them now because it will look bad. She said the guards will think I have something to hide."

"Lilly's right," I say. "It's important for you to tell the guards everything you know. Did Zuzanna tell you who she was going to talk to?"

He shakes his head.

"Do you think Agnieska knows who it was?"

He looks up quickly then back down at his lap. "I don't know."

"You need to tell the guards," I say. "The sooner the better. Just say that you were still in shock and you got flustered and forgot to report an additional conversation with Zuzanna. Your brother can go with you to make a statement or one of us can." I look at Conor, who nods.

"Tomasz can come with me," he says. "Thank you. Will she . . . will she find it suspicious?"

"She will," I say. "It looks strange. But the fact that you're correcting the record will help."

"Thank you," he says. I feel a surge of sympathy for him and, at the same time, a surge of caution. I don't want Lilly wrapped up in an investigation just because she's spending time with him, but he obviously felt guilty about his omission and was honest with her about it, which says something. I study his face for a moment in the wash of yellow light coming from the lamps next to the couch, trying to see what he's really thinking. As I told Conor, I'm good at detecting evasion, and I think there might be something Alex isn't saying, but I have no idea if it's related to Zuzanna's death. Lilly walks him outside, and when she comes back, she says Alex is going to go talk to Ann Tobin in the morning with his brother.

"Lill," I say. "You did the right thing telling him to go back to the guards. I'm proud of you."

"I knew they'd make a big deal if they found out," she says. "The police are always discriminating against Polish people here. It's really outrageous."

I take a breath before saying, "I think it's a good sign that he was honest with you. But if there's anything else he knows, he should tell her now. Investigators are good at finding things out. She may already know a lot more than what she told us. Her questioning us, her questioning Alex, it may have just been to see if we lied about anything, to see if our stories matched those of the witnesses in the pub."

Lilly's wearing a sundress, black with red chrysanthemums, under her leather jacket, and her cheeks flush nearly to the color of the flowers. "You think he's lying, after he came to ask your advice? He didn't have to tell me and he didn't have to tell you, but he wanted to because he was worried you might hear about it and think he's not honest, since you're a cop. But you just think that because he has an accent he's got to be guilty of something."

"Lilly, that's ridiculous. I don't think that at all. I'm just telling you."

She gives me a nasty look and stalks off to her room.

Conor comes up behind me and puts his hands on my shoulders. He kisses my neck, but I'm so exhausted, I don't respond.

"I'm sorry. I'm wrecked," I say.

He takes my hand and shuts off the kitchen lights. "Let's get some sleep," he says. "Things will look better in the morning."

Twenty-Five

Ann Tobin gets a mug of tea and takes it into the incident room, getting a few envious looks as fragrant steam wafts from the mug. The room is full, everyone at all involved with the Lukas Adamik case crowding in for the briefing. She sees a few detectives she knows from the West Cork divisional drugs unit and the uniforms they've brought from Bandon to supplement what they have in Bantry. Someone has decided that they're going to solve this thing. Katya Grzeskiewicz, the detective from Dublin, told Ann yesterday that it feels to her like someone, somewhere, was waiting for this, like they had their eye on Rosscliffe in case something happened there. She's right.

And that someone is Padraig Fiero.

He's come down from what they all call the super unit, the combined drugs and organized crime unit that was created a few years ago as a way to save money and to bring down the organized criminal gangs responsible for most of the drug trafficking in Ireland.

Four years ago, he was a member of the divisional drugs unit, so he's come up in the world despite his failure to get Anton Dorda in 2013.

Because they all know it's about Anton Dorda.

Superintendent Cleary welcomes everyone. "The second post-mortem should be done in the next couple of days, but we're not expecting anything too surprising as the body was found immediately. She certainly seems to have died from drowning and it looks like she did in fact go in on Ross Head. The question, of course, is, did she jump or was she pushed?"

"Just like your man Humpty Dumpty, eh?" someone calls out.

Cleary smiles. "Yeah, so what's the connection with Adamik's death?"

Ann watches him let one of the newer detectives from Bandon say it. "She was his girlfriend. She knew who killed him, right? She was going to tell."

"That's the one that comes to mind for me," Cleary says. "But how do we go about finding out who it was?"

One of the divisional guys looks up. "Nothing to link Lukas Adamik to Colin Nugent?"

"No." Fiero shakes his head. "Not a fucking thing we can use. Not yet, anyway. Except for the fact that it's the same profile. It's possible we'll get something from the body, but as you know we never found out where Nugent's body was kept, so there's nothing to compare it to. Nugent was found without clothes and so was Adamik. There might have been forensics off the clothes, like, but . . ." He shrugs. "The lab's still working on the remains. I'm not optimistic."

"Can youse refresh our memories about Nugent," someone calls out.

Everyone looks around, waiting for someone else to do it. Finally Ann says, "Colin Nugent, age twenty-three, failed to come home to his parents' residence in Dunmanway on the eleventh of June, 2013. He had been involved in the drugs trade in West Cork and Cork City, known to the guards. That October—I'm sorry, I can find the exact date in a bit—his body was found in the water by a fisherman. But, as you all know, postmortem showed he'd been stabbed soon after disappearing, but had only been in the water a week or so."

Fiero says, "Thank you, Sergeant Tobin. That's right, so similar time frame, not identical. Adamik wasn't stabbed. He had damage to his skull that suggests blunt-force trauma was the cause of death."

"Lukas Adamik had a cannabis possession charge from last year, right?" someone calls out.

"Right," Ann tells them. "But it was . . . like, hardly anything. More than personal use, but . . . He paid a fine."

"I'm still interested," Fiero says. "Was he dealing? Is he connected with Dorda?"

"We haven't found a hard connection," Cleary says. "Adamik knew Dorda, of course. The village is small and the Polish community in Rosscliffe sticks together." Ann watches Katya Grzeskiewicz frown and turn her eyes away from Cleary. "Adamik worked on the building sites. Dorda did some work for Sam Nevin early on in his development of Ross Head. He was a builder before he bought the takeaway and the dry cleaners."

"You searched both of those after Nugent was found, I assume," Katya says.

Fiero shrugs. "Best we could. There wasn't anything for a warrant, but we kept an eye on things, poked around a bit. He had some other buildings too, warehouses and so forth."

"I think the guy who supervised Adamik knows something," one of the uniforms says. "Tomasz Sadowski. When I was taking his statement, I got the sense he was holding back."

Ann speaks up. "I did, too. I spoke with him a couple of days ago and there was definitely something off there. He seemed scared. And his brother came in this morning and added something to the statement we took just after Zuzanna Brol's body was found. He says that in the pub that night, Zuzanna asked him what he remembered about the day Lukas disappeared. She said she thought that someone hadn't told the truth."

Some of the people in the room already know about Alex Sadowski's statement, but she can hear a little murmur of excitement come up from those who didn't.

"That's all she said?" Cleary asks.

Ann shrugs. "By his account anyway. I believed him though."

Fiero, triumphant, says, "Look here, all signs point to Adamik having been killed because of his role in a criminal enterprise. I think we can be fairly sure that Zuzanna Brol was asking questions and someone got scared. Tomasz Sadowski was here in 2013. I remember him. We never connected him to Dorda definitively, but, Detective Grzeskiewicz, you've been talking to some of the Polish workers. What do you think?"

Katya steps up to the front. Ann catches a little gleam of annoyance in her eyes as she glances at Fiero. "I think Agnieska Tarnowski is afraid of something. She was Zuzanna's closest friend and she knew Lukas as well. I talked to her for a long time yesterday, but she seemed really . . . contained. I had the sense that she was trying not to tell me something, but was keeping herself kind of locked up, if you know what I mean. Her story about where she was the night Zuzanna died is shite, like. She says she wandered around the village, then went home. We need to look at the CCTV, but I think she was somewhere else. I think she knows something."

"What?" Fiero asks.

"I don't know. Something Zuzanna told her? Something Lukas told her? Say Lukas was killed by Dorda. It must have been because of something he knew, right? About Dorda and his business. If Zuzanna knew that Lukas was dealing drugs for Dorda, maybe she told her best friend Agnieska. In fact, she probably did."

"But we don't know Zuzanna *was* killed," someone says. "There wasn't a mark on her. She drowned, remember?"

Fiero rolls his eyes. "You think she *just happened* to fucking step off the cliff that night?"

There's an uncomfortable silence and Griz breaks it by saying, "This probably isn't related, but it sounds like Lissa Crawford told Maggie D'arcy a story about a woman who may have lived at her family's home in the 1970s. She seems to have disappeared around that time and Mrs. Crawford had a . . . a dream, I guess, about something violent happening to this woman. I doubt there's anything to it, but it might be worth checking into."

Ann says, "I looked into that when Lissa mentioned it to me a few months ago. There were no reports of a missing woman here in 1973, nothing in the files at all. The guards were never called up there, no one ever went missing. I think it's probably one of those strange memory things. She was only ten at the time."

"What about electronics?" someone asks.

"Zuzanna's phone wasn't with the body when they recovered it," Ann says. "Neither was Lukas Adamik's. We're in the process of getting her texts and a call record. No other devices. We've looked at both of their social media and nothing jumps out. They liked taking selfies of the two of them before he went missing." She shrugs. "His family seems willing to be patient, but hers wants us to release the body so they can fly it home. I don't blame them."

Fiero nods and says, "Now, Anton Dorda. For those of you who haven't been as close to the case, he owns a few businesses in the area. We've had suspicions that some of them were laundering profits from the drug trafficking, but we haven't been able to prove anything. From the outside, he looks brilliant, absolutely clean. I don't know how he's doing it."

No one says anything and he goes on. "This may be our chance. I want to focus on putting pressure on Agnieska Tarnowski and Tomasz Sadowski. I think one of them knows something, right?"

"What about Barry Mahoney?" someone else asks. "He knew Zuzanna because she worked at the pub. Did the interview with him yield anything?"

"Not really," Ann tells them. "He said she'd been depressed since Lukas's disappearance. When the remains were found, he thought she'd at least have some certainty but she seemed worse if anything. The other thing I'm following up on is the graffiti up at the building site. It was probably just kids having a laugh, but since the vandalism happened the night Zuzanna died, those kids may have seen something. I've already questioned a lot of people in the village and we'll be checking CCTV and asking around at the shops about who might have purchased the orange paint."

Fiero nods and says, "Okay, we're going to solve this by putting pressure on people in the village. Someone knows something.

Someone saw something. But they're all afraid of Dorda. We need him to make a misstep so we can get out to his place and search it. Lukas Adamik's body was somewhere for three months. Colin Nugent's, too. If they can get us some forensic evidence from the remains and we can tie it to him, we've got him." His eyes are glittery, excited. "CCTV might give us something, too. That's where I want a fucking miracle, yeah? Forensics off Adamik's remains and who was doing what in the village the night Zuzanna Brol died. That's what I want you all to bring me."

As they all go off to their tasks, Ann catches Fiero's eye across the table. He tries to hide it, but he looks embarrassed, and she feels herself flushing. At some point, they're going to have to talk about it. They can't have the unspoken history mucking up the investigation.

But for the moment, she's happy to let it go.

Twenty-Six

Lilly is friendlier the next day and says that Alex talked to Ann To-bin already. She doesn't apologize for snapping at me last night, but she thanks me for making her grilled cheese just the way she likes it and even kisses me on her way to the shower. Conor is preoccupied. He's driving to Dublin the day after tomorrow to get Adrien and he's behind where he wants to be on his book.

I get dressed for a run and set out just as it starts to drizzle. I don't turn back though; I need the exercise and the time to think. I'm passing the gastropub when I spot Rochelle, also in running clothes, up ahead on the sidewalk. I call her name and she stops and turns, smiling broadly when she sees me. "Want to run together?" I call out.

"Yes, I'm feeling grumpy about getting my miles in this morn-ing," she says. "I'd love some company."

We settle into an easy pace, chatting about the weather and, ten-tatively, about the investigation and the arrival of Griz and Fiero. "I didn't get a chance to thank you for the party," I say. "It was lovely."

"Until the end, anyway," she says grimly. "Then it became the worst party ever. We shouldn't have gone ahead with it. Sam knew a lot of the investors had made travel plans and he felt badly about canceling, but . . ." She shrugs and runs a little faster, causing me to adjust to keep up.

"I'm sure everyone understood," I say.

"Maybe." She turns to look at me. "I heard you and Ellen had a bit of a row. Are you okay? She can be a bitch sometimes. I should know. I've been her sister-in-law for seventeen years now." She smiles. "I love her, but we've had our share of run-ins. She's hot-tempered, just like Sam, but she usually gets over it quickly enough. She's his favorite sister and he'd do anything for her, as you can imagine."

"She had every right to be annoyed," I say. "I was acting like a cop, even though I'm not a cop. Not anymore. Lissa Crawford told me about something that may or may not have happened when she was a child at Rosscliffe House and when I asked Matt Mahoney about it, he seemed like he didn't want to talk about it. I should have left it."

"Don't worry about it," Rochelle says. "Ellen will have forgotten all about it in a few days. Barry has had his share of troubles and he's struggling a bit right now. I think it's made her extra touchy."

"I'm sorry he's struggling. I'm sure all of this isn't helping. I imagine the police have questioned him because Zuzanna worked for him."

She slows her pace a bit and says, "Yes, and . . . well, he's had run-ins with the guards before. Don't tell anyone I told you that." Suddenly, she looks almost scared. "As Ellen implied the other day, Barry was troubled for a long time. He struggled with addiction. He's turned things around the last few years and I think we're all just terrified that this will set him . . . back, if you see what I mean."

We run for a bit before I say, "Sam didn't remember anything about this Dorothea in 1973, did he? I'm still looking into it for Lissa."

"Sorry, I forgot to ask. But Sam has always had a thing about the house. He doesn't like going in there alone. He said his mother told him a story once that terrified him. Frankly, I was surprised when he wanted to buy it from Lissa. I don't think he's been in there more than once or twice since he bought it in 2013. She probably told you he stole it from her or something."

"No, but she sounded regretful. What happened between them?"

"To be fair, Sam probably did play down the chances that he was going to develop the house. But she knew it was a possibility and she certainly didn't ask for anything in the sales agreement. I've learned that with things like this, people often engage in magical thinking. She wanted to believe that nothing would change and so she heard what she wanted to hear. Sam felt betrayed when she spoke out against the hotel, but I tried to tell him it was natural she would have a hard time with things moving forward on the peninsula."

I nod and we run in silence for a bit. I'm not at my best, my lungs sluggish and fighting for air. A Garda car passes us driving slowly, no one I've met at the wheel, and after it's gone, I say, "When we were at the pub the other night, someone referred to Ann Tobin as 'poor Annie Tobin.' Do you know why?"

Rochelle shakes her head. "Oh, poor Ann. It's horrible, Maggie. Her son, Dáithí, died from a drug overdose a couple of years ago. He had been sort of a troubled kid, but nothing too terrible, if you know what I mean. Ann's husband, Sean, was a lovely man, principal at the village school, and Dáithí was their only child. We weren't down as much then, but apparently she was the one to find him, out by Rosscliffe House . . ."

I turn to her, shocked. "How horrible."

"I know. Whenever I see her, I just think that I don't know how I'd even go on . . . She looks terrible these days, haunted, you know? But of course you would be, wouldn't you?" She shivers despite the fact that she's sweating.

We're almost back to the village when she says, "Have you decided if you're going to move to Ireland?"

I reach up to wipe sweat out of my eyes. "Not exactly," I say. "I think we're proceeding as if we are, but I haven't actually made the decision yet, you know? If we are moving here, I need to finalize Lilly's school, I need to make a decision about my career. It's complicated, relationships when you've been divorced, when you're older." We stop in front of the gastropub, breathing hard. "Do you ever regret moving here?"

She smiles and looks a bit wistfully out toward the sea. "Every day," she says. "I love it here, I really do, and my boys are Irish through and through, but I'll never feel like I'm home, not really. I'll never have friends who've known me all my life. Almost twenty years of that isn't easy. When my father died, I didn't get back in time. I've never forgiven myself for that and then lately, well . . . as you say, it's complicated." She smiles. "It's lovely having you here, you know." She looks sad for a moment. "Thank you. I needed to talk."

I leave her at the pub and stop on the peninsula road, looking down toward Rosscliffe House. It doesn't look like work has started yet, probably because Sam Nevin still needs to get the planning approval for the renovation. The windows are all blank, the house benign in the strong morning light. Remembering Lissa Crawford's story, I try to make out the layout of the house. There must be a central staircase and then another staircase up to the third floor. *I was going up the stairs to the third floor, where my room was, and in this little pocket or compartment next to the stairs . . . I saw that someone had stuffed a piece of cloth or linen inside, something nice, and it was stained with blood, absolutely soaked with it.*

The thought appears quickly before I can reject it. One way to find out whether there's anything to her story would be to corroborate the details. Is there a pocket or compartment along the stairs going up to the third floor? If there's not, maybe she dreamed it. If I find it, if the house is as she described, well, it might warrant a bit more looking into. It's even possible there's still evidence there, I realize suddenly. If it's really true that no one's set foot in the house but local teens.

I think about just jogging over to look around, but I don't know if anyone's watching. The guards seem to have finished searching along the cliffs, but I have no idea who else may be out here. I need an excuse. I walk quickly to the cottage and get Mr. Bean and his leash, calling out to Conor that I'm taking him for a walk.

The headlands are quiet, no one but us on the walking paths. A lone bird calls once, then twice, causing Mr. Bean to prick up his ears and start toward the sound. I don't see the birdwatcher today, so I let the little dog off his leash and he races along the little walking paths toward the sound, searching the sky, leaping and then racing in circles looking for the now departed winged creature.

We reach Rosscliffe House as the sun reaches a solid vantage point over the water. It looks almost majestic for a moment, the bright light blurring the decay and restoring the overgrown gardens to their former glory. The ruins are eerie in the thin light.

Mr. Bean is exploring the porch, sniffing away at something on the ground. Checking to make sure no one's watching, I try the handle of the back door. It's locked tight and there's a new-looking keypad on it. Checking again, I try "1234." No luck. But the window to the right of the door is open just a little at the bottom, the rock still wedged beneath it to keep it open. That must be how teenagers sneak into the house. I cup my hands around my eyes and peer through the glass, seeing piled furniture, a few boxes, an old-fashioned room with a large hearth. Carefully, I get my fingers under the window and lift. At first, it holds fast, but when I lean in and rock it back and forth in the casement, it breaks free in a cloud of paint flakes and dust. It's low enough that I could climb in without too much trouble.

The sound has unnerved me though and I stop and let the window slide back down again. The house belongs to Sam Nevin's development company. If there are workmen in there or if someone sees me going inside, I could be charged with trespassing.

But it doesn't *feel* like anyone's inside. It doesn't feel like anyone's been inside for a long time. I hesitate. There are still a few empty cans and food wrappers in one corner, but they've been there for a while, the wrappers faded from the sun and the rain. I almost miss it, the flash of color on the ground next to the stone railing: a small piece of painted wood. An earring, distinctive and one of a kind. One of the pair I've seen Agnieska wearing twice now. She had them on at McCarthy's, I think, and it occurs to me she must have lost it since then.

Something about the earring decides me. I pick it up and tuck it into my pocket, and then, checking to make sure no one's watching, lift up the window and wedge it open with the rock again. I'm not sure what to do about Mr. Bean. I could tie him up out here, but I could also use him as justification for going into the house if anyone finds me. The window's low enough that he could have jumped through it after a scent or sound. *Sorry, the window was left open and my dog jumped through. I had to go in and get him out.*

"Okay, Mr. Bean," I say, lifting him up and through the window. "You're going to be my alibi."

The house, cold and silent, is still mostly furnished. It's as though the Crawford family just walked out one day, leaving everything exactly the way it was. The interior is frozen in time, the chairs and tables like silent witnesses to the decades. Some of the furniture is covered with sheets and a thick layer of dust frosts everything. The paintings have been taken down though, and darker rectangles where they once hung stack up along the walls, the faded wallpaper peeling and traced with black.

Even with the dust and dirt, the tattered curtains hanging at the windows, the smell of mildew and something else, sharp and unpleasant, a decaying mouse or bird perhaps, I have a sense of what the house once was. The main foyer is backed by a wide staircase, leading to the second floor. The public rooms on the first floor are huge, graceful, many of them oriented to look out at the sea. Heavy velvet drapes, hanging in shreds from the rods, match the upholstered furniture, the colors corrupted by stains and dark deposits of grime. Rodents have been at the chairs, chewing through the upholstery and tugging out tufts for their nests.

I could look around for hours, but I can't afford to get caught trespassing here and it's the third floor I need to examine. I look up. The staircase opens in front of me, climbing to a half landing where it splits and runs around the second floor toward darkness. The rippling light angling through the windows on the landing is throwing strange patterns on the wood, vaguely human shapes that make me think of bodies floating in water. I climb the stairs slowly, dread washing over me as I reach the windows and stand there for a moment looking out at the water. Despite the summer day outside, it's chilly in here, the house's thick walls keeping the rooms the same temperature as a wine cellar. My legs feel heavy, resistant. I don't want to go any higher, but I take the right-hand staircase, which creaks and moans with every step. Rows of closed doors greet me around the second-floor landing and I stand at the bottom of the single staircase to the third floor. But I can't make myself take a step. The hallway seems to shrink and a wave of cold dread sweeps over me; I nearly stagger. I feel something heavy and dark rising up within me, as though all my doubts and suspicions were finding one another and forming together into a mass of dark bile. The stairs seem to move.

Something above me rustles, a whisper of movement.

I turn around, running all the way down the stairs and calling for Mr. Bean. He comes galloping, his tongue lolling, unaware of my terror, and I snatch him up, lift him through the window, and practically sprint back to the cottage, off-kilter and shaken.

"Are you okay? You're awfully quiet tonight," Conor asks me later. We're sitting next to each other out on the deck, holding hands and drinking wine. Lilly and Alex are practicing a song inside, and we can hear their voices harmonizing, trying out a new song Alex wrote. When he arrived, I asked if everything was okay and he said that he told Ann Tobin what Zuzanna had said and she seemed to accept that he'd just been stressed. She thanked him for coming in, he told me, looking relieved, and told him not to worry. Now, I listen to his voice rising and falling, trying to make out the words. My experience in Rosscliffe House, which I haven't told Conor about, has put me in a dark mood and I can't help thinking Alex is still hiding something.

"Yeah, I'm just struggling a little. I think this whole thing has me out of sorts," I say. "I want to be working this case, you know? I can't stand that they're out there, asking questions, getting evidence, and I'm not there."

He hesitates, then says with a little smile, "But surely, even if you were working as a guard, you couldn't solve *every* mystery."

"I know I can't. I just . . . I don't know. It's hard to explain. I can't stand that they won't tell me what's going on. Anyway, have you talked to Adrien?"

"Yeah, they'll definitely be back in Dublin on Thursday. He sounded a bit down when I talked to him. I'm worried that Bláithín's told him she's moving to Paris."

"Did he say that?"

"No, but . . . I know him. And . . ." He hesitates for a long moment. "I didn't tell you before, but when she was here, she mentioned something about selling the house."

"Your house?"

"Well, our house. When we signed the divorce papers, the

understanding was that I'd stay in it until Adrien goes to university and then we'd sell and split the sale price, but she was wondering about selling sooner, and I . . . I think it might be because she wants to move to Paris."

Panic surges through me. I should just let it go, but I say, "She can't expect you to just pick up and find a new house. Especially when she knows I'm moving over here. And it's the house Lilly knows. It's the only thing she knows here."

He turns his face to look at me and I can see how worried he is. "I know it. I don't think she cares about that. It *is* a large house. If she's starting a new life in Paris, she'll want to be able to buy something there, so Adrien will have a home when he's with her."

"Well, that's not your fault."

"It's not about me," he says, "It's what's best for Adrien. It's just . . . I might need to take him over there more to see her, if she does move, or take him to spend his holidays there."

"But we're moving over here." I don't like the whiny tone that's crept into my voice. There's a long silence. I stare down at Conor's hand, entwined with mine, but loosely now.

I hear Lilly's voice, finishing the song on a clear high note, Alex's guitar capping it. "Well, you may not be in Dublin during the week, anyway," he says carefully, not looking at me.

I feel it like a stab. "Conor, it's not the same thing. You know that. It's only for a short time."

"A year." He meets my eyes.

"That's not fair. We're the ones moving over here. I'm just trying to figure out how to make a living."

He reaches for me. "You're right. I'm sorry. It's just . . . I don't know. I don't like the idea of you being away so much."

"I don't either." I let him pull me in.

He sighs. "I'm sorry, Maggie. I'm just feeling really overwhelmed. I'm nowhere near to finishing this chapter and I really wanted to get it done before driving to Dublin. I feel like I'll be so preoccupied when Adrien gets back and . . . I'm just tired."

We sit there like that for a bit, hanging on to each other, a new discomfort between us now, the evening settling down around us.

"Hey," I say, pulling away and turning to look at him. "Why don't I go? I think I need to get away from here for a day or two. This place is beautiful. I love it here, but everything going on is doing my head in. I can go talk to the school about Lilly, get everything set up. Maybe she'll even come with me."

"But it's such a long drive." His forehead furrows in worry.

"Honestly, I could use the practice and that way you'll be more relaxed when he gets home."

"Really?" The hopeful look in his eyes tells me I've done the right thing.

"Yeah. I could leave tomorrow morning and spend the night at your place. I can check in on things, get the mail, and then I can stop by the school on Thursday morning before picking Adrien up."

"Are you sure? That would be great. I can really push it here and I'll be done by the time you get home." He smiles, looking happier already.

"Yeah, and we'll figure all of this out. I'll see if I can get some more information about the other possibilities for jobs for me.

Okay?" I'm conscious of how desperately I want to smooth things over, how falsely cheery I've made my voice.

He nods and smiles and I lean over to put my head on his chest, listening to the soft receding and returning waves of his heart beating inside the darkness of his body.

Twenty-Seven

Griz looks down Rosscliffe's main street, thinking about history.

The village is like a library, she realizes, containing all the experiences of the people who live here, each building, each brick, each stone a historical text.

If only the stones could talk, she thinks. *Because the people don't have a lot to say.*

It's not that she has the strong feeling that anyone other than Agnieska is holding out on them, but rather that no one is going to offer anything that could help the guards unless they're forced to. There are relationships and secrets here that run under the surface like a subterranean river and Griz and Ann Tobin are walking around looking for a way in. They've interviewed all of the business owners and workers, asking about the day Lukas went missing, asking about whether anyone saw anything the night of Zuzanna's death.

Broome has some CCTV from outside Donnelly's store and he's taken it back to Bantry to start going through it. It's probably their best bet, but she's still hoping someone will have seen something.

They find Gwynedd Williams at the health food store, stocking bottles of herbal remedies and tinctures on the shelves. He greets them when they come in and Griz thinks he seems a bit apprehensive, but then that would be natural with everything going on in the village.

"Hi, Gwynedd," Ann says. "I don't know if you've met Detective Grzeskiewicz. She's helping out with the investigation into Lukas Adamik's death."

He looks up from his work, settles his eyes on Griz for a moment, and nods. "Have you found out anything?" he asks, carefully placing a small white box on the shelf and then turning back to face them.

"We've made some good progress," Ann says. "We're just wondering if you remember anything about the day Lukas Adamik went missing. We asked you at the time and I have all those statements, but if you could refresh our memory, that would be wonderful."

He frowns, clearly nervous, and Griz steps closer, to put a little pressure on him and because she wants to see his face. She has the feeling he's holding something back.

Gwynedd, continuing to unpack the boxes of remedies, tells them that he doesn't have any CCTV on the outside of the shop, because of the "privacy concerns," and that he doesn't remember anything in particular from either of the days in which they are interested.

They move on, stopping in at the other shops and hearing almost nothing of value.

"What do you think?" Ann asks out on the street. "I'm not sure there's anything here we haven't gotten already." They watch an older couple make their way slowly along the footpath, looking into shop windows. A group of boys in school uniforms, freed for the day, dart past, slowing respectfully so they don't careen into the couple.

"Yeah, you're probably right." But Griz feels uncertain.

They're about to finish for the afternoon when Griz hears someone calling out Ann's name and they turn around to find Gwynedd waving them down from across the street. He indicates that he's coming to them and they wait for him next to Donnelly's shop, watching as he dashes across the street like an awkward stork, his arms flapping and his head bobbing on his long neck.

"What is it, Gwynedd?" Ann asks kindly.

He starts to talk, then stops, looking away, embarrassed. "Mairead said I was to tell you," he says finally. "She said it's gone far enough."

"Tell us what?"

He watches a young mother with two toddlers in a pram make her way out of the shop, laden with parcels. Finally he says forcefully, "That it's I who's been protesting up at the building sites through sabotage!"

Ann looks shocked. "That was you? Up at the building sites? You're the one who's been vandalizing and taking things from the sites?"

He draws himself up, looking a bit indignant. "You may know that I am very opposed to the development of Ross Head," he says proudly. "I have been quite open and public about my opposition, but I have also been engaging in, well, guerrilla warfare, you might call it, in order to advance my cause." Griz has to resist the urge to laugh.

"Vandalism," Ann says.

"Well, I prefer to think of it as a justified interruption of a capitalist enterprise. I was going to tell you today. I swear to it. It was Mairead who told me I had to, after we heard about that poor girl, Zuzanna." He hesitates, then continues, "I saw something you should know about, that night."

Griz is alert now. "The night Zuzanna Brol died?"

Gwynedd nods.

"I went up there about midnight. I thought there wouldn't be anyone on the peninsula then. I've seen people out and about there, torchlights in Rosscliffe House a few times and so forth, so I went to the pub and I had a few and waited until I was pretty sure everyone would be asleep."

Impatient, Ann says, "What did you see, Gwynedd?"

"Zuzanna was out on the peninsula, not far from Rosscliffe House." He hesitates, and it's not until Ann nods encouragingly that he says, "She wasn't alone. There was someone with her."

Twenty-Eight

In the morning, I ask Lilly if she'd like to drive to Dublin with me. When she says she wants to stay in Rosscliffe to practice for a music festival later in the summer, I try not to examine too hard the flood of relief I feel. There's something a bit claustrophobic about Rosscliffe, even without the suspicious deaths. I'm looking forward to getting away and, I realize, to some time alone.

I stop at the gastropub on my way out of town.

The recognition hits me as soon as I walk in the door: wood polish, industrial dishwashing detergent, last night's beer. It's the morning smell of bars and pubs, everything clean and wiped down, glasses dry and waiting for the night ahead, a fresh breeze drifting in from an open window somewhere, all the conversation of the night before still hanging on the air.

Agnieska is standing at a table, her back to me, folding napkins. A cup of coffee steams next to her, and the sun is angling through a side window, lighting up the sharp planes of her face. She's daydreaming, her hands on autopilot with the napkins, a small smile on her face that makes her beautiful, and I hesitate to interrupt her. She's so wholly solitary, reveling in this bit of space that's hers and hers alone. She lives over the pub, she works all the time, she's grieving her friend, she probably gets very little time to herself, and here I am, intruding on it.

"My family owns a bar in the States," I say quietly, so as not to startle her. "My favorite thing was coming in for an early shift, opening up by myself. I loved the way the bar smelled, the way the tables shone, the way everything was clean and . . . ready. I'm sorry to bother you."

She turns around, her blue eyes friendly and open for a moment. "I like it," she says. "Folding the napkins is . . . It lets your mind float free while your hands are busy. My grandmother used to say that about knitting."

"It's true," I say. "I used to like polishing glasses, too. Same reason. I'd fight the guys who worked behind the bar to polish glasses. Make them do the floors."

"I hate it, mopping the floor," she says. "Was it a pub like this? Your bar?"

"Yeah, an Irish bar. On Long Island. Big Irish-American community. It's called Flaherty's. I miss it."

Agnieska keeps folding, her hands quickly turning and doubling the fabric. "But you are moving here?"

I realize she must have overheard our conversation the night we had dinner here. I wonder if she's said anything to Lilly. "Maybe," I say. "It's hard, being away from home, moving to a new place. But I don't have to tell you that. How long have you been in Ireland?"

"Two years. I came with Zuzanna. I like it, but . . ."

She looks sad and I jump in, a little awkwardly, "I'm so sorry about Zuzanna. It must be awful." She acknowledges my words with a dip of her head but doesn't say anything.

"Will you stay?" I ask.

"Probably, yes." She looks up, something secretive in her eyes I can't quite read. "Rosscliffe feels like home now. I like the people." She smiles and turns back to the napkins. "Can I help you with something?"

"No," I say. "I just wanted to drop by and give this to you. I found it while I was out walking near Rosscliffe House. I think it's yours. I remembered you were wearing them the other night." I watch her face carefully as I take the earring out of my pocket and offer it to her in my open hand.

She blanches. I see fear sweep through her eyes and she takes it quickly and puts it in the pocket of her apron. "Thank you," she says. "I was looking for it."

"It's so pretty. What did you call it?"

"*Wycinanki.* It's, like, paper cutting, to make flowers and birds and things. This is a painted kind of that."

I jump in, aware that it's my only chance. "Agnieska, did Zuzanna say anything to you about Lukas's death the night she died? It sounds like she had some questions and may have been talking to some of her friends. I'm sorry to ask, but it could be important for the guards to know about it."

She looks toward the door, as though she's expecting someone to come in, then starts folding the napkins again. "No, she did not say anything."

"Are you sure?" I watch her body language carefully. She's defensive suddenly, turning away from me, the pile of napkins like a wall she thinks will protect her.

"No, she . . . she did not think Lukas went off the cliffs on purpose, but . . . that night she did not say anything."

The door to the pub opens and her eyes dart up to see who it is.

"Ah, hello. May I get a coffee, Agnieska?" asks Anton Dorda. He's smiling and it makes him almost boyish. Behind him on the street, I can see his car, waiting for him.

She nods, a hand plucking nervously at the pocket where she's tucked the earring, and goes to the bar, pouring a cup of steaming coffee in a to-go cup and adding a splash of milk. I smile at him and he nods back. Now that I'm close to him, I can see the tattoo that starts behind one ear and disappears into the collar of his jacket. It's a dolphin, leaping over a stylized wave.

Agnieska hands him the coffee and murmurs something in Polish. She stumbles a little walking toward him and blushes, but he takes the coffee and says something back, watching her closely.

"Are you going out on the boat?" she asks, looking down at the ground.

"Yes, before the weather gets bad." His accent matches hers, but it's softer, more Irish. He's been here longer.

"Do you have a sailboat?" I ask him.

He turns to look at me and I know he recognizes me from the way he meets my gaze and waits a moment before saying, "No, I am not so skilled. I have just a . . . powerboat." He gestures with the coffee and grins at me.

"I'm Maggie D'arcy," I tell him, offering my hand, hoping he'll introduce himself. "My family and I are renting one of Mrs. Crawford's cottages."

"You are the American cop," he says. He shakes my hand and I can feel Agnieska's stress wafting up around her. She's nervous about something. About him? Me? "I have not met you yet. I am Anton Dorda."

"I hope it won't rain while you're out on the water," I say.

"Ah yes, I had better get out there." He murmurs something else in Polish to Agnieska and then he nods to me and goes back out, leaving behind a faint smell of expensive cologne and new car.

Before I can ask her anything else, she looks toward the back of the pub and says she needs to get started on setting tables. When I follow her gaze, I see Barry Mahoney standing in the doorway, his expression steely. I don't know how long he's been there or how much he's heard.

Agnieska moves toward the door and I know she wants me to leave. "Thank you," she says quietly. "For the . . ." She gestures to her ear.

When I go out on to the street, the Mercedes is parked there, idling, but Anton Dorda is nowhere to be seen. The morning skies are still unsettled over the village, clouds pressing in, the rain holding off for the moment but threatening from the horizon.

As I drive back through the interior of West Cork on the narrow, local roads, I can feel my anxiety lifting a bit. I listen to the radio for a while and then turn it off, enjoying the silence and the time to think. The route takes me up through Cork and Tipperary and Portlaoise, where I stop for gas and coffee, and once I settle into motorway driving, I find my mind is free to think, to organize all my preoccupations and concerns.

How will things change if Bláithín moves to Paris? I know that Conor feels like Adrien's finally back on track after a rough period during the divorce. I know he'd do anything for Adrien.

When my mother or I would get upset about something or other, my father used to tell us that most of the things you worry about never end up happening and that worrying about maybes is just a waste of time. He was mostly right. The thing is, we have no idea if Bláithín is really moving to Paris. Until I know that for sure, any time I spend worrying about it is wasted time.

Knowing that doesn't melt the little hard knot of anxiety in my stomach though.

And then there's Lilly. I just don't know if I'm doing the right thing letting her spend so much time with Alex. I remember something Uncle Danny said to me once, that parenting is hard because you won't know if you've done a good job until it's too late to change course. I think of his voice, the way it feels to hug him, and I feel a wave of homesickness.

What am I doing, anyway? Uprooting Lilly from everything she's ever known and bringing her to a place where not only does she not know anyone, but where everything is different and strange. After my last case, when it became clear that I wouldn't be working for the Suffolk County Police Department again, the move to Ireland seemed like the fresh start Lilly and I needed. But now I've brought us here and we've been dropped into the middle of a criminal investigation. It's like I can't keep Lilly away from trauma and death, no matter how hard I try.

And apparently I can't keep away from it, either. If I'm honest with myself, as soon as Ellen Mahoney mentioned her sister, I started thinking about trying to talk to Bridget.

I get to Kildare by two. It's a busy and seemingly prosperous market town, lots of horse-racing-related businesses, signs for the Irish National Stud horse-breeding facility and the Curragh Racecourse, the great flat expanse of the plain always looming to the east. The word *curragh* means "boat" in Irish, and there's something about the landscape that makes you feel nestled in a canoe or a kayak, adrift on the great green sea of Ireland's interior.

When I searched last night, I found an address for a Bridget Nevin in a townland just outside Kildare, but it's just the name of a house, Hawthorne Cottage, and when Google Maps tells me I've arrived, I don't see anything indicating that there's a Hawthorne Cottage anywhere. I'm thinking I'm out of luck when I see a woman and a child approaching on the road, a small spaniel jumping around their legs, tangling them in its leash. I get out and ask her if she can give me directions to Bridget Nevin's house.

"Ah, your one who makes the pots?" she asks, her eyes telling me she doesn't think too much of the pots. I nod, even though I don't know if it's the same Bridget Nevin. Ellen didn't say anything about pots. "Keep going up here and you'll see it on the left-hand side. They think a lot of their gardens." She smirks and looks away.

When I pull into the driveway of a small cottage surrounded by greenery, there's someone out in the garden plot out front, a tall older man with thinning gray hair and spectacles, stooped over and trimming rosebushes with a pair of hand clippers. He looks up and waves as though he was expecting me, so I get out and say, "I'm so sorry to bother you, but I'm wondering if a Bridget Nevin who grew up in Rosscliffe lives here."

"Yes," he says cheerfully. "That's my partner. I'll just get her now." I feel my hopes rise just a little. His accent is mostly English, clipped and aristocratic. He doesn't seem in the least bit suspicious; he doesn't ask what I want and disappears inside. The garden is beautiful, laid out in a grid, with complementary flowers in each rectangle, different colors and textures that create a pleasing impression. But what I really notice are the pieces of pottery placed around among the beds, large brown earthenware planters, fanciful things, with scrollwork decorations and little clay animals clinging to them.

When the man comes back out, he's trailed by a small woman with bowl-cut silver hair and an elfin face; she's wearing an apron covered in red stains, clay, I think. "Hello," she says warily, looking up at me, and I can see both Sam and Ellen in her face, a preview of what they'll look like as they age. "Rodney says you want to speak to me." She doesn't offer a hand and I see that they, too, are crusted with clay.

"I'm sorry to interrupt your work," I say, "but my name is Maggie D'arcy and I'm involved in a bit of a research project, trying to learn a bit more about Rosscliffe House in the 1970s, around the time Lissa Crawford's family left."

"Ah, do you know Lissa?" She looks confused.

"We're renting one of her cottages for the summer. I'm looking into something she talked to me about and I was told that you worked there when you were a teenager and might be able to help me out."

"Ah," says Rodney. "Rosscliffe House." The words are heavy with meaning.

Bridget Nevin doesn't question my motives in asking. "Yes, well, I was a sort of, well, housekeeper, I suppose you'd say. Though not in any traditional sense of the word. I lived in the village, of course, and my mam was the cook. It was casual. I cleaned a bit, but it was . . . there wasn't much to be done." She smiles. "Those poor people. They had no money, but she couldn't handle any of it; I was all they could afford. A sixteen-year-old who didn't know the first thing about keeping a house. I only did it for a short time and then they were leaving and of course he . . . died. Very sad."

"Do you remember anything about the houseguests they had that summer?" I ask. "I'd heard there was someone named Dorothea staying at the house around that time."

To my surprise, she gives Rodney a flirtatious smile. "Oh, yes. They always had people staying, but Rodney could tell you more about the family. He's the posh one."

Rodney lets out an ironic "Ha! For all the good it did me."

"Sorry, you knew them too?" I ask.

"Ah, I thought you knew," he says. "Yes, my name is Rodney Allerton. My father was a third cousin of Felix Crawford's. We lived in Dublin, but we spent quite a lot of time with them down there in those years. But then we went to London and I suppose they lost touch. I was sixteen that summer. Just like Bridget." He smiles at her again and she looks pleased.

"What do you remember about it?" I ask him. "I received information that there may have been some sort of . . . incident. That a woman who lived at the house disappeared and everyone left quite soon after."

"We did leave very suddenly," he says, thinking hard. "I remember that. But I don't know why. One day, my mother just said that we had to pack up and we were leaving. My father stayed to help, but everyone seemed upset."

"Did either of you know this woman, Dorothea? I've seen a photo; she had black hair with a white streak, kind of distinctive. Supposedly, she was living at Rosscliffe House that summer, too. She was perhaps in her early twenties."

"They had so many people staying with them," Bridget says. "It's hard to remember."

Rodney inspects the leaves of the rosebush and then looks back at me. "I remember her giving out to us when we were naughty. We boys liked to run around the place. It was on the site of an old castle, you know, and there were towers and root cellars and things. Good places to hide, out in the gardens. But she'd complain about us dashing around everywhere, said we were too noisy, told us to stay out of the ruins. She was some sort of governess, I think. She seemed like that, anyway, fussing over the Crawford children."

"Yes, that's what Lissa Crawford thought, too. You don't remember her disappearing, though?"

"No, surely someone would have said? A thing like that? It's all quite murky, you know. She wasn't who I was interested in in that house." He smirks at Bridget.

"So that's where you met?"

Bridget says, "Well, initially. I remember thinking he was very handsome. But then everyone left suddenly and I didn't think I'd see him again. But a few years later, I went to art college in London and the first day, there he was." She reaches out and takes his hand. "I recognized him right away, but I wasn't sure he recognized me."

"But I did, right away," Rodney says, smiling. "When we left so suddenly, I remember being despondent that I didn't get to say goodbye. It leaves a mark on you, something like that. I thought about her a lot."

I smile at him and at his obvious affection for Bridget Nevin. "Is there anything else about this Dorothea that you remember? Anything at all? Her last name, where she was from?"

Bridget shakes her head, but Rodney looks up at me. "You know," he says. "I've just remembered something. A few of the boys, my brothers who were a bit older, were bothering her, asking why she didn't like any of them, and one of them said something about how being married to Jesus must be awfully boring. Something about her being a Sister of Mercy. I remembered because it seemed so funny. She wasn't like any nun I'd seen before. She wore bell-bottoms! She put them in their places, said she was very happy, thank you very much."

"Really? That's very interesting."

"But why would the Crawfords have had a young Catholic nun staying?" Bridget asks. "They weren't observant in any way and they would have been Church of Ireland if anything."

"I don't know. It does seem odd. But I've just remembered it," he says.

"And there's nothing else you remember about that summer?" I ask. Bridget shakes her head. "Your mother worked there as well. Did anyone else in your family help out?"

"I don't think so," she says. "The boys may have gone up to help Matt Mahoney with the gardening once in a while. You could ask Sam if he remembers. He was quite young though. I'm not much in touch with my family in Rosscliffe, but I talk to Ellen and Sam every so often. Rochelle's lovely and she's always made an effort." Her eyes dart to the ground. When she looks up, they're sad. "I've lived a different sort of life to them, I suppose. But we're fond of each other."

"I met Matt Mahoney," I tell them.

Bridget clucks. "He's an old character. I'm sure he worries about Barry."

I assume she's referring to his drinking, but something in her face makes me ask, "Why?"

Bridget hesitates for a minute. "Ellen and Barry, they . . . They've been together since they were sixteen. There's been a lot of water under the bridge." Rodney snorts and Bridget glances at him and says, "Barry's had his troubles. Ellen's the best thing that ever happened to him. I don't know where he'd be without her."

"Without Sam, I'd say," Rodney mutters. "Sam's the one who keeps saving him."

"What do you mean?" I ask.

Bridget chooses her words carefully. "Oh, Barry was quite . . . wild. He got into a few legal scrapes over the years and Sam always got him out. But it was putting him in charge of the pub that really saved him, gave him a purpose, you know. Sam's always been like that. He knows what people need to succeed. That's what he and Rochelle are trying to do for Rosscliffe, I think." She rubs her hands on her apron. The clay is starting to dry in the warm air and she looks back toward the house, eager to get back to work.

I need to let her go, but I've just thought of something else. "What about Lissa's brother? What was he like?"

Bridget wrinkles her nose. "Arthur his name was. He was only, what, fourteen? He was quite tall, though, and he was, well, odd. Aggressive. I didn't like being left alone with him. It made me nervous. But he was just a boy, after all."

"Well, I'll let you go, but thank you for your help," I say. "Your garden's beautiful. And I love your pots."

"Thank you so much." She smiles at Rodney, but he has a small frown on his face.

"You know," he says. "When I saw the news that Sam was going to turn Rosscliffe House into a hotel, I was happy for him. But I won't ever stay there. I didn't like that house. My brother Randall used to tell us stories to scare us, say that the house was haunted. I had a bad feeling whenever I went upstairs to the third floor. I told my mother once and she said she got a bad feeling from it, too, but Dad and Felix were so tight, we kept going back. I told you that, didn't I, Bridge?"

"Yes, you did," she says. "You did tell me that." She smiles at him indulgently and then turns to me. "Rosscliffe is so lovely. But I never feel quite right there. The house, you know, looming over everything. I always felt that it had absorbed too much of the history of the place, too much of the things that had happened there."

Twenty-Nine

Griz sounds tired when I get her on her mobile as the traffic slows on the motorway outside Dublin. She's on her way back to the bed-and-breakfast, and when I tell her about finding Agnieska's earring near Rosscliffe House and recount Rodney Allerton's memory of Dorothea being a Sister of Mercy, she doesn't sound very interested. "It just seems so long ago," she says. "Look, I need to get some food into me before I collapse. I'll talk to you soon, yeah?" I can't help but feel vaguely *handled*, like one of those crazy people who love to call up police tip lines and report obscure leads to investigators.

The traffic only gets worse and it's six before I pull into the little driveway in front of Conor's Donnybrook semi-detached and sit there for a moment, looking up at it, trying to feel a sense of homecoming.

The house is silent, dark. He's had a neighbor stop in a few times to check on things and I see a pile of mail on the table that must have arrived before the forwarding order started. I stand in the kitchen and look around at all of the things that he's brought into the house over twenty years, the ceramic fruit bowl with apples painted on it, the stack of books on a counter, a wine rack holding two bottles of red we meant to bring with us.

It's strange being alone in a place so associated with him and I wander through the rooms, getting reacquainted with the details of his life: the books on the shelves in his living room, the layout of the kitchen. There's a picture of Adrien as a baby on the refrigerator and I stare at it, feeling the weight of all those years I'll never have with them, all those things we'll never know about each other. The house contains so much history, so much laughter, so much pain. Could I live here? Could I make it mine?

And will I have the chance? If Bláithín does want him to sell, it's a desirable address and I know it will go fast in Dublin's feverish real estate market. There should be enough profit for them each to buy something smaller, but what about me and Lilly?

When I go upstairs, it takes me five minutes to find a light switch for the hallway and it feels like the house is taunting me, keeping me out. A long hot shower improves my mood and I get dressed and try to decide what to do about dinner. Conor cleaned the fridge out before we left, so there isn't anything in the house, and though I usually don't mind eating out alone, for some reason I don't want to tonight. I think about who I know in Dublin. Roly and Griz, of course, but Roly's away and Griz is in Rosscliffe. There's Emer Nolan. Emer was my cousin Erin's roommate and I reconnected with her when I was in Dublin last year and we've stayed in touch ever since. I love her company, but she and her girlfriend are having a baby in August and I know Emer is feeling exhausted by pregnancy and probably won't want to go out.

If I'm going to move to Dublin, I'm going to have to make some friends.

But then I remember that I do have another friend in Dublin. Or a kind of friend. In truth, we started out as enemies, but since

March we've chatted on the phone a few times and he knows I'm spending the summer in Cork. Stephen Hines, crime reporter for the *Irish Independent,* might be an interesting dinner companion. And maybe he knows something about Anton Dorda and Operation Waves.

I dial the number and he answers on the second ring, like he's been waiting for a call. "Maggie D'arcy," he says. "To what do I owe the pleasure?"

"Well, I'm in Dublin for the night. I'm picking up Conor's son tomorrow to take him back to West Cork and I was wondering if you'd like to have dinner."

"I'm intrigued. Certainly, but I won't be able to meet you until eight. Is that all right?"

"Yes, you name the place."

"Mmm. There's a ramen place off Grafton Street that's very good. That okay for you? I'll text you the address."

I tell him I'll see him there and decide to walk into the city center since the weather is so nice. Morehampton Road is quiet, but as I walk up Lower Leeson Street and over the canal, the sidewalks become more and more crowded, Dubliners out enjoying the weather. I walk around St. Stephen's Green, stopping to watch the ducks in the pond, everything still and warm in the midsummer evening. Then I walk down Grafton Street, dodging groups of teenagers, trying to imagine Lilly among them and laughing with her friends, and I remember the first time I explored the city. It feels like a homecoming now, the little lanes familiar and some of the shops and pubs ones that I now have associations with. I stop to listen to a busker playing the tarantella on an acoustic guitar and the music tugs at me, invoking a strange sense of déjà vu. How does a place start to feel like home? I guess it's those associations, the connection of emotionally fraught experiences to a place that fixes it in your mind.

Stephen is already waiting for me when I come down the narrow staircase and into the dark restaurant. He isn't a hugger; in fact, I have the sense that he doesn't like to be touched at all, so I nod and slide into the booth. "How is it to be back in Dublin?" he asks. He's let his hair grow long again and has it in a ponytail. His usual tweed jacket has been replaced by a thin cotton shirt left open over his turtleneck. I feel hot and uncomfortable just looking at him.

"It's nice actually," I say. "West Cork is beautiful, but it's good to get a dose of city life. It's interesting down there. Though we've had a couple of suspicious deaths."

"I did hear about that. We have a correspondent there or I might have gone down myself. What's your sense of things? Drugs activity, organized crime, was the assessment I heard."

"Maybe. They seem to be looking at a guy named Anton Dorda. Local businessman, widely rumored to be involved in the drug trade."

"They won't let you in on the inside information?" He's teasing me. "That must drive you mad."

I smile. "Just a little."

"How do you like it otherwise? It's quite nice down there in West Cork, very posh, lots of famous Americans, I hear." He smiles. "Like you."

"Very funny. Yeah, this village we're in, it's a weird combination. Lots of history, but lots of newcomers, too. There are all these . . . undercurrents, layers of relationships. I can't quite figure it out. There's a big Anglo-Irish house that belonged to the painter Felix

Crawford that they're turning into a luxury hotel and some people in the village think it's great, some are horrified."

"Is it Nevin, the guy who's developing down there?"

"Yeah, that's him. Sam Nevin." I see something on his face that makes me ask, "Why? You know him?"

"No, no. Scruffy journalists don't mix with the likes of him. The name is familiar, that's all. I think a friend of mine was working on a story about him a few years back."

"What, related to crime? He's not connected to drug dealing, is he?" Suddenly I'm thinking of the possibilities. Maybe Sam Nevin was in league with Anton Dorda. Maybe he got the Polish guys working on his building sites to deal drugs for him.

"No, nothing like that," Stephen says. "Calm yourself now. It was a colleague who covers banking and finance. I think he was writing a story about developers post-recession, investment schemes and how financing had changed after the crash, and such. Hang on." He takes out his phone and types for a minute, then says, "Bill Daly's his name. I just sent him a text to see what he remembers. We'll see if he gets back to us."

"Thanks. It's interesting about Sam Nevin. Yeah, he's this sort of glamorous rich guy and they have this incredible place on the cliffs. But he grew up there, one of seven kids. His mother was the cook up at the Big House, which was a whole other story, like something out of a novel." I tell him a little bit about Lissa Crawford and her memories and the paintings, though I hold back when it comes to what I've found about Dorothea and the summer of 1973. I'm not sure why, except that my investigation, such as it is, isn't complete yet and I don't want to give anything away that I'm not sure of.

"That's quite gothic, Maggie D'arcy," he says. "Do you think there's anything to it?"

"Seems like there must be, but the question is, what can she do about it? If something did happen to this Dorothea, most of the people who were around then are long gone. I suppose it's more to scratch an itch than anything." But as I say the words it occurs to me that I'm wrong. Quite a few of the people from Lissa Crawford's list are still alive.

Our food comes and we slurp happily in silence. "My father's mother came from one of those families," he says after a bit. "I had a great-aunt who lived in this pile near Ballinasloe. She had a ghost called Frederick. She talked to him and everything. I think he may have been the most important relationship of her life. Before she died, it was all Frederick this and Frederick that. We went along with it, asked after him and all."

"Really? You didn't believe in it though, did you?"

"I didn't. I think my grandmother did though. She'd grown up in the house, too. I'll tell you something. After my great-aunt died, I think we all missed Frederick a bit."

"So where did you grow up?" I ask him. "I don't actually know anything about you."

"Here mostly," he says, gesturing around at the restaurant and the city. "I had a bit of a strange childhood, Maggie D'arcy. My father was the product of a mixed marriage—his father was the Catholic, his mother the Protestant—and my mother came from an old Portobello family of Lithuanian Jews. That unique combination of influences doesn't set me apart so much now in the new Dublin, but it did when I was a boy, I'll tell you."

He asks about Lilly and Conor and tells me about a story he's working on, which involves a gangland shooting, and says, "When my friend rings me back, I'll see if he remembers anything about Sam Nevin. Okay to give him your number?"

"Sure. What about this Anton Dorda guy? He ever come across your radar?"

He thinks for a moment. "Mmmm. I remember Operation Waves, of course. I covered a murder near there a few years back. There was a fella killed. Seemed like a gangland thing, maybe, related to the drugs trade. His body wasn't found until months later."

I look up quickly. *His body wasn't found until months later.*

"What was the victim's name? Colin Nugent?"

"Mmmm. I think that's it."

"When was this?"

"I'd say 2013, 2014, something like that. I'd have to find the piece. Anyway, no one was charged, but I heard Anton Dorda's name come up. I got the sense that Nugent was an informant."

We finish eating and I get another beer. "So, are you moving to Dublin?" he asks me.

I take a long sip. "I don't know. That's the plan, but the question of what I'll do for work is complicated."

"Couldn't you get a lateral transfer? With your connections?"

"Not really. I'd still have to do the training college, do a year in uniform. I don't know. Anyway, if you hear of any other jobs for a frustrated detective, let me know."

"You could be a private detective," he says, winking at me. "Maggie D'arcy, P.I."

I grin. I'm already a private detective of sorts. "And help blondes in distress? Maybe. I'll have to think about that. And thanks for meeting me for dinner."

"Anytime, Maggie D'arcy," he says. "By the way, there's a good exhibit on at the National Gallery at the moment. They've just reopened after the renovations. Twentieth-century Irish painters. There are a couple of lovely Felix Crawfords. You might like to see them if you have the time."

"I'll do that. The Crawfords' Dublin address was on Mount Street. I thought I might walk home that way and have a look."

"I'll come with you. That's along my way, too."

We walk along the side of St. Stephen's Green and then down Fitzwilliam Street to Mount Street. The Georgian town house where the Crawfords had a flat is nondescript, a respectable address, I think from my reading, but a flat rather than a whole house. Stephen and I stare up at it.

"Doesn't say much of anything, does it?" I say. I'm trying to imagine Elizabeth and her children hurrying into their flat after the long trip, to the news that Felix was dead. What had Elizabeth Crawford's reaction been? The flat, gray front of the building offers nothing.

"No. It really doesn't."

We say goodbye on Baggott Street, and by the time I'm walking home down Morehampton Road, it's quiet and dark, the streetlights creating little shadows under the trees along the sidewalk. My mood has improved from the conversation and the two beers and I'm thinking about what Stephen told me. Now I understand why Padraig Fiero came down so suddenly. As soon as they got the results of the postmortem, he must have jumped to Colin Nugent and the connection with Anton Dorda.

When I call Conor at ten, he says Lilly saw Alex but came home to have dinner with him and seems okay. They took Mr. Bean for a walk but otherwise they've stayed close to home.

"She's fine. I've gotten loads done." He hesitates. "Are you . . . are you okay, Maggie? I'm sorry about our conversation. I'm stressed about Bláithín and it's hard to think of us finally living together and then you, not being here a lot of the time, you know?"

"I know," I say. "I feel the same way. I'm going to check in with my FBI contact, find out some more about that work." I tell him about Stephen Hines's suggestion that I become a private detective.

"I like it," he says. "I'll come and try to hire you. I'll wear a trench coat."

I laugh. "Is that a promise?"

"Yeah." He sighs. "I can't wait to see Adrien tomorrow. Thank you for doing the drive."

"Of course. See ya tomorrow, okay?"

Thirty

Griz is sitting on a bench in the little park down by Rosscliffe's small harbor with Padraig Fiero, eating the cheese and tomato sandwich she bought at Donnelly's, the one shop in the village. The sandwich is soggy and at least a day old, but it's sustenance.

"Yours okay?" she asks Fiero. He's frowning, hunched over his own sandwich, looking miserable.

"It's shite," he says. "But I'm not here for the cuisine."

Griz looks over at him. "Really, because there's a Michelin-starred restaurant thirty kilometers from here." She wants to try to get a laugh out of him. He's respectful and considerate to work with, but he's so serious. She hasn't seen him crack a smile since she met him the day they arrived.

It doesn't work.

"How did you meet Colin Nugent?" Griz asks Fiero.

"He'd been on my radar for a bit," Fiero says, balling up the cling film that had been around the sandwich and stuffing it into the paper bag. "We were pretty sure he was responsible for the drugs trade around Bandon in 2010, 2011. We never managed to get him, but we had a few informants who mentioned his name or implied that he was if not the top of the pyramid, an important layer of it. So I started looking at lower-level offenses, just trying to get a sense of who might be working with him. I didn't get very far. Dorda was either out of the business or very, very careful. Then, in late 2012, Colin Nugent was stopped by gardaí on his way out of Cork City. He had five thousand euros worth of cocaine and heroin and four thousand euros in cash. He was likely going to sell the drugs across West Cork, and combined with a previous charge, he was looking at a significant prison sentence."

"So you recruited him?" Griz says.

"Yeah, I recruited him. He was a useless little shite, never got into the spirit of it, but he got in touch in March of 2013 and said he'd 'heard' that something big was going to happen in May, that they had a boat and they would be bringing it in off Ross Head."

"Did you believe him?"

"Not at first, but then we got some intel from another source and everything lined up in the Caribbean. That's when the lads from Lisbon got involved and I started to trust that he was giving me good intel. We organized Operation Waves and we made the seizure. And then we got into the hold."

"Was that when you knew?"

"Ah, to be fair now, I started to have a bad feeling when we boarded. Those two fellas, the English guys, they seemed like they were playing a part, you know? But then we got in the hold and there were five bales, much less than what all the intel had told us."

"They off-loaded it earlier. Did you ever figure out how?"

"No. But if Lukas Adamik was involved, that might have been motivation for his killing."

Griz finishes for him. "And if he told Zuzanna, it was motivation for hers." Knowing that she was with someone out on Ross Head the night she died has made Griz even more certain that Zuzanna was murdered and that her murder was related to Lukas's.

"What did you think about Nugent?" She can feel his anger, still just as strong four years after the fact. It worries her, makes her wonder if she should trust him.

"I went back to him. He swore that he didn't know, that they put one over on him, too. I fucked up, went to his house. But I was so fucking angry at him." He takes a deep breath. "Three days later he was gone. I thought maybe he'd run. The drugs started to leach out into the community. We saw them there, could feel them coming. There were a bunch of overdoses, kids. Fucking horrible." He shakes his head, some specific memory plucking at him. He's furious. "Then Colin Nugent's body showed up."

"We'll get him," Griz says. "Don't worry. We're going to get him."

"That's his boat," Fiero says suddenly, pointing to the small gathering of sailboats and motorboats beyond the pier. "We need to talk to him. One way or the other."

Griz looks where he's pointing. There are letters on the white hull, crisp and clean, painted in blue: SZCZĘŚCIE. No one's on board and the boat rocks gently on its moorings.

"It means happiness," she says.

Thirty-One

The Sisters of Mercy have a congregation in Cork City, I discover when I search for them online the next morning. I dial the number and when a woman answers, her voice younger sounding than I'd been expecting, I say that I'm trying to track down a sister who worked for a West Cork family in the 1970s. In my imagination, the nun who answers the phone will say, "Oh, Sister Dorothea. Yes, she went to work for a family in 1973 and no one ever heard from her again," but instead she says, "I'm sorry, where are you calling from?"

The temptation to lie and identify myself as a police detective is strong, but when it comes down to it, I'm still a Catholic and I can't bring myself to tell a fib to someone who may be a nun.

"I'm doing some, uh, historical research and I'm trying to locate her. Would it be possible for you to look in your records and—"

"Those records are confidential," she says. "Is this a family member?"

I hesitate. "No, but I was hoping you could just look and tell me if you can find her in your records."

"I'm sorry," the woman says. "I can't help you. That would all be confidential now."

I can't help wondering if it's my accent that sealed the deal.

I get coffee on the walk over to the school. It's a nice day, with a hint of a chill in the air that means the weather's turning, and I find it easy to imagine Lilly walking to school on a crisp autumn morning, her backpack slung over one shoulder, hurrying to get there before the first bell. If they have bells.

St. Theresa's is bucolic, a gated campus with playing fields and gardens only five minutes from Conor's house. There aren't students around, of course, but a glossy brochure showing girls in red tartan skirts and red sweaters over neat white shirts gives me an idea of what it must look like during the school year. A young woman who works in the admissions office takes me around, showing off science labs and bright classrooms and then brings me into the office of the school's principal.

Her name is Barbara Geary and she's younger than I expected, with a blond bob and wearing jeans and sneakers. "It's lovely to meet you, Ms. D'arcy," she says. "We're so pleased to hear that Lilly may be joining us in September."

I must look surprised because she says, "Were you expecting a habit? Americans always expect me to be in a habit. I'm not a sister."

I laugh. "Sorry. I went to Catholic school up until third grade and I think I just assumed. But that was the 1970s."

"Well, the school was founded by Dominican sisters and it's

an important part of our legacy," she says. "But they'll be moving the convent next year and the last sister on the teaching staff will depart in May." She explains the ins and outs of the Irish educational system, telling me that usually Lilly would be coming off her "Transitional Year" during which she would have traveled or done work experience. "It's not a bad time for her to join us," she says. "The girls will all be embarking on their fifth year together." I know some of it from Conor's explanation of Adrien's schooling, but she explains that college-bound Irish high school students use their fifth and sixth years, the last two years of their secondary educations, to prepare for the Leaving Certificate exams, which are used for college admission.

"Lilly's always been a good student," I tell her. "But the last year has been rough. She missed a lot of school last spring and fall, after her father died. She seems to be caught up now though. I've asked her high school on Long Island to send all of her records and test scores. But I don't know how it will all translate."

"Her mental health is the most important thing," Barbara Geary says. "Stability, relationships with her teachers and peers. We'll emphasize all of that for Lilly to make sure she makes a good transition. If she needs more time, she can take more time. And we have an excellent counselor on staff who she can chat to any time she needs it." I can feel my heart rate slowing, a sense of relaxation washing over me. Barbara Geary is better than a Valium. She tells me about the courses Lilly will take, the subjects of the Leaving Cert exams, the opportunities for singing and music at St. Theresa's.

When she's finished, I hesitate and then decide to go for it. "Can I ask you something? I'm trying to figure out my own . . . career prospects here in Ireland. One of the options would have me out of the city during the week. Lilly would be with my partner and his son, who she is close to. What do you think about that? My partner is supportive, but . . ."

She smiles. "I think that it depends so much on the girl, on how much maturity she's attained, on whether she's ready for the independence. It probably depends, too, on your relationship. I've known girls who really thrived on a bit of independence and some who suffered. I'm sorry that's not helpful. Obviously a lot will depend on how she's adjusting to a new city."

"No, that's helpful. I think . . . I have a lot to think about. Anyway, thank you. The school seems wonderful. We're very excited." I'm flustered suddenly.

"You're so welcome."

I'm on my way out the door when I see a framed black-and-white photograph of two rows of nuns in habits. Most of them have serious expressions, but a few have little smiles or smirks, hints of the personalities behind the identical clothes.

I hesitate in the doorway. "That picture. I'm trying to get in touch with a woman who was a young Sister of Mercy in the 1970s. How would I go about finding her? She'd be in her seventies now, I suppose. I've tried the congregation in Cork, but they quite rightly didn't want to just give out confidential information to a random American. I can promise you it's nothing . . . invasive. It's really just making sure she's all right, if that makes sense."

Mrs. Geary smiles. "Knowing your line of work, Ms. D'arcy, I wonder if it isn't a bit more than that. But I have an acquaintance who's a Sister of Mercy. I could ask her. What's the name?"

"Dorothea," I say. "No last name. That's the difficulty. She would have been employed as a governess in West Cork in 1973. I'm just trying to figure out what happened to her after that."

She writes it down. "I'll ask my friend," she says. "It's probably a long shot, but I'll be back to you if she has anything. Please tell Lilly we look forward to meeting her."

I'm picking Adrien up at four, so I decide to take Stephen's advice and stop at the National Gallery to see the Felix Crawford paintings. It's been closed for renovations and has just reopened, so it's busier than it might be otherwise, but I still find pockets of peace and quiet as I wander through the galleries. The Irish painters exhibit is small but contains a good selection of Irish landscape painters, including three canvases by Felix Crawford. Transported back to West Cork, I stand back and take them in. The earliest one is from the forties and shows Ross Head on a sunny day. It's pretty but unremarkable. The second painting, dated 1969, is more interesting, a moody scene of Rosscliffe House and the cliffs at the end of the peninsula from a vantage point I judge to be not far from our cottage. There are dark clouds overhead and the sea is gray and white, churning with energy. The size of the house is exaggerated, I think, its windows like staring eyes. It looks angry and powerful, like it wants to overtake the viewer. But the cliffs are what make an impression. He's painted them in a more abstract style than the rest of the landscape so that they're made up of snakelike dark lines, almost like vines, reaching up from the water. There's something creepy about it, as though the cliffs themselves were reaching up to ensnare passersby.

The final landscape is even more experimental. The card below it makes the point that by 1972, when it was painted, many Irish artists had begun to create more abstract works of art. But when

I look at it, all I can see is the way the cliffs have moved into the foreground of the painting, as though they were moving toward the viewer. The twining black and gray lines that make up the rock face are thicker, ropier, even more disturbing. And the more I stare at it, the more I think that I see faces in the rock, ghostly faces hiding, a woman's figure lurking on the edges.

I pick up Adrien at four. Bláithín doesn't say anything about the engagement, so I choose to leave it alone. "Thank you for driving all the way up to get him, Maggie," she says, uncharacteristically sincere. She hugs Adrien, holding on, and when he says he'll see her in a few weeks, I see a sadness I recognize all too well cross her face. Transitions and handovers are the worst. Adrien doesn't seem to want to talk, so we listen to the radio. By five, we're driving past the exit for Portlaoise when he says, "Did Dad tell you they got engaged in France?"

"He did tell me."

I'm not sure what to say, whether to congratulate him, whether he wants to be congratulated. But he keeps going, answering the question for me. "I'm happy for her, I guess. She seems happy." He glances over at me. "He proposed in front of her whole family. They thought it was cringey, I could tell. But she was delighted."

"You're a good kid," I tell him. "It's hard sometimes, isn't it? This divorce thing."

"Yeah, but it's okay. I just hope that they don't want to live in Paris."

I hesitate, not sure what to say, then settle on, "Well, you know your dad is here for you and he'll help you figure this all out. And you can talk to me any time you want."

"I know," he says. "Thanks, Maggie."

We stop for gas—*petrol, Maggie,* I tell myself—near Thurles, and I text Conor to let him know our ETA. *How's Lilly?* I text and he texts back, *Good, but making me watch a horrible film about cheerleaders! Send help.*

Adrien goes to use the restroom and I'm starting the car up again when my phone rings and I see an unfamiliar number on the screen.

"Mrs. D'arcy?" a male voice asks.

"Yes?"

"This is Bill Daly. I'm a colleague of Stephen Hines's. He said you're interested in Sam Nevin's big development down in West Cork?"

"That's right, thanks for getting in touch."

There's an awkward silence. Finally he says, "Stephen thought you might have something for me."

I smile. Stephen must have gotten him to call me back so quickly by suggesting mysteriously that I had something on Sam Nevin.

"Well, look," I say, watching for Adrien to come out of the petrol station, "I'm down there for the summer and there have been these suspicious deaths. The guards seem to think they're connected to Operation Waves, that big cocaine seizure a few years ago."

"Oh, yeah, I remember." He sounds interested now.

"Sam Nevin owns everything down there and Stephen Hines said you were working on some story about him, about mortgages or something? Was there anything off about the mortgages? Anything that made you think he'd bought the house and land with money he'd gotten in, well, an illegal way? It seems odd, that just after losing so much in the crash, he'd be able to buy up all this property. I guess I . . . wondered."

I can hear traffic behind him, cars revving their engines, horns honking. The city sounds are incongruous with the scene in front of me. Daly says, "Yeah, I had the same thought, though I didn't go to drug trafficking. I was thinking more along the lines of dodgy loans. I was interested in how he was financing it. That was after the banking crisis and the recession and he seemed to be taking on a lot of debt. But it was all on the up-and-up. His father-in-law was some real estate magnate in Toronto and died at the end of 2010 and they inherited a boatload of money. Big bucks. That's what they used to buy up all the properties and to secure the financing."

So it's all aboveboard then. I feel a little disappointed. I don't know what I was thinking. Of course Sam Nevin didn't finance his development with drug money. "So there isn't anything else about the development that seemed suspicious to you?" I ask.

"Well, I didn't say that."

"What do you mean?"

"So you know about the banking crisis here in Ireland, yeah?" I say I know a little. "I've been covering the financial beat, looking for things that don't seem quite right. Everyone wants to avoid another crash and I'm sort of looking out for warning signs, things that seem off."

"Yeah?" Adrien walks out of the petrol station, checking for traffic and I wave to him and point to the phone, mouthing, *I'll just be a minute.*

"Between you and me, there's an investor in that development down there who raises some red flags, if you see what I mean."

"Nevin?" I ask.

Bill Daly hesitates. "Not Nevin. A fella named Lorcan Murphy."

Daly doesn't give me much more than that, just a few vague statements about the development being *overleveraged* or something. I think he's hoping I'll tell him something about Lorcan, but when it becomes clear that I don't know anything about Lorcan's investment portfolio, he makes an excuse to get off the phone pretty quickly.

I'm thoughtful, trying to put the pieces of it all together, and we've been driving for twenty minutes when Adrien, looking out the window as the fields flash by, asks, "How's Lilly doing?" The sun has dropped toward the low hills in the distance, somewhere near Clonmel.

"She's fine. Your dad told you about Zuzanna, the young woman who worked at the pub?" He nods. "It has me a bit worried about her hanging out with Alex so much. It just seems like she's gotten so serious about him so fast, you know? And I don't really know him at all." As I say it, I think about Alex's face when he told me about his conversation with Zuzanna the night she died. Was he withholding something? My instinct tells me yes and suddenly I'm sure that there's more to the story, that he knows more about Lukas and Zuzanna than he's letting on.

Adrien says, "Lilly has pretty good judgment about people, I think. A few times I've noticed that she sees when someone's, well, not worth the time, you know? I don't think she'd like him if he was going to hurt her."

I nod. I'm thinking, *Yeah, but the man she loved most in the world hurt her. What if Brian destroyed her judgment?* "Have I told you how grateful I am that you're in Lilly's life?" I ask him. "I can't thank you enough for being such a good friend to her."

He doesn't say anything, just nods and smiles as he looks out the window again.

The drive feels endless, still another hour and a half once we're past Cork City. The village is quiet as we turn on to the road up to Ross Head at seven thirty. I roll down my window and listen to the sea, smell the sweet saltiness of it as it drifts across my face. Adrien's fallen asleep in the front seat, but he wakes up as we pass Lissa Crawford's cottage. Across the peninsula, Rosscliffe House is a dark blot on the horizon. A word pops into my head, surprising me: *Home.*

Adrien and I get out of the car and stand there for a moment, looking out at the ocean.

"It's nice here," he says. "I missed it when I was gone."

"Your dad is so excited to see you," I say. "You better go in."

After he goes, pulling his suitcase behind him, I stand there for a moment, watching the sea beyond the peninsula. There's a light out there somewhere, a boat, I suppose, though what it's doing out there at night I can't imagine.

There would have been lights out here in May 2013, when Fiero lay in wait and then swooped in on the men transferring bales of cocaine to a rowboat. There must have been some lights, too, when the real shipment was transferred, when whoever was the local connection took the shipment off the boat and brought it ashore.

Did anyone see them? Did anyone know what was going on?

What was everyone on Ross Head doing that night? Only a few of the houses out here would have been finished and it was the óff-season, so none of the holiday houses were occupied, but Lissa Crawford was at home.

Did she see something?

And where was Lukas Adamik that night?

My brain is exhausted from the drive, and though something is there, knocking at the surface of my subconscious, I lock the car, turn my back to the cliffs, and go inside.

Thirty-Two

Griz sits at the big table in the incident room, pushing stacks of paper around, making piles, trying to organize the different threads of the investigation. The Lukas Adamik pile contains printouts of the original report from April that he was missing, the interviews that Ann Tobin had done with all of his known associates.

And now it contains the statement from Alex Sadowski about what Zuzanna said to him the night she died. Griz reads it over carefully; there's not a lot there. Alex said that Zuzanna wasn't making a lot of sense, that she kept asking him what he remembered from the day Lukas died, that she said something about a car and asked a few times about whether he had gone to Lukas's flat, a small studio over Ellen Mahoney's shop.

Ann looks as tired as Griz feels, stopping every once in a while to rub her eyes or get yet another cup of tea from the staff room. Not that she's counting, but Griz wonders how she sleeps with that much caffeine running through her veins.

"Why do you think Alex Sadowski didn't say anything at first?" Griz asks her.

"He said he was upset, in shock, and he wasn't sure it was important. I think he was worried we'd suspect his brother or Zuzanna," Tobin says.

Griz looks up. "Was there a connection between the brother and Zuzanna?"

"They knew each other."

Pointing to the sentence in the statement, Griz asks, "He said that she said something about the flat. Lukas's flat?"

"Yeah. She said something, like, did he remember anything about the day Lukas went missing? She had remembered something about Lukas's flat and she was confused and she needed to talk to someone."

"She went back to the flat. You don't think it was something she found there the day he disappeared, do you?"

"I don't know," Ann says. "She went twice actually. Once that evening of the tenth and then again the next day before she reported him missing. We checked the flat, but there wasn't anything there that would have raised our suspicions. We were looking for his wallet, passport, phone. None of that was there."

Griz looks up. "No passport?"

"No, that seemed strange to me, too." Ann shrugs.

Fiero's been listening and now he gets up and comes over. "Flat's right there, isn't it? Can we look at the CCTV from the street?"

"Well, yeah, we got it when he went missing, to see if we could find him on it, which we couldn't," Ann says. "But just about everyone in the village must have walked by it at some point that evening."

"Including Anton Dorda?"

"The fella haunts the main street like a ghost, so yeah, I'd imagine."

"Why does he do that? Sit in his car like that, watching?"

"Because he's a fucking sociopath," Ann says. Griz studies her face. There's something there. Something personal. She thought she detected it a few times, but now she's sure. "He says he's keeping an eye on his businesses, like. I don't know. Maybe he's stalking someone."

Griz watches her face. Ann is flushed now, her eyes narrowed. "Okay," Griz says finally. "Let's see what we've got."

Fiero and Griz come over and they look at the footage from April tenth. Ann writes down the names of anyone she can identify for sure, along with the time they appeared on the video.

But after an hour, Griz realizes that it's just as she feared. Everyone in Rosscliffe walked by the camera outside Charlie Dunne's real estate and property agents office on the main street at some point on April tenth. There's Gwynedd Williams, there's Barry Mahoney, there's Ellen Mahoney, there's Anton Dorda, there's Charlie Dunne, everyone going back and forth multiple times.

"There's Adamik," Ann tells them. She points to a grainy figure on the computer screen. "On his way to work in the morning." They watch him pass by the camera.

"He didn't come back to the flat," Griz says. "He only walks by the once."

Ann shrugs. "He didn't walk that way, anyway. He could have come back one of four or five ways that wouldn't have required him to walk past that camera. But yeah. That's why we got the coast guard out, that's why we kept searching for days."

Griz thinks, *The flat.* There's something there that's bothering her, knocking at the door. "The passport," she says. "You must have thought he took his passport with him because he was planning on disappearing. But he didn't disappear. So why did he have his passport on the building site?"

Ann considers that. "Maybe he needed it for identification?"

Griz sighs. "This is a waste of our time if everyone in the whole village really did pass by the real estate office. I suppose it will be the same with the reg plates. Every resident of the village must drive by once or twice a day."

"I'll get one of the uniforms to write them down and look them up," Ann says, "but yeah, it's probably going to be a waste of time."

Griz hears something in her voice that makes her ask, "Are you okay?"

Ann seems to sway for a moment, then recovers her balance and says, "Yes, just tired. Sorry. I'm going to get some more tea. Want some?"

Griz shakes her head and watches her go.

Thirty-Three

It's overcast the next morning with a chill in the air that almost makes me turn off my phone alarm and snuggle back up next to Conor for another couple of hours of sleep, but I've been thinking about my swim the other day and I could use some of the exhilaration I felt submerging myself in that cold water.

There's a lone swimmer, far out in the bay and moving fast, when I get to the beach. I stand there for a moment just taking in the sight of the green hills on either side of the little bay, the white cottages settled into the folds and slowly moving sheep that seem to lower my pulse as I watch them. I agree with Adrien: *It's nice here,* and I can't help smiling at the new day. I strip off my sweatshirt and shorts and run across the sand and rocks, splashing and then diving in and striking out for the open water. The cold wakes up my brain and I settle into a nice rhythm, crawl, then breaststroke, then backstroke, until I'm pretty far out.

I think of Zuzanna falling from the cliff. I'm remembering what she said to me about the water, that it was too cold for her, and I feel quite certain suddenly that she wouldn't have gone in on purpose, wouldn't have gotten close enough to fall accidentally. So how did she go in? If Alex was right and it was because she knew something about Lukas's death, then whoever pushed her must have killed Lukas, too.

I stop to catch my breath, treading water. The other swimmer has made a triangle and is now swimming parallel to the shore. Whoever they are, they're fast and skilled and I watch as the small figure stops swimming and then starts for shore.

Something about the profile is familiar and it comes to me in a flash: Ann Tobin. I strike out for land and when I wade up on the beach, breathing hard, she's already toweling her hair. "Hello," I call out. "Nice morning for it."

"It is." She pulls a hoodie and sweatpants on over her suit and takes a bottle of water out of her bag. "But I'm here every morning. Even when it's not so nice."

"I can see why. It's addictive," I say. "I live near the beach at home, but the water's warmer, in the summer, anyway, and then in the winter it's actually frozen. I like it here."

"Where it's Baltic all year long. You should feel it in February. You need a wetsuit to even get in. But I like the way it . . . takes over your brain, you know? You can't worry while your body is screaming at you."

I smile. "That's the attraction for me, too. It clears the cobwebs out. How's it going? How's the investigation?"

She doesn't answer my question, but she says, "Thank you for telling Alex Sadowski to come talk to us."

"Of course. I think I understood why he didn't say anything right away, but I knew how it would look."

"You think he told us everything?" I'm conscious that she's only asking me because we're on a beach in the early morning. She wouldn't ask it if I was sitting in an interview room at the Bantry Garda station.

And I'm conscious of my own honesty, too. "I don't know. There might be something else. He's protective of his brother."

"Yeah. He's a nice lad. I've known him a long time. He was friends with my son. Not close, but . . ."

I hesitate before saying, "Rochelle Nevin told me about your son. I'm so sorry."

She turns away, picking up her damp towel from the rocks, and says, "Thank you."

I don't know what to do. The energy is awkward now and I'm about to make an excuse to leave when she continues, "There were a bunch of overdoses around 2014, teenagers in the village and surrounding towns. Some people think it was the cocaine that came from Operation Waves, the drugs we didn't get." She takes a deep breath. "My only child, my son, my Dáithí, was one of them." She doesn't look at me. "He didn't come home and I went looking for him. We were still finishing up the investigation and some of the detectives from the divisional unit were still around. Everyone went out to help and we . . . we found him out on the peninsula, not far from the Big House. Whoever he was with left him there by himself. The doctors said he had a mild heart defect that made him high risk, but he would have been okay if it hadn't been for the cocaine."

I have nothing to say. All I can do is sit with the pain.

After a minute, she goes on. "You have so much love for your child. When they're gone, you still have it, but you have nowhere to put it. It's huge, tidal, like. Sometimes it feels like you're drowning in it."

"I can't imagine," I whisper, overcome now. "I'm so, so sorry. No wonder you want to get him."

She smiles a small, pained smile. "Yes, well—" Her phone rings from the bag and she bends down to extract it from a tangle of clothes and goggles.

"Sorry," she says. She looks at it, puts it to her ear, and says, "Yeah?" She listens for a minute and says, "On my way." I can tell from her body language that there's been a development.

"Enjoy the morning," she throws back over her shoulder. I watch her climb up the hillside toward the road where she must have left her car and every bone in my body wants to chase after her and force her to tell me.

We have a leisurely breakfast when I get back, a full Irish breakfast made by Conor and served on the patio, and we eat and drink coffee while Adrien and Lilly catch up. I try not to obsess about Ann Tobin's call. At eleven, I find Lissa Crawford in front of her cottage, deadheading the lilies growing along the foundation and tossing the browned blossoms into a pail.

"I'm on my way down to the village," I tell her. "But I wanted to let you know that I talked to Bridget Nevin. She lives in Kildare now, with a man named Rodney Allerton, who was also at the house that summer. It's how they met."

She stares at me, her eyes wide. "Not the same Rodney Allerton, not my Rodney Allerton, my cousin? Ellen never said."

"Yes, the same. They were happy to talk to me and they had an interesting memory about Dorothea." I tell her about Rodney's recollection that Dorothea was a Sister of Mercy. "Does that make any sense to you, that your parents would have hired a governess who was a Catholic nun?"

Lissa laughs. "It does in a way, I suppose. They were quite open-minded about religion. We weren't religious in any way our-selves. I suppose that she may have come cheap, if you see what I mean. They would have liked that. Did they know anything about her?"

"I'm afraid not," I say. "But I've made some inquiries. I'll let you know if anything comes of it."

"Thank you," she says. "It's so interesting. I've been thinking quite a lot about the house lately, you know, remembering it, re-membering the way it was . . ." She smiles, then goes back to the garden.

Thirty-Four

When we tell Lilly and Adrien that we're going for a drive, Adrien nods neutrally and Lilly groans and says, "What, sightseeing? I hate sightseeing. I mean, I'm happy to go somewhere and, like, go to a museum or something, but just driving around, looking out the window? Ugh."

"It'll be fun," I tell her firmly. "I found the place where my nana Nellie was born and we're going to go check it out. I promised Uncle Danny we'd send him a picture of the old homestead, if it's still there."

Lilly presses her lips together and flips her hair. "I think I'll just stay here," she says. I catch a little gleam of interest in her eye. She thinks we'll go off for the day and she can invite Alex over.

"Nope," I say. "You're coming. No arguments." I put a bowl of granola in front of her.

She doesn't say anything, just grumpily eats her cereal and then goes to get dressed.

Conor and Adrien are game, ignoring Lilly's and my bickering and her last-minute attempt to get out of the trip by "remembering" she was going to have a phone catch-up with her friend Zoe back home.

We drive up through the West Cork interior, the sweeping ocean views on the hillsides quickly giving way to the more familiar Irish scenes: green patchwork fields and small houses nestled into the borders between them. We pass through a few tiny villages, but it's much less populated here than it is on the coast.

If it weren't for Google maps, I wouldn't even know that the narrow stretch of dirt road is a townland at all. Shanakeel, it's called, the mysterious name I first heard on the lips of my grandmother Nellie, when she told me about her childhood there. Before we left, I promised Uncle Danny that Lilly and I would go find it, since we're so close. "We'll do the legwork so we can take you there when you come over to visit," I told him. Uncle Danny grinned and rubbed his hands together. "You tell 'em we're coming, okay, Mags? Maybe we'll build a little vacation place there now."

I smile, remembering his face, his certainty that all the Egans and Flahertys would still be here and would come out en masse to meet us.

Fields stretch out on both sides beyond the hedgerow and there's a bit of a view, more fields unfolding in the distance, a small hill dotted with yellow gorse. One newish house interrupts the delineated pasture, but there doesn't seem to be anyone home. We hike out into the center of the field labeled Shanakeel on the map on my phone and stand there for a moment, letting the air wash over us. I take a picture of Lilly, Adrien, and Conor and he takes one of me and Lilly to send to Uncle Danny.

"This is the place," I say. I'm not sure if I feel anything or not. The road is quiet. There are no cars. "I wouldn't exist if it weren't for this place. Lilly, you wouldn't exist if it weren't for this place."

Lilly just looks bored.

"Are you sure?" Adrien asks.

"I can see why your grandmother left anyway," Conor says, looking around.

"Yeah. Funny, I thought there'd be a house at least."

"It may have been pulled down for the stones," Conor says. "Or it may be somewhere under the grass."

"She left Ireland when she was just a teenager," I say, "but she talked about this place all the time. I remember her describing that hill there." I point to the hill, a gentle slope at the back of the field. "It must be that hill, anyway."

"Did her whole family leave?" Lilly asks.

"No, just Nellie and an older brother went to America. They never saw their parents again."

She looks surprised at that. "Really? Why didn't they visit?"

"They didn't have the money. By the time Grandma Nellie and Grampy had the bar and had enough money, her family was mostly gone or I guess she lost touch with them."

"How many siblings were there?" Conor asks. "It wasn't just the two of them, was it?"

"No," I say. "I think there were six or seven. I'll have to ask Uncle Danny. I guess some of them could still be around, right?"

"We should track them down," Lilly says. "We might have relatives right here."

"Do you have your grandmother's birth certificate?" Conor asks me.

"You know, I don't know. I can ask Uncle Danny. Maybe he has it somewhere."

Lilly and Adrien go off to look around for evidence of former houses, and Conor and I walk hand in hand to the edge of the field.

"If you're going to try to get your citizenship through your grandmother, we'll have to find a record of her birth," he says. We've talked about me getting Irish citizenship so I can work here, but apparently it's a years-long process and more complicated than just having an Irish-born grandparent. "I'll see if I can track some of the records down."

"Am I your history project?" I ask, leaning into him.

"Mmmm." He puts an arm around me and kisses the top of my head. His body is a known entity now and I let the familiarity comfort me.

We stand there for another few minutes and then because there's nothing left to see, I take a few more pictures to send to Uncle Danny and we walk back toward the road. We're almost there when Conor says, "Here now, this looks like a foundation. Do you see that?" He's pointing to a couple of large stones set in a line. There are a few more opposite, poking above the dense thatch.

"Was that their house?" Even Lilly's excited now, bending down to explore. There are more of them when she parts the grass, smaller stones tumbled down. My imagination fills in the lines of the foundation, the walls, the roof.

"It may have been," I say. "We need to do some more research and see if we can figure out exactly where they lived. Maybe someone in the nearest village knows."

"Do you want to stop?" Conor asks. "We can ask at the church and look up the family name."

"Not today. We'll come back another time. It's not a long drive. Here, Lilly, take one of those little stones, in case this is it." The stone she finds and hands me is gray and smooth, worn by time and weather. I look around at the fields, the stone walls marking them off, the thick grass and blooming walls of gorse, the shades of green and yellow so specifically of this place that I think you could show me a square inch of a photograph of the scene in front of me and I'd know where I was. I rub the rock, thinking about how it may have been touched by my grandmother, by her grandmother, by people who looked like me. Who looked like Erin. Like Lilly.

"What are you thinking about?" Conor asks me. "You look contemplative all of a sudden."

I smile up at him. "I'm thinking about rocks." His eyebrows ask the question and I explain, "I'm thinking about how rocks hold memories, how we build houses out of rocks, how this house would have held all the history of the people who built it, all the people who collected the rocks. When they built Rosscliffe House, they used rocks that already had a history in them and so maybe they were doomed to fail, those Cromwellian planters and everyone who came after, because they couldn't own the rocks; the rocks already had a life."

"I'm glad I asked. You're right, you know. Stone is history. Even if your grandmother's house isn't here, everything that happened there is in those rocks, this mud, that grass. That's why place matters."

Lilly falls asleep as we drive back down toward the coast and Adrien looks out the window wistfully, full of his own secret thoughts about his life and how it might and might not be changing. Conor is lost in his thoughts, too, listening to the news on the radio.

"You okay?" he asks, feeling my eyes on him.

I nod. The sun is still strong overhead. I can feel it on my face through the glass, though it's started its drop toward the water.

Thirty-Five

Lilly is out of sorts for the rest of the evening. I know Alex is playing a gig in Skibbereen tonight and she seems overly obsessed with her phone, checking to see if he's called, putting her phone down, checking it again. After dinner, we find a stack of playing cards in the kitchen and play a raucous game of hearts that Adrien dominates, Conor ribbing him the whole time. But Lilly keeps checking her phone, and every time I look up at her she seems more and more anxious.

"Do you think there's trouble in paradise?" Conor asks me in bed.

"I don't know. He must have stayed out late and not called her," I whisper.

The rain starts up around midnight and I sleep fitfully, waking every hour or so, thinking I've heard something outside and going to the window. At three, the sound of a car on the road drifts through our window.

It stops outside the cottage.

I sit up, my heart beating, my hand going to the bedside table. But there's no service weapon there and I get out of bed and listen to footsteps out in the kitchen. I fling the door open and find Lilly standing in the hallway, shaking out the leather jacket that Alex must have just taken off. He looks pale, shell-shocked.

"What's going on?" I ask them angrily, my reach for my service weapon still hovering uncomfortably. "Do you know what time it is?"

"Jeez, Mom," Lilly says. "It's just Alex."

"I'm sorry, I know it's late," Alex says.

"Mom, they just took Alex's brother to Bantry for questioning," Lilly says. She hangs the jacket on a hook and takes his hand, leading him over to the couch.

"Did they arrest him, Alex? Has he been charged? What did they tell you?"

"They didn't tell me anything," he says. "I was playing at a pub in Skibbereen and when I got home they were there and they were asking him all these questions, saying did he know what they would find if they looked in the bathroom press and did he know anything about Lukas's death and then one of the guards, he said he was going to open the press. I told Tomasz to say no, but he just . . . stood there, like he was frozen. They opened it and there was a bag of clothes, hidden behind towels and things like that. I don't know where it came from, but they took it out and looked at it and put it in a plastic bag and then they took Tomasz away."

I feel a wave of guilt wash over me. I told Ann Tobin that Alex might be protecting his brother. Is that why they searched the apartment?

Conor comes out of the bedroom and listens as Alex tells him again what happened. "Did you recognize the clothes? Were they Tomasz's?"

Alex looks up at us. He's still processing whatever it is he's about to say. "I . . . I think they were Lukas's," he says slowly. "I recognized a shirt he . . . wore sometimes, and I only saw them quickly, from the other room, but I think they had blood on them."

I meet Conor's eyes. If Tomasz had the clothes Lukas Adamik was wearing when he was killed, that's a pretty damning piece of evidence.

Lilly pleads with me, "We have to help him get a lawyer for Tomasz. You can find out what's going on from Griz, right? You can help?"

She looks so little, sitting there in her pink pajamas next to the boy she loves. I nod, already getting my phone out of my pocket and dialing Griz's number. It goes straight to voice mail.

"Were Tomasz and Lukas friends? Did they ever have a fight about anything? It's important to know if there's any way Tomasz could have been involved in his death, Alex, by accident or just being in the wrong place at the wrong time."

He takes a long sip of the hot tea Conor brings him. "They were . . . not friends exactly. Tomasz was the boss. But Lukas liked him, I think." He sounds uncertain.

"Around the time that Lukas went missing, do you remember how Tomasz seemed? Was he upset? Worried?"

"No . . . Well, he was worried. I know he went to Lukas's flat to help Zuzanna look for him. Because she was worried, and Lukas worked for him. So Tomasz wanted to find him. They needed him on the site."

"Where was Tomasz that day? Was he at the other building site?"

He shakes his head. "I think he had to drive to Cork for supplies.

He took one of the trucks and he was gone all day. When he got back at night, that's when Zuzanna said Lukas wasn't answering his phone."

"Alex, is there anything you're not telling me? Is there anything that could help us find out the truth?" *Even if the truth is that Tomasz killed Lukas and Zuzanna.*

His face is so smooth in the light streaming in from the kitchen. He looks young, angelic. I want to pat him on the shoulder and assure him that everything will be okay.

He meets my eyes, then looks away. "One time, I came home early when I was supposed to be at a gig and Agnieska was there and . . . she said Tomasz gave her the key so she could sleep. It was loud at the bed-and-breakfast over the pub. She was embarrassed though and I thought maybe, well . . . The way Tomasz looked at her sometimes, I think they were more than friends."

"But why wouldn't Tomasz and Agnieska want you to know?" I ask.

"Because of Mr. Dorda. I think Agnieska used to be his girl-friend." He shrugs. "But I don't know for sure. I saw them together sometimes."

"Is Tomasz afraid of Mr. Dorda?"

"He . . . Mr. Dorda helped us when we first came here. He gave Tomasz work to do. He helps out the Poles in Rosscliffe and Tomasz didn't want to . . . make him mad." He looks away once more. There's something there he doesn't want to say.

"Did Tomasz ever help Mr. Dorda with anything other than construction work, building work? Did he ever do anything illegal?"

He speaks too quickly. "No. Tomasz wouldn't do that."

But what if there was no other way to support you? I want to ask. Suddenly I'm tired and sad. I need to talk to Griz later, need to find out what they have on Tomasz.

I stand up and pat his shoulder. "Alex, why don't you stay the night and we'll see who we can reach in the morning," I tell him. He nods, looking confused and shaken, and I make up a bed for him on the couch. "Get some sleep," I say. "It will all look better in the morning."

In bed, I snuggle up against Conor's back and we roll over so that his arms are around me, encircling me.

"I don't know what to do, Conor," I whisper. "What if Tomasz had something to do with all of this? What if he's guilty? Alex wants our help. He wants Lilly's help."

I feel him brush my hair with his lips. He holds me tighter. "We help him," he whispers. "We help him because he's a kid and he's all alone and because it's the right thing to do, even if Tomasz is guilty." His low voice in my ear makes me turn, slowly, and press myself into him, looking for comfort, looking for him. What I really want to ask is *What will happen to us?* But I don't and our bodies find each other as the ocean rushes at the cliffs outside.

I sleep for a bit, but wake again as the sky is just beginning to lighten in the east. I finally give up and tiptoe into the kitchen to make coffee, trying not to wake Alex.

The coffee is almost done when I hear footsteps behind me and whirl around to find Alex standing there, a blanket draped around his shoulders.

"Sorry, I didn't mean to scare you. I couldn't sleep," he says. "I'm too worried."

"It's okay," I say. "I couldn't sleep either. Want some coffee and toast?"

"Sure." He wraps the blanket around himself and goes to the door, opening it and looking outside at the sunrise, barely discernible through the fog.

"Try not to worry," I tell him. "I'll see what I can find out from my friends and we'll help you find a lawyer, or solicitor, for Tomasz."

He takes the coffee from me when it's done and takes a long sip. "Thank you," he says. "I shouldn't have come here, but I didn't know what else to do. I'm sorry."

"No, Alex. I'm glad you came."

"I want you to know that I would never put Lilly in danger," he says earnestly. "I would never let anything happen to her. I care about her." He puts up a hand. "I know how that sounds. We haven't known each other very long. But I do, I . . . I care for her." He looks up at me and I feel a surge of genuine affection for him. He's so open. So vulnerable.

I feel my whole body resisting it. *You're seventeen,* I want to yell at him. *You have no idea what caring for someone means. That girl asleep in the other room watched as her father said goodbye to her and then ran into the ocean and drowned himself. She stood on the beach for twenty whole minutes before they got her back to the house. She watched as I dragged him out and tried to make him breathe again and pounded on his chest for what he did to my family. You have no idea how much I love her.*

But instead I say, "I know you do. She cares for you, too, Alex. The two of you, you've had so much loss for people your age. It hardly seems fair." We both sit there for a few minutes, drinking our coffee. Finally, I ask, "How old were you when your parents died?"

He shrugs. His face is like white marble in the light coming in from the kitchen. "My father when I was five. He had liver cancer, did not know until it was too late. To be honest, I barely knew him. But my . . . my mother, I was almost eight. She and I were close. Tomasz was already out of the house. He was eighteen and he lived with his father in Gdansk—he had a different father—I didn't really know him very well. My mother was crossing the street on her way to work and a bus . . . hit her. The driver was tired. They said he fell asleep. I was at school and the teacher took me home with her. No one said why. They waited until Tomasz came to tell me my mother was gone." He looks up from his tea and meets my eyes. "He was already planning to come to Ireland. This was just before the crash, when construction was everywhere. There was a lot of money. He didn't have to bring me, but he did. At first we were in Dublin, but then Tomasz heard about a job in Bantry, and he started working for Mr. Nevin when that job ended. Someone told him we could live in one of Mrs. Crawford's cottages in exchange for him working on it for her. He fixed it on the weekends and I helped, too. Mrs. Crawford let me stay at her cottage after school, so I wouldn't be alone. She is . . ." His voice breaks and I put a hand on his shoulder. "She helped me so much." Something crosses his face and then he says, "I think she sold Rosscliffe House to Sam Nevin because she wanted to give the money to me. I think she thought something was going to happen to Tomasz, that he was going to be arrested."

"What? When was this?" Suddenly I remember her words to me. *I needed the money or . . . thought I did and I believed him.*

Alex starts to speak, stops, and then says, "Around the time the guards caught the men on the boat with drugs. Four years ago."

"Do you think Tomasz was involved, Alex? It's very important that anyone who's trying to help him—and you—knows the truth."

He puts his head in his hands and I think maybe he's trying not to cry. He says, "I don't know. I was only thirteen then. He came home one day and he told me that if anything happened to him, if he disappeared or he was arrested, that I should go to Mrs. Crawford's cottage. He said that she knew, too, and she would take care of me. But he never told me what he thought was going to happen. A few months later he said everything was okay and I didn't need to worry. But since Lukas was found he has seemed . . . worried again. After they took him, I tried to find Agnieska to see if she knew anything, but she didn't respond to my text. Then I went to Mrs. Crawford's cottage to see if she knew what was going on, but she wasn't there either. I didn't know what else to do."

I start to stand up, to go make the toast, then turn back to him. "This morning, just before you got here, she wasn't there?"

"I knocked on the door. The lights were on, but she wasn't there. Her car was gone." Now he looks worried. "Do you think she's okay? I didn't even think! I'm so stupid! I'll go check on her right now." He jumps up and goes into the den to put a sweatshirt on over his T-shirt and jeans.

"I'll come with you," I say. "It's starting to get light now, but let me go find a flashlight or what do you call it, a torch?"

I find one in the drawer next to the sink and we slip out into the early morning. A light rain is falling now and we walk quickly down the road to her cottage. Her car's not in the drive, but the lights are on in the kitchen and the living room, and when we try the front door, it's open. "Lissa?" I call out. "Are you here?"

Silence.

"Do you know where her bedroom is?" I ask him. He nods and disappears into the back of the cottage. When he comes out a few minutes later, he shakes his head. "There's no one here."

The kitchen table is covered with more of the watercolor drawings. She seems to have drawn each of the rooms in the house. I recognize a few of them from my exploration the day I found Agnieska's earring.

There's a glass of paint-muddy water on the table and I touch the paintbrush sitting on top of the open pan of paints. It's still just a little damp. She must have been working on them yesterday. I leaf through them, finding quick watercolors of the entryway, the kitchen, and then the landing, the gardens, and the castle ruins; she was painting her memories.

I look up from the artwork. "I'm going to just walk down toward Rosscliffe House and see if her car's there," I tell Alex. "Just to make sure. Go back to the cottage and wake up Conor. I don't have my phone, but I'll see if she's down there and let you know."

He nods. "You sure you don't want me to come with you?"

"Yeah. It's light now. I'll be fine. Okay?" We close the door behind us and he nods and sets off across the road. I start walking toward the looming shape of Rosscliffe House, the sun still sunk below the horizon, the sky starting to color a little over the ocean.

Thirty-Six

....

I see Lissa Crawford's car as soon as I get out onto the headlands. It's pulled up next to the front entrance, as though it had been hurriedly parked, one door slightly open and the keys still in the ignition. The house seems very still, the ruins of the castle surrounded by a thick mist in the early morning cool.

Around the back of the house, the window is still open, propped open now with a long stick. Inside, I call her name but don't get any answer. Someone has been here though; I can see new muddy footprints crisscrossing the foyer. I wouldn't want to be here at night, but somehow the early morning light takes away some of the gloom I remember from my last visit.

I call her name again, but there's no answer, and I can feel alarm starting in my stomach. Something's very wrong here. I should really take her car and go back up to the cottage to call the guards, but I'm worried she's hurt somewhere in the house. I keep calling her name and walk quickly through the first-floor rooms, past the covered furniture and peeling wallpaper. The sitting room contains stacks of stretched canvases and dried-up paints on a desk, a room with a long dining table is lined with shelves containing a few old books, warped by moisture, their pages crumbling, and little porcelain curios and a few pieces of silver tarnished black. The empty spaces on the shelves make me think some of the teenagers who have broken in over the years have helped themselves to the more valuable items.

"Lissa? Are you upstairs?" I slowly climb the stairs to the second floor. I check each of the doors, but they look the way they did the other day; I don't think anyone's been in them. Standing there, I now imagine Bridget Nevin, sweeping these floors, scrubbing the bathtub and toilets, trying, against all odds, to bring some order to the chaos.

I go back out into the hallway and find the staircase up to the third floor. I try to imagine Lissa Crawford as a little girl, scared and confused, wandering up the stairs. Halfway up, I look to the right and, sure enough, there's a small compartment there, a sort of wooden pocket on the paneling. It must have been used by the servants to stash cleaning supplies or things they needed to hand but didn't want to leave out. It's empty now.

I keep going.

And that's when I feel it, the distinct chill in the air I felt the last time, but something more than that even, a sense of *gloom* that only increases as I climb, and when I reach the top, it's all I can do not to turn around and run out of the house as fast as I can. I gather all my courage to push open the first door I see. It's simple, with a metal bedstand and a dark blanket hanging over the top, a thick layer of dust everywhere, rodent droppings along the baseboards. The room is unadorned. *Servants' quarters,* I think. The next one I open is the same.

When I push open the last door, though, it's a different story. Someone has swept and cleaned in here and the rusty brass four-poster bed in the center has been made up recently with clean linens.

A half-full bottle of water sits on the floor next to the bed. An incense holder filled with ash sits next to a box of matches on the bedside table.

Someone's been using the house as a hideout—or a love nest.

Back downstairs, I call Lissa's name again, but there's no one in the house. It's silent and frigid. I can't wait to get outside again.

The sun is up now, golden light reflected in the clouds over the water.

Lissa's car is still there, solitary, somehow ominous, the driver's-side door open. I don't want to touch it, in case there are fingerprints; it's clear to me that something's happened to her, and as soon as I get back to the cottage I need to call the guards and start the search for her. A sinking feeling comes over me as I glance in the direction of the cliffs.

Another one.

What's going on here?

The peninsula glows green and brown and yellow, white sparks of rock here and there. The ruins of the old castle seem softer in the light somehow and I'm remembering what Rodney Allerton told me about the boys in residence at Rosscliffe House in 1973 hiding and running in the castle ruins.

An idea is starting to form and before it's really taken shape, I'm running into the gardens, toward the rows of stones and the old structures. *It was on the site of an old castle, you know, and there were towers and root cellars and things. Good places to hide, out in the gardens.*

Lissa's paintings of the gardens and the ruins.

Root cellars. The most intact part of the ruins is a rectangular structure with low, tumbling walls incorporated into the garden design and surrounded by what must have once been neatly laid out garden beds. Now tall grasses fill the beds, hedges overtaking the flowers and vegetable plots.

I walk carefully through the space, looking for stairs or an entrance, then turn to the rest of the ruins.

The other structures in the garden are less discernible; there's one round pile of stones that might once have been a tower or a keep, and a few smaller rectangular structures, but I don't see anything that could be the entrance to a cellar.

"Lissa," I call out. "Are you out here?" I'm imagining her looking for . . . something, remembering something, retracing the steps she took so many times as a child. Perhaps the solution to her mystery lies out here, in the ruins of those earlier inhabitants of Ross Head.

I'm about to give up when a pile of stones closer to the road catches my attention. There's something studied about the way the stones have been arranged in a low wall, and when I examine it further, I see why it stands out. The stones are paler in color, newer. They've been moved here.

And next to them, nearly completely obscured by a tangle of hedge, is a bulkhead door opening into the ground.

"Lissa," I call out. With effort, I lift the door, which groans and creaks on hinges pulling away from rotting wood. But when I have it up, I see a shallow set of well-maintained stairs. The opening to the cellar seems to be carved into the bedrock, curving away from the house toward the water, and when I shine my flashlight into it, I catch a gleam of white along a passageway. This must be an old root cellar associated with the castle or with the original Crawfords. It makes sense. Produce from the gardens would have been easily put up here after the harvest. I call out again. There's no answer, but I just want to make sure she's not there, so I use the sloping entrance, ducking my head under the low ceiling of what turns out to be a corridor, lined with plywood. There's a padlocked door at the end. I shine the light around the entrance and the plastic lining carefully water- and weather-proofing the interior and suddenly I know that someone has been in here much more recently than 1973.

I turn off my light and start climbing back out again. I've got to get back to the cottage to call the guards and tell them what I've found. My mind is occupied by next steps: tell Conor, call Griz, take the car to look for her farther out on the peninsula.

But suddenly a man appears before me and I go into self-defense mode, shouting at him to back off. My heart is pounding, my whole body on alert. I raise my hands to defend myself and charge at him.

It's Padraig Fiero.

"What are you doing here?" he yells at me, and we're both moving too fast to prevent the collision. He slams into me and I step back and falter, tripping on the uneven ground, and fall hard on my knee, pain flashing through it.

I clutch my knee and look up at him. "There's a hiding place down there." I gasp. "Someone's fixed it up recently. I don't think there's anyone there now, but I think this might be what you've been looking for. This might be where they kept the bodies and the drugs. And I think something's happened to Lissa Crawford."

Thirty-Seven

They get there quickly, Griz first and then Ann Tobin and car after car of techs and uniforms. I sit in the back seat of Fiero's car with my leg sticking out through the door so they can look me over, and watch as uniformed guards and techs swarm the house and the grounds. I tell them about the room upstairs and they say they'll see if they can figure out who's been using it, though I think I know: Agnieska and Tomasz.

But what they have to do with the rest of it, I haven't figured out yet.

I didn't fracture my kneecap, but it hurts like hell and the nice young guy who bandages it up for me says I'm going to have a bruise in the morning and should stay off it as much as I can for the next few days.

Once they know I'm okay, Fiero comes over and says, "What made you go into the house, Mrs. D'arcy? I don't have to tell you that you were trespassing on private property." He looks angry, his eyes narrowed, the veins bulging on his right temple.

I tell my story, explaining about going to Lissa's cottage, seeing the watercolors, and realizing that she might have wanted to go down to the house and refresh her memory about the details herself. "She may have been painting," I say. "She probably just meant to have a quick look around. But something happened to her. Do you think she's in the water?"

"We don't know," Griz tells me. "The coast guard has been deployed and they'll look carefully. But something is very, very wrong here. If she found the cellar, it's possible that she surprised whoever has been using it. Don't worry, Maggie. We'll do our best to find her."

"Why did you come down here?" I ask Fiero. "Did you see Lissa's car?"

Fiero looks at Griz. "I was distracted when you told me about finding Agnieska's earring," she says. "I didn't really take in what it meant. But I was thinking about her last night and I started to be pretty sure she was hiding something. Then I remembered what you said. I went to talk to her, but she didn't come back to her room at the pub last night, and after waiting for a few hours, I started to worry. I rang Fiero early this morning and told him it might be worth checking out the house and grounds, since that's where you found the earring. I was meeting him here."

Fiero points to the flashlight still clutched in my hand. "I saw your light," he says. "I wasn't ready for you to scream at me though."

"Do you think she had something to do with it?" I ask them. "Agnieska?"

Griz sighs. "We just don't know. But if she did, I'm starting to be very worried about her. Come on, you look exhausted. Let me drive you home."

She tells me they're launching a full-scale search for Lissa and Agnieska and helps me into her car. My knee is throbbing now. She drives slowly back up toward the cottage, parking in front and leaving the car running. "You should go rest," she says. "You must be in pain." She leans back against the seat and I can see how tired she is. But it's not just the lack of sleep and the hard work of this case.

"What's going on with you, Griz?" I ask her. "Yeah, this case is tough. I know you're not going to tell me anything about what you all are looking at. Yeah, you're tired. But it's something more than that. I know you pretty well now." She sighs again, deflated. I say, "Come on, Griz. What happened? Did you and Peter Mooney get together and it all went wrong?" I'm teasing her—Peter Mooney is a Garda detective we met on a case and he had an obvious crush on Griz—but the look on her face tells me to stop.

"Okay," she says finally. "But you can't tell Roly. I need to handle it on my own. I don't want anyone knowing, okay?"

"I won't say a word."

She closes her eyes for a moment, letting the cool wind coming off the water wash across her face through the open window and then she says, "Back in the winter, just before Christmas, I went home with a fella, a detective on one of the other specialty squads. You know the story. We'd been flirting for a while, had a great night out at the pub, one thing led to another. We had fun, but he was a bit intense for my taste. Like, he started talking about all the things we were going to do together. He sent me flowers the next day. I went out with him again because he seemed so enthusiastic, but he was . . . There was something off and I stopped returning his texts and calls after that. That was stupid. I keep wondering what would have happened if I'd just told him right then that I wasn't interested."

"What did he do?" I ask.

She sighs and tucks a piece of hair behind her right ear. "He started coming by as I was getting off duty, waiting outside for me. I told him I was busy, couldn't go for a drink, but he didn't like that. He started creating scenes, saying loudly that I'd led him on and I couldn't just ignore him."

"Oh, Griz. Did anyone else on the team hear?"

"One of the lads did. He asked if I needed help, but I didn't want him to think I couldn't handle it. Roly still doesn't know. When you were here in February, it had just started. It went on for a while and finally I told him that if he didn't leave me alone, I'd report him. He knew there were cameras, so he stopped coming by work."

She doesn't even need to say it. "He started coming by your flat?" I ask.

"Well, not exactly. I saw him a few times outside on the street; he clearly was following me, but he knew where the CCTV was and he never got close enough to be caught. I'd see him at a pub where I was meeting someone or the place where I get coffee. That kind of thing."

"What happened?"

"Nothing, that's the thing. He hasn't approached me, hasn't actually done anything. So there's nothing I can do. It was kind of a relief coming down here, honestly. But I know when I go back that he'll be waiting, somewhere."

"Oh, Griz." I start to tell her that she needs to tell Roly, that she needs to tell someone. But I know what this guy is doing. He's riding a line here. There's nothing anyone can do. Griz is stuck. If she tells Roly or her detective inspector, they're not going to find anything on the guy. And they're going to think less of her after that, imagine her going home with a guy she just met. They just are. "You feel like you can keep yourself safe?"

"I guess," she says. "Yeah, of course. But having to *think* about it all the time is doing my head in, you know?"

"Yeah." We just sit there for a bit, watching the view. "What's his name?" I ask finally.

"You going to beat him up for me?"

"No. But I'm not an active guard. I can look up a few things maybe."

"Oh, come on, Maggie."

"What's his name?"

"I'm not going to tell you. You'll go beat him up." Griz smiles.

"Well, he sounds like an asshole," I say, smiling back. "He sounds like he might deserve it."

"It helps to talk about it," she says. "Thanks. It's stopped me doing things, you know? Because I'm worried he'll show up. Peter was in town a few weeks ago and asked if I wanted to go for a meal. I might have said yes, but I knew if I did this fella would turn up and I just didn't want the hassle. So I told him I was working."

"Oh, Griz." I lean across the gearshift and give her a hug, feeling the sharp points of her shoulder blades. She feels like she's melting away.

"Thanks," she says. "I meant what I said. It helps to talk about it. A thing like this, it makes you . . . question your own judgment. I blamed myself for a while, but I'm not fucking doing that anymore." She looks out toward the end of the peninsula. "Anyway, we need to find Lissa Crawford and Agnieska Tarnowski."

"Alex is inside," I tell her. "I don't know what to tell him. Do you think Tomasz knows what happened to them? Do you think he really had anything to do with Lukas's death?"

"I don't know, Maggie. We'll be questioning him today." She hesitates. "It doesn't look good."

"Because of the clothes?"

She smiles and I can see a glimmer of the Griz I know, sarcastic, full of energy. "I'm not telling you. You go rest now."

Inside, I let Conor fuss over me a bit and I'm on my way to take a shower when my phone rings with an unfamiliar number and the person on the other end says, "Ms. D'arcy?"

"Yes? This is Maggie D'arcy."

"You won't know me, but Barbara Geary from St. Theresa's in Dublin has been in touch with a former colleague of mine. She said you might want to talk to me."

"I'm sorry, what's your name?" My brain is sluggish and I realize who she must be just as she says the words.

"My name is Dorothea Reynolds and I think you've been looking for me."

Thirty-Eight

Dorothea Reynolds tells me she'll be sixty-nine next month and that she lives in Clonakilty. When I explain that I'm looking for some information about the summer of 1973, when she was working in a house in Rosscliffe, there's a long silence before she says, "I wondered if that would ever come up, you know, if she would ever come to ask me about it. And here you are. Did you say you're a guard?"

"No, I . . . I was a police officer in the States, but I'm living in Rosscliffe and I've gotten to know Lissa a bit and that's why I'm asking."

That seems to satisfy her. "I don't think I want to tell you over the phone though," she says. "Might you be able to meet me for a coffee? I don't drive anymore, but if you can come to Clonakilty, I'll meet you."

I hesitate, then say, "There's quite a bit going on here at the moment. I don't know when I'll be able to get away. Are you sure you couldn't just give me the outline over the phone and then I could come see you in a few days."

She's firm. "Quite sure. I don't like the telephone. You lose so much."

"Well, okay. What about later today then? Late afternoon? I could drive over."

She sounds pleased and we set a time for me to meet her.

When I tell Conor what I want to do, he protests, saying he needs to come, too, that I shouldn't be driving with my knee. But I tell him I want him to stay here to keep an eye on Lilly and Alex. Alex has been trying to get some information about whether Tomasz is being held or charged, and he says he's going to go to Bantry to find out what's going on. "If they go, I want you to go with them," I tell him. "I need to find out what this woman has to tell me, but I don't want Lilly off alone with Alex until we know more. Ring me if there's anything on Lissa or Agnieska."

By afternoon a giant bank of clouds has settled in over the peninsula. When I open the front door, I can't see the cliffs, can't see beyond the rooflines of Rosscliffe House.

My knee behaves and I make it to Dorothea Reynolds's flat by three. I call her number and she comes down to meet me on the street, carefully stepping through what are now large puddles and holding an umbrella over her head. She's tall, her dark hair steel gray now and cut in a short bob. She points to a parking spot, and when I've pulled into it, we walk down to a little café at the end of her street. She waits until we're seated, with sandwiches and coffees in front of us, to start talking.

She's been retired for five years now, she tells me, after a long career as a psychiatric nurse. I explain a little bit about how I got interested in Rosscliffe House and what happened there in 1973 and she nods along and then says, "I read a story about Lissa Crawford a few years ago. About her work. I thought about going over and visiting her, but I wasn't sure she'd want to, well, go back there, if you see what I mean."

"Were you friends with the family?" I ask. "How did you come to be living with them?"

She looks surprised. "No, I had just finished nursing school and one of the sisters told me there had been an inquiry. A wealthy family in West Cork needed a private nurse. I assumed it was for someone with cancer, a debilitating illness, that sort of thing. But the sister told me that this was slightly different. It was for a poor man who was disturbed—that's the word she used, can you imagine?—and his family wanted someone to keep an eye on him, but that he couldn't *know* I'd been hired to keep an eye on him. That he wouldn't like it, wouldn't accept it. So I needed to pretend I was just there as a . . . well, as a governess for the children, but actually it would be for him." She looks up at me and smiles a mischievous smile. "I always had a bit of an interest in spy films, thrillers, that sort of thing. It appealed to me, more than working on a hospital ward, I suppose. I was twenty-five. And the way the sister made it sound was that I'd be living in a mansion and I'd have a glamorous sort of summer before going back to Dublin and getting a nursing job."

"And it wasn't like that?"

"No!" She laughs. "It wasn't like that at all. The house was big, that was true, but it was freezing cold, even on a hot day, and it was in terrible disrepair. Peeling wallpaper and damp everywhere and not enough food to go around. There was a woman from the village who did the cooking and she did her best to stretch it, but they had no money. I knew my wages were coming out of the food budget, but she—Mrs. Crawford, I mean—was desperate. She couldn't manage him anymore."

I wait to see if she's going to explain. She seems to be thinking about how to explain it. "He needed . . . he needed to be in a hospital," she says finally. "It was so sad. He could have been medicated, he could have been helped. But there was so much we didn't know. At one point, she said to me, 'You know, his father was mad, too. I didn't realize when I married him.' And she was embarrassed. They were still trying to pretend, for their friends. He didn't like to be alone, so she thought a nurse . . ."

"What did your job entail?" I ask her.

"Babysitting, essentially. I sat with him while he painted, to make sure he didn't start getting maudlin, and I watched him to make sure he didn't throw himself off the cliffs. It was too much. I'm tall and I was strong as a young woman, but . . . as the summer went on, I could see that he was getting worse. One morning, I found him out on the cliffs, looking down at the water. I started chatting to him, redirected him. You could sometimes do that. I told Mrs. Crawford that she needed to keep him locked in at night. Then he lashed out, accused me of all kinds of terrible things, ranting about poor Elizabeth and how she was disloyal. I was . . . scared. He was much stronger than I was and it occurred to me suddenly that he could hurt me. I told Mrs. Crawford that I couldn't do it anymore, that he was worse." She looks up at me. I can see the trauma still there all these years later.

"The next day we couldn't find him. I checked the cliffs. I didn't see him. I searched everywhere. He was nowhere to be found. Some friends of theirs were staying, the Allertons. And I found Mr. Allerton and said I couldn't find Mr. Crawford and he went to look. He found him, but . . ." She looks up at me. "Everything was in disarray that day. Mrs. Crawford came and told me that she was facing facts, she couldn't care for him, and she asked me to go to Dublin and find doctors for him, set everything up so that when they got to the city, everything would be ready. She was crying, saying she didn't know how she'd pay for it, but I packed a few things and they took me to the train that night."

"Lissa Crawford thought something happened to you," I say. "Because you disappeared. Wasn't Mrs. Crawford worried about what he would do?"

"There was a man who did the gardening, Mr. Mahoney, and she said he and Mr. Allerton would help her make sure nothing went wrong until they could leave." She sighs. "I did everything she asked. The house in Dublin was ready and I'd found someone who was willing to treat him."

"But then he died."

"Yes, Mrs. Crawford and the children had already left Rosscliffe House. They got to Dublin and then we got the call that something had happened, that he'd thrown himself from the cliffs. They called it an accident, of course. That was what you did. His father died in the same way. He told me that once, when he was talking about the cliffs. He used to talk about a woman who would appear to him out on Ross Head. He said she appeared to his father, too. I never knew if she was real or a figment of his imagination."

"Lissa found a cloth stained with blood on it," I say. "Do you remember that? Do you know what that might have been?"

She looks genuinely shocked. "Blood . . . No. They . . . they said that he ran in the night and tried to throw himself off the cliffs, but maybe . . . it happened differently." She looks uncertain now. "You don't think . . . How awful. I suppose Mr. Allerton is long dead. I wonder if Mr. Mahoney is still around. He was a young man then. His father had worked for the Crawfords for many years, fixing things, helping around the gardens. I liked him. He was kind. He taught me about flowers and birds, country things I wasn't used to."

"He still lives in the village," I say. "I'll try to speak with him."

She shakes her head. "It was the shame, you know. I wish they could have been open about it, could have talked about it. I went into psychiatric nursing because of that experience, so I guess something good came out of it."

"I'm grateful to you for telling me the story," I say. The café is getting busier. She's tired now. She takes her purse from the back of the chair and pats her hair into place.

"When I heard about the deaths, I wondered, you know. There's something about that place, about the cliffs. I don't believe places are haunted." She hesitates and I wonder suddenly if there's something she's not telling me. "But I do believe that secrets and shame, well, they end up being nearly the same thing, don't they? They infect a place, get into the very stone of it."

Thirty-Nine

Griz and Fiero let Tomasz Sadowski stew a few minutes before they go into the interview room.

He looks up. "Is Agnieska okay?" he asks desperately.

They don't answer. They can use his panic to their advantage.

"You remember me from the last time I was down here, don't you, Tomasz?" Fiero says finally, his voice low and serious. Tomasz nods. He looks terrible, every second of the sleepless night etched on his face, the scar red and angry against the paleness of his skin. "You said then that you didn't know who was working with the British men who were arrested on the boat, that you knew absolutely nothing about the cocaine, how it got there, how it was supposed to be transported once it was loaded off the yacht."

"I didn't," Tomasz says, almost in a whisper. He and his brother are good-looking men, blond and thin, muscular and high-cheekboned and Slavic in a way that still seems a bit exotic in Ireland. Tomasz is harder than his brother, though, with the scar on his forehead and something in his eyes that says his life hasn't been easy.

Fiero starts in and Griz tries to paste a sympathetic smile on her face, her best good cop attitude. "Look, Tomasz. We know most of it already. Anton Dorda was behind it. He arranged for someone in the village to get the bales off the boat the day before. Then they stored them in the cellar of the ruins at Rosscliffe House. Was it you?"

"No."

Fiero studies him. "Come on, Tomasz. We know you were involved. If you provide information about Dorda's operation, we can help you. We can help Agnieska."

He shakes his head. "Can you just tell me if she is okay?" he asks.

Griz sighs. "We don't know. She and Lissa Crawford are missing. Do you know where they could be, Tomasz? If you know where they are and you help us find them safely, this could all go much better for you."

She feels something uncertain snake through her veins when she sees his face, the genuine surprise in his eyes. The fear. He doesn't know where they are.

He looks up at them helplessly. The room is cold. Griz can see that his hands, splayed on the table, are pale and bluish. She can smell his breath. She feels so tired suddenly that she thinks she might collapse.

"I want a solicitor," Tomasz says very quietly. "I want a solicitor and I want you to promise to keep Agnieska out of it and then I'll tell you."

Forty

I drive back toward Rosscliffe, thinking about Dorothea's story. What happened after she left for Dublin that night? What did all the people in the house do next? I'm remembering Lissa's suspicions about her mother and Matt Mahoney, then remember I can't ask her. Panic washes over me. Where are she and Agnieska?

Traffic is bad on the N71 and I call Conor just as I'm passing Skibbereen. His voice is constrained, too formal, and when I ask him if he's okay, he says loudly, "Hang on, I'll just go in the other room," and a few seconds later he says, "Sorry, Grace is here. She and Lorcan have had a huge row and she's going to leave him."

"Really? What happened?"

He lowers his voice so that I can barely hear it. "He's had affairs before," he says. "I knew about one of them with a woman in Dublin. Bastard. But she's just found out he's sleeping with someone in Rosscliffe. I guess he's been coming down alone to manage the development. It was the last straw for her."

"Who?" I'm trying to think of who it could be.

"Danielle Donnelly," Conor whispers. "At the shop."

"What?"

"That's right. Grace is furious. I don't know quite what to do with her."

"Good luck. Are Alex and Lilly there?"

"Lilly is. Alex was able to talk to Tomasz's solicitor and then he was going back to their flat to get some clothes."

"Okay, I'll be back in a bit. I just need to talk to Matt Mahoney."

Ellen and Barry's house is a white bungalow on a large plot of land, with a little iron gate at the end of the drive, cheerful yellow shutters, and a yellow door. Everything looks new and clean and I wonder if they built the house after Barry started running the pub. Another example of how Sam's largesse in the village improved someone's life.

I knock on the door, but the house looks unoccupied, no cars in the drive. Ellen is probably still at the store and I'm sure Barry is at the pub.

There's another bungalow across from the drive, though, and the worn path tells me there's a connection between Barry and Ellen's house and this one.

When I knock at the door, I hear a shouted greeting and the blare of the television. It takes Matt Mahoney a few minutes to get there and when he opens the door and sees me, the expectation on his face turns to suspicion. He seems diminished since the last time I saw him, his hair uncombed, a few days of gray stubble on his face.

"Oh, Mrs. . . ."

"D'arcy," I say. "I need to ask you about something, Mr. Mahoney. Something that happened a long time ago, around the time that Felix Crawford died. Can I come in?"

He looks up quickly, his eyes wary now.

"I don't know if you know that Lissa Crawford and Agnieska Tarnowski are missing. They may be in danger and knowing more about Rosscliffe House may help us find them."

He tries to open the door, but his hands are shaking, so I open it myself. I follow him inside and watch as he sits in an armchair and mutes the television.

"You a guard?" He seems confused. "I thought they'd . . . Ah, well, I guess I can tell you." His eyes are bloodshot, slightly yellow. I know I should correct him, but I want to hear what he has to say. He's wearing the same cardigan he had on at McCarthy's, a yellow the color of mustard and stained down the front with brown liquid.

"You worked at the Big House?" I prompt him. "That's where you met Dorothea Reynolds, the nurse who was caring for Felix Crawford? I asked you about her before."

"Dorothea? Eh . . . I loved working at Rosscliffe House," he says. "My father worked there, you see, and I had grown up at the house, spending time there. When he died, I got the job."

"Were they able to pay you much?"

"No, but I had other work, building and so forth, and I would go when I could and take care of the gardens. Elizabeth, that was her name, Mrs. Crawford, loved her flowers and we planned things . . . together. She couldn't buy things, but I knew how to take cuttings, how to grow flowers from seed."

He stops talking then and stares off into space for a moment.

"Lissa Crawford thought that maybe you and her mother had a . . . well, a special friendship. That you were close."

He sighs. I'm not sure what he's going to say, but he surprises me by saying, "I loved her. I would have done anything for her. I was a married man, with three children and another on the way, but I loved her. Sure, it can't hurt anyone now to say it. Her husband was mad, you know. The famous painter. Absolutely mad."

I wait. I sense him organizing his thoughts. He's struggling. But he tells me the story of that summer, of how Dorothea came and how Felix Crawford got worse and worse, until Elizabeth Crawford realized that he needed to go back to Dublin.

"I took that young one, the sister, to the train, saw her off. Elizabeth was going to have her find a hospital in Dublin. And when I came back to the house, I found her in the garden. It was dark, late at night, and she was crying. She saw me and she ran toward me and clung to me, like . . . her arms. I'll always remember that. She was wearing a dress with no sleeves and her arms were pale, her shoulders . . . I had thought about that for so long, Mrs. D'arcy. God help me, I was a married man. But that night, we . . . we were together, in the garden. My garden. It was warm and everything smelled good and I thought I'd never been as happy as I was right then. Mad things came into my head. That we'd run away, go to America and be together. I even thought . . . so help me . . . that maybe he would die."

He slumps in the chair, drained from telling the story. His hands are shaking violently on the arms of the chair. The little bungalow is absolutely quiet. Actors move silently on the television screen.

"What happened?" I ask gently.

"He saw us. I don't know how much, but . . . enough. He was

shouting, going for Elizabeth. He got his hands around her neck and he was . . . I pulled him off. His friend, Mr. Allerton, was there, too. He tried to help, but Felix, he was raging, furious. He kept screaming about how I was the devil and then he ran off. We were . . . we were relieved, I think."

I can hear a clock ticking somewhere, the gentle beat of the rain on the roof.

"Mr. Allerton, uh, found him in his study. He'd taken a knife from the kitchen and he was cutting himself, in the stomach, and he'd managed to create a lot of blood, but not to do any real harm. Mr. Allerton tried to take the knife from him and he went after him with it. Mr. Allerton was stabbed, too. It was terrifying. We got him to the bedroom, locked him in. I thought we could . . . Elizabeth knew she needed to get the children out of there. They packed up. Mr. Allerton and I kept Felix under lock and key." He pauses, his eyes filling. "She, Elizabeth, said goodbye and that she would be back when she could. I thought she . . . but she never came back."

"Because he killed himself the day she left?"

Matt Mahoney nods heavily.

"Lissa Crawford thought something happened to Dorothea," I say. "She found a bloody cloth and she connected it with her disappearing."

"Poor lamb. They should have told her. I was cleaning up the blood and I must have left one of the rags on the stairs. Poor lamb, poor lamb. I don't remember the whole . . . I'm sorry." His limbs are vibrating again; he's trying to hold one hand with the other to stop it.

"Mr. Mahoney," I say. "The root cellar out in the garden. Who else knew about it?"

But he's somewhere else. "I don't understand. To hurt yourself like that, to do yourself in. I'll never understand it. My boy, Barry, in some ways it was the same except with that poison, the drugs. I never understood his addiction. It made him . . . someone else. It made him do terrible things. I never understood. I never did. That . . . man. It was his fault. He did it."

I meet his eyes. "Sorry, which man, Mr. Mahoney?"

He looks confused, but he speaks clearly. "Dorda. *He's* the devil. Barry wouldn't have done it if it wasn't for him. I knew when I heard they hid it. Was it . . . ? I'd told Barry, you see. About the cellar. I'd let him play there when he was a boy. We used it to store bulbs and things. Elizabeth and I would go there to talk. Barry liked it, he thought it was a secret tunnel . . . stories, you know, about boys finding caves. He liked all that . . ."

"I'm sorry. What did Barry do for Dorda?"

He realizes what he's done, puts his head in his hands, and then he says, "He's back at it, you know. My Barry. Back to the drink, maybe the rest of it. Just like before. I think he's done terrible things." He's crying now, big tears falling from his eyes onto the cardigan.

"Mr. Mahoney, where is Barry now?"

"I don't know. Ellen said she was going to the store. Barry . . ." He looks up and I follow his gaze. Ellen Mahoney has come silently into the room while we've been talking. "Ellen, Ellen, I'm sorry. Where is he? Where's Barry?" His voice is growing weak.

Ellen goes to him, touches his shoulder. She's wearing a raincoat and it's dripping onto the carpet, but she doesn't seem to notice.

"It's okay, Matt. He's okay. I'll make you some tea." She looks at me and says quietly, "He's not well, you know. You shouldn't have talked to him."

"Where is he?" I ask her. "Where's Barry?"

She sighs. "I think he went to talk to Lorcan and Sam."

Forty-One

....

The solicitor gets there at seven. Ann joins them in the interview room at Griz's request, gulping a ham sandwich before she goes in. She's jittery, feeling the effects of too much tea, not enough sleep.

"When did you become aware of Anton Dorda's illegal activities?" Fiero asks, once they've settled in.

Tomasz Sadowski starts. "We all knew that Dorda sold drugs, at least the Polish here did. When I first arrived, I was working on a site in Bantry and some of the guys, they said to watch out for him, that he was good to the Polish who came here, but that he would try to get you to work for him, in the illegal part of the business. He was very careful, I guess you would say. Not to get caught. I even thought maybe he had stopped. He bought the takeaway and some of the guys, they said he did not do that anymore. But then after you caught those men, in the boat?" He looks up at them and Ann nods. "After that, well, I started to think that something wasn't right." He sighs and sits back, thinking. "I realized they were using the trucks from the building sites. One night, I saw Barry Mahoney and Mr. Dorda loading boxes into one of the trucks. They went down to Rosscliffe House and came back to the site and I saw them putting some bags into these bigger bags of concrete. I realized that they must have been the ones who took the drugs off the boat before you caught those men. Everyone in the village was talking about it, about how there must be someone local involved.

"They let me see what they were doing. I think that was their point. To see if I would do anything. Barry was my boss. I was scared that he would sack me, and one day he came and told me to drive a truck to Cork. He said he needed someone who could be very discreet and was I discreet. I said yes. I was afraid. I needed the job. I thought . . . hoped . . . maybe it was something else. Stolen equipment maybe.

"I drove toward Limerick, like I was supposed to, but I pulled over on a small road and I looked in one bag. It was full of taped-up bags of a powder. . . . I knew what it was. Not cement."

"Dorda was using the building projects, the trucks, to move the drugs from Operation Waves around, wasn't he?" Ann asks.

Tomasz nods.

Fiero is furious. Ann can feel his fury. She feels it, too. "Did Mr. Nevin know?" Fiero asks.

"No, I don't think so. I think Dorda was using Barry, but this was before Mr. Nevin had a house down here and he didn't come down so much."

"Why didn't you tell anyone?"

Tomasz looks embarrassed. "I was afraid. I took the truck where I was supposed to take it. Some men there unloaded the bags. I pretended I didn't know. When I got back, I told Barry I didn't want to drive anymore. He said that I had driven the truck. I was involved. They would tell someone. And then he told me that Mr. Dorda had killed a boy who knew about what he was doing. He said he had seen him, that he had to help Mr. Dorda dump the body, and that if I didn't keep quiet, Mr. Dorda would kill me, too, now that I knew. He was scared, I think. I think he was taking drugs, too. He said that he couldn't help himself, that he'd gotten into trouble." His eyes are wide. Ann can see the terror in them.

"I went to Mrs. Crawford and I told her that if anything happened to me, she should take care of Alex. I thought they were going to kill me. I was sure of it. But . . . they didn't. Time passed. I thought maybe it was . . . all over."

Ann feels rage rise up in her. *But it wasn't over. The drugs were making their way into the community. They were doing their work. And the money was rolling in.*

"But then you fell in love with Agnieska," Griz says gently. "How did it start?"

He smiles a little. "Just . . . we were friends first and then . . . it was more. I realized one night and I told her and she . . . she said she loved me, too. But she told me that Mr. Dorda had tried to . . . ask her out. He wanted to marry her. When she said she wasn't interested in him like that, he became angry. He started watching her. One night, she came to my flat and she was crying. She said he told her that he knew something about me, something that could get me in trouble with the guards, and that if she kept seeing me, he would tell the guards about what I did. He told her he had evidence."

"When was this, Tomasz?" Griz asks.

"In the winter, February. It was cold. We couldn't meet outside, and we didn't want him to know, so that is why we got the idea of meeting at Rosscliffe House."

"Was Lukas involved in the drug dealing with Dorda?" Fiero asks. "Is that why he was killed?"

Tomasz looks up. "I don't think so," he says. "He wasn't one of the guys. I never saw him talking to Dorda or anything like that."

"What about Zuzanna?" Fiero sounds desperate now. "Did she have any connection to Dorda? Do you know who Zuzanna was with the night she died?"

"No, I don't know."

"But how did Lukas's clothes get into your flat, Tomasz? That's what I don't understand," Ann asks him. She's sure he's telling the truth.

"I think someone placed them there. I think someone must have broken in or taken a key. Maybe Alex left it somewhere by mistake and someone took it, or he forgot to lock up."

Alex. Ann's thinking about the statement he gave about Zuzanna's movements on the night she died. *She said something about the flat, how she'd realized something about the flat.* What had Griz said about the passport? *You must have thought he brought his passport with him because he was planning on disappearing. But he didn't disappear. So why did he have the passport?*

Suddenly Fiero's phone buzzes and he looks down at it, then pushes it over so that she can read the text. They've sent two uniforms over to get Dorda.

Dorda's not home and his car is gone.

"Is Agnieska okay?" Tomasz asks uncertainly. "Where is she?"

"That's what we're trying to find out," Fiero tells him. "Stay here please. We'll be right back."

They leave Tomasz with the solicitor for a moment and huddle out in the hallway.

"Get cars out looking for him right now," Fiero shouts at someone. "I want him in custody tonight! Barry Mahoney, too. Someone get to the pub and arrest him."

Broome is standing awkwardly underneath a poster warning of the dangers of driving under the influence.

"Hiya, Broome," Ann says. "I want you to do something for me. Ring up Charlie Dunne right now and ask him who owns the flat where Lukas Adamik lived and who owns the Sadowskis' flat. I know he manages them, but who owns them? Who's got keys besides him? That's what I want to know, okay?"

Broome nods and goes off to do it. Ann sits there for a moment, thinking. She uses the bathroom and then she and Fiero go back into the interview room while Griz goes off to try to find Barry Mahoney.

"Tomasz," she says, "if Dorda were going to take someone somewhere and hide her, or them, what are the options? His house, obviously, the takeaway, the dry cleaners, his boat, but where else? Does he own any other buildings that you know about?"

Tomasz is quiet, considering. "There's a warehouse on the way to Dureen. I don't know if he owns it, but he had me bring lumber there once to store it. That's the only thing I can think of."

Out in the hallway again, Ann tells Fiero, "I'll drive out there right now. I can take Broome or you can send a uniform for backup."

He shakes his head. The air in the hallway is heavy, full of their memories. She flashes back to his face over her that November day, his eyes panicked as he listened to her screaming. They'd gone looking for Dáithí, once she'd realized he was missing. Fiero had come down from Bandon to check on something and he'd offered to go along while she searched. They'd been walking the peninsula road when he saw something in the grass near Rosscliffe House and went to look. He tried to stop her following him, but of course he couldn't. He was paralyzed at first that day, staring at her cradling her son's body, until he snapped out of it and called for help, touched her shoulder, tried to peel her away from the body.

She knows he's remembering too.

He says, "No. I'm coming with you."

Forty-Two

After I leave Matt Mahoney's bungalow, I leave a message for Griz, telling her about Barry Mahoney and what Ellen said about him talking to Sam, and drive slowly back up to Ross Head. The rain is coming fast now and I'm hunched over the steering wheel, trying to see the road through the deluge. I'm trying to see the picture behind the fog, the relationships that matter amid the ones that have only served to confuse us. What does Sam Nevin know? Did Barry Mahoney kill Lukas and Zuzanna? Was Tomasz Sadowski involved in their deaths too?

When I pull up in front of the cottage, Conor comes running out to meet me, holding an umbrella over my head as we dash back inside. Grace is still there, crumpled in a corner of the couch.

I dry off and put on new clothes while Conor makes tea. Lilly and Adrien come in, having heard my voice.

"Mom?" Lilly asks. "What's going on? Are you okay?"

"Yes, love, but where's Alex? I need to ask him something," I say.

"He went back to the apartment to get some clothes," she says. "He should be back soon."

Gratefully, I take a mug of tea from Conor and turn to Grace. "Are you okay?" I ask her. I put a hand on her arm and she leans into me, looking for comfort.

"No," she says. "But I need to get it together and go back to pack up and get the girls." Her face is pale, her eyes puffy but bright with anger.

"Are you going back to Dublin?"

"Yeah. He can have his ugly house. I've never liked it. We asked if we could build something smaller, but Rochelle was responsible for the design and she said they all had to look alike." She closes her eyes, swaying against the couch cushions. "Fuck! Did Conor tell you what happened?"

"Not really." I check on Lilly and Adrien. They're listening but trying to pretend they're not, looking at their phones and giving each other guilty glances.

Grace hardly knows they're there. "I found Lorcan at the store, in the back room, like some kind of fucking soap opera! You should have seen Danielle's face. She looked so smug, until he buttoned his trousers and came running after me. When I asked him why he did it, he said he was stressed. Can you imagine? *Stressed!* Because of the development, the investors. He said it felt like everything was falling down around them and he needed something simple. *Simple!*"

She's crying now and I pat her shoulder ineffectually. Lilly's phone buzzes and she looks down at the screen for a few seconds. Something on her face makes me say, "Was that Alex?"

Her eyes are wide, worried. "He said he's not coming back here. He said he realized something and he has to go talk to

Mr. Nevin. Mom, I'm really worried now. He was acting weird before."

"Do you think we should ring the Nevins?" Conor asks. "See if he's there?"

"Stay here," I tell them, putting my tea down and standing up. "I'll go see if I can find him."

Forty-Three

He's locked them in a small room, an office of some sort, with a desk and files along one side and a dusty couch on which they got a little sleep a few hours ago, Agnieska with her head at one end and Mrs. Crawford with her head at the other. Agnieska feels weak, her brain sluggish, not processing correctly. She knows they need to make a plan to fight back for when he returns, but he's tied their hands behind their backs and she's just so tired; he hasn't told them what he wants, what he's going to do.

Everything since last night is blurry in her mind, the shock and lack of sleep making the memories fuzzy. She and Tomasz had agreed to meet at Rosscliffe House at ten, after she was finished at the pub. She was a little late; they were busier than usual, and when she got there and he wasn't there yet she waited around the back on the patio. Ever since she told Tomasz that she thought Mr. Dorda was following her, he insisted that she wait for him inside. But it was dark last night and she didn't like being in the house alone. She sent a few texts, but Tomasz didn't open them, and she was about to ring his mobile when she got a text from Alex. *You there? I need to talk 2U!!!* he had written. She studied it for a moment and was about to write back when she saw the lights. A car was coming along the road and, thinking it was Tomasz, she ran out to greet it.

But it wasn't Tomasz.

It was Anton Dorda.

He pulled over and got out. "Hello, Agnieska," he called to her. "Are you okay?" He was wearing a black coat, long, like the ones in cowboy films.

She felt a cold line of fear run down her back. She needed to move her legs, get out of the middle of the road, but she was frozen, stuck there as though her feet were in cement. He must have seen the terror on her face because he put his hands out and walked toward her and said, in Polish, "Please, Agnieska. Why are you afraid of me? That is all I want to know."

The lights from the car were shining on her face. She put a hand up to shield her eyes, but she felt like the animals she sometimes saw at night, surprised in the middle of the road, when she and Tomasz were driving.

"I have to go," she managed, barely loud enough for him to hear.

"Why are you afraid of me?" he asked. "Tell me and I will let you go." She heard a car somewhere in the distance, or perhaps it was just the sound carrying across the water in the inlet. His headlights lit up the house like a haunted mansion in a horror movie.

It took her almost twenty seconds to choke it out. "The way you look at me," she said. "You look like you are a hunter and I am the deer."

He crossed the distance between them, grasping her hand and

saying, "Agnieska, that is only because I love you, because we belong together. You are meant to be with me. I need to explain, I just want to tell you." He had both of her hands in his now, and he pulled her in, crushing her against his body, trying to kiss her, his face rough against hers, his hands on her body, squeezing, pinching, grabbing. She tried to wrench free, twisting away from him, knowing she wasn't strong enough to free herself. And then they both looked up and saw Mrs. Crawford's car, saw her get out, protesting, asking what was happening. *Get back in your car,* Agnieska wanted to say. But it was too late.

He was the frozen animal then. In the bright light she could see the thoughts move across his brain, his realization that there was no way to explain away what Mrs. Crawford had seen, that if he let them go they would tell the guards. He made the decision quickly, pushing them into his car, taking Agnieska's mobile, locking the doors as they pounded on the windows.

It was the middle of the night. There was no one on the road to see or hear.

Now, Agnieska and Mrs. Crawford hear the sound of a key in the office door. He comes in with bags of fish and chips, the smell so delicious Agnieska feels her stomach rumble.

"Do you think anyone knows where you are?" he asks them. He's nervous, preoccupied, still wearing the black coat. They shake their heads, too scared to talk. He unties their hands and spreads the food out on the desk. Agnieska hesitates, then gets up and takes some. Mrs. Crawford shakes her head. She's barely spoken since they've been here. Agnieska thinks she's in shock.

"I'm not going to hurt you," he says. "That's not why I brought you here. I just want to explain, so you'll understand. Agnieska." He gestures to the couch, and when her eyes go wide and she shakes her head, he sighs and says, "Not for . . . that. Agnieska, I only want to talk to you."

She stands up, stretching her hands to bring the blood back, and sits down. Mrs. Crawford, sitting in the desk chair, meets her eyes. *Careful,* Agnieska thinks she's saying.

His black raincoat is dripping on the carpet, and in the low-ceilinged space he looks huge, imposing.

"What did he tell you, Tomasz? Did he tell you about me, what did he say?" She can hear how insecure he is, how much he cares about her opinion, and it sparks a wave of pity, mixed with fear, that confuses her.

She doesn't say anything.

His eyes flash with impatience. "What did he say, you can tell me. I won't be mad."

She takes a breath. "He said that you were a dealer, a drug dealer, that you were the one behind the big shipment that the guards got, that you tricked them and there was more that they didn't get."

He nods. "This is true. It was their own fault."

She thinks he isn't going to say anything else. She wants to ask him if he killed Lukas and Zuzanna.

But he goes on, sitting down on the couch next to her, but not too close, trying to show respect for her fear, she thinks, which confuses her even more.

"When I first came here, I worked as a builder, in Cork," he tells them. "One day, I came out to work on a site here, to build a house for a rich man from Dublin who wanted to have a holiday house. I loved it here. I made a plan for myself. When we finished the house, I decided to move here. I knew a man in Dublin who said that I could be his local representative for different things that people wanted. I did not like doing this and I didn't want to do it forever, you see, but I needed money. Well . . ." He shrugs. "When I could, I bought the laundry business, I bought the chip shop. I needed legitimate businesses. You cannot be greedy. That was why I did so well. I was . . . disciplined. I only did what I needed to do, never more, even if the men from Dublin always wanted more, more, more. I was close to my plan being finished, Agnieska. This is what I want you to understand. In 2013. We set it up so the guards would think it was happening in one place, but in fact . . . like a magic trick, it had already happened. The guys who they caught, they were willing to do some time in jail if there was money waiting on the other side. That's what it was about, Agnieska, enough money to be able to . . . not do this anymore. To have a beautiful life. I wanted you to be part of that life."

She feels a cold chill run down her spine. His eyes on her are desperate, needy.

"I knew the first time I saw you," he says. "I walked into the restaurant and you were standing there in your apron, ready to greet me, and I thought you were the most beautiful girl I have ever seen. I fell in love with you."

Agnieska remembers it suddenly. He had walked in and she had been scared of him, right then, right from the beginning. There was something about the way he had looked at her that terrified her. It was like he'd decided something, like he had a plan for her and it didn't matter what she thought about it.

"You made Tomasz drive with the drugs. He told me," she says. "You saw us kissing outside the pub one time and he was scared, and when I asked him why, he told me that you had made him drive the load of drugs to Cork and you told him that if he told anyone you would kill him, like you killed the boy who was talking to the guards. He thought you were going to kill him. He even told Mrs. Crawford that something might happen to him, because he wanted her to take care of Alex if it did."

"Is that what he said?"

"Yes, he is scared of you. He said we had to meet at Rosscliffe House because you were watching his flat to see if we would meet there. He had the code to the lock because he worked for Mr. Nevin. He didn't want you to know because he thought you would hurt us."

Dorda sighs heavily. "Look, Tomasz is . . . just a builder. He is not worthy of you, Agnieska. I know you'll see that. He has no plan. I have a plan. And until this . . . until *this* happened, the plan was working." He sighs and stands up. He looks tired and it gives Agnieska courage.

She sits up straight and looks right at him. "So why did you kill Lukas? Why did you kill Zuzanna? Were they involved, too?"

Mrs. Crawford is watching and listening from the corner of the room. Agnieska doesn't dare look at her.

Dorda turns to her. "This is what I wanted to tell you, Agnieska," he says. "I could see how sad that made you. I could see how you could never love me if you thought I killed your friend. That is why I brought you here, so I can tell you about that. That wasn't me at all, though I know who it was." He bends down on one knee, as though he's going to propose, and spreads his hands out, imploring her. "That was something else completely."

Forty-Four

....

I make good time to the Nevins', coming up on the drive as the rain suddenly intensifies, falling in sheets and running along the road in silvery streams. The house is lit up, every window like a lantern in the rain, the sky over the peninsula a strange yellow gray. There are five cars in the driveway and I feel my heart speed up when I recognize Alex's. I need to make sure he's okay and get him out of here and then let Griz, Fiero, and Ann Tobin deal with the rest of it. Maybe I can say something's happened to Lilly, that he needs to come with me, that there's been an emergency.

Grace's voice is in my head. *He said it felt like everything was falling down around them.*

I walk carefully toward the terrace where Lilly and Alex's band played the night of the party, wanting to get a sense of where everyone is before I go to the door. There's enough light from the house that I can mostly see where I'm walking and I'm almost around the house when I hear Barry Mahoney's voice and press myself against the exterior wall to listen.

"It's your fault," Barry's shouting. "It's all your fault. Everything was good. I got it all together. But you, you made me help you! You caused all of this!"

"What's he talking about?" It's Alex's voice, outside too.

"Barry, you're being ridiculous," Sam Nevin is saying. They must be standing under the little roof that covers half the terrace. "Why don't we go inside and have a drink, get warm and dry. I know you're upset, but I think it's made you think strange things."

Alex shouts, "No, I want to hear this. I want to hear what you have to say. I know you put the clothes in our flat. Lukas's clothes. I realized when I was back just now. We pay the rent to Mr. Dunne, but you own the flat. You have a key. I realized I saw Jack's car that weekend. Zuzanna said something about a car and I think that's what she meant. He was here in Rosscliffe when Lukas died."

"Let's just go inside, Alex."

"No! I want to know about Lukas. I think you know what happened to Lukas. Zuzanna kept talking about the flat. I didn't realize it, but she saw something, or realized something, after Lukas went missing. Was it you? Did you kill him?"

I think he's talking to Sam, but then I hear Barry Mahoney's voice. "I didn't kill Lukas."

"What about Zuzanna?" Alex asks him. "What about her."

"Alex, you know this. Zuzanna was upset about Lukas. She killed herself." That's Sam.

"No," Alex says. "She didn't. Yes, she was upset about Lukas, but she was convinced someone killed him. She told me."

"What do you mean, Alex?" Sam asks.

I move around the side of the house, just a little, so that I can see part of the terrace. Sam and Alex are standing under the roof, but Barry is in the rain, his clothes soaked, his face dripping wet. He looks desperate, his eyes wild in the light filtering out through the open French doors.

"Zuzanna said she was going to talk to someone. I think she

had an idea of who killed Lukas," Alex says. "The night she died. She told me she realized something about the flat. I think she realized that someone had come back and taken Lukas's wallet and his passport, to make it look like he went away. And I think she remembered seeing Jack's car when Lukas disappeared."

"Jack's car? Barry, what's going on here?" Sam asks.

I'm starting to shiver now and I know that my body's going to start losing strength. If I'm going to get help for Alex, I need to do it now. But I also know that they'll stop talking if I announce myself.

I wrap my arms around my body and listen.

"*You* killed her. Did you kill Lukas, too?" Alex asks. "My brother is sitting in jail. They think he killed Lukas. Did you kill him?"

And then I hear, from the road, the very faint sound of a car pulling into the drive. *Griz,* I think. It must be Griz. I want to let her know we're around the back of the house, but I don't want to miss anything they're saying.

There's a long silence. "Look, Alex," Barry says. "You need to know. No one killed Lukas. It was an accident. It was . . . I didn't kill him. I didn't." He's almost crying, his voice catching and rasping.

"What do you mean?" Alex asks. "What do you mean it was an accident? He was killed and you threw him in the ocean."

There's a long silence.

I have to strain to hear Barry's voice over the sound of the rain. "He was killed on the building site, in an accident. A girder swung and bashed his head in and there was nothing we could do. He was dead before Piotr even got to him." Barry's crying. "Tomasz didn't know. He had to drive to Cork that day and Piotr rang me, and, well, we decided not to tell Tomasz. I knew Sam was so worried about the project. I'd been his building manager. I knew what would happen if the guards got involved. If we went to them, everything would be shut down while they investigated. They would discover any shortcuts that he'd taken . . . So, we paid off Piotr, told him to go home, told everyone his father died back in Poland and he'd had to go."

"What?" Sam asks. "When was this, Barry? When his body was found, you told me you thought Dorda did it, that he killed him because Lukas was dealing drugs and was going to go to the police. You told me I had to stay quiet because you would be charged with what happened in 2013."

"I'm sorry, Sam," Barry says. "I'm so sorry. We did it to protect you. You were in Germany and I thought if we could just take care of it, if we could just—"

"What the fuck are you talking about?" Sam asks. "Who is *we*? Will someone tell me what the fuck he's talking about?" He's looking toward the interior of the house now, his hands out in front of him, upturned, looking for answers.

"Okay, Sam," says a new voice, steady and commanding. "Let's just calm down, everyone, and see if we can talk about this like adults."

Forty-Five

....

Ann spots the low-slung warehouse building eleven kilometers out of Rosscliffe. It's almost to Dureen, not far from Dorda's house, and though a sign out front reads DUREEN AUTO REPAIR, it's pretty clear that no one's fixed anything here for many years. Grass and brambles have grown up all around, but there's what looks like a drive of sorts, and they pull in and Fiero shuts off the car.

"He's not here," Fiero says.

"His car's not here," Ann says. "If he's smart he would have left it somewhere else or hidden it. He must know we're looking for him now."

They get out, pulling up the hoods of their waterproofs against the driving rain. The warehouse is in good repair, Ann can see now. She sweeps her torchlight across the façade, noting the new siding and freshly painted foundation. Fiero nods to the entrance at one end of the building and they make their way through the tall grass, feeling it soak their trousers as they go.

Ann tries the handle on the outside of the door and, to their surprise, it turns. She pushes it halfway open and when nothing happens, she swings it all the way in and Fiero enters the small space on the other side. She follows. There's light coming from a small fixture overhead and she can see that the warehouse has been set up as a storage facility for boxes of napkins and paper sacks used by the takeaway.

She's about to tell Fiero to keep going down the corridor when they hear Dorda's voice.

Ann nods toward the half-open door along the corridor, and Fiero holds his personal weapon next to his leg and covers her so she can get closer.

Dorda's voice is loud, easy to hear. "This is what I want you to understand," he's saying. "In 2013 we set it up so the guards would think it was happening in one place, but in fact . . . like a magic trick, it had already happened. The guys who they caught, they were willing to do some time in jail if there was money waiting on the other side. That's what it was about, Agnieska, enough money to be able to . . . not do this anymore. To have a beautiful life. I wanted you to be part of that life."

Ann's heart seizes. This is it. He's admitting to everything. Right now. She wants to move closer to see if Lissa Crawford is in there with them, but she wants to hear what else he says. When she looks over at Fiero, she can see the same triumph she's feeling on his face. They've got him. Any second now he's going to admit to killing Lukas Adamik and Zuzanna Brol. That will be their moment. They'll arrest him and take him in to get a statement. Agnieska Tarnowski is a witness to his confession.

Fiero moves closer to the door.

Dorda goes on, explaining himself, pleading.

Agnieska asks him if he killed her friends. Ann can see the veins on Fiero's neck standing out. It's taking every ounce of willpower he's got not to burst in and arrest Dorda right now.

But Dorda's answer surprises her.

"That was something else completely," he says. "Agnieska, you have to understand," And then he tells her.

Fiero nods toward the door, puts up three fingers. *Three, two, one.*

"Armed gardaí," Fiero announces. They enter the room. Ann has imagined this moment so many times she almost feels as though it's already happened. In her fantasies, Dorda is defiant, yelling that he won't go easily, that they'll have to kill him before he'll let himself be taken in for questioning. She's imagined him swinging for her, pulling a weapon. She's imagined aiming, pulling the trigger . . .

But when Fiero gets to him, he's already put his hands out in front of him. "I wanted you to love me," he says. "That is all I wanted, Agnieska." His shoulders are slumped. He's deflated, smaller somehow.

Once they have him cuffed, Ann calls over to dispatch. "Get the armed response unit out to Ross Head right now," she says. "To the Nevins'. As soon as you can."

As Fiero leads Dorda out of the room, Ann hears Agnieska, her voice strong and clear, say, "You cannot make someone love you. It isn't up to you."

Forty-Six

They're all out on the terrace now and I move carefully around so I can see the whole scene, Sam and Alex at one end and Rochelle and Barry at the other, the rain falling on them in relentless sheets. If any one of them turns, they'll see me standing there. But they're completely focused on one another. "But Lukas was found in the water," Sam says. "I don't understand."

"Sam," Rochelle says. "Stop asking questions. We need to get ahold of this situation."

But Barry keeps going. Tears streaming down his face, he says, "I'm sorry, Sam. The kid, Piotr, called me. He couldn't get Tomasz. I knew you were in Germany. I called Rochelle, asked her what we should do. I knew if we went to the guards, everything would get shut down. I knew they'd start looking around. When I helped Dorda with that kid, the one who was talking to the guards, it worked, Sam, hiding the body in the old cellar at Rosscliffe House until things died down, then throwing it into the ocean. It was Dorda's idea. Rochelle thought it would work again."

"Barry, shut up," Rochelle says. Her voice is furious.

"Come on, Rochelle." Barry's really crying now. "You never should have asked me to help you. The lads . . . Sam, you were away. Rochelle said if we called the guards, if we reported the death, they'd shut down the development project for months, maybe years. You wouldn't get the planning permission for the hotel. She said we couldn't let that happen. All the money, all her father's money, would be down the drain. She took Jack's car and drove down here. She knew that people would remember her car, but Jack's was less familiar."

It's starting to make sense to me. Sam and Lorcan are overleveraged on the project and they need the investors to re-up with more financing or they're finished. I'm still not quite sure what Lorcan did to secure the loans and whether it was illegal or just reckless, but they needed the houses to be finished so that they could sell them to finance the renovation of the hotel. If they reported Lukas's death on the site, construction would have been shut down for months. The whole thing would have fallen apart. They never would have gotten the planning approval for the hotel.

"But why did you do it?" Alex asks. "Why did you help her hide his body?"

"I had to," Barry says. "She said she'd go to the guards with what she knows about me, about what I did before I got clean, about helping Dorda in 2013, about that boy."

"Barry?" Sam asks hesitantly, as though he's afraid of the answer. "Did you have something to do with the death of that boy? Barry?"

Barry sobs. "They killed him. Dorda and some fella. They had to do it. Colin Nugent was working with that detective, Fiero. Dorda found out and decided to feed him information about the wrong transfer point. The night before, I borrowed a fishing boat and diving equipment. They wrapped everything, dropped it in the water at night off Mizen Head, and I retrieved it, then took it ashore and hid it in the old root cellar in the ruins at Rosscliffe House. We fixed it up and there was a hidden entrance in the grounds that my father told me about."

"What about Mrs. Crawford?" Alex says. "It was her house."

"She didn't know," Barry said. "She hadn't been in it in years. Months later, when everything was over, Dorda moved it."

"And then he sold it all," Sam says bitterly.

"I didn't kill Colin Nugent," Barry says, turning to him. "I thought we were just going to scare him. I knew him a little and I went to his house to pick him up. Dorda made me take him to that cellar. We went down there and Dorda made him admit he was the informant and then this guy put a knife in his stomach. I didn't do it. I didn't do it, Sam. That's why I stopped all of it. After seeing that, I got out, I stopped drinking, stopped everything. You know that. I only wanted to work at the pub. Ellen . . . I only wanted to . . . I was happy. I'm so sorry, Sam."

"I know, Bar," Sam says. "I know that." He's watching his brother-in-law's face with a tenderness that almost takes my breath away. "That's why I bought the house, to make the hotel, that's why we put you in charge of the pub. I knew you just needed a chance."

"I was sober until Rochelle called me in April. Until she made me help her. The stress . . ."

Sam turns to look at her. "Why didn't you tell me? We could have dealt with it together."

Her face is turned away from me, but I can hear the scorn in her voice. "You would have called the guards. The whole thing would have been shut down. You know that."

Suddenly, lights sweep the lawn. I hear the cars and go back around to the driveway to see Griz and a phalanx of uniformed guards.

"They're around back," I call to her.

"Armed gardaí!" Griz calls out when she reaches the terrace. "Everyone get on the ground. Put your hands where we can see them!"

Barry sees them and the panic that sweeps over his face sounds a note of caution in my brain. *He'll do anything now. He knows it's over.*

"Armed gardaí!" Griz shouts again. "Get on the ground."

But Barry doesn't get on the ground. He grabs Alex, pinning his arms behind him, and drags him toward the cliffs.

Sam calls out, "Barry, no, please!" and he and Rochelle run after him as Griz comes up on the terrace.

We can all see them in the strong lights from the cars, frozen there at the edge of the peninsula. The rain lashes our faces, pelting us with what feel like tiny frozen needles.

"Everyone step away from the edge," Griz shouts. But it's hard to make herself heard over the rain.

"Stay back," Barry shouts. "Stay back or he goes over."

Griz and I stop walking. Barry, at the cliff's edge, is holding Alex's arms behind his back. One wrong step and Alex will fall over. I can feel Griz calculating, trying to decide if we can get around behind them and herd them away from the edge.

We can't.

"Let Alex go," she calls out. "We won't make a move on the rest of you. We just want Alex to be safe."

Someone laughs. I think it's Rochelle. Griz and I wait.

Barry screams. "I don't even care anymore. It's over, Rochelle. I deserve to go to jail. You do, too. For Zuzanna. And for putting the clothes in Tomasz's flat. And Dorda deserves to be locked up. I should just go over, too. I'll take us both over!"

"What the fuck are you talking about?" Sam asks him. "Barry . . ." I can hear the anguish in his voice. "Zuzanna?"

Barry sobs, "It wasn't me, Sam. It wasn't me."

Sam yells, "What about Zuzanna? What about Zuzanna, Rochelle?"

Rochelle steps forward. "Sam," she says. "Zuzanna was upset. She killed herself after Lukas's body was found."

"That's what happened," Sam says desperately, looking around at all of them. "Right?" He knows though.

I step out into the pool of light from the house. "I don't think it was. I think Zuzanna wasn't despondent. I think she was angry. All those months, thinking he'd left her without a word. And then to find out he was actually dead. She wasn't suicidal. She was furious. And she wanted someone to pay. She realized that she'd seen Lukas's passport earlier in the evening at his flat and then the next morning it was gone. She remembered that you owned the flat, that you had a key. I think she wondered about Sam, so she thought it would be safe to talk to you, Rochelle. To ask you if it was possible Sam had come down to Rosscliffe in April. I think she may have remembered seeing Jack's car in the village. But she never thought of you."

Sam is staring at me, horror washing his face pale. He turns back to Rochelle. "But . . . Did you, Rochelle?" he asks her. "Why?"

"Oh, don't be ridiculous. I didn't kill her. She fell." But I can see the evasiveness on her face. I know she's lying. "She came by the house late that night and asked to speak to me about Lukas. She said she saw Jack's car when she and Agnieska were going into the pub and she realized she'd seen it the night she went to Lukas's flat to look for him. She wondered if Jack, or maybe you, had been down here, if they knew anything. I tried to talk to her but she was angry and she lost her footing and . . ." She looks toward the water.

I imagine them standing there. How did Rochelle do it? Did she beckon to Zuzanna, say she'd show her what had actually happened? How easy it would have been to just put out a hand and . . . push.

"Look," Rochelle says. "This is ridiculous."

Alex looks terrified, Barry's arms around him, the cliffs at his back. *Move back as much as you can,* I think. *Just a little, just to buy yourself some time.*

"Everyone move away from the edge," Griz says. "Everyone just move away."

We're all waiting, breathing. *This is it,* I think. They'll arrest them. It's almost over.

But then Rochelle darts forward and, before anyone can react, she shoves Barry and Alex toward the edge.

Forty-Seven

....

Barry's arms reach out into the empty space above the cliffs, and it's Sam who grabs his arm and pulls him back, the two of them collapsing on the ground.

Everything slows.

The rain stings my face.

Somewhere behind me, I hear a familiar voice call Alex's name.

He starts to fall. We all watch him teeter for a second, everyone screaming through the rain. I try to organize my mind and muscles into action, but I'm sluggish, too slow, too cold. I feel my knee balk at the pivot I need to make.

I won't get there in time. He's going to go over.

And then I hear Alex's name again and I see a tall figure sprinting across the space between them and it takes my brain a second to realize who it is.

Lilly.

Maybe he texted her again or maybe she followed me, running through the night across the headlands, knowing Alex was in danger. She's here.

She runs forward, her legs churning the air around her. She is speed, motion, bending the laws of physics to save Alex and I reach out for her but I can't stop her. As Alex's arms pinwheel, it's Lilly he reaches for.

And then they both start to fall.

I leap forward, ignoring the pain flashing through my knee. I don't care about anything else. I don't care if Alex goes over, if I go over. I only want to grasp Lilly's hand and pull her to safety. I don't care about anyone else. But I'm not fast enough. My knee fails, my legs don't move fast enough.

Lilly, I realize suddenly, doesn't care about anyone but Alex. I could go over, any one of us could go over; all she cares about is saving him.

Saving the boy she loves.

Her love is so big it fills the air around the cliffs, it fills the ocean. She grasps for his hands and she does it, she gets purchase, and her strong arms pull him back so that they're safe on the edge as Griz tackles Rochelle and uniformed guards come up behind us and put Barry Mahoney in handcuffs.

Forty-Eight

It's still hot the September day we drive south, the back of the car packed with boxes, the green of the fields along the motorway diminished at the end of the summer. Conor plays jazz on the radio and the kids sit in the back of the car with their headphones on, listening to their own music, checking their phones. Lilly hums along to a song, something Alex sent her for them to perform together once he gets to Dublin in October.

We get to Templemore by noon, making our way through the town and following the directions to the Garda Training College. They help me carry all my things up to my room, a small chamber that reminds me of my freshman dorm room at Notre Dame. I walk them back down to the car, reminding Lilly and Conor to pick up her school uniforms and what time school starts on Monday.

"It feels like college," I say. "My parents dropping me off, except it's you guys."

"It is college," Conor says. "Now, be good. Remember to stop after two pints."

"Ha ha, very funny. I'm going to be the weird old lady. No one's going to want to ask me to go for pints. Besides, I won't even be here on the weekends."

"Ah, I bet you'll make lots of friends, Mom," Lilly says. "You'll see."

I make a face at her and hug her hard. "Call me after the first day," I tell her. "Promise?"

"I promise," she says. She's been happy, excited about school starting, excited about Alex coming to Dublin to start a music course later this fall.

"I'll call you later," I tell Conor. "And I'll be back Friday on the bus."

The kids drift away and I hug him. The sun is hot on the asphalt. It smells like autumn.

"Thank you," I say. There's so much more I want to tell him. But the rest of it is big and messy, my love and gratitude filling all the air between us.

So I leave it at that.

"I love you," he says. And I have the feeling that he has so much more he wants to tell me, too. He's afraid and hopeful and nervous. But he leaves it at that.

"I love you, too." I hug him hard, soaking in the feel of his back and his rib cage and the smell of him.

Then I watch them drive away. The leaves have started to turn a bit. Nothing like Long Island in the fall, the banks of red maples and yellow oaks, but it's pretty in a different way here.

"Are these the dorms?" I turn around to find a young woman standing there. She's tall, friendly looking, dark-haired, and surrounded by boxes.

"Yeah, you want a hand with those?"

"Sure," she says. "Are you an instructor or . . ."

"No," I say. "I'm a trainee. Just like you. Maggie."

"Hannah." She shakes my hand. "I'd love some help. Thanks. My boyfriend just dropped me off. Arsehole. I can't believe he didn't help me carry them in."

I pick up a box and we head in together.

Forty-Nine

....

Agnieska looks out over the peninsula, smiling at the warm day, at the sun lighting up the tops of the whitecaps out on the water. They had a lot of rain in August and now it seems like the weather has turned for a bit.

When they moved into the middle cottage a few weeks ago, Tomasz and Alex helped her dig a few plants out of Mrs. Crawford's garden and put them into the ground here. When she said she was giving Tomasz and Alex the cottage, Mrs. Crawford said they could take some cuttings and that she would give them a few chickens if Tomasz could build a coop for them. "You should have fresh eggs," she said. "For the baby."

When Tomasz gets back, they'll work together to fix the patio. It will be nice to have a place to sit outside in the evenings, when she isn't working. And once the baby comes, they can play out here in the evenings, let her lie on the grass in the sun.

Rosscliffe House sits empty, the windows blank, the hulk of it somehow diminished.

It feels different, Agnieska thinks. It feels at rest, too. Everyone in the village says that nothing's going to happen to it now. By the time the legal issues with the Nevins get sorted out, no one's going to be interested. Gwynedd and Mairead are making a pamphlet for visiting birders, describing all the species one can see on Ross Head. They're going to lead birding hikes, and Sam has made it known he doesn't mind, though he hasn't been back to Rosscliffe since Rochelle was charged.

The house seems . . . relaxed, she thinks. No longer angry.

In the garden, a bee buzzes from one flower to another. The sun warms her back. She smiles and turns away from the sea. She's had enough of the sea. It's the soil she wants now on her hands, the smell of it in her nose, the feeling of living, growing things all around her, beauty, new life, love.

Acknowledgments

Huge, huge thanks to my agent Esmond Harmsworth for his hard work on my behalf and to the whole team at Aevitas Creative Management.

I am grateful to all the brilliant folks at Minotaur Books and in particular to Kelley Ragland, Madeline Houpt, Sarah Melnyk, and Allison Ziegler.

Gillian Fallon once again provided absolutely invaluable editing and perspective from Dublin. A big thank-you to Paula McLoughlin (and Mundo) for hosting me on my visits, and to everyone in West Cork who told me stories and taught me some history.

As always, I send huge thanks to the law enforcement professionals in Ireland who shared their expertise with me and answered my questions.

And, of course, my biggest thanks go out to my family. I love you all so much.

Turn the page for a sneak peek at
Sarah Stewart Taylor's new novel

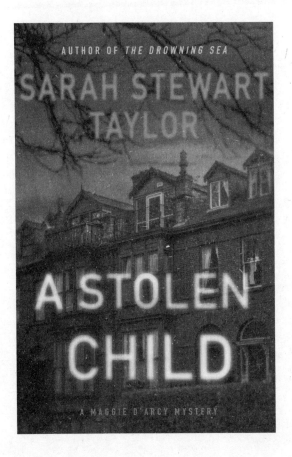

Available Spring 2023

One

....

"Guard! Guard and American Guard! Guard and American Guard!"

My partner, Garda Jason Savage, and I are just finishing up our community patrol when we see two boys beckoning to us along the South Circular Road. Jason rolls his eyes at me. We've tried to get to know this little gang of kids who live and go to school in the neighborhood so that we'll come to seem as familiar as the houses and shops they pass by every day. But they picked up on my accent right away and now when they address me, it's always qualified by my nationality.

The younger one, a runty blond-haired kid named Luke, calls again, "Guards, guards! American Guard and Guard!"

"What is it, Luke?" Jason asks when the boys reach us. "Are you all right, so?"

Luke, all baggy school uniform and spindly limbs, looks up at us, his eyes wide. "Guards, you've got to come, Donald's in the drain!"

Jason and I exchange a skeptical glance. Are they playing a prank? It wouldn't be the first time the kids have tried to trick us. Our first week on the beat, they put a large doll in a baby stroller and rolled it along the sidewalk, yelling, "The baby! The baby!" and laughed when we raced to retrieve it.

But Luke seems genuinely upset, so we follow him to the end of

Carlisle Street, almost running to keep up with him. Up ahead, I can see a crowd of kids clustered in front of a house that's under construction. In a perfect little microcosm of the flavor of the neighborhood, the house next to it is already sleekly renovated, with a tasteful glossy charcoal front door and two planters filled with topiary. The house on the other side has a peeling facade, a rampantly growing rose garden overtaking the iron fence, and row upon row of small animal figurines in the dusty windows. FOR SALE signs are posted in front of a third of the houses in the neighborhood.

"Let's see now," Jason says soothingly as we get close. "What's the trouble?"

The kids shuffle aside, and we step into the small front garden. It's been completely dug up and there's a pile of gravel and debris to one side. Luke points to a large, half-covered drain hole, from which we can hear loud and insistent quacking.

"Donald's a duck?" I ask stupidly.

"Yeah, he's going to starve down there. We've got to get him out," Luke is saying, hopping around excitedly and getting in the way of us seeing anything. Most of the kids in the little gang are Luke's age, ten or eleven, but there are three teenagers, two girls and a boy, watching from the sidewalk. Their younger counterparts seem to generally trust us, but I've seen these three around, and they exude waves of teenage resentment and skepticism about law enforcement. One of the girls has dyed black hair in a severe bob-and-bangs cut, her school uniform too big on her thin frame, paired with black tights and heavy black shoes. Her friend has stringy dark blond hair worn long and straight, a smear of too-bright pink lipstick on her mouth, and small eyes surrounded by dark eyeliner. The boy just looks furious with the world. He's tall, broad-shouldered, his face troubled by acne, and he looks like he'd rather be doing anything than participating in the duck rescue mission.

"Now then," Jason says. "Youse all step aside and I'll see what the situation is here." The kids move to the edge of the sidewalk as he looks down into the darkness. "Hello there, Donald. Have you gotten yourself into a fix?"

A loud battery of quacking comes from the drain.

"He's got a wife down by the canal," one of the kids says. "I'd say he's worried about whether she thinks he's run off." Jason and I exchange a glance and try not to smile.

"Can you get him out, guards?" Luke asks, his voice high and a little hysterical.

"Of course we can," Jason tells him in a calm, soothing voice. "Now, I'll just move the cover away. Garda D'arcy, will you help me?"

The two of us drag the heavy metal cover to the side. "He must be pretty far down," I say quietly. Jason takes the flashlight from his vest and shines it into the hole. There's more quacking and then, out of the blackness, we see the head of a duck, his iridescent head-feathers set off by the flashlight. "I think I can reach him," Jason tells me. "You'll have to hold my feet."

"No problem. I didn't start lifting at the gym for nothing."

I turn to the kids. "Does anyone have a jumper or a coat we can put on the ground so Garda Savage can lie down?"

"Tina," Luke calls out. "Give us your jumper." The blond girl tosses him her fleece jacket—now I can see a family resemblance between them, which explains the girl's presence here—and he rushes over to lay it down.

Jason rolls up his shirt sleeves and gets down on his belly. Once I've got a good grip on his feet, he inches over the drain and I start lowering him down. The quacking becomes louder the lower he goes, and I can feel all the kids waiting behind me. Jason's voice drifts back up to me. "Come on, Donald. I'm trying to help you here. The sooner you let me get you, the sooner you'll be back to your wife in the canal."

"Come on, Donald," Luke blurts out. "Let him catch ya!"

"I've got you," I call down to Jason. "If you need another few inches."

"C'mere to me, Donald," I hear him say. "C'mere, you." I feel him swinging his arms around and then he yells out, "Got him!"

"Give me a hand," I say to the kids, and they all help me pull Jason back up to the edge of the drain and onto the sidewalk. He's tucked the duck under one arm and as soon as they're back in the light, Donald starts quacking wildly again and trying to break free.

"You got 'im!" Luke shouts.

I help Jason stand up. "Now, let's take him back to his wife," he says and gives an indignant Donald a pat on his head. Making a noisy but triumphant procession, we all follow Jason along the little side streets and back down toward the canal as passersby stop to find the source of the commotion. Amid lots of quacking and flapping on Donald's part, Jason stoops at the water's edge to release him. There's already a small group of waterfowl there, three swans and a half dozen mallard ducks, and Donald gives a few final quacks and then goes to join them, propelling his feathery body smoothly beneath an overhanging willow tree, the wispy pale green branches reflected on the surface of the water.

"There, now, I think he was saying thanks a million," Jason tells the kids. "He'll be all right. Job well done."

"Thanks, guard," Luke says.

There are a few more *Thanks, guard*s and then they all melt away, the teens, still looking bored, bringing up the rear. The dark-haired girl hangs back a bit to walk with the boy and I watch them go, a little thread of worry tugging at me. I'd guess they're about fifteen, and I remember what a tough age that was for my own daughter, Lilly, and her friends. Jason and I have learned a bit about some of these kids' home lives, and they're not very stable. The neighborhood is gentrifying quickly and from what Jason's said, it's lost some of the community watchfulness that existed for children when he was growing up here; there are smoothie shops and fancy coffee and million-euro-houses, but the neighborhood is full of danger for kids on their own in the afternoons.

As if to drive the point home, a familiar figure comes around the corner. I recognize him as a low-level drug dealer named Cameron Murphy whom Jason and I have interacted with before. He's spent a few months here and there in jail for minor offenses, but he doesn't have the air of a hardened criminal. He's not much taller than I am, but he's pumped up every muscle he's got, and he keeps his hair longer and gelled on top to give him an extra couple of inches. He has a Sylvester and Tweety Bird tattoo on his neck and when he turns his head, his skin wrinkles and Tweety takes on a demonic attitude.

Cameron is sucking furiously at a cigarette, keeping his eyes down while still scanning the street for someone he's either looking for or trying to avoid. He slows when he spots us along the canal bank, but he's too smooth to stop or change direction. His body goes rigid, but he keeps coming, still surreptitiously checking for whoever it is in his sights.

"Hiya, Cameron," I call out to him. "How are you today?"

"Ah, good, very good, now," he says. "What's the story yourselves, guards?"

Jason says, "Fine, thanks. Anything going on we should know about?"

"Ah, I wouldn't say so, now. I'm just out for bit of a stroll meself." He nods and walks past us, heading in the same direction as the kids, which makes me nervous. I'm seen him talking to Tina and her friend a few times, and I'm pretty sure nothing good is going to come of any friendship between them.

"Well now," Jason says once Cameron's gone, straightening his high visibility vest and patting his chest in a self-satisfied way. "That feels like a good day's work. Though we'll have to keep it quiet. The lads hear about this and we'll never get out from under it. You'll be Donald Duck D'arcy for the rest of your life. And I'll be responding to fake calls for injured waterfowl until the day I retire. Yeah, I'd say best not to spread this one around."

"My bill is sealed." I gaze up at the blue sky and sunshine and the green dome of St. Mary Immaculate across the canal in Rathmines, hardly a cloud in sight. "I thought it was supposed to rain today."

"Ah, sure, it'll be coming later," Jason says wisely, reaching up to scratch his forehead. "I'd say about four o'clock." He's only thirty, with thinning hair he's started rearranging over his scalp in a way that makes him look older. Contemplating the upper atmosphere, patting the beginnings of a belly under his uniform, he could be an ancient country farmer, gauging his chances of getting the hay in today. Jason is a city boy, born and bred only a few streets from where we're standing, but his first posting was as a guard in a small-ish town in County Offaly and he seems to have incorporated a rural sensibility into his personality even though he's back in Dublin. His blunt, kindly face inspires trust and he's physically imposing enough to make people think twice before misbehaving.

"I wore my fleece because it was supposed to be cold and now I'm sweating," I grumble.

Jason just nods and looks upward again as if things might have shifted in the last thirty seconds. They haven't. The sky is still clear, reflected in the calm ribbon of water. I tug at the collar of my dress shirt and too-warm jacket.

My uniform still feels strange, too heavy, too conspicuous after so many years in plainclothes as a detective. I resigned from my job on Long Island a year and a half ago and then finished at the Garda Training College in Templemore in August. My friend Roly Byrne, a detective inspector with the Garda's criminal investigation bureau, pulled some strings to get me posted to Dublin, where my boyfriend, Conor, and his son live and where my daughter, Lilly, is going to school. It feels like I'm right back where I started when I was twenty-five and a new officer with the Suffolk County Police Department, patrolling the streets, arresting drunks, driving by beaches and parking lots and high schools to make sure nobody was up to anything they shouldn't be, spending enough time on the beat so when something really bad happened, people wouldn't hesitate to let you know.

Jason's and my scheduled community patrol has already brought us all the way down Clanbrassil Street to the Grand Canal. We'll keep walking along the canal until we reach Portobello Bridge and then head north again up Richmond Street as it turns into Camden Street and then back to the newly finished Garda Station on Kevin Street. The skinnier-at-the-top rectangle—on the south side of the Liffey and not far from Dublin's city center—that we'll have described once we're done is loosely our patrol area. For the past two months, since I finished the training I need to work as a Garda officer in Ireland and was paired up with Jason, it's been our job to get to know it, to get to know the people, the businesses, the houses that are empty, the ones that are under construction, the ones that are occupied by families who have been in the Portobello neighborhood for generations, the ones that have sold to young couples flush with cash from the red-hot Dublin real estate market, and the ones where suspected drug dealers or gang members or pedophiles live.

It's taken time to figure it out, to understand how the roads and lanes and alleys all flow together, the networks of streets between the canal and the South Circular Road, once called Little Jerusalem because of the Jewish community that settled there in the early twentieth century, and the quiet residential neighborhoods above that that run parallel to Synge Street and up toward Camden Row. I'm just figuring out where the good coffee and lunch places are off Camden Street Lower, the hipster espresso places and health food cafés within easy walking distance of the increasing number of tech-related start-ups and creative industry offices in the neighborhood. Our patch is gentrifying quickly, though there's still plenty of street crime, robberies and drug dealers bleeding east from Rialto and Dolphin's Barn, and many of the kids we come across in the course of our work live in one of two older social housing complexes at the northern end of our beat.

I worried about how Jason would adjust to being partnered with a middle-aged American woman with twenty years of police work already under her belt, but he seems to take it all with a relaxed acceptance that will stand him in good stead his whole career. He doesn't have the kind of edgy, multilayered intelligence that gets you into the specialist bureaus or promotes you to detective, but he has street smarts and an overwhelming sense of calm about him. He's expert at defusing tensions—in particular talking down belligerent drunks, which I've seen him do quite a few times now—and he has the look of an Irish grandfather from a photograph of the 1950s. People think they know him, even when they don't, and he works it to his advantage. He also has a good rapport with the kids; kind, but a little stern.

We're passing the neighborhood pub just off the canal when my radio unit crackles and the dispatcher gives our call signs.

I respond and a voice comes through with a bit of static. "You near the canal?"

"Roger that."

The dispatcher says there's been a report of a possible homicide at an apartment complex called Canal Landing. "You know where it is? Unit 201." Jason is listening and his head snaps up.

"Roger that," I say.

"Bureau is on the way," the dispatcher says.

I tell him we'll head right over.

"Shite," Jason says. "That's where we responded to that possible domestic Saturday night."

Dread sweeps through me. "Yeah, I know."

We were on a four to midnight patrol Saturday night, talking to a neighborhood resident about some graffiti on the South Circular Road, when we got a call about a possible domestic violence situation in an apartment complex right on the canal; someone had heard screaming and fighting and called in to the emergency number.

I'd walked by the gated development of apartments many times, one of a pair next to a vacant lot on that section of the canal. Canal Landing is the shabbier one, built on the cheap in the late 90s, with twenty duplex units, four to a block, wrapped around a parking lot and small courtyard. The development next to it, called Harbour Quay, is more solid, newer, higher end. On Saturday night, we waited for Canal Landing's property manager to let us in through the gate, and when we asked him if he'd heard the screaming himself, he said, "I didn't hear anything," shrugging as he led us through the quiet parking area, dodging a child's bike lying on the ground and two plastic trucks. "I've got a place there on the first floor by the gate and one of the tenants knocked on my door, said there was screaming in one of the apartments, and to call the guards."

When we knocked at 201 though, a young woman answered the door, dressed in a bathrobe and looking confused when she saw our uniforms. She struck me as legitimately surprised to see us and when we said we'd received a call about a disturbance, she apologized for the noise, explaining she was watching a loud movie. She gestured to the large-screen television, where a now-muted action film was playing, and she seemed fine to us, with no visible injuries on her lovely, fine-boned face. We looked past her into the apartment, which seemed to be otherwise unoccupied, gave her the usual spiel about feeling comfortable reaching out for help and even left her a card with the number of the domestic violence prevention hotline. We felt fine about leaving and filed a report indicating that we hadn't located the caller but that the sound was likely the movie the woman in 201 was watching. That was it. I can't even remember her name, though we took it down for the report.

When you've responded to a possible domestic and left without arresting anyone, a follow-up call to the address is bad news. A possible homicide at the address is pretty much your worst nightmare.

Jason's normally placid face is twisted in worry now. "I guess we'd better get down there and see what's going on," he says, casting a final glance at the canal, at Donald and his wife and the other birds carving rippling channels through the water. The skies are darkening now, and I think he must be right. It's going to rain tonight.

SARAH STEWART TAYLOR is the author of the Sweeney St. George series and the Maggie D'arcy mysteries. She grew up on Long Island and was educated at Middlebury College and Trinity College, Dublin. A former journalist and teacher, she writes and lives with her family on a farm in Vermont where they raise sheep and grow blueberries. Taylor spends as much time in Ireland as she can and loves to explore new corners of the island. You can visit her online at SarahStewartTaylor.com.